"Connor's ability t   plot
thread is fascinating even when the horror is reserved...
the constricting pressure as the dread piles on makes this
book hard to put down and even harder to go to sleep after
reading. This is a great novel..."
                    -David J. Sharp, *Horror Underground*

SECOND UNIT

"Intricately plotted and vividly layered with suspense,
emotional intensity and strategic violence."
            -Michael Price, *Fort Worth Business Press*

"Drips with eeriness...an enjoyable book by a promising
author."
        -Kyle White, *The Harrow Fantasy and Horror Journal*

FINDING MISERY

"Major-league action, car chases, subterfuge, plot twists,
with a smear of rough sex on top. Sublime."
        -Arianne "Tex" Thompson, author of *Medicine for the
                    Dead* and *One Night in Sixes*

THE JACKAL MAN

"Connor delivers a brisk, action-packed tale that explores
the dark forests of the human--and inhuman--heart. Sure to
thrill creature fans everywhere."
        -Scott Nicholson, author of *They Hunger* and *The Red
                    Church*

Also by Russell C. Connor

SARGASSO

RUSSELL C. CONNOR

DARKFILAMENT BOOKS

Visit us online at

DARKFILAMENT.COM

Contact the author at
facebook.com/russellcconnor
Or follow on Twitter @russellcconnor

Cover Art by SaberCore23 Artwork Studio
For commissions, visit sabercore23art.com

ISBN:
978-1-952968-01-3

Second Edition: 2020

Radiolog transcript between US Coast Guard vessel *Miami 18* (crew of 8) and privately-owned houseboat *Holy Mackerel*, registered to Farhad Iravani (believed to have 5 passengers onboard).

June 18, 1984, 14:33 Eastern Time

Holy Mackerel (HM): Mayday, mayday, mayday, this is the *Holy Mackerel*! Any channel receiving, please respond!

Miami 18 (M18): Attention crew of the *Mackerel*, this is Coast Guard *Miami 18*. We read you. Over.

HM: (*sounds of cheering*) Oh, thank god! My wife and I have been broadcasting for two hours! I thought we were too far out for anyone to receive us! Over!

M18: What seems to be the problem? Over.

HM: I do not know sir, something is wrong with our damn engine. We are dead and drifting! Over.

M18: Can you confirm your location, *Mackerel*? Over.

HM: Looks like...81 degrees west by 25 degrees north. Do you copy that? Over.

M18: We copy you. We're twenty minutes out from your position. Just stay calm, sit tight, and we'll get you folks towed back stateside, all right? Over.

HM: Bless you good sir, my wife and children—(*long burst of static, timed at approximately 1:43*)—going on?

M18: *Mackerel*, we didn't catch that last transmission. Please repeat. Over.

HM: Your signal faded, sir. For a moment, we were picking up another broadcast. Over.

M18: What was the nature of this broadcast? Over.

HM: It...it wasn't in English, it sounded...well, foreign. Very unsettling. I attempted to reply in both English and Farsi, and when it responded, it told me only, 'Go.' Over.

M18: Wait, we need a clarification on that. Do you mean this other transmission answered you in Farsi? It actually spoke the language? Over.

HM: Yes, and then...dear lord.

M18: *Mackerel*? You still with me? Over.

HM: There are other ships out here. They all seem to be adrift also. O-over.

M18: I'm still not sure we're reading your correctly, Mackerel. What kind of ships? Over.

HM: Some sailboats...a few fishing vessels—(*sounds of excited shouting*)—very old, like something from the Middle Ages!

M18: *Mackerel*, stay clear of any vessels in your area. This region is notorious for smugglers and pirates. They congregate in international waters to make contraband exchanges. We'll be to you in fifteen minutes. Over.

HM: We are about to drift into one of them...hold on, children! We bumped against one, but we are fine! And...there is some kind of blue beacon flashing to the north!

M18: What the...? *Mackerel*? Over.

HM: Oh no, oh my lord, no! Amira, get the children back! Look out! (*running footsteps, screams*) Help us—under attack—!

M18: *Mackerel*, what's going on? Has someone boarded you? Over.

HM: —came from the other boat—

M18: Who has boarded you? (*aside*) I know, but their goddamn mic must be stuck open!

HM: (*growling noise followed by a scream; loud, building static*)

M18: Come in, *Mackerel*! Anyone on board, please respond!

HM: (*loud mechanical noises followed by roar*)

M18: Shit, what the hell was that? (*Miami 18 switches channels*) Base...this is 18. We...we just saw a blue flash on the horizon ahead, bright enough to light up the entire goddamn sky. It looked like...well, like a miniature nuclear explosion, for Christ's sake. The water out here has gotten rough and we're all feeling a little seasick suddenly. We'll proceed with caution. Over and out.

No trace of the *Holy Mackerel* or her crew was ever recovered.

1

A SOB STORY

THE CUSTOMERS AT TABLE NINE

WHERE CARLOS WENT

ERIC MAKES A CALL

1

The squinty bartender put two frosty beer bottles on the bar, along with a fruit-juice-heavy concoction adorned with a pineapple slice and a plastic umbrella. His breath, blowing over the three or four yellow teeth left in his head, smelled to Eric like a potent mix of dead fish and the contents of the shelves behind him. His skin was leathery from lifetime exposure to sun and sea air, his nose bulbous, pockmarked and straining against the boundary created by the beady eyes above.

This, Eric Renquist thought, *is the kind of local you meet when you go slumming off the guidebook.*

The old man looked up from his wares and asked, "You kids ain't headin out Sargasso way, are ya?"

Tension straightened Eric's spine. He gave one furtive glance around the dank seaside bar before answering but had no idea what he was looking for. Suspicious bulges under clothing? Eyes that stared back a bit too long before dropping? Earpieces, maybe, like something from a cheesy cop TV show? For a guy used to being the center of attention, remaining inconspicuous was a new way of life for him. But his father's lessons in caution had sunk into his head a lot deeper than anything he'd learned at Penn U the last four years.

Which was not, admittedly, all that much.

As far as he could see, there was nothing to get nervous about. The other patrons—most of them as homely as the bartender himself—were too busy getting shitfaced in the warm Caribbean air to notice him. The bar was only three walls and a thatched roof, with dining tables arranged on a patio beyond the shade of the interior, overlooking the beach and the bustling panorama of the Nassau docks. Out there, the sun was scorchingly bright, but in this dive the only lighting was over the bar; it turned every wrinkle and fold of the ancient man's face into fat black lines. From somewhere back there, static-laden speakers pumped a bass-heavy Calypso remix of Will Smith's "Miami".

Eric leaned toward the old fart across the bar. "How'd you know that?"

"Heard you and your friends talkin earlier." His accent sounded like a mish-mash of Cajun, Irish, and the local Bahama patois.

"So what if we are? What's it to you?"

He shrugged. "Just a warnin, friend. Bad time for it, s'all."

"Oh really, old timer? And why's that?"

The bartender made a business of wiping out some used mugs. "Air feels wrong out there. Like it's fulla electris'ty." Each syllable of this last word was sounded out carefully. "Strange things happ'n when tha air gets like that. Trust me."

Ah, so he wasn't really prying, just looking for an excuse to yammer. Eric slung a leg around the closest bar stool. "Sounds like you got a Triangle story."

"Aye. A *story*."

"Unburden yourself, brother." Eric caught the eye of a native goddess with tightly braided cornrows at the other end of the bar. He winked before remembering he was wearing sunglasses.

"Nearly ten years ago," the old man began, still cleaning glasses as he spoke, "my son and his wife—pregnant she was, with their first child—they set sail for tha Florida coast. He'd just bought hisself a new yacht, christened tha *Fam'ly Way*, and come down here ta show me. They left from yonder port, same way you 'bout to. A perfectly calm day, nary a cloud in tha sky, but I amember thinkin tha air felt wrong then, too. Almost like… you could taste it on your tongue. Kindly bitter." He smacked his lips to illustrate this. "Few hours later, 'nother ship picked up a distress call less'n four miles from their position. I spoke ta tha guy who heard it later on, and he said my boy was babblin 'bout monsters, and lights in tha sky. Said…said he sounded terr'fied." The bartender seemed to wind down as he said this last, his rag freezing in mid-wipe as he stared off into memory. Gathered tears made his dull eyes look gummy. "By tha time they got there, just thirty minutes later, tha seas had got rough, even though there still weren't no wind. But my boy…he was gone. They never found him, his wife or tha *Fam'ly Way*." He inhaled sharply as he came back to life behind the bar.

"Okay, my man, I gotta know." Eric hopped up, gathered the drinks, and tossed a twenty on the bartop. "Do you spin that moldy old tale for everyone stupid enough to come in here for a drink? Complete wit tears and everything?"

"I…I don't…"

"Seriously, it's a good story. Only problem is, I've read just about every book written on the Bermuda Triangle, and I've never heard of any boat called the *Family Way*."

The bartender tucked away his pain, wiped his eyes with the bar rag, and said defensively, "There ain't enou' books in tha world to talk 'bout every person Sargasso's swallowed. Gets mighty repe'tive, I guess. But *I* know it's true."

"Yeah, I'm sure you do." Eric gave a last smirk and strolled away.

The bartender watched him weave across the bar into the sunlight, back to his table where three other early twenty-somethings sat, one of them a buxom blonde all but popping out of her string bikini. He'd seen more rich young men with musclebound bodies come through here than he could count, all of them obnoxious, all of them thinking the world had been created solely for them to carry around in the back pocket of their designer khaki shorts.

He shook his head, jowls jiggling, and took the next drink order.

2

As Eric came back from the bar, Justin Bushe recognized the smug smile on his friend's lips all too well. It meant he'd handed someone their ass, gotten to feel superior to another human being if only for a few seconds. Eric used to get the same look on his face daily in high school, a sure indicator there was an underclassman somewhere whose wet head now smelled like the hormone-riddled piss of a hundred teenage boys.

"Beer for the bro," he said, handing Justin a bottle as he slid into the unoccupied plastic patio chair beside him.

"Thanks, man." Justin saluted with a finger.

"Rum sunrise for the hottie."

On the other side of the table, the girl Eric had introduced to Justin and Amber only as 'Cherrywine' giggled, creating a low-grade earthquake of bouncing flesh on her chest. Her pink bikini top barely had enough material to cover her nipples. She accepted the drink, popped the straw between collagen-thick lips, and sucked down half of it in one pull. "Yummy!" she cooed. "Thank you, baby!"

"And a great big, fat nothing for the killjoy who brought a fucking library with her."

Across from Justin, Amber didn't even look up from her textbook as she said, "Eat a dick, Eric. I told you if I came, I was going to study."

"Woah, nice mouth on your girl over there! Just told me to eat a dick!"

Justin shrugged. "And yet you're still talking. If you can get a word out around a mouthful of manmeat, that usually means you're doing it wrong."

"You would know, bro." Eric leaned back in his chair, the unbuttoned sides of his designer guayabera flopping open. "I'm just saying, what's the point in coming if you ain't gonna enjoy it?"

"Life doesn't stop when you have a party." Amber looked up now, eyes flashing beneath the rim of her ball cap, and Justin recognized the look on her face, too. "Some of us are taking real classes, not just wasting Daddy's money."

"Screw you, I did awesome last semester!"

"In what, Coloring Inside the Lines? How much does the professor charge for an A?"

Eric's expression darkened. Justin rushed to distract him before a war broke out, pointing the neck of his beer at the bar. "What was that about?"

"Who, the bartender? Old bastard was just yanking my chain. Telling boogeyman stories about the Triangle."

"Like what?"

"You know, warning us not to go out. Said the air was bad or some crazy shit like that." He took a swig from his bottle. "Only thing bad around here is this stuff. Shoulda stayed at the hotel bar. Don't know why I let you bring me to the cheap places."

"Because the cheap places are all I can afford, asshole."

"I said I was buying!"

"Is it...is it *really* dangerous?" Cherrywine twisted a lock of curly blond hair around one finger as she spoke.

"The beer? I think I'll live, babe."

"No, the Bermuda Triangle! I watched this movie where all these ships went missing for a while and then, when they came back, everyone was a ghost!"

"That's called fiction, sweetheart," Amber muttered.

"It is?" Cherrywine frowned at her. "I thought it was called *Death Ship*. But anyway, I don't wanna go if people really disappear out there!"

"Relax, it's all bullshit." Eric brought a leg up and rested it on the tabletop, almost spilling Cherrywine's drink.

"How do you know?"

"He did his end-of-year science report on it in the ninth grade." Justin grinned at Eric. "You used to be fascinated by the most morbid stuff back then. Remember when you went on your serial killer kick and started drawing all those bloody pictures? The school nurse told his mom he was 'disturbed.'"

"Yeah, whatever." Eric held up an open hand, as though trying to slap the words away. "The point is, once you really start digging, most—not all, but *most*—of that Triangle stuff is just a buncha crap. People tell stories to explain away wrecks and piracy, just like the shit that bartender tried to feed me. And the more they tell them, the bigger the legends get."

"Gotta be something to it," Justin argued, actually interested in the topic now. He could remember Eric's little fascinations when they were kids, the glazed sheen to his eyes when he found Justin before school and described whatever disaster or gory accident he'd read about online or in the nonfiction books he checked out from the library. Back then, when all they had was each other, and popularity was a distant concern, Justin hadn't thought this was strange at all (*still* didn't, considering he now knew who Eric's father was), but as his hobbies started to make him look weird to their teachers and classmates—in other words, when he started getting tackled the hardest in football practice, and girls began avoiding him like the plague—Eric's interest in the macabre suddenly faded away. Now, hearing him talk like this, Justin wondered if they'd actually just been *hidden* away. "I mean, what about that old ship they found abandoned from the 1800's? What was it, the *Mary Celeste*? We learned about that in school, for god's sake."

"Bro, have you ever *read* the actual accounts of the *Celeste*?" That superior grin came back to Eric's face. "Most of the facts people give about it are from a fucking Arthur Conan Doyle story. That ship was found abandoned off the coast of *Portugal*, not anywhere near the Triangle, and there wasn't anything mysterious about it."

"Amazing." Amber snorted, finally pushing back from the stack of books and highlighters in front of her. "You've never studied for a test in your life, but you know all that useless crap."

"History Channel." Eric finished his beer and tossed the bottle at a nearby trashcan. It missed, shattering against the concrete. He belched and laughed. "So you see, Cherrywine, there's no reason to get those edible panties of yours in a bunch. Nothing scary is gonna happen out there."

Justin raised an eyebrow. "Then why do you wanna go through it so bad?"

"To say I did it! Like jumping out of an airplane or some shit. I figure, if I gotta take the boat back to my father anyway, might as well make it interesting." His smile drooped. "Besides, like I said, there are a few Sargasso stories that don't add up."

"What's a 'sargasm?'" Cherrywine asked.

"It's when women tell Eric he's good in bed," Amber answered. Justin put a hand over his mouth to hold back laughter.

"*Sargasso*," Eric corrected, shooting Amber a black look, "is the sea where the Triangle's at. There are a few ships that just... BLINK!...vanished out there. Nobody knows where they went. No wreckage, no nothing."

Cherrywine shook her head vehemently. "Uh uh, no way. I don't wanna go."

Eric swung his leg down, leaned over the table, and took off his sunglasses. When he spoke, his voice was little more than a whisper. "Okay, listen. It's dangerous, sure, but I know the secret for getting through in one piece."

Cherrywine came forward also, straining to hear him, her eyes big and round and moist. "What?"

"Whatever you do...you have to make sure...you stay in your room...*and fuck the whole time you're there!*" He punctuated this by grabbing her arm, yanking her up from her seat, and pulling her into his lap. His hands roamed across her while she tittered and made feeble attempts to stop him. Justin tried not to use the opportunity to admire her, but it was hard. These were the type of women Eric surrounded himself with in a never-ending parade: completely reconditioned chassis, but the engine never fired on all cylinders. They didn't stick around more than a week or two, and a few of them—usually the ones of Cherrywine's social caliber—seemed to get a perpetual beaten-dog look in their eye when Eric got finished with them. Justin would see them slinking around campus days or weeks later, but they invariably scurried away whenever he tried to talk to them.

He realized Amber was watching him watch her. He expected a frown, but instead there was an oddly contemplative pucker to her thin lips.

"*Hey!*" Eric shouted suddenly, pounding a fist on the table-top. "What the fuck're you staring at?"

Justin jumped. He thought at first Eric was talking to him, but his gaze was directed elsewhere.

Their table sat at beach level, an easy stroll down to the sand and the small vessel piers sandwiched between the enormous cruise ship docks. The restaurant next door, a seafood joint called Bahama Best, had an outdoor area as well, but theirs was on an elevated sundeck overlooking the ocean. The table closest to the railing just above them was taken by five men, and all of them were staring down at Cherrywine as she squirmed in Eric's lap.

"What's up, shitheads?" Eric flew out of his chair, almost throwing Cherrywine to the ground. She managed to land awkwardly on her hands and one foot and then hurried to get out of Eric's way.

Above them, the five men stayed perfectly still. One black man, one white, and three olive-skinned. Had to be locals. Three of them were pretty big too, muscles on top of muscles, the shirtless white guy a rippling tapestry of tattoos.

They looked like hard men, little more than big, hairy gorillas, and Justin had no doubt they could take Eric apart piece-by-piece without even breaking a sweat.

"Hey Eric...dude...maybe that's not such a good idea."

"You looking at her?" Eric shouted, pointing at Cherrywine. Her cheeks reddened as she looked at the ground. "Or maybe it's *my* sweet ass you want, you faggots!"

"Eric, this is serious!" Amber hissed. "Those guys are gonna rip your spine out!"

"I ain't scared of those island trash rump-riders! Hey fuckers, look somewhere else right now, or we're gonna have a serious problem!"

Justin waited for them to respond. Waited for them to stand up, come down here, and administer a much-deserved beating that would put them both in the hospital.

Because Eric would never back down. Never had, in his entire life. And whatever obstacle he couldn't squash with his fists, Donnie Renquist did with his money. Not to mention, if a fight started now, Justin would have to back Eric up, right? The guy was his best friend, had been since elementary school, and just because they hadn't hung out much the last couple of years—with Eric taking up residence at the Delta Sig frat house, and Justin still living at home with his folks so he could afford to go to school—didn't mean he could stand by and watch while Eric was used as a punching bag.

But, to Justin's utter amazement, one of the men signaled the others, and they all looked away, toward where the ocean and sky seemed to stretch to infinity.

3

"That's right, bitches!" Eric couldn't resist shouting as he sat down. Probably a mistake to be stirring up a brawl—the less attention drawn to them right now, the better—but he just felt too good, too...*invincible*. He fervently believed in destiny, and it wasn't part of his to get pinched by whatever passed for backwater Caribbean law enforcement around here.

"Goddamn you." Amber shoved her chair back as she stood, slamming textbooks and throwing them into her bag. He caught the title of a couple: *The Essence of Language*, and *Speech Mechanics*. What was this bitch studying again? Poetry? Latin? Justin had told him once, but he'd forgotten. "You truly make me sick, you know that?"

"Oh boo hoo, Amber. I don't know if I can go on living without your respect."

She grabbed her bag and stormed off, walking barefoot across the hot sand. Justin ran after her, pussywhipped as ever, but she pulled away and stomped her narrow ass up the sidewalk toward the hotel. If any woman had ever tried that bullshit with Eric, she'd be walking home. Or, in this case, swimming home. He heard her say something to Justin about 'needing to be alone.' Bitch had to be on the rag, with a menstrual flow as heavy as the Mississippi.

Justin came back and sank into his chair. "Thanks a lot."

"Not my fault, bro. I told you to never date a woman who can form her own opinions."

"Advice from the master. You should write a book."

"If she's not back by four, we set sail without her."

Justin frowned at him.

"I'm just saying, we're on a schedule here!"

"I can go after her, if you want," Cherrywine offered. "Sometimes a girl just needs to talk to another girl, ya know?"

Eric almost laughed at that. Judging from those uptight, frigid bitches Amber surrounded herself with at school, being saddled with this airhead probably wouldn't improve her disposition. Which was exactly why he said, "You go do that, babe."

"Okay!" Cherrywine paused in the act of getting up and gave him a beseeching, sidelong glance. "But don't leave without me, honey, okay?"

"Wouldn't dream of it."

He reached out and grabbed a handful of her ass cheek as she stood, a mound so perfect and tightly curved it looked like half a basketball. She squealed and playfully slapped at him, but he thought he caught the slightest look of annoyance on her face. Maybe ol' Cherrywine had a bit more fight in her than he thought.

He'd find out tonight, one way or another.

From the corner of his eye, he caught Justin staring after her too.

"Nice, huh?" he asked. "You wanna take her for a test drive when I get finished?"

"No thanks, I'm watching my syphilis intake. So what strip club did you pick this one up in?"

"*Love Makers*. Place down by the airport. Had her give me a lap dance while I was waiting to check in for the flight."

Justin's jaw dropped. "I was joking, man. You really mean to tell me you just met that girl and you asked her to go to the Bahamas with you?"

"Sure, why not? She quit her job on the spot." Eric shrugged. The stripper—who'd been wearing a g-string that had more in common with dental floss than clothing when he'd met her—was so excited, you'd think he just told her there was a half-off sale in the skank section of Victoria's Secret. "I thought it was just gonna be the two of us trolling for women on the islands, but I had to bring someone after you invited the Ice Queen."

Justin sighed. "Seriously man, you gotta cool it with that shit. I need you and Amber to get along. Preferably for the long term, but if not, at least for this trip."

"Why? It's not like you're marrying her." Eric noticed the look that passed over his friend's face. "No."

"Yeah."

"You're not."

"Brought the ring with me. I figured, you know, we're out on the ocean, it's romantic…"

"Bro…you've known her, what? A month?"

"Asshole. We've been together since sophomore year."

"You are one sorry sack of whipped shit, my friend. Getting married to the first piece of ass that comes along? You *will* regret that."

"I disagree. And I really just want everything to go smoothly when I ask her tonight." Justin stuck a finger in his face. "You swear we'll be back before Spring Break is over?"

"One night on the ocean tonight, a quick stop in Bermuda tomorrow, and then it's straight back to Philly. My dad wants the boat back by Friday."

"And why are we stopping in Bermuda again?"

Eric waved the question away. "Don't worry about it. It'll take five minutes, tops. You don't even have to get off the boat."

"All right. I'm holding you to that."

"C'mon, let's get the supplies aboard. I wanna be ready to shag ass when they get back."

They stood and plowed across the beach, heading toward the wharf where his father's boat, the *MishMasher*, stayed docked for nine months of the year.

As they reached the first of the wooden planks, Eric glanced back at the table of locals he'd taunted.

All five men stared right back, silent and still as gargoyles.

4

Damon knew it was going to be a shitty day.

First, his alarm didn't go off. His roommate had eaten all the Froot Loops again, leaving him without breakfast. His boss at Bahama Best harangued him for being late and threatened to fire him.

But, when he saw the customers at table nine, he figured things were about to get worse.

Mambo, the bloated Bahamian who cooked in the back, slid Damon a tray with a large pitcher of beer and five mugs.

"Who's this go to?" Damon asked, rushing to tie the strings on his Bahama Best apron. The restaurant logo—a picture of a boiling lobster with little sad brows floating above the eyes on their stalks—had made him swear off seafood forever.

"Table nine, near da railin, *mon*."

Damon looked.

The five men seated at table nine were all staring intently over the edge of the sundeck, so he could study them without being noticed. Three were Latin descent; either Cubano or maybe Puerto Rican. Two of these were fit and muscled, but the third was a scrawny little dude with the build of a toothpick. One was black, definitely a native, sporting a nest of short dreadlocks as thick as snakes. The handle of a machete was visible over one shoulder, strapped to his back in a sheath. And the last man was a huge, shirtless hulking white guy, possibly American, whose biceps were as big around as Damon's head. His chest, back and arms were covered in a rainbow of tattoos; barely an inch of non-pigmented skin remained. Damon might have said they were construction workers, but the closest work being done was the renovation of the Ocean Towers Hotel, nearly two miles down the beach. Long way to go to grab a beer during your break.

"Watch your step, white boy," Mambo cautioned, flipping a filet on the grill.

"Right." Rough customers occasionally came into the restaurant, but they were mostly tourists that got drunk and ran their mouths. Damon slid the tray off the counter and started across the sundeck, holding up a hand to keep the sun out of his eyes. Halfway there, the group turned in their chairs and spotted him.

He reached the table, tray balanced on his shoulder, and was opening his mouth to greet them when a shape lunged from the shadows under the table with a roar like an 8-cylinder engine.

Damon let out a squawk. His feet tangled as he tried to jump away. He felt himself falling backward. The tray of beer flew into the air as his hands followed instinct and moved to catch him. He sprawled on the wooden deck and looked up.

In front of him was the ugliest, mangiest pitbull he'd ever seen, its face nothing but scars and hardened flesh and crooked teeth. It lunged at him again, and he yelped and covered his face before realizing it was chained to the bottom of the table. It regarded him with cloudy eyes as growls and saliva spilled out of it slack jowls.

"Down, Cheech," someone at the table above said in a thick, Spanish accent. The dog reluctantly retreated back under the table, where it scowled at him.

"Jesus!" Damon bounded to his feet. "You know, we don't allow dogs in…"

He trailed.

The tray and mugs had rolled out of the way on the deck, the glass not even cracking. At least *that* wouldn't come out of his paycheck. But the large pitcher of beer had somehow landed upside down in the lap of the tattooed guy, on a pair of black leather pants slick and shiny with alcohol.

Now that he was closer, Damon could see the tattoos were all intricate drawings of interwoven animals. Hawks, snakes, wolves, bears, sharks; anything and everything predatory. The guy's face was rugged as stone, with a jaw big enough to chew through steel. Long, blonde, greasy hair fell to his shoulders. His eyes, cold chips of dull mica, regarded Damon without moving.

The thin, wiry Hispanic guy seated next to him cackled shrilly. "Oooo, little *cabrón*, you done messed the fuck up now!"

Tattoo picked back up the pitcher and set it on the table with smooth, measured movements. Then he opened his mouth and said slowly, "This was my favorite pair of pants, mate."

"I…I'm really sorry, I—"

"*Sorry* ain't gonna take the lager out of 'em, now is it? *Sorry* ain't gonna make you any less of a dumb shit."

"I…I-I…" Damon looked around the table for help. The dreadlocked native reclined in his chair, looking up at the sky, eyes hidden behind mirrored sunglasses, but there was a lopsided grin on his lips as he listened. The skinny guy bounced in his seat with anticipation. That left the two Latino men on the far side of the table; one with a ponytail that had his face planted in one palm, the other watching Damon with a serene, neutral expression.

"Speak up, mate," Tattoo prompted. The accent leaned toward British or Australian. He put a giant-sized hand against Damon's shoulder and gave him a half-hearted shove that nearly threw him back off his feet. The little one laughed like a hyena, his voice as squeaky as a teenager breaching puberty. "Whatcha gonna do about this?"

"I'll...bring you some more beer?"

Ponytail gave a sad shake of his head.

Tattoo moved fast. A muscular arm grabbed Damon by the front of his apron and dragged him almost down into the chair until their faces were an inch apart. The man used his free hand to reach down to his boot, and the next thing Damon knew, the blade of a wickedly thin knife was pressed against the underside of his jaw. From the angle, he knew his body blocked anyone else in the restaurant from seeing what was happening. A shivering numbness froze up his muscles even in the day's heat.

"Maybe I oughta make you pay for 'em, mate," his tormentor rasped in his ear.

"Make 'im pay, Rabid!" the skinny dude agreed.

"Make you pay in *blood*," Tattoo continued. The knife pressed against Damon's unprotected throat felt like a razor-thin line of fire.

"*I'm sorry*," Damon squeaked. He was afraid to move. Any more pressure and that blade would begin cutting through flesh. Warm piss pressed against the floodgate of his bladder.

"That's enough." This came from the Latino that had yet to speak. His eyes, two clear ovals the color of ripe kiwi skin, were almost unnaturally calm.

Tattoo glanced at him across the table. "But Cap'n—"

"Let him go. *Now*."

The pressure on Damon's throat disappeared. Tattoo flipped the knife and made it disappear as expertly as a magician before releasing his grip on the apron. Damon straightened and backed out of reach.

The man that had saved him—tall and lean, with short-cropped black hair and a floral-pattern Tommy Bahama shirt unbuttoned far enough to reveal the smooth, tanned expanse of his chest—said, "Just bring us another round, kid."

Damon nodded quickly and found the strength to run. He looked over his shoulder several times on his way across the restaurant and back to the cook's counter.

"Mambo," he gasped. "Mambo, those guys threatened me with a knife!"

The cook looked up from his grill. "Who, Lito's crew?" He chuckled. "Didn't I tell you to watch your step?"

"You *know* them?" Damon looked back at the table. Once more, their attention was focused in the direction of the docks.

"Sure, dey come in whenever dey in port. Hadn't seen dem much lately. Heard a rumor dey mighta pissed off de wrooooong people."

"Well, who the hell are they?"

Mambo grinned, revealing nicotine-stained teeth. "White boy, you just met your first real live Caribbean *pirates*!"

5

After the waiter left, Lito Porto looked around the table at the crew of the *Steel Runner*. Most of them had been in his employ for better than five years, but their stupidity still amazed him at times. He took a moment to center his inner chi before demanding, "How many times? How many times I ask you not to start shit in port?"

"Oh c'mon Cap'n, the little wanker had it comin." Marcus 'Rabid' Jackson raised his leg and slid the folded switchblade back into his boot. "'Sides, you gotta admit that was funny."

"Yeah, man!" This from Jorge Lopez-Esperanza, the skinny Cubano sitting next to him. He gave a nasally guffaw and said, "Dude looked like his pants were wet too, but it wadn't from no beer!"

"We'll see how funny it is when he calls the cops, *idiotas*. Like we don't have enough heat on us right now."

Rabid shrugged and looked away. His pecs twitched with irritation, making the animals tattooed there look like they were moving and fighting.

"And *you*." Lito elbowed his fellow Puerto Rican with the ponytail beside him. "Control that ugly mutt or leave him on the boat."

Raymundo Vargas, his second-in-command, reached under the table to stroke the pitbull's misshapen head. "You know Cheech, Lito. He got a mind of his own."

"He ain't even got *half* a mind of his own." Lito lashed out with a foot under the table and hit the dog in the side. This did nothing except cause the flies nesting on him to rise in a little cloud before resettling. "Which is more'n I can say for the rest of you."

They got quiet. From the bar next door, where the little *gringo* had been yelling at them, the last strains of "Margaritaville" drifted out. Lito hated that song; when you lived anywhere near a beach that American tourists frequented—as he had his whole life—you heard Jimmy Buffet's contribution to seaside culture at least twenty times a day. So instead he looked back over the railing at the boat far down the docks, which the two white brats had just boarded. He realized the rest of his crew was doing likewise, their greedy gazes drawn as surely as compass needles swinging north.

Jericho Trellis, his native mechanic, produced a pair of binoculars from his satchel under the table. He studied the boat through them for a long minute until Lito asked, "So what is it?"

"Looks like...a Halverson. Fifty-footer, *mon*. Luxury cabin, twin V10 hemi engines. Prob'ly do 60 or 70 miles per hour out in de open. Fuckin t'ing looks brand new, too."

Ray whistled. "That's a five hundred thousand dollar boat."

"Bet we could squeeze Dully for three, easy," Rabid added. "Plus any other goodies on board."

"I tell you what, man," Jorge said, his thick accent putting a 'g' at the end of the last word. "I wouldn't mind takin my cut outta those two *putas* of theirs, know what I'm sayin?"

Rabid gave him a high five. "I'd have that sweet piece in the bikini ridin my dick like it's a fuckin pogo stick! After I slap some manners into her brainless boyfriend!"

"You see de way he yelled at us?" Jericho lowered the binoculars. "Dude is seriously overcompensatin."

"We'll see how fulla piss he is with a semi-automatic to his bloody forehead."

Lito let them jaw on for a few minutes, while a new waiter brought them a fresh pitcher of beer. Then Ray asked, "So whatcha think, Lito? This the one?"

All conversation stopped as they awaited his answer.

"What do I think?" Lito set his glass on the table and pulled sunglasses from his pocket. "I think we got four rich *bastardos* that'll fold quicker than a sack of laundry under a little pressure, in a luxury boat worth more than what all of us together made the last two years, and, based on their yappin, it sounds like they're gonna voluntarily drop anchor in the middle of the Sargasso tonight, miles away from civilization. I think, boys... that life just got very, *very* good."

Laughter broke out all around, Rabid pounding the tabletop like a barbarian. Lito's confirmation had lifted a tension that had only been growing the last few weeks. Probably because they were almost out of money. And supplies. And fuel. And it probably didn't help that the Dominican had his entire force keeping an eye out for them after the incident in January. Lito had heard the bounty on his head alone was hovering at the hundred grand mark.

Three days ago, when they'd docked in Havana, a coked-up street peddler wanting to make a name for himself had stowed away aboard the *Steel Runner* with a machine gun big enough to shoot Mars, and attempted to take them all hostage as gifts for the man who ran the biggest drug cartel in Caribbean waters.

There was barely enough of him left to feed the sharks after Rabid went to work.

Still, it sent a clear message: the Dominican wasn't going to forget, and the sooner they had some coin in their pockets, the sooner they would have options. Like finding someplace to lie low for a year until the heat was off. That's why they'd come to the one place the man would never think to look for them while they sought another big job.

The very island where his base of operations was located.

"So what's de orders, Cap'n?" Jericho asked.

"We move, and move *now*. Jericho, get one of your trackers on board their ship. Rabid, Jorge, get the *Steel Runner* ready to leave port. And make sure Carlos and Mondo finished emptyin out the holds. I wanna transfer as much cargo from their yacht as possible after we take it tonight, just in case."

They all suddenly had somewhere else to look.

"What?"

Ray told them, "Get goin guys." The other three pushed away from the table and started down the staircase from the sundeck to the beach. Ray waited until they reached the pier before saying, in Spanish, "Carlos bugged out this morning, right before you left. Said he had somethin to take care of in the city."

"Shit." Lito sighed. "Why didn't you tell me earlier?"

"Because we had more important things to do."

"You try to stop him?"

"Nope."

"Ray, *Jesus Christo*! If someone recognizes him and it gets back to the Dominican—"

"Then some poor sucker's gonna have ground Degas in their tacos tomorrow afternoon. Knowing that kid, he'll probably give 'em wicked shits, too." Then, when Lito didn't laugh, "He knows all that, and he went anyway. I ain't his father. Neither are you, last I checked."

Lito's fist curled up on the table, but he forced it to open again. "Goddamn it. I told him…"

"Don't matter what you told him. Boy don't wanna listen. He's nineteen, mad at the whole world in general, and you in particular. Sooner or later, you gonna have to cut him loose."

Lito closed his eyes and said, "It's gonna be sooner if he's not back by the time we go after those rich kids. I'm not missin this opportunity."

"All for the best," Ray said. "Mark my words: the longer that kid's with us…the worse things are gonna get."

6

Carlos Degas gripped the steering wheel of the little Toyota in frustration. The vehicle cost him twenty-eight bucks to rent for the day, all the money he had left in the world—plus a baggie of weed to convince the clerk to let him have it without a valid driver's license—but you couldn't exactly take a cab where he was going. Now he was caught in a traffic jam from an overturned fish truck, and the cars in front of him hadn't moved in ten minutes.

Time crunched down like a vice with teeth. Life felt like a giant conspiracy sometimes, had ever since his mother died choking on her own blood in a county hospital in Daytona Beach nearly four years ago. He flipped stations on the radio, trying not to look at the time.

No good. One o'clock already. Not only was he late for his appointment, he'd been gone from the *Steel Runner* for almost three hours now. He'd tried to slip out before the rest of the crew roused from their drunken slumbers, but Vargas caught him going out the door and stuck his nose in, as usual. Fucker was always hassling him, tattling to Lito anytime he stepped out of line. Carlos mumbled something about having business in town, which was technically true. It took him a half hour to get the car, another hour to get out of New Providence and take Carmichael down to South West Bay, and now here he was, sitting in muggy island traffic with no air conditioning and sweat soaking the back of his Tampa Bay Rays jersey. He had to get back before suspicions were raised too high for him to lie his way out.

Then again, if things went well this afternoon, maybe he wouldn't be going back at all.

And if they *didn't* go well…shit, then he still wouldn't be going back, but only because he'd be dead.

Ahead of him, the driver of the fish truck argued with a pedestrian. Carlos pounded the steering wheel and honked the horn. When the car in front of him moved up another foot, he squeezed into the mouth of a nearby alley and jetted away.

The buildings that made up this industrial dock were riddled with interconnected backstreets. Carlos drove past warehouses and dank alleyways, looking for the place his contact had instructed him to go. Import boats and fishing vessels unloaded cargo all around him, some of them with cranes. One of the many places that kept the islands functioning, but few tourists ever saw. Finally, he spotted the place.

A shabby building in need of a paint job sat at the end of a small, private alley, with a large overhead door in front standing open. Two fishermen-types stood on the loading dock out front, one black and one white, in rubber gloves and waders, moving empty wooden crates. Beyond them, the interior of the warehouse appeared to house a wall of duplicate crates, but again, nothing in them. The longer he watched the two men, the more their actions seemed robotic, perfunctory.

He stopped out front and sat in the car, trying to calm his nerves. He'd brought a pistol with him—a little Grand Power semi-auto he'd picked up at a pawn shop the last time they docked in Florida—but he didn't dare bring it inside. Carlos pulled the gun from his pocket and tossed it in the rental's glovebox.

When he got out and headed toward the front of the building, the fishermen dropped the act and turned toward him on the loading dock. The white one lifted a flap on his wader to show the submachine pistol shoved in his waistband.

"Hol' up right dere," the black one said, his Jamaican accent thicker than the local dialect. This had to be Vishon the Vicious, the Dominican's local enforcer. His head was shaved high on the sides, with a thick hunk of greasy dreads tied in a ponytail that hung down his back. "You Degas?"

"That's me." He started to tack on an apology for being late, but decided against it.

"You packin?"

Carlos lifted his shirttail and spun around. "Naw man, I'm clean."

Vishon laughed. Most of his front teeth on the top were capped in glittering gold. "*Bomba claat*, you must be sky high you t'ink dat's good enou'. Get up 'ere and lemme search you."

A pulse of anger beat at Carlos's temple, but he held his tongue as he climbed up onto the loading dock. Vishon stripped off his thick rubber gloves and set about the most thorough pat-down the world had ever known, one that ended with him giving each of Carlos's pecs a healthy squeeze just south of painful. His partner watched with one hand on the uzi.

"God*damn* homey," Carlos said. "This ain't the strip club. I feel like we fixin to get engaged or some shit, you feelin on my titties like that."

Vishon slapped him across the back of the head.

"Ow! What the fuck, man?"

"Lesson numbah one: always show some respect for de *bredda* who just 'ad yo' balls in 'is hand."

"Yo, you done picked the wrong profession if you want respect for holdin another guy's junk, muhfuckah."

The other man grinned, displaying more gold in his mouth than enamel. "Gotta make sure dere ain't no uddah ears listenin in, *batty*. Follow I."

The two of them led the way into the warehouse. Past the open bay door was nothing but more of those empty crates stacked around an open concrete floor. This couldn't be the right place. The door trundled closed behind them, leaving the illumination to flickering fluorescents high above. Carlos's heart started to pound until the man with the gun pulled a chain against the wall, and a section of the floor dropped down, revealing a staircase.

"Aftah you," Vishon offered.

Carlos hesitated. He could probably still make it out at this point, as long as he went for the one with the gun first. If he went down those stairs…and things went sour…he had no one to blame but himself.

But once he thought about the alternative—another few months at sea on that stinking ship with the collection of retards that ran it—his choice was clear.

Carlos descended and entered a bustling chamber that made him see the abandoned warehouse floor above for the façade that it was. A long, rectangular room held rows upon rows of tables with men and women in their underwear standing in front of them, cutting cocaine and weed into street bags, while still others sorted pills and gallon baggies of crystal meth into affordable—and concealable—packets. Along the wall, others pulled in bales of coke as big as engine blocks through an assembly line that ran up through a hole in the wall, from a ship outside, he figured. They handled the heavy packages as delicately as packed dynamite.

All told, the product in this room must've been worth over two hundred million dollars, easy.

"Is this it?" Carlos asked in amazement.

"Whatchoo t'ink, it's Willy Wonka's fact'ry? Keep movin."

He kept moving. The people working with the drugs watched him wearily, their eyes little more than haunted hollows. Carlos spotted closed circuit cameras behind each of the workstations, the lenses glaring.

Another door waited at the far end of the room, locked with a heavy hydraulic system, like a bank vault. The Jamaican rang the buzzer on an intercom next to it.

"It be I, boss. Got de gennleman callah wit me."

No response, but a hiss from the hydraulics signaled the door opening. They had to move back to allow the thick metal slab to swing freely. Beyond was darkness.

Carlos stepped inside.

7

The room beyond looked like it had once been a large storage area, back when this place was an import warehouse or fish packing plant. Now it had been transformed into a lavishly decorated bedroom suite. The only thing separating it from a high class New York hotel room was the absence of a view. Or windows of any kind, for that matter.

Carlos stood looking around as the escorts came in behind him and the door swung shut. Lush shag carpeting swallowed his sneakers. The only light came from torchiere-style lamps in the corners, turned low, and the illumination they gave off was absorbed by dark blue velvet draperies that covered the walls. The effect reminded Carlos of the sitting room of some British royalty. A home entertainment center stood against the far wall, next to a bank of monitors that displayed the workers outside from every conceivable angle. The muted television displayed a violent porno where a dark-skinned male barbarian screwed the ass of a white woman bound and hung upside down.

To the left of the door was a four-poster bed with gauzy, see-through curtains hanging down. On the blood-red coverlet sat the man Carlos had come to see, snorting a line of coke as thick and long as an index finger off a shaving mirror. Three naked, sleeping Latino women surrounded him on the bed.

"Well...fucking hell." Romero Felix Santiago—known all over the Caribbean as 'the Dominican,'—rubbed the last of the coke on his gums and set the mirror aside. Carlos didn't know if the guy was actually from the Republic or not; rumor placed his origin anywhere from a tribe deep in the Amazon to the dark side of the fucking moon. He was dressed in red silk pajamas that actually matched the bedspread. Dude must've been in his fifties, but extensive plastic surgery let his dark face pass for around thirty. His hair was a mess of tight, gray curls perched on his scalp. "*You're* Carlos Degas?"

Carlos couldn't stop looking at the women long enough to respond. *Shit, now ain't the time to get a fuckin stiffy.* He shoved his hands in the pockets of his baggy jeans and nodded.

As he slid off the bed, throwing toned legs out of his way, Santiago said, in a refined, well-spoken voice that Carlos never would've expected, "You're a lot younger than I imagined. Just a boy, really. I wish I could say that's going to make this harder... but I didn't get where I am today with sentimentality."

Before Carlos could react, Vishon and his silent partner tackled him, wrenching one arm behind his back and sending him to his knees in that luxurious carpet. The silent one held him where he was by standing on his calves and keeping his left hand pulled tight between his shoulder blades, while Vishon stretched his right arm above his head and then bent it at the wrist in such a way that the fingers were forced to uncurl, like he was preparing Carlos for a manicure.

"Oh! Oh, *shit*, that hurt! Leggo man, whatchoo doin?"

"Lesson numbah two," Vishon purred above him, his gold teeth flashing in the dim light. "Nevah walk into de home of de man who 'as a bounty on yo' 'ead, and expect to walk back out again."

"Mr. Santiago, please, you gotta listen to me, you don't understand—!"

"Understand?" Santiago padded across the room to a full wet bar and set about pouring himself a slug of rum. "What I understand is that you are a crew member of the *Steel Runner*, that rustbucket pirate vessel captained by Lito Porto. Now, please do not misunderstand: I have nothing against a pirate. Here in the Caribbean, you all still sail under the romantic notion that you're Blackbeard on the high seas, when you're really just a bunch of petty thugs mugging wayward tourists, but you do occasionally serve a purpose. What I *don't* like…what I *cannot* tolerate…" He knocked the rum back and then threw the glass into the basin, where it shattered. "Is when a group of pirates boards one of my smuggling ships."

"*It was an accident!*" Carlos screeched. Oh god, it was all going wrong, he'd been an idiot for coming here, and now he was going to die for it. "We didn't know it was yours, I swear, we didn't even take nuttin, we left as soon as we realized who it belonged to!"

"After you killed the entire crew."

"They was shootin at us! It was self-defense! Lito don't even want us killin unless we got to!"

Santiago crossed the room in the span of a second. He bent over Carlos and snarled, "That may very well be, but you left my fucking ship derelict. The Coast Guard picked it up two days later. Whether it was an honest mistake or your captain being a moron, *I'm* out five-million dollars and, my friend, you better believe someone will pay for that!"

"I'm sorry Mr. Santiago, so sorry, if you'll just listen…!"

"Do you know what bottlecapping is, Carlos?"

Carlos stopped his whimpering and stared into Santiago's bloodshot eyes. "Huh?"

"I'll take that as a no." The drug lord reached out to the hand that Vishon still held stretched upward and pinched the loose skin on the middle knuckle of Carlos's index finger. "Bottlecapping is where you take a knife and slice right here, through all those delicate tendons over the joint of each finger. When you peel it back to the bone, it becomes a perfect little circle of flapping skin, like a bottlecap. I'm told it's excruciatingly painful, and cripples the finger for life. Which, in your case, won't be that long anyway."

With his free hand, Vishon pulled a straight razor from his breast pocket.

Carlos's testicles leapt up into his stomach. "*NO!* Oh my god, Mr. Santiago, *PLEASE* don't do this!"

On the bed, one of the naked women rolled over and mumbled something about them keeping it down.

"Sorry, sweetie," Santiago called, then to Carlos, in a more subdued tone, "Then tell me who arranged this meeting."

Again the direction of the conversation changed so abruptly that Carlos could only give a confused, "Huh?"

"Someone gave you the name and cell number of one of my lieutenants, who delivered your meeting request to me. I agreed, giving you only a time and not a location, and yet you found your way here. That means you're being fed information by someone who works right here, at this facility. And if this person talked to you, then who *else* might they be willing to talk to?"

Carlos swallowed. The Dominican was just as crafty as the rumors said. "He didn't mean nothin by it, Mr. Santiago. He was just tryin to help a brother out. We went to grade school together and shit, right here on the island."

Santiago shook his head. "The Coast Guard, the Bahamian government, and even the FBI have formed an alliance to infiltrate my organization. What's left of Sullis Carbini's drug cartel in Miami has a death warrant out on me. I can't have my people dropping the address of my home and business around the island, especially to a member of the group that's at the top of my own personal shit list right now. *Someone's* getting bottlecapped today, Carlos. It's up to you to decide who."

"Diego. Diego Palacios."

Santiago snapped his head up to the silent guard holding Carlos from behind. "One of the outside dock workers. Bring him."

And just like that, Carlos was released. He fell limp to the ground and lay panting with his cheek against the carpet. Plush fucking rug was more comfortable than his bed back on the *Steel*

Runner. He heard the door hiss open and shut again while he tried to figure out what had just happened and, worse yet, what might still be to come.

8

Carlos finally risked looking back up. Vishon stood against the wall with his arms crossed, and Santiago was back on the edge of the bed. He held up a peace sign in front of his broad chest. "I can assume two things by your presence here, Carlos Degas. The first is that you want a job. To jump ship, so to speak, and work for me. The second is that the *Steel Runner* is in port somewhere right here on the island. Correct?"

Carlos nodded while climbing warily back to his feet. "Over at Prince George."

Santiago gave a self-satisfied grin and held up a hand. "Let's speak of one, and then the other. What could you bring to my organization? You want to handle drugs, like those people out there?"

A disgusted shiver worked through Carlos at the thought of the zombies he'd walked through on the way here. "No, sir. I was thinkin I could smuggle. I got ship experience."

The other man chuckled. "I suppose you do. So I would... what? Place you aboard one of my vessels?"

"Well...I don't know...I was thinkin...maybe I could be in charge of one or somethin..."

Now Santiago threw back his head and roared with laughter, his belly shaking, until one of the women on the bed flopped over on her back and dug a heel into his side. He slapped her hip with the back of his hand and said to Carlos. "So I am to turn over command of one of my ships to a boy I barely know, eh?"

Carlos shrugged and looked away. It had been a pipe dream, but in his head it somehow all made sense. Now he just felt stupid and embarrassed.

"That I cannot do, Carlos. But...if you had a ship of your own...and wanted to offer it up for service...that would be something else entirely."

"I don't."

"Oh really?" Santiago cocked his head to the side as if he knew different. "Let me ask you, Carlos...why do you want to work for me?"

"Because...I wanna make some real money."

"That you could certainly do. My people are rewarded for their work. But I find it interesting you wanted this so badly you thought coming here—risking your life—was worth it."

Carlos sighed. He'd been trying to come up with the right responses, but now he just let his anger flow and said what was in his heart. "Yo, I'm sick of bein treated like a fuckin cabin boy. I'm sick of those muhfuckahs and the way they live. Mostly...I'm just sick of bein under Lito's thumb."

He thought Santiago might laugh again, but the man only studied Carlos with those piercing eyes. "You're ambitious. Hungry. Like me, when I was your age. What if I told you I had a way you could square your debt with me for your part in the raid on my ship, *and* make yourself captain of your own smuggling vessel?"

"Tell me."

"It's simple." Santiago's smile was almost feral, the grin of a wolf closing its jaws around a plump rabbit. Carlos suddenly understood that whatever the man was about to say was the only reason he'd been allowed to live this long. "Kill Lito, and his entire crew. Bring me the man's head and the *Steel Runner*. You and I start fresh, and you have your own ship, which I will provide with a crew."

"I'll do it." The answer came so fast, he figured the man could've asked him for just about anything. Judging by the look on Santiago's face, he knew it too. But, even so, if this was all that stood in the way of Carlos's dreams, it was a small price to pay.

And, who knows? Maybe killin Lito and Ray and Jericho and all the others won't just get you in good with this dude.

It might even be fun.

"Good boy. Contact the same man when the deed is done, and you'll receive further instructions."

The door opened behind Carlos. Vishon ushered him toward it just as his partner came through from the other side, dragging Diego Palacios behind him.

"Carlos!" his old friend pleaded, as they pulled him past. He hadn't talked to Diego in nearly seven years before hearing that he worked for the Dominican, and then tracking him down to ask for a favor. "Help me!"

Carlos held up his hands and shrugged.

"You promised! *You promised you wouldn't give him my name!*"

And then his words became nothing but muffled shouts as they threw him to the carpet. The white man held him there while Vishon spread out a plastic tarp beside him.

"And Carlos?" Santiago gestured, and Carlos tore his attention away from the situation unfolding in the floor. "If I see you again without Lito Porto's head...bottlecapping will be the least of what I do to you."

Carlos left. The door swung shut behind him, just as Diego began to scream.

9

The torture was over, and what was left of Palacios was being loaded into plastic garbage bags.

Vishon asked Santiago, "You rilly trust dat *bomba* ta get de job done, boss?"

"Stranger things have happened," Santiago answered. He scratched his chin thoughtfully. "But I'm certainly not going to let them slip away without some insurance. Take a few men and get out to Prince George so you can follow them. If the job's not done by midnight, kill them all—including Degas—and burn that sad excuse for a boat to ashes."

10

When Cherrywine found her, Amber was sitting cross-legged on the narrow strip of beach that ran in front of the hotel they'd stayed in last night, after getting to Nassau at two in the morning. They'd sat apart on the flight down—her and Justin together in coach, Eric and his blonde up in first class—so Amber barely had a chance to say two words to the other girl since meeting her at the airport. She'd joked with Justin that the girl had to be a stripper.

"Hey girlfriend!" Cherrywine flopped down beside her, stretching out long, bronzed legs that caught the eye of every male walking by. The two of them would never be mistaken for relatives, not even distant. Amber was athletically thin compared to the other girl's curves, with dark hair so short it barely peeked out from under the edges of her ball cap, and dressed in a conservative pair of khaki shorts, t-shirt, and flip flops. She looked down to find Cherrywine had worn four-inch, zebra stripe heels to walk on the beach. The other girl noticed Amber's gaze and slid the footwear off so she could dig her pink toenails into the sand. "Yeah, I totally know. They're not the most practical beachwear, right? But when Eric asked me go on this trip, I didn't have time to go home and pack anything. I'm just glad one of the other girls at *Love Makers* had a bikini that fit me!"

Well, that answered the stripper question. Although Cherrywine's definition of 'fit' seemed questionable, considering her breasts were one jiggle away from full release.

Amber didn't answer. She didn't want company, she wanted to think. She turned back to the sliver of blue ocean stretched out in front of her and pretended to be engrossed by the people windsurfing and snorkeling out there, even though her mind was light years away.

"So what're you studying?" Cherrywine asked, looking around her at the bag on the sand.

"Linguistics."

"Do you wanna be an Italian chef or something?"

Amber had to kick that one over in her head a few times before saying, "No, *linguistics*. Language."

"Oh. What can you do with that?"

"I can tell that most people probably believe you're from California, but you're really from Oregon. Somewhere up north, but inland. More rural than Portland. Am I right?"

Cherrywine squealed in delight and slapped Amber on the shoulder. "Oh my god, I was born in Condon! How'd you *know* that?"

"The vowels phonemes in the way you said 'totally.' The vowels always tell."

"That's like a magic trick or something! They taught you that in college?"

Amber shrugged. "I've always had an ear for language."

They lapsed into uncomfortable silence for only a few seconds before Cherrywine pointed at one of the windsurfers and exclaimed, "I did that once! It was really fun! But when I did it, the instructor said we had to be strapped together. You know, for safety." Her face scrunched up. "Don't know why he held on to my tits, though."

Amber sighed. Probably best to confront this problem head-on. "Why are you here, Cherrywine?"

"We flew here together, remember?"

"No, I mean, *here*, talking to me."

"The guys asked me to see if you were okay."

"Which means Eric wanted you to make sure I got on the boat in a timely fashion, so he's not inconvenienced in any way."

The other girl squinted. "I guess. You don't really like him, huh?"

"No. But he's Justin's best friend for reasons I'll never under-stand, so I have to tolerate him. What's your excuse?"

"My excuse?"

"Yeah, I mean, how can you stand that asshole? You're a... reasonably intelligent girl. What made you want to spend more than five minutes around him? Is it the money, the looks, what?"

"Um, hello? It was a free trip to the Bahamas! Who's gonna turn that down?"

"Cherrywine, *nothing's* free. Just because there was no cost for you to come down here, doesn't mean there's no debt to be paid. If you didn't find that out yesterday, I guarantee you will tonight."

From the way her eyes dropped to the sand and watched her wiggling toes, Amber suspected the girl knew this already. For a moment, she felt bad. She wasn't mad at Cherrywine, after all. She wasn't even mad at Eric. They were just convenient targets. In a way, she was mad at herself.

And Justin too, if she were being honest.

"I don't know," Cherrywine muttered. "He just seemed nice. And way hot. And I just kinda thought..."

"That he would be your Prince Charming. Sweep you off your stripper heels, and ride away with you into the sunset for a happy ending."

Cherrywine smiled cautiously. "It happened to some of the other girls. One of them married this guy that owns a Jaguar dealership and he gave her one with the cutest little license plate on it. I guess I thought, why not me?"

"Because there are no happy endings." Amber could feel tears gathering at the corners of her eyes and hated it. She hoped they were in the shadow cast by the brim of her ball cap. "And defi-nitely no Prince Charmings."

"Hey sweetie...you all right?"

Amber nodded. Wiped at her eyes. Said nothing.

"Well, okay then. I guess I'll leave you alone. See you on the boat."

Cherrywine got up, and Amber had the sudden, undeniable urge to talk to *someone* about this, to unload on another human being, and since all of her friends were a thousand miles away, she would have to make do with this Barbie blow-up doll.

"I'm scared, okay?"

"Oh my god, totally me too!" Cherrywine plopped back down and clutched at her arm. "All that talk about the Bermuda Triangle earlier has got me frrrreaked out!"

Amber shook her head. "Not about that. If Eric Renquist has ever been right about anything in his whole miserable life, it's that the Bermuda Triangle is just a bunch of garbage."

"Well then, what are you scared of?"

She spoke in a distant voice, cramming words into a series of halting phrases as she relived the horror all over again. "Last night...when we got to the hotel...Justin passed out...but I needed some toothpaste...so I looked in his bag...and...that's when I found it."

Cherrywine gasped. "Another woman's panties?"

"Uh...no."

"A severed head?"

"That's a pretty big leap from underwear to decapitation. No, it was an engagement ring. I think he's planning to propose tonight."

Cherrywine opened her mouth to gasp again, then slowly closed it. "I don't get it. Isn't that good?"

Amber pulled the cap as low as it could go over her eyes and raked the sand with her fingers. "You would think so. We've been dating two years now. We both graduate in a few months. And, until I saw that ring with my own eyes, I would've sworn that I loved him."

"Soooo...you don't then?"

She hesitated, unable to find the words to explain this to herself, let alone anyone else. She was a linguistics major for Christ's sake, this shouldn't be so hard. "Did you...did you ever have one of those prisms as a kid?"

"Nope. My parents drove a Mitsubishi."

Amber blinked at her for several long seconds. "A *toy* prism. You look through it and it breaks up everything you see into a series of repeating images."

"Oh, you mean a fly's eye!"

"...you lost me again."

"That's what my brother called 'em, a fly's eye. Cause he said that's what everything looks like to a fly."

"Okay, yes, a fly's eye. Well, when I was a kid, I had one that I looked through a lot, and I used to think about how all those reflections could be different universes. Alternate dimensions, I mean. Where I was another person, with a different name or different parents."

"Don't take this wrong way sweetie, but, uh...you were kinda weird."

A laugh escaped Amber. "Yeah, I guess so. But the point I'm trying to make is, the last few years, I've just been complacently rolling along through life, as if there were only one path to take. But when I saw that diamond glittering at me from the bottom of Justin's bag...I thought about that prism again for the first time in years." She tilted her head back and looked up at the cloudless sky, which was only a few shades lighter than the ocean. "I mean, I haven't even really settled on what I'm gonna do with my degree yet. There's this lab position open in Russia, an experiment working with a form of electronic sign language that one of my professors said I'd be perfect for. But Justin can't come with me for that. I don't know, it felt like I still had time to decide all this, but now things are moving so fast and I'm just...terrified of what'll come out of my mouth when he asks. I wish he hadn't picked now to do it."

To her surprise, Cherrywine wrapped an arm around her shoulders, a familiar gesture that even the friends Amber had known for years wouldn't have tried. "My grandma used to say, 'a short truth hurts less than a long lie.' Then again, my grandpa tried to tell her that after he admitted to sleeping with the neighbor, and she almost took his eye out with a nail file!"

Amber laughed again. "Thanks, Cherrywine. That actually helps."

At this, the other girl beamed. "Great! I wanted us to be friends, seeing as how we're gonna be crammed up on the boat together for a few days!"

"Yeah. Me too."

Amber was even more surprised to find that she actually meant this.

11

The *Steel Runner* had started out life as a commercial fishing ship, but so many modifications had been made to it over the years, it was more of a hybrid now. Lito had stolen it from a police impound dock in Miami nearly eight years ago, where it had been sitting after the previous owners were arrested for human trafficking out of Cuba. With a wheelhouse on deck and ample space below for crew berths and cargo holds, it had served their needs as he and Ray began to pick up crew members.

Most of the gunmetal gray hull was slowly surrendering to rust, but Jericho had completely upgraded the innards, integrating a state-of-the-art electrical conversion system for the engine that improved fuel economy and drain on the batteries. She was in deceptively great shape, which was exactly how Lito wanted it. Some pirate crews working these waters couldn't resist painting skull and crossbones on their bows, or running up the black flag every chance they got. When you asked these guys why they did it—these men who were usually the meanest, the most violent, and had the least hesitation over killing—they invariably said it was for the intimidation factor, but the truth was, they were all head-over-heels in love with some very outdated ideas about the profession.

Lito ran his hand along the *Steel Runner's* side as he and Ray arrived back from the city, with Cheech hobbling along at the end of his leash in front of them. The book he was reading suggested making some object in one's life a 'center'—a sort of compass needle that pointed toward inner peace—and his ship served readily.

Ahead, Mondo, their cook and part-time cabin boy, looked up with bloodshot eyes from where he sat on the dock with his feet dangling in the water. Tufts of shockingly white hair stood up on either side of his otherwise bald scalp.

"Yo Mondo, what's for dinner?" Ray called.

"Fuck you, tha's what's fo dinnah," Mondo growled. "You wanna know befo I cook, get in there and do it yo'self. Till then, don't fuck up my buzz, cuz."

Ray planted a knee in the small of his back and gave a little shove. The old black man screeched and clutched at the pier.

"*Whadaya do that fo? I can't be swimmin when I'm high!*"

"You smoke up the last of my stash old man?"

"I don't need yo' cheap-ass weed to get up, Vargas! I go for premium shit! And if you evah do that again…"

"What? You gonna put one of your voodoo curses on me, old man?"

Mondo fixed Ray with a glare from his left eye, the one that bulged from its socket. "No. But you keep pokin fun at my religion, I might have ta sue you fo harassment in the workplace." Ray laughed.

"Mondo." Lito snapped his fingers in the man's heavily-creased face to get his attention. "Everything ready to go?"

"Yeah, but Cap'n…I think we oughta call it off." He pointed toward the bay in front of them, and the open seas beyond. "Somethin out there just don't feel right. I read the bones this mornin, and they came up bad."

Ray rolled his eyes. "You say that every time, Mondo."

"I'll take it under advisement," Lito told him. "The others get back yet?"

Mondo shrugged bony shoulders. "Rabid and Jorge're fartin around somewhere. Ain't seen Jericho or yo' boy Carlos. Who didn't help me with shit, by the way!"

Lito was on the verge of commenting when Ray tapped him and pointed over his shoulder. Strolling up the pier from the direction they'd just come was Carlos Degas.

"Get ready to leave port, you two. I wanna be gone before those rich kids pull out."

Mondo saluted, got slowly to his feet, and limped up the short gangplank on his bad leg, mumbling under his breath the whole way. Ray followed behind the older man, leading the dog.

Lito walked out to meet Carlos. The kid's swagger never faltered. He met Lito's gaze with open defiance. "'Sup?"

"Where you been, Carlos?"

"Had some bidness in the city."

"What kinda business?"

The kid shrugged. "You know how we do, homey."

Lito crossed his arms, flexed the muscles beneath his floral print shirt. "No, I don't know, Carlos. I don't know, because you don't have any business that's not *my* business."

"What's that supposed ta mean?"

"I gave you an order. You didn't follow it."

"Said I was busy. Hadda go into the city ta make that green. Call it a...secondary income."

"Yeah, well, as long as I'm your captain, you clear it with me. You know what woulda happened if someone had recognized you while you were out earnin your 'secondary income?'"

Carlos snorted and stared at the dock. Lito had first met the kid when he was thirteen, giving his mother hell, running with a street gang, in-and-out of jail every other week. He had a real problem with authority figures, and his attitude hadn't improved much since then. This life didn't suit him, but Lito had promised Marisol Degas, who he'd been madly in love with before she contracted an aggressive stomach cancer, that he would look after the boy when she died. Maybe piracy wasn't exactly what the woman had in mind, but Lito had always figured it was just until the kid was old enough to find his own way.

Carlos said, "Maybe if my cuts were a little bigger, I wouldn't hafta do stuff like this."

"You get bigger cuts when you help out with the jobs. I told you, you gotta pay your dues. If I can't trust you to clean out the holds, how am I gonna trust you to help us take a ship?"

Carlos rolled his eyes and muttered something that sounded like, "Least I'm man enough to do what needs to be done."

Lito wanted to grab him. Wanted to smack him one across the jaw. But that would've been the technique employed by his own father, a man who'd been plagued by so much rage that it finally burst his heart at the age of 48. Instead, Lito took a deep, cleansing breath and flushed his negativity before speaking. "Look, you made it clear you don't wanna be part of this crew. I get that. But nobody's keepin you here. You're free to go whenever you want—"

"Go *where*? I ain't got a home or a fuckin dollar to my name since you been draggin me around!"

"—but until you do, you follow orders," Lito finished.

"Okay, fine, whatevah. Lemme give your boots a spit shine, massa!" Carlos held up his hands. "We done here?"

Lito nodded. The kid walked around him and mounted the gangplank of the boat. When he was halfway up, Lito said, "Carlos...if you were anybody else, I woulda kicked your ass off this boat a long time ago. I don't need someone givin me attitude. I kept you around cause I promised your mom. Even so...I think after this job is over, we're gonna need to have a serious talk about your future aboard the *Steel Runner*."

To his amazement, the kid threw back his head and started laughing. "Oh yeah, homey. Definitely. I'm lookin forward to that one."

12

Justin had gotten his first look at the *MishMasher* in a picture when Donnie Rehnquist bought it last year. Eric went around the

Penn U. campus for a week, shoving the yacht under everyone's nose. But, Justin had to admit, the photo hadn't done the craft justice. It was a huge, sleek machine, glossed to perfection and glaring white in the sun, with a razor-sharp belly designed to slice through the waves, and massive twin inboard diesels that sounded like jet engines. The steering and controls were up a short staircase in a small compartment that overlooked the front bow. Reclining deck chairs were laid out there, and at the stern was a quartet of plush, padded benches arranged in a square around a built-in fire pit. Justin had never even been on a boat before, and had to get used to the feeling of the deck moving and rocking beneath him.

Truth be told, the invite to come on this trip had taken him by surprise. Eric had a crew of Delta Sig lackeys at school, any of which would've killed to come with him. Instead, Eric caught him one day on the quad and, with that old, hungry gleam in his eye, begged Justin to come to the Bermuda Triangle over Spring Break. Only now was the reason obvious: Eric couldn't risk exposing his morbid obsessions to the brainless lunks that followed him around, so he'd turned to good ol' reliable Justin.

"You gonna let me drive this baby?" he asked, when they stepped aboard the yacht.

"Not on your life, shithead. Nobody drives this thing but me."

The concierge from the hotel delivered their luggage dockside after a huge tip, and Eric left Justin to bring the bags on board while he ran an errand. After getting his and Amber's stuff into their cabin—not too spacious but nice, everything carved from a rich shade of mahogany—he took off his shirt and changed into his trunks, then dug into his bag and found the purple, velvet-covered box at the bottom.

He opened it, made sure the diamond ring was perfectly positioned inside. He'd worked an extra shift every week for the past eight months at the answering service just so he could afford the thing, then bought it as soon as Amber agreed to come with them.

Justin closed the lid and slipped the box into the pocket of his shorts. He had no idea when or how he would do this, he just wanted it on hand for when the moment was right. Amber deserved nothing less. He'd known she was the one almost as soon as he met her, but he never felt rushed to propose.

Until recently.

There had been this niggling little voice in the back of his head lately that told him if he didn't close the deal soon, it might never happen.

To take his mind off this, he explored the rest of the below-deck area: the ship's single bathroom, a game room complete with a ping pong table, and the kitchenette, where he popped the tab on a beer from the fully stocked fridge. Then he slid aside the door to the larger bedroom down the hall, meaning to just poke his head in and have a look around.

The master cabin was *gorgeous*. It took up probably the front third of the boat, with an oval porthole across one wall that looked out on the harbor. The bed was a king, with a framed painting of Paris above it that—knowing Donnie Renquist—was probably worth a small fortune itself.

A series of mounted cabinets lined the wall to the left of the door. Justin popped one open to sneak a peek. They contained a fully stocked bar with every liquor known to man, and a few bottles of vintage wine. He was just closing the door again when he noticed the knob protruding from the back wall of the cabinet.

He moved aside glass bottles to get a better look. There was a panel back there, expertly cut into the bulkhead so that it was almost camouflaged. Half of him knew he should walk away, but the other half knew the curiosity would kill him if he didn't see what treasures Eric's old man was hiding in there.

Justin reached in and pulled the knob. The trap door flopped open just as a wave moved the boat against the dock, causing the floor to tilt at a sudden grade. He stumbled back a step as something about the size and shape of a tube of toothpaste wrapped in brown parcel paper came rolling out of the liquor cabinet. Justin tried to catch it, but it squirted through his fingers and struck the floor beside the bed.

He squatted next to the object. The paper had shredded up one side, revealing a narrow, ornate statue of a horned figure, made of an opaque glass. It looked like a satanic Oscar. As he studied it, he noticed one of the horns ended in a ragged edge.

"Shit. Ah, goddamn it." Had he done that? There was no telling what the thing had been worth. He dropped to his knees and ran his hands through the carpet. The missing piece, judging from the other side, would be about the length of his pinky from the second knuckle up but much thinner, and incredibly hard to see against the dark rug.

Footsteps and voices drifted above his head. He scooped up the statue and went back to the compartment. This time, he spotted the other objects that took up residence in the small space: a snub-nosed .38 revolver and a gallon baggie of white powder. Justin carefully laid the figurine beside them and closed the panel.

He moved the bottles back, closed everything behind him, and hurried up to the deck.

13

Eric waited until Justin was settled aboard the *MishMasher* before feeding him some story about needing to run back to the hotel. Luckily, his best friend—who spent most of his life in naïve bliss, in Eric's opinion; always had, ever since they were kids—didn't offer to come with him. Eric slipped away, stepped onto the dock, and almost stumbled over a dark, dreadlocked native kneeling down in front of the yacht's prow as he came around the corner of the pier.

"What the fuck, man?"

The native picked up a satchel from the dock, stood up, and gave him a big grin. "Sorry, *mon*. Just tyin me shoe."

"Yeah, well do it away from my boat, asshole." He might've said more, might've pounded the guy's smarmy, big-lipped face, but the order of the day was low-key. Just because he had a destiny didn't mean he should tempt fate. After the drop off in Bermuda tomorrow, he could resume his regularly scheduled programming and stop feeling so goddamn tense.

So he went around the guy and kept walking, heading all the way back to the boardwalk. From here he jogged another two blocks to the west, until he came to a payphone he'd spotted earlier, jammed far back in a little alley niche between island trinket stores.

As he picked up the receiver, he heard a plaintive mewling behind him. Across the narrow alley, far back in the shadows of a dumpster, a bloated, orange and white tabby had made a nest to give birth in. She lay on her side, looking frazzled and exhausted, as four kittens rolled and crawled across her. Eric made kissy noises at them as he dialed a number with a Philadelphia area code.

On the other end, the great Donald Renquist picked up after three rings. "Christ, *what*?"

"Hey, it's me."

"*Me?* Who the fuck is *me?*"

"It's Eric, Dad."

"Oh. Son." There was a split second while this was digested by his father before he continued yelling, with his usual habit of emphasizing all the important words. "Well, what the hell are you doing calling me on *this* line? I told you not to call me here! This is where you call me when you're my *son*, but when you're out on a job for me, you are *not* my son, you're an *employee*, and *employees* call me on the employee *line*, you got that through your head this time?"

"Yeah, Dad, I got it, I'm sorry." None of Eric's friends, not even Justin, had ever heard the subservient tone coming out of his mouth. Most would never have even guessed him capable of it.

"Hang on a sec." There was the sound of shuffling movement over the phone, then the click of a door being closed. He imagined his father sealing himself into the Closet, a small room at the back of his office that he regularly swept for bugs. "Okay, what is it, kid? I'm in the middle of business."

Business. Eric had found out all about his father's *business* when he was in the fifth grade, and two men had tried to ambush their limo on the way to school. He never made it to class that day, was instead brought along to an empty warehouse to watch as his father and three associates beat the men to death. A lesson on the importance of ethics, he'd been told, and far more important than anything he'd learn in school. The only thing Eric could remember from that day was Big Donnie Renquist kicking those two would-be hitmen in the face while he screamed, "*You don't touch my family!*"

"I'm just calling to, you know, tell you everything's all right. I made the pick up last night at the airport, and it's on the boat now."

His father's voice softened. "That's good, kid. Real good. You just drop it off to my guy in Bermuda and get back here. You do a good job on this, and I'll see if maybe I can get you some other work."

"Yes sir. But...what is that thing, Dad? Is it, like, an antique or something?"

"Who knows? Ol' Carbini was into all sortsa weird shit. I'm sure it's worth a fortune to the right people, but he asked me to deliver it if anything happened to him, so that's what I'm doing. All you need to keep in mind is that it's probably hot enough to get you a nice stint behind bars if you get caught with it."

"Okay. I'll be careful."

"Good boy. Now, you need anything else? Some more money, maybe?"

"Naw, we're pretty much set. We're about to leave in just a few—"

"Wait a minute, what the hell're you talking about, *we*? Who's there with you?"

Eric's lungs gave a sudden hitch. "I-I brought down some people, Justin and a couple of girls. We're gonna go through the Bermuda Triangle, just like I always wanted..."

"*You fucking moron!*" Donnie Renquist roared over the phone line. "Did I *tell* you to bring anybody with you? *Did* I?"

"No sir." Eric's hand began to shake, his fingers gripping the pay phone receiver so hard, the knuckles turned a ghostly white. A vein pulsed at his forehead, throbbing with a beat he could actually feel.

"This ain't a goddamn *pleasure cruise*, you're fucking *smuggling* contraband through international waters! If I wanted you to *party* and get your *dick* wet, I'd've sent you back to that school you've been *failing* at for the past four years!"

"I'm sorry, sir. I just didn't realize." His whole body quivered with tension now. A red ring crept in at the edges of his vision.

His father gave an exasperated sigh. "Just get it done, Eric. You think you can manage that? Just get it done and get your dumb ass back here with my boat." He hung up.

Eric stood where he was for several long seconds, with the receiver pressed to his ear. He had to force his cramped fingers to uncurl and let the receiver fall. It dangled at the end of its cord. The whole world seemed to stand out in harsh tones, a palette of blues and greens and reds that all hurt his eyes. He walked out of the little niche with the pay phone and crossed the alley in short, robotic steps.

The family of kittens looked up just as he brought his heel down on them.

Eric stomped and stomped and stomped, until all the squealing cries of pain stopped, until there was nothing but a lumpy puddle of bones and fur under his foot, until the splatter of blood on the alley wall came up almost as high as his knee. Later, he would recall none of this, just as he didn't remember any of the other animals he'd mutilated over the years, or that townie girl last spring, the one that had been on the missing posters all around campus for a few months...

He pulled a newspaper out of the dumpster and used it to wipe the worst of the blood from his sandals and legs, then started back to the boat.

2

WEEDS

MORE STORIES

A MODEST PROPOSAL

CHERRYWINE GETS THE BILL

1

The *MishMasher* pulled out of dock at Prince George around two in the afternoon, with the sun straddling the ocean off the port bow and casting ripples of golden fire across the water. The sky was still gorgeous and clear besides an ink spot of dark clouds to the south. Eric throttled the engines up to a steady roar, blasting the yacht over the surface at close to 40 miles per hour. Within minutes, Nassau fell away behind them, the whole island sinking into the pencil-thin line of the horizon.

The solitude made Amber feel a little helpless. She imagined how they must look from high above, a tiny speck on an endless blue field. She'd been on boats, but always within view of a shoreline. Out here, with only ocean on all sides…it was a little disorienting. She tried to compare the experience to long road trips she'd taken—one in particular through the Mojave, where the only things around had been scrub grass and sand dunes—but being miles away from civilization in a boat wasn't like being in a car; you could get out of a car if you needed to, and it wouldn't ever sink out from under you.

More than anything though, it just made her feel trapped. Sort of smothered. She finally had to push these thoughts away before she freaked herself out.

Eric remained upstairs at the controls, blasting Pantera and Megadeth over the boat's stereo system. Cherrywine spent the time stretched out on one of the deck chairs, sunbathing with her top off. Usually behavior like that would've annoyed the piss out of her, but the new Amber—the one that had looked through the fly's eye and come out the other side—found it amusing. She couldn't help but think how much easier it would make things if Cherrywine seduced Justin...and maybe they slipped away... and then Amber caught the two of them together, giving her the perfect, guilt-free excuse to break up with him.

Yeah, right. As far as she could see, the big boy scout wasn't even trying to ogle anymore. Was it so much to ask for him to just cheat on her?

For the first time, the odd sense of apathy for him that had been growing in her since last night was replaced by full-on annoyance.

He tried to get her to go to the back of the boat, where they'd have some privacy, but she grabbed her textbooks and took a seat near the front, overlooking the brilliant blue water as it rushed beneath them. The wind in her face felt wonderful. She took off her hat to enjoy it, freeing her short mop of dark hair. Justin followed like a little lost puppy, taking the opposite end of the bench, and that annoyed her, too.

"*It's beautiful, don't you think?*" he asked, leaning close to her and shouting over the sound of music, motors and wind.

She pointed at her ear, shook her head, and buried her nose in her studying.

At some point, she dozed, and the next time her eyes opened, the world had been painted with black. A bloated spring moon hung in the sky, surrounded by more stars than she'd ever seen in her life, each one with a duplicate reflected on the face of the black water surrounding them. Across from her, Justin was passed out with drool glistening at the corner of his mouth. His eyes fluttered open and he gave her a smile.

The music snapped off and the engines throttled back, leaving them in silence save for the splash of the boat's wake. Their speed slowed drastically as water sucked at the hull. Floodlights blazed down on the deck from the top of the control booth.

Amber checked her watch, pressing the button on the side to light up the face. Just before seven o'clock. It was chilly now that the sun had gone down, and the air felt crackly with the threat of discharge. She thought she caught a faint whiff of ozone on the breeze. Amber rubbed at the goose bumps spreading up her arms, and a giant spark of static electricity jumped from the vinyl back of the couch to her bare flesh. She couldn't stop a small squeak of surprise from escaping her, but no one noticed.

Eric came down with a beer in one hand and a joint in the other. He blew a ream of sweet smoke into the crisp sea air. "Welcome to Sargasso, ladies and gentleman."

"*Ewww!*" Cherrywine's voice came from the railing, where she was tying her skimpy top back on. Eric started toward her. Justin and Amber followed, leaning over beside the stripper as she asked, "What is that stuff?"

"That is what gave this place its name," Eric said. "'Sargasso' means a whole shitload of seaweed."

Around the boat, as far as the floodlights could reach, the calm, even surface of the water was interrupted by floating mats of vegetation. Amber figured they must be brown or green, but they had an oily sheen in the light that almost made them look blue. Their previous speed had created a wave that shoved the plants out of their path, but now that they were drifting, the seaweed crept back in to caress the side of the hull at the waterline.

A wave of fresh goose pimples moved up Amber's arms.

Justin stuck out his tongue. "Ugh. I guess going for a night swim's out."

Eric grinned. "Plenty of stories about this stuff too. Sailors used to be scared of it." He grabbed the waist-high railing and twisted his hands on the metal. "Just think: every part of the

Bermuda Triangle legend—every boat or plane that's ever disappeared—happened right out here."

"I thought all those stories were fake," Amber muttered.

"I said *most*. Still a few mysteries they haven't solved, and people gone missing. Think about it: their bodies are probably right under our feet!"

"Must be nice to pick and choose what you believe."

"What can I say, I'm a skeptic that wants to be proven wrong."

"I don't like it!" Cherrywine complained. "Can we go somewhere else?"

"Not while it's dark. I don't wanna get this stuff caught in the props. This is where we set up shop for the night."

Amber thought that excuse stank of bullshit—a way to make sure they stayed put until morning—but she said nothing.

"Where are we, exactly?" Justin asked.

"About halfway between the Bahamas and Bermuda. Three hundred miles from the closest land."

"You're *sure* you know how to get there?" Justin sounded a little unnerved himself. Maybe Amber wasn't the only one feeling claustrophobic.

"Dude, what do you think, I'm navigating by the stars? This ship has fully-functional GPS. *I* don't have to know jack shit."

"And we have enough gas?"

"Jesus, yes, what the hell's wrong with you, man? Your dick fall off on the way here?"

Amber was only half-listening to this exchange as she watched the endless stretch of ocean ahead of them. Everything was a flat, featureless landscape beyond the floodlights, but, for just a second, she could've sworn she saw a tiny blip in the distance, a shape silhouetted against the bruised purple line of the horizon. She scanned the darkness, trying to pick it out again.

Eric passed the joint to Justin, who took a hit. "All right people, let's party."

2

Lito harbored no hope of keeping up with the rich kids' boat. The *Steel Runner* wasn't made for speed, but it didn't matter. The GPS screen beside him showed the exact location of their prey, thanks to the tracker Jericho put on their hull. It took another two hours after their dot stopped moving to catch up, even with the *Runner*'s engines opened all the way. When the distance between them closed to ten miles, Lito throttled back to a crawl but continued forward until he spotted the gleam of their running lights ahead.

He took a pair of binoculars from under the wheel and trained them on the yacht. The Halverson blazed out there. Figures moved around on the deck.

"Jesus, it's like these kids *wanna* get jacked," Ray said in Spanish behind him.

"I know. That's what money does to these rich assholes. No self-preservation instinct."

"They'll learn tonight." Ray chuckled and lit up a cigarette, then offered the pack to Lito, who declined. "You decide what we're gonna do with 'em?"

Lito shrugged. They'd never attempted to take an entire boat. It was much easier to board, subdue the passengers, strip the ship down, and leave. Taking prisoners was an added complication…but that gleaming white yacht—parked a good three or four hours from help of any kind—was too tempting to pass up. "Dump 'em in the water off the nearest port, I guess."

"Alive?"

Lito paused to think about that. "Unless they force us to do otherwise."

"Guess that would fuck up this whole yin-yang thing you got goin, huh?"

Ray's tone, not to mention the smirk on his face, told Lito how funny he thought his friend's recent interest in the eastern philosophies was. The rest of the crew hadn't taken too kindly to his avoid-murder-at-all-costs edict either. "Well, killin *is* bad for the soul, Ray, but this is more about business, plain and simple. The more tourists turn up missin or dead around here, the sooner we're gonna have Coast Guard and police boats shoved up our ass on routine patrols."

"Yeah, like just takin their half-a-million-dollar boat is gonna be any better." Ray shook his head. "In any case, you better tell the others the plan then. Rabid and Jorge are downstairs right now playin poker to decide who gets the blonde."

"Where's Carlos?" Lito tried not to sound too interested.

"Locked in his bunk like a fuckin teenager."

"He *is* a fuckin teenager."

"He's a disrespectful shithead who don't belong here, Lito. He ain't cut out for this lifestyle."

"Give him time."

"We've given him two years. I don't trust him. And that's not ever gonna change."

Lito said nothing, just stared out the wheelhouse window at the distant lights of the yacht off the starboard bow. Ray smoked his cigarette down to the filter and asked, "If we manage to move that boat for three-hundred thou, your cut will be somewhere just north of a hundred. What're you gonna do with that much money?"

"Fix up the *Runner*, probably. You?"

Ray took his time answering. "Been meanin to talk to you about that. This whole deal goes okay...I'm out. Headin into the states."

"Bullshit."

"I'm serious, Lito."

"Believe it when I see it."

"It's true. I'm goin, and Jericho's comin with me. Maybe Mondo, too."

Lito frowned. "Really? They said that?"

"Yep. Woulda asked Rabid and his little sidekick, but they're a bit too trigger-happy for the straight life."

"But why now, all of a sudden?"

"Because we'll have the cash. Because that fucker back in Cuba was a wake-up call. The Dominican wants our blood, and sooner or later he's gonna get it. We've had a good run, but I want out before I end up dead. Or worse, like Brewster."

Brewster, their last captain, had been caught by the Coast Guard down south of Key Largo just a few weeks after Lito and Ray had stolen the *Steel Runner*. Due to some jurisdictional quirk of the maritime law, he'd been remanded to Mexico, where he was serving out his time in a fleabag prison that only saw sunlight for fifteen minutes each day.

Ray said, "You could come too, you know."

"And do what?"

"Me and Jericho wanna open up a shop on the beach. Maybe in California. Fixin boat engines. Mondo can sell sandwiches to the tourists."

Lito burst out laughing.

"What's up?" Ray sounded pissed.

"Sorry man, I was just imaginin the three of you livin together like the fuckin Cleaver family."

Ray's lips puckered. "Yeah, well, suit yourself, man. I'll go get the others ready to move." He walked out of the wheelhouse, then poked his head back in. "And just so you know, if you decide to come, Carlos ain't invited to tag along."

Lito was still laughing, but it soon tapered. He'd been friends with Ray a long time. He couldn't imagine what life would be like without the man watching his back, or the *Steel Runner* with a new crew.

He turned to watch the rich kids' yacht...and that was when he saw the stuttered explosion of blue light somewhere far beyond the other ship.

"Whoa. What the hell?"

The sky lit up in an irregular series of muted flashes, like lightning wrapped in the heart of thick clouds, except, judging by the angle of its fade, the origin had to be somewhere on the water's surface. The color was beautiful, the pure blue of a clean-cut sapphire. He'd seen *green* flashes before, the phenomenon that occurs at dusk on the high seas, but, besides the fact that this was the wrong color, it was far too late in the day for one to appear, and they were one single burst rather than quick blips. These faded away as fast as they'd begun, cycling down like the last reverbs of an echo.

His stomach gave an odd twinge, as though dinner wasn't quite sitting right.

Lito stepped out of the wheelhouse and walked to the bow of the ship. The night was still and utterly silent, the sky clear except for a high bank of building thunderheads that blotted out the stars behind them, to the southeast. Barely a wave stirred the unending mats of seaweed. The ocean was like a sheet of black glass.

But the breeze carried a hint of something sharp and almost bitter.

He scanned the horizon to the west with the binoculars. It did no good; with the moon only a crescent above, the night was pitch. It was doubtful the rich kids would've seen the distant blue sparks with their floodlights on, but he kept an eye on their boat for movement anyway.

If there was another ship out there...they would have to reconsider their approach to this operation.

3

Carlos locked himself in his microscopic bunk after leaving port, but he'd gotten no sleep. He just stared at the ceiling and, to keep from remembering the way Diego had screamed, he daydreamed about how things would be different once this ship was his.

But how the hell was he supposed to carry out Santiago's orders? It all seemed so easy when he was standing in front of the man, but, then again, he supposed the prospect of climbing Kilimanjaro in your underwear looked like a cakewalk when the alternative was torture and death. Now though...? He couldn't just walk out there and start shooting. He wasn't the greatest shot, and he had no doubts a straight firefight against the entire crew would end badly for him.

And issat somethin you could really do anyway? Kill 'em all in cold blood? They the closest thing you had to family since your mom died.

Rather than answer, he tucked the pistol in the back of his pants, pulled the tail of his wife-beater over it, and stepped out of his bunk.

A small common area was just outside. Rabid, Jorge, and Jericho sat at a rickety folding table amidst the remains of several cases of beer and two bottles of tequila, playing cards. Mondo stood at the ancient range stove against the bulkhead, grilling up hamburgers that always tasted like fish and copper to Carlos. A cloud of cigarette and weed smoke hung over the scene.

Rabid's eyes rolled up from his cards to Carlos. "Well well, mates, the li'l bunny rabbit poked his head outta his hole. Whatcha think bunny, we gettin six more weeks of winter?"

Jorge cackled. Mondo turned and gave him a squinty stinkeye. The old man was pissed about Carlos bugging out earlier.

"That's groundhogs, you Aussie redneck," he muttered, and headed for the stairs up to the main deck.

Rabid was up in a heartbeat, throwing down his cards and shoving the table aside. He put one thick arm across the door. A hammerhead shark stretched from wrist to elbow. Behind him, Jorge sat forward to watch. Jericho groaned and said, "Leave de boy alone and let's play, Rabid."

The hulking Australian paid no attention to them, just leaned down and snarled, "What'd you say, you faggot?"

Carlos knew the smart thing to do. Rabid was that special steroid brand of nuts, where a person's brains leaked into their muscles and got converted to pure violent fury. Provoking him was as dangerous as poking a sleeping bear with your dick.

But things felt different today. *He* felt different.

"Get your arm out my way, muhfuckah," he said slowly. "Or else."

"Else what? You'll go tell daddy on me?"

"Lito ain't my father."

"That's right. You don't know who your bloody father is, do ya?"

The pistol was in Carlos's hand before his brain registered he was reaching for it. He pressed the barrel against the forehead of the wolf tattooed in the middle of Rabid's chest. Jorge's snickering laughter stopped.

"You pointin a gun at me, son?" Rabid leaned into him, forcing Carlos to push even harder. His hard eyes glittered.

"Don't," Carlos warned. The trigger of the gun felt like ice beneath his finger.

"You better not *ever* pull a bloody gun on me unless you got the balls to finish business, mate. Cause unlike Lito, I don't give a shit about you. I got no qualms about breakin every bone in your body while you're asleep, slittin your throat, and dumpin you overboard for the barracudas while you're still squirmin."

Carlos wanted to kill him. *Pow.* One bullet straight through the heart, and one of his six problems was solved.

But if he did, there would be no turning back. He'd have to finish as many of them as he could right now.

Rabid didn't look intimidated in the least. "I'm givin you one chance, you li'l pig fucker. Put that pussy peashooter away and get outta my face."

Carlos let the weight of the gun drag his arm down.

Rabid's open hand came up and then smashed across his cheek. Carlos was spun halfway around by the force of the belt. He touched the right side of his jaw, which already felt swollen.

Without a word, Rabid went to sit back down at the table and resume his game.

Carlos took the stairs up to the main deck two at a time, feeling broken, humiliated and a little dizzy from the teeth-loosening blow. Jorge's laughter followed him out. The salt air hit him, helping to wake him out of his stupor.

This was family?

He put the pistol back in his waistband and started toward the stern. As he passed by the narrow opening leading to the maintenance hatch for the engine room, he almost ran into Ray.

"We need to talk," the other man said.

"Jesus. What now?"

"I'll make this quick and simple: you need to get off this ship. Disappear at the next port. You've never fit in around here, and you ain't never goin to."

A sudden moment of panic speared Carlos. Leaving on his own terms was one thing, but getting outcast? He clung to the one thing that could save him. "Yeah, and what's Lito gotta say 'bout that, homey?"

"Don't know, and don't care. Lito still thinks you're a child who's eventually gonna grow up, but you and me...we know different, don't we?"

Carlos tried not to let the shock—or worse, the truth—show on his face. "You can't do nuttin to me."

Ray nodded his head thoughtfully. "You should remember, Carlos: it's Lito that gave up on violence, not me. Now get up front. We're about to make a move and as long as you're still here and gettin a cut, you're gonna work for it."

He shoved past Carlos and shouted downstairs that it was showtime. Carlos waited until the others had filed out and then glanced back at the maintenance hatch as an idea began to form. He made a sudden pledge to himself.

Whatever else happened tonight...not one of his fellow crewmembers was coming back from this alive.

4

"The best story I ever heard about the Bermuda Triangle goes like this."

Eric took another hit off the huge bong, then passed it and his lighter to Cherrywine. "Guy comes through here back in 1970, probably right about where we are now. He's sailing around the world or some shit like that. Anyway, in the middle of the night, he comes up on this old ship just floating, free-anchor. And when I say 'old,' I mean Mayflower-Spanish-Armada kind of old."

"I don't think I wanna hear this," Cherrywine whimpered, smoke dribbling from her nostrils.

Amber wasn't sure if she did either. She'd never been the skittish type—she hated those girls at school who insisted they couldn't watch horror movies—but she was beginning to feel uneasy again.

She declined the bong this time as it made a circuit around to her. Eric had built a cozy campfire in the pit at the stern of the yacht, and they'd sprawled on the four benches around the crackling flames for a couple of hours, eating sandwiches from the fridge, drinking Red Stripe and blazing through the bag of weed Eric had gotten on the island. She was already buzzed far beyond her usual limit, but it just felt so good to turn off her mind for a while. School felt deliciously far away, and, in an effort to forget all her problems, she'd made a point of avoiding eye contact with Justin across from her.

Eric ignored Cherrywine and continued. He'd obviously been waiting for just the right moment to tell his ghost story. "This guy, his name was Bidwell, he boards this ship, intending to claim it under maritime salvage. He said the thing looked brand new: no barnacles, no mildew or rot, food still on plates, not even spoiled, the whole deal." He held up a finger and lowered his voice. "So he's trying to figure a way to tow this thing into port when he starts hearing these moans from the holds downstairs."

Justin motioned for him to continue, eager for blood the way only a guy can be.

"He goes down with only a flashlight, but something attacks him. He doesn't get a good look at whatever's in there. There's too many, they're moving too fast, and all he sees are shadows coming after him."

Cherrywine covered her eyes. Amber tried closing hers, but her dizzy head amplified the slight rocking of the boat. She had to open them before she got queasy.

"Bidwell gets scratched on the arm by whatever it is, drops his flashlight, and takes off. He runs without looking back, jumps onto his ship, and sails for the horizon. He marks the location on a map and radios in to the Coast Guard. Help gets there, he takes them back to the area where he found the ship...but there's no trace of it."

"That's it?" Justin shrugged. "That's lame, it sounds just like every other Triangle story."

"Yeah, except I think this one's actually true."

"How come?"

"Three reasons." Eric leaned forward on the bench. "First of all, the guy was some kinda wall street tycoon. Got no reason to lie about it."

"Yeah, unless he just wanted the attention. Or he's nuts."

Eric shrugged. "Second, he was very specific about the fact that he dropped his flashlight aboard that ship."

"Yeah? So?"

"So it's just the kind of little detail that rings true to me. Most of the other stories you hear are so vague."

"He probably got drunk and dropped it in the ocean. What's the third reason?"

"Okay, so get this: the only reason anybody knows this story at all is because Bidwell talked to this reporter for a local paper when he got back to land to get his arm stitched up. After that... he disappeared. Nobody's seen him since."

"You think he went back to the Triangle?"

"No way, the guy was terrified. But the reporter said he was sick during the interview, like he had the flu or something. And the manager at the hotel where he stayed that night said some very men-in-black-type government guys came and took him away. They probably quarantined him. Or interrogated him. I mean, who knows what he *really* saw out here?"

Justin still looked skeptical. "Where'd you hear this one anyway?"

"Found it in a library book about conspiracy theories when we were in high school."

Amber let a harsh bark of laughter escape her. "Sounds like a reliable source."

Eric jumped to his feet, but not before Amber saw the scowl on his face. Little baby didn't like having his precious Bermuda Triangle stories doubted. He made a show of stretching and said, "Time for bed. Let's go Cherrywine."

"But I'm not tired yet!"

"That's good, cause we're not gonna be sleeping."

He grabbed her wrist and pulled her up, all but slinging her over his shoulder like a caveman.

Sudden panic knifed through Amber. She stood on wobbly legs and ran to cut them off before they made it to the stairs. "Wait, wait, don't you wanna stay up a little longer? We can… we can…uh…toast marshmallows?"

"Oh, I love marshmallows!" Cherrywine squealed.

Eric snorted. "What're you, in the fifth grade? Besides…" He shot a knowing glance at Justin that made her stomach drop. "I think your boyfriend over there wants some privacy. So he can make the biggest mistake of his life."

"Shut the fuck up, man," Justin muttered.

Eric went past her, still dragging Cherrywine behind him. The girl whispered to Amber as she went by, "Remember sweetie, just be honest."

Honest. Yeah, right. Anyway you sliced it—no matter how delicately she chose her words—this week cooped up on a boat was going to get incredibly long and uncomfortable after she told Justin he might as well take that huge diamond and toss it in the ocean *Titanic*-style for all the good it would do him.

Unless you just say yes for now…and then tell him the truth when you get home.

That option seemed even crueler. Unbelievably so.

As they reached the stairs, Eric flipped a switch on the deck that shut down the floodlights, leaving them in the glow from the last few burning embers of the fire. The stars seemed to jump out at her from the heavens. "For ambiance," he said, pronouncing the word like a snooty French waiter. They disappeared below deck.

5

Lito waited until the crew was gathered on deck before handing out assignments. He'd spotted no more of the blue flashes, and from what he could see on the yacht, the party was winding down for the night. The floodlights were off, and the deck looked empty.

"I want this to go smooth. No bloodshed, and no gunfire if possible. First and foremost, they do *not* see our faces. As long as they're on this ship, everyone wears a mask. Got me?"

They grumbled agreement.

"Who's goin over, Cap?" Jorge asked.

"Rabid. *Just* Rabid," he added quickly, before anyone could protest. To the Australian, he said, "Take one of the rowboats, get on board, and get those kids under control. Bound, gagged and blindfolded. When you signal the ship is yours, we'll dock. The prisoners come over first. Mondo, you're on jailer duty. Everybody else, transfer cargo over to the holds. Once the ship is stripped down, Ray will pilot. We're not stoppin till we're in port at Miami. I'll call Dully when we get close and let him know we're comin. Any questions?"

There were none. The group broke up. Carlos stomped away without looking at him. Rabid—who had put on a black leather biker vest to cover the majority of his tattoos—headed to the port side of the ship, where two fiberglass rowboats were lashed to the deck. Lito and Ray lowered one into the water while Rabid pulled on a black ski mask and checked the cylinder of his magnum. The huge gun was one of the few that looked correctly proportioned in his hand. Jericho offered him one of their walkies, but Rabid refused.

Lito stopped him as he swung a leg over the *Steel Runner*'s side.

"Don't hurt 'em if you don't have to. That includes the women, Rabid. They're just a bunch of college kids out lookin for a good time. Threaten 'em a little, they'll be eatin outta the palm of your hand."

Rabid's grin was a perfect example of how he'd gotten his nickname. "Oh yeah, Cap'n. Those two sheilas over there are gonna be eatin *somethin* all right, but it won't be my hand."

He dropped over the railing and landed with a thud in the smaller boat below.

6

Amber turned back to face Justin. "I know I've told you this before, but...your friend is a real dickhead."

Justin gave her a slightly drunken wave. "You gotta understand, his father...he didn't have an easy life."

"Oh yeah, poor little rich boy, woe is me. What, did Daddy not fork over his allowance on time every week?"

He raised his beer bottle and blew across the top, producing a lonely whistle, then said, "You try having a father that's the head of one of the last mob families in Philadelphia and see how normal you turn out."

"What? How do you...did *he* tell you that?"

"Nope. He hardly ever talks about his old man. Never let me meet him. I found out when we were twelve or thirteen, and his father got indicted. His face was all over the news for like a week. I was too young to really understand what it meant, but my parents didn't want me to hang out with Eric after that. His dad beat the charges and kept a pretty low profile since, so not a lot of people even remember that about Eric."

And Amber got the feeling the only reason she was getting the inside scoop now was because the alcohol had loosened Justin's tongue.

She made a show of checking her watch. It was just rounding to ten. "So you wanna go to bed too?"

"Not quite yet."

"You sure? We don't have to sleep either, you know." She tried on a seductive smile. As awful as it sounded, it would be so much easier to fuck him right now than talk to him. Anything to delay what must be coming. She'd even be willing to do that thing with her tongue he loved so much.

But instead, he patted the bench beside him. "Why don't you come over here? I feel like I haven't been able to spend any real time with you since the plane ride." He frowned. "Plus, I'm not too eager to listen to Eric and Cherrywine get it on."

Because that one wasn't exactly on her wish list either, Amber went. She sat next to him. He put an arm around her shoulders and pulled her over against his bare chest. There used to be comfort in that, but now...it felt empty. It was like there was a switch in her head, one that had been flipped by the mere sight of that ring in his bag.

"You okay?"

"Uh huh." She couldn't do this right now. Her head was swimming from the booze and weed. The boat's motion was beginning to feel like some carnival tilt ride, even with her eyes open.

"You seem tense. You've seemed tense all day."

"Just...school."

"You'll be fine. You're one of the most smart, capable people I've ever met. That's one of the things I love about you."

"Great. Thanks." Her stomach felt like the inside of a washing machine.

"I'm really glad we got a chance to do this. It's kinda romantic being out here, huh?"

Gag me, was this it? Was this really how he was going to do it? It sounded like the speech she'd gotten from the guy who took her to prom, his not-so-subtle way of trying to finagle a blowjob. She wasn't the type to expect her proposal to be written in the sky with fireworks like in a movie, but the reality was sadly hysterical.

Amber started laughing against him. She tried to smother it and couldn't.

"What's so funny?" Most guys would've been annoyed, but he sounded amused, a perfect prince, and she hated him for it and hated herself for hating him.

She opened her mouth to say something, *anything* to derail this train before it could pull into the station with its bomb attached, and instead felt her stomach throw the works in reverse. It was all she could do to reach the back of the boat and lean over the guardrail before chunks of half-digested sandwich spewed from her lips. They hit the water below with tiny splashes.

"Oh honey." Justin was there, brushing her hair back out of her face, helping her back to the couch. She sat down heavily, and he knelt in front of her to rub her bare thighs. "Was it the beer, or are you just seasick?"

"I don't know. But I feel better now." And she did; the fog in her head was dissipating.

"Okay, good. Because, well...there's something I wanted to ask you."

His hand stole down to the cargo pocket of his shorts. It seemed to happen in slow motion. She would give anything not to have to face this moment.

And then her wish was granted, as a huge man in a ski mask appeared over Justin's shoulder.

7

Cherrywine—whose real name was actually Cheryl Windsor, although she hadn't gone by it since she left home at the age of 16—allowed herself to be dragged into the master cabin in the bottom of the yacht. Once inside, she rushed past Eric with a giggle and flopped down on the king-size bed with its fluffy comforter and kicked her legs in the air.

Who would've thought she'd end up in a place like this? Certainly not her mother (whose only other pearl of wisdom seemed to be that her daughter's head manufactured stupid faster than the Chinese did everything else) or her stepfather (who was still, to this day, the only man she'd been in a relationship with for longer than a month) or any of the other girls at the club. And yet here she was, jetting through the Caribbean with a man that wasn't even twice her age.

She looked up. Eric stood in the doorway, watching her with an intense, spaced-out grin on his face.

Cherrywine thought about what Amber told her, that there was a debt to be paid for this trip. And now, she was about to get the bill. She'd known sex would be required, and it really didn't bother her; she'd fucked other guys for a lot less.

The thing was though, Eric really *was* gorgeous...and rich... kind of overbearing, sure, but funny...and she thought she liked him. And if she wanted this to last, then maybe she shouldn't treat the situation like normal. She should make him *respect* her. She couldn't remember what women's magazine she might've read this in, but the idea seemed sound.

"Poor Justin," she said, desperate to make conversation. "I feel bad for him."

"Poor Justin what?"

"He's gonna ask Amber to marry him."

"You know about that?"

"Yeah. Amber does too. She's gonna turn him down."

To her surprise, Eric laughed. It had a mean-natured ring to it. "Good. Asshole needs to have his heart broken. Then maybe he'll learn the one thing women are truly good for."

With that, he stalked toward the bed, shrugging out of his unbuttoned shirt to reveal a chiseled six-pack, and dropping his swim trunks. His dick wasn't quite erect but getting there, dangling from the trimmed thatch of his pubic hair. Something about his brazen intensity was frightening.

"Hey, wait," she said, propping up on her elbows.

"What for?"

"I was thinking—"

"Don't."

"...don't what?"

"Think. You ain't so hot at it, honey. It'll just get you into trouble."

She blushed with embarrassment. She hated when people called her stupid. "Maybe we could...you know...talk a little bit. Get to know one another. Kind of...take it slow."

He grunted. "Yeah, right." Eric grabbed hold of her ankles and yanked her to the edge of the bed. His hands—rough hands, she was suddenly aware—slid down her waist, found the thin band of her bikini bottoms and jerked them down, manhandling them off her feet.

Sudden panic kicked in. Cherrywine squirmed and tried to cover herself. "No, stop, I don't wanna do it like this!"

"Too late for that." He grinned savagely, but his eyes were glassed over in a way that completely changed his rugged face into a blank mask. Her struggles only seemed to excite him more. She felt the tip of his cock pressing at the cleft between her legs as he held her against the bed.

This was unexplored sexual territory for her. The bouncers at the club had always kept the grabbiest guys off her, and, even at the age of 15, when her stepfather first began his midnight excursions to her bedroom, the acts had been consensual.

But now...

She was about to be raped.

A small voice spoke up in Cherrywine's head, listing her only two options. She could lay back, stay still, and get this over with...or she could find a way to skip out on the check.

As Eric forced his way into her—the full length of his penis like a burning rod—she got one of her hands loose and pistoned it upward, as she used to do when her brother tried to wrestle her. It was a blind shot, more panic than instinct, but she felt the heel of her palm strike him directly in the nose.

There was a brittle *crunch*. He grunted and fell back off the bed, pulling out of her but leaving a dripping scarlet trail down the length of her naked body. Cherrywine sat up and scooted away from him across the covers.

Eric stood hunched over, holding his broken nose as blood leaked between his fingers. She expected anger, expected him to be coming back at her any second, but instead his eyes were rooted on the floor beside the bed. He reached down and came up holding what looked like a shard of smoky glass.

He stared at it, lowering his hand from his face to reveal the ruins of his nose, then glanced toward a cabinet mounted on the wall beside the door. "You been snooping in here?"

"Huh?"

Eric moved toward the cabinet. He flung open the doors and shoved liquor bottles out of the way, spilling several of them on the thin carpet. He reached in and pulled open some kind of door in the wall behind them, then brought out a tube wrapped in shredded paper.

"Oh my god," he snarled. "You fucking whore."

"But Eric, I didn't do anyth—"

He came for her again, but this time it wasn't sex on his mind. His eyes were wild, crazed, but still with that faraway look in them, as if Eric Renquist had taken a step back in his own head and a more primitive identity had hopped in the driver's seat. He leapt on the bed and threw his weight on her before she could react. His hands stole up to wrap around her throat. They squeezed.

She felt her air supply trickle to a stop. Her eyes bulged as she tried to pry his fingers off.

"You *whore*, you *bitch*, you fucking *tramp*," he chanted, emphasizing each insult. "You're trying to *stop* me but you *can't*, nobody can, I have a *destiny*, one that makes me invincible to a *cunt* like you."

She didn't know what to do. The world was going dim. She screamed, but it sounded far away, and then she realized that it couldn't have been her, because she didn't have air to breathe, let alone scream.

"What the hell?" Eric blinked, seeming to come back to himself. He released her and jumped to his feet to pull back on his swim trunks and shirt. Cherrywine sucked in air, coughing and clutching at her raw throat while he shoved the statue in his pocket, then reached into the door at the back of the cabinet and drew out a gun.

He flew out of the bedroom, and she heard him pounding up the stairs to the deck.

Cherrywine grabbed for clothes—a new pair of panties and the long t-shirt she'd brought to sleep in the only items at hand—and followed him.

8

Justin at first took Amber's reaction to the impending proposal—which involved screaming and clutching at him—to be good, if slightly out of character. Then he realized she was looking over his shoulder.

He turned...and saw stars as a fist smashed into his forehead and left eye. He sprawled backward, narrowly avoiding taking a header into the still-smoldering fire pit. Through a film of tears, Justin blinked up at the huge guy in the ski mask standing over him.

"Get up! Now!" the man growled, a trace of accent to his words. "Both of you, lay on the couches, face down! *Do it!*"

The whole side of Justin's face throbbed as he tried to make sense of this. Where had the guy come from? Did he stowaway somewhere on the *MishMasher* before they set out?

The stranger knelt so their eyes were level. He casually pulled a knife from the inside of his boot and tapped the blade under the shelf of Justin's chin. Justin swallowed, feeling the metal tip press against his jugular.

"Tell ya what, mate," the stranger said calmly. "You don't move your ass, I'm gonna stick you fulla so many holes, we'll be able to use you for a sprinkler. Or maybe I'll start with *her*." His eyes moved up to Amber, who was studying him with as much intensity as she did her textbooks.

"Don't hurt her," Justin whispered.

Pounding footsteps came from the stairs. Eric ran onto the deck, blood pouring down his face and holding the revolver that Justin had seen behind the trapdoor in the liquor cabinet. He spotted the stranger, skidded to a stop, and leveled the weapon with both hands. "Drop the knife, asshole!"

The stranger stood and turned around slowly. Justin was struck all over again by just how big he was. He held up his hands, but kept the knife in his right. "'Ey now, mate, careful with that li'l thing, you wouldn't wanna hurt y'self."

Eric snuffled blood through his crooked nose. "Drop the knife or we'll see how little it is."

The intruder lowered one tattooed arm and tossed the knife across the deck to Eric's left. Eric's eyes tracked the object, causing the .38 to drift away…

Timing the distraction, the stranger whipped his hand back and scrabbled under the vest he wore for a huge gun tucked in his waistband.

"Eric, look out!" Justin shouted.

His friend reacted fast, whipping the gun back on target and firing wildly. Because of the angle, Justin and Amber were as much in the line of fire as the other guy. The first shot punched a hole through the deck several inches from where Justin sat, but the second hit the intruder in the right thigh, just above the knee. He cried out and fell across the deck facedown, the large revolver in his hand flying away to strike the bulkhead next to the stairs.

Cherrywine emerged into the night behind Eric and started screaming also, one long, hoarse note that rolled away across the ocean.

"Shut up!" Eric told her. To Justin he shouted, "What the hell is this, where'd he come from?"

"I don't know! What happened to you?"

Eric wiped at the blood across his lips with the back of his forearm, but only succeeded in smearing it further. "Nothing, I'm fine."

The intruder on the deck turned on his side. He clutched his leg as blood pooled beneath him and cursed from the side of his mouth. Eric walked over and kicked him in the shoulder, forcing him over onto his back. He stuck the .38 in his face. "Who are you, fuckhead? What are you doing on my boat?"

The intruder's lips, visible through the bottom hole of his black ski mask, stretched into something halfway between a snarl and a grin. "*You li'l rich shitstains…just bought y'selves…a world of hurt…*"

From behind them, a bright light blazed, throwing their shadows long across the deck.

9

Lito saw the muzzle flashes from the yacht when the two shots went off. They'd drifted closer after Rabid left, and the other boat was only fifty yards away now.

He glanced at Ray, who frowned and shook his head. "That was too small to be Rabid's gun."

"Goddamn it, how could he fuck this up? Get your masks on, everybody!"

Up and down the bow, the rest of the crew pulled on their own ski masks. Jericho—whose dreadlocks made a lumpy mess of the mask's tight-knit fabric—handed a bullhorn to Lito. "All right boys, keep a cool head and we can still pull this off."

A high-beam searchlight was mounted on the front of the *Steel Runner*. Lito switched it on and trained it on the yacht. He saw several figures moving toward the stern, raising their hands to shield their eyes from the light.

He said through the bullhorn, "ALL OF YOU ON THE YACHT! PUT DOWN YOUR WEAPONS AND LAY FACE-DOWN ON THE DECK! NO HARM WILL COME TO YOU IF YOU SURRENDER NOW!"

In response to this, there were more muzzle flashes, and bullets spanged off the hull of the *Runner*.

Jorge whipped his AR-15 up—a weapon almost bigger than he was—and opened fire. The figures on the yacht leapt for cover.

"Stop!" Lito shouted. "For Christ's sake, *stop*!"

"They're shootin at us!"

"Yeah, and every bullet you put in that boat is comin outta *your* cut!"

From his other side, Ray asked, "What do you wanna do, Lito?"

"Let's get in closer. We need to end this fast."

10

From where Amber lay between the railing at the stern and the padded benches, she heard Justin ask, "Who are these guys, the Coast Guard? We didn't do anything wrong!"

"Does the Coast Guard wear ski masks and carry automatic weapons?" Eric yelled from behind the bench opposite them. "Whoever they are, they're after *me*, to get to my father!"

"Cherrywine, are you okay?" Amber shouted.

"Yes." It sounded like the squeak came from the stairwell to the lower deck.

The growl of an engine drifted across the water. Amber rose up enough to peek over the railing. "They're coming!"

Eric popped up and fired again at the approaching ship. After one shot, the hammer clicked on empty cylinders. "Shit, where's that other guy's gun?"

Justin got to his knees to look across the fire pit. "Eric, man, don't shoot at them!"

"What am I supposed to do, flash my dick?"

"Don't make them mad! Let's just do what they say!"

"Are you fucking nuts? They're gonna kill us!"

"They said they wouldn't!"

"Listen to 'im, mate," the wounded man said through clenched teeth. He was still stretched across the deck between the benches, with a sizable blood puddle around his leg. "We ain't gonna do shit to you. All we want's the boat…"

"Oh, right! I'm supposed to believe you're just pirates? And you just happened to pick *this* boat to hijack?"

"Maybe it's true!" Justin insisted. "Just cooperate, we don't have any other choice!"

"Eric's right." Amber grabbed Justin, forcing him to face her, and sank her nails into his bare shoulders. "If these guys are here because of his father, then the rest of us are just collateral. And if they really are pirates…they're gonna kill you guys, and rape me and Cherrywine. They *cannot* get on this boat."

This seemed to get through to him. His eyes grew large…then he stood and pounded away across the deck.

"Hey, where you going?" Eric demanded, his voice nasal from whatever had happened to his nose. He dropped to hands and knees, scrabbling around on the deck to look for the wounded pirate's gun.

Amber looked behind them. The other ship, which looked like a dirty garbage scow compared to the yacht, had closed to within thirty yards, and was churning up a mass of seaweed in front of them as they approached. She could see a line of men standing in its bow, all wearing masks.

Beneath her, the engines of the *MishMasher* roared to life.

Eric's head came up. "Christ, what's he doing? The anchor's down!"

The boat was in motion. Eric ran to the control box for the anchor mounted on the bow. They picked up speed fast, the searchlight from the other boat falling away to leave them in darkness. A small rowboat slipped aside in their wake, probably what the injured man had used to get from the other boat to theirs. As the distance between the ships increased, Amber stood up. Cherrywine came to join her.

The other girl was in tears. Even in the dark, Amber could see the ring of dark bruises around her throat, above the collar of the much more modest t-shirt she wore.

"Oh my god. Cherrywine...what did he do to you?"

The girl fell against her, sobbing. Amber held her as the wind whipped their hair. "It's okay. We're safe." This seemed to be true, at least as far as their attackers went; the other ship was falling further behind each second, unable to keep up.

The pirate on the ground gave a chuckle that sounded full of pain.

Eric stood at the bottom of the small set of stairs leading up to the yacht's control room and shouted, "Bro! What the fuck are you doing?"

Justin leaned out of the compartment and looked down at him. "I'm getting us outta here!"

"Get down here now! Nobody drives this thing but me!"

Cherrywine shrieked in Amber's arms and jabbed a finger toward the front of the boat. "*Look out!*"

Amber glanced up in time to see what appeared to be a wooden wall loom out of the darkness directly in the yacht's path. They rushed toward it. She had time to see the bow of the *MishMasher* strike this surface dead-on before the world tilted, and water enveloped her.

3

VIKINGS IN THE END ZONE

SWIMMING AND SABOTAGE

DESERTED MACKEREL

PRISONERS

1

Ray pounded a fist on the outside of the wheelhouse window. "We're losin 'em!"

"I can see that, but they gotta be doin forty knots!" Lito shouted back. "I got her opened all the way up, but we just can't compete with that thing for pure speed!"

On the foredeck, Jorge bounced on the balls of his feet, while Jericho, Carlos, and Mondo watched their payday speed into the night, taking a member of their crew with it. The nervous tension had even dragged Cheech from his bed downstairs. The dog paced back and forth across the planks, more restless than Lito had ever seen him.

Just as the yacht passed beyond the edge of visibility, a tremendous, rumbling crash rolled back to the *Steel Runner*, followed by the squall of tortured fiberglass.

Lito ordered, "Get that spotlight up!"

Jericho swept the light across the ocean's surface, the yellow beam cleaving through the night to illuminate the fertile bed of seaweed around them. He trained it on a shape coming up fast off the port bow, and Lito cut the engines to let them drift as he tried to make sense of what he was seeing.

The pleasure yacht had crashed into another vessel midship.

A curious wooden craft, long and narrow with a rounded hull, whose bulwark rose only a little taller than that of the yacht. A huge square sail—blood red with a yellow sun—flew proudly from a crooked mainmast that had been cracked by the impact, and an ornate dragon's head stared from the prow. A row of square holes ran down the length of the hull up near the deck; it took Lito several seconds to figure out what they were.

Oar slots. The kind that men with horns on their helmets rowed from. Because what you're looking at is a real-life Viking ship.

He shook his head. He'd seen pictures of such things before, on TV or maybe even in school, and this vessel matched his mental picture so closely—not to mention looked so fresh and new—that it had to be a fake, some sort of prop rig built to look like those old seagoing Norsemen ships.

In any case, he wouldn't be able to look for long. The yacht had hit the wooden ship with enough force to punch right through, almost tearing the thing in half. The rear end of the vessel was quickly sinking beneath the weed-infested surface of the Sargasso Sea. A stream of sharp cracks and pops sounded as stressed timbers snapped. The mast broke completely and hit the water with a splash.

Ray stuck his head in the door of the wheelhouse. His eyes seemed to float in his black ski mask. "Are you seein this?"

Lito nodded and angled the rudders so they coasted within fifty feet of the Viking ship's bow. The dragon head stared at them briefly before the weight of the sinking ship forced it to turn skyward and then pulled it down toward the ocean floor. *Vikings in the end zone*, he thought giddily.

On the deck, Cheech began to bark his head off.

The rich kids' sleek craft was just beyond the remains of the Viking ship, listing at a nearly forty-five degree angle to starboard. The bow had been crushed from the impact, and the port side of the fiberglass hull had a crack several yards long and as wide as a basketball running up it. The water had rushed in with enough weight to cause the boat to roll the opposite direction. This had bought the yacht some time, but not nearly enough to save it.

All their work—not to mention all that *money*—was minutes away from sinking.

And there was nothing they could do to stop it.

Bodies flailed in the water. He couldn't tell who was who. Lito leaned out the wheelhouse door, trying to catch a better glimpse of the figures in the splashing and chaos as they passed, and heard panicked shouts from the foredeck in front of him. He looked forward and heard himself yelp.

Now the *Steel Runner* was about to collide with another vessel. A large pontoon fishing boat floated diagonally across their path just twenty yards ahead, no more than a rectangular raft with a cabin in the middle.

Lito dove for the controls and threw the engines into full reverse. "Brace yourselves!"

The crew grabbed the railing. Lito gripped the wheel and turned hard to port, hoping to give them a few extra seconds to slow. The *Runner*'s hull was hardened steel, and their speed hadn't been too great to begin with, but he still didn't want to risk plowing into the heavy aluminum pontoons head on. He squeezed his eyes shut and waited for the verdict.

2

Amber tried to swim beneath the water, but her limbs felt heavy. At first she thought it was disorientation, or perhaps the lingering effects of the alcohol, but after struggling for a few seconds, she realized she was tangled in some kind of slick, slimy rope. She opened her eyes in the murk. The salt water burned, but she could make out the shadowy fronds of seaweed all around her.

It was everywhere she turned, brushing against her face, wrapping around her arms and legs. The stuff was so thick, it made her feel like she was swimming in molasses. And the more she moved, the more ensnared she became.

In fact, in her panic, it almost felt like the seaweed moved with *purpose*, creeping around her wrists and ankles and tugging her ever so gently toward the dark depths of the ocean.

Her lungs ached. She made one last titanic effort, ripping the plants away from her with one hand and then kicking hard toward where her natural buoyancy told her the surface lay. At last the seaweed parted, and her head breached. She sucked in a lungful of new air, coughing and spluttering.

Someone was shouting. Amber didn't recognize the voice. She wiped water out of her eyes and dogpaddled in a circle.

The *MishMasher* was behind her, nearly on its side in the water, cast in muted light by the full moon. It was surreal to see the benches where'd she just sat and the deck she'd just stood on, now nearly vertical.

She vaguely remembered the boat crashing into—and then through—something, and then she'd been pitched into the air like a rock from a catapult. A good twenty feet separated her from the ship. If she'd been thrown this far in a car wreck, she'd be dead, nothing more than a smear on the asphalt. Even as it was, she felt bruised and sore along her right side from impacting on the water.

The screamer turned out to be the huge pirate Eric had shot. He clung to the guardrail of the yacht, working his way up as more and more of it sank beneath the water, and bellowed for help. Probably couldn't swim with that wounded leg.

"Justin!" she yelled, her cries competing with the pirate's. The water around her was full of floating debris from the yacht; one of her textbooks bobbed past. "*Anybody!*"

Something breached the surface like a rocket a few feet away. Amber almost shrieked until she spotted blonde hair. Cherrywine gasped and slapped at the water, flinging seaweed everywhere. Amber grabbed her arm to steady her. "It's okay, you're all right!"

"Ew, ew, this stuff is *gross!*"

Amber agreed. The slimy vegetation clung to her everywhere. She was already getting exhausted from trying to swim with it on her.

"*Fuuuuck! Fuck, shit!*" The new shouts came from the front of the yacht. Amber spotted Eric treading water and shaking his fist at the night sky.

"This way!" she told Cherrywine. She swam toward him and, after a moment's hesitation, the other girl trailed behind, making sure to keep Amber between her and Eric.

"*Nooo!*" Eric howled. The water had cleaned the blood off his face, leaving his nose a bulbous lump that pulled to the left. "I can't goddamn believe this!"

Amber fought to keep her head above water. "Where's Justin?"

He ignored her. "Look at this, he wrecked my father's boat! I'm gonna kill that son of a bitch!"

"What did we hit?"

"I don't know, I didn't see!" Eric submerged briefly, thrashed, and came up choking. "Maybe I can still save it!"

He put his head facedown in the water in preparation to breaststroke, but Amber caught his arm. "You can't do anything, it's going to sink! We have to get away in case it rolls over on top of us!"

"Leggo of me!" Eric swung around, struggling like a maniac. He raised a fist as though to hit her, but it took too much effort to stay afloat. Then, all at once, he calmed down and stared over her shoulder.

Amber saw movement from the corner of her eye. A searchlight swept across them. The pirate boat coasted by, cutting a silent swath through the mats of seaweed, then its engines kicked on and it veered left to keep from hitting another small boat that floated in its path. It was beginning to look like the arena at a demolition derby out here.

She grabbed Cherrywine's hand and waved the other in the air to flag them. "*Help! Over here!*"

Eric splashed water in her face. "What're you, crazy? Don't fucking call them! You just said they were gonna kill us!"

"It's them or nothing! If they don't pick us up, we'll drown out here!"

"I can't swim anymore!" Cherrywine pleaded. "I need to get outta the water!"

Eric pointed over the sinking prow of the *MishMasher*, where the boxy shape of yet another boat was visible. "There! Head toward that! Anything's better than them!"

They began to swim (except in the thick mat of seaweed, it was really more like pushing through Jell-o), and Amber kept an eye out for Justin. She wanted to search for him on the other side of the yacht, but Cherrywine was right; she could feel herself getting heavier with each passing second, her lungs working harder and harder to pull in oxygen. Their path took them on a diagonal past the end of Eric's boat, and, as they drew closer, the pirate screamed, "*Wait!* Wait, please don't leave me, my fuckin leg, I'm gonna drown!"

Amber started to swim on, but a kernel of guilt blossomed inside her. She angled toward him.

"What're you *doing*?" Eric yelled.

"Keep going!" she called over her shoulder. She reached the edge of the yacht and held the railing with a shaking hand, letting it support her weight. It felt so good to rest for a moment. She waited till her breathing slowed and some of her strength came back, then looked at the pirate. He'd taken off his ski mask; beneath was a grizzled face with tattoos creeping up the neck. His eyes were filled with panic.

"You're a lot bigger than me," she told him. "If you struggle, you'll take us both under. Just relax and float and I'll drag you.

And if you try to hurt us when we get out, I swear to Christ, I'll kill you myself."

"Bless you li'l sheila, no worries, you got my word." He took the hand she offered and let go of the yacht, then laid over on his back to float. She began to swim again, towing the behemoth behind her like a barge. From the pirates' ship, a searchlight played across the water. She tried to avoid it. They'd crossed half the distance to their destination—a good-sized houseboat, she thought—before she looked back.

Only the *MishMasher*'s belly showed now, and even that was quickly disappearing beneath the ocean surface.

3

A hollow *thump* rang across the *Steel Runner* and vibrated through Lito's feet. He opened his eyes.

They'd nudged the fishing vessel with the starboard side of their hull, and were now drifting to a stop right up against it, like two cars in a parking lot. The top of its cabin peaked just above the *Runner*'s bulwark.

Lito shut down the engines and emerged from the wheel-house. In their current position, they were sandwiched between the yacht a few dozen yards away on their left, and the fishing boat up against them on the right.

The rest of the crew picked themselves up off the deck. Cheech was still barking—shrill, frightened yips unlike anything Lito had ever heard the ugly animal make. The pitbull stood on his hind legs, hanging over the guardrail and barking down at the boat against them.

"*Someone shut him up!*" Lito hissed. The last thing they needed was to get the owner of this other boat involved. Mondo grabbed Cheech's collar and dragged the dog away with some effort. He settled on his haunches with a whimpering growl.

"Rabid, man, we gotta find him!" Jorge squealed, running to the port side of the ship.

"Just a sec! Let's see if this is trouble!"

Of course, what he really meant was, find out if it was time to shag ass, either with or without Rabid. Lito went to the starboard bow and looked down at the fishing boat with Ray. Jericho turned the spotlight around and shone it along the length of the vessel.

It was upscale for a fishing boat, designed for multiple-day excursions. The aluminum deck measured ten yards by six and was held aloft two feet out of the water by the pontoons beneath. Big outboard motor, two jet skis parked on folding ramps to either side of it, and a narrow fiberglass cabin in the middle would sleep two or three comfortably. The kind of boat a true fisherman would cherish...but all the same, Lito figured his worries about waking the owner were groundless.

Unlike the Viking ship, this thing looked to be in *baaaad* shape. Rust and barnacles covered every inch of the two barrel pontoons, the deck sagged in several places, and the white paint on the cabin was sun faded. The door hung slightly open, the hinges so rusted it couldn't swing freely in the strengthening breeze. The interior was too steeped in darkness to make out.

Lito didn't think anyone had owned this vessel in a long time.

"Over there." Ray nodded his head to their left. Again, Jericho directed the searchlight.

Yet *another* ship floated thirty or forty yards away, in the nocturnal shadows just beyond the foundering yacht. This one looked to be an even larger houseboat, and in just as poor condition as the pontoon. Moss covered the railings along the lip of the deck. The searchlight's beam skittered across two words painted on the hull, barely visibly under a layer of grime and barnacles.

HOLY MACKEREL.

That wasn't all, either. Lito could see more vessels out there now that he was looking, beyond the range of their light and too far away for the moonlight to illuminate, nothing more than silhouettes against the black horizon. They all just seemed adrift in a loose congregation.

And the air...the air was heavy with that burnt ozone he'd smelled earlier, so thick even the salt-laden scent of the ocean was overpowered.

For some reason, those ghostly sparks of blue light replayed in his head.

"What is dis, *mon*?" Jericho whispered.

Lito didn't know if his mechanic expected an answer, but it was Mondo—standing behind them and forking some kind of evil eye sign with both hands—that said solemnly, "Bad omens. I'm tellin you Cap'n, ain't nuttin good gonna come from this. You best belie' *that*. We need ta turn our asses around and leave, right now."

"Knock it off," Lito told him. A prickle teased the nape of his neck.

"I don't know 'bout no bad omens," Ray said, "but this is fuckin weird as shit, Lito. Maybe we should think about makin a run for it. The yacht's trashed, there's no reason to stay."

Lito held out a hand. "Don't freak out. Let's think about this before we go runnin away with our tail between our legs."

"Yeah, but this many boats...it's too much activity, and we're sittin here with our hand practically in the cookie jar. This is the quickest way to get pinched."

"By *who*, Ray?" Lito couldn't keep the frustration from his voice. "These things have gotta be abandoned, and even if they aren't, none of 'em look like cops to me."

"Yeah, but Cap'n," Jericho said quietly, "what if dis got somet'in to do wit de Dominican? A blockade, maybe?"

Lito looked out at the flotilla of dark boats once more, then at the rest of the gathering night around them. He hadn't considered that idea, but it felt like paranoia. How could the man with a price on their heads possibly know they would come through here, when they hadn't known themselves?

Unless...he was working with these rich kids in the first place. Unless they'd been *led* here.

Suddenly, the whole business of the yacht falling into their lap seemed entirely too convenient.

"We're gonna find Rabid," he told them, "and then see how things play out."

They left off their inspection of the fishing vessel and hurried to the opposite side. Off their port, the yacht performed a lazy roll before slipping under the water amid a flurry of bubbles. A group of four figures swam away from it, making for the house-boat on the other side. Jericho followed them with the spotlight, but Lito couldn't determine their identities. The entire crew stood at the edge of the railing, straining to see what was going on.

Well, almost the entire crew. As Lito looked around at the faces of his men, he realized Carlos was not among them.

4

It was Romero Felix Santiago that Carlos focused on while he hurried down the starboard gangway of the *Steel Runner*. Santiago, and his damn 'bottlecapping,' which was almost certainly not a medical procedure recognized by any doctor. And the screams of Diego Palacios as he'd been thrown down on a plastic tarp.

As useful as blind ambition had been to motivate most of Carlos's actions, he was finding fear an even better spur.

He didn't know what to make of their current situation, but right now, he didn't care. The abandoned ships were a useful distraction, and he didn't want to waste it. His first priority was to make sure this boat couldn't go another inch until he could plan his next move. Once the others were all dead, he would try to figure out what the ships were about.

He could look over the railing and see the old fishing boat below, right up against them, like the ships were spooning. Every few seconds there was a teeth-grinding *creeeeak* when the motion of the sea lifted one vessel or the other and the two metals rubbed against one another.

The engine room maintenance hatch was just ahead on his right. Carlos checked to make sure no one was looking. He could still hear their voices from the opposite side of the ship, watching the yacht sink. He raised the door and climbed down the ladder three rungs at a time.

Below deck was a dark, hot, cramped space that smelled of oil and gas fumes, but it was better than that constant burnt-hair stench floating through the air out in the open. The compartment couldn't be any bigger than five-by-five, and most of it was taken up by the twin diesel engines. Heat baked off them, causing an instant flood of sweat from nearly every pore on his body. He reached bottom and inspected the metal conglomeration.

Now that he was down here, this no longer seemed like the greatest idea. He had a basic working knowledge of engines, but Jericho had made so many modifications, the thing looked like some kind of demented pipe organ now. Plus, whatever Carlos did to sabotage them would have to be reversible, so he could get the ship running again after he'd taken care of the others. And what could he do that Jericho wouldn't be able to fix even easier than him?

Then he spotted the solution. The fuel line. He could just unscrew it from both ends, and take the whole damn thing. They wouldn't get far without that.

A toolbox lay nearby. Carlos grabbed a pair of pliers and loosened the couplings at both ends of the fuel hose. It was a thick coil, maybe six inches long and an inch in diameter; too big to try and stuff in his pocket. He gripped it in one hand and started back up the ladder.

At the top, he closed the maintenance hatch. The gangway was still empty. So far, so good. He stood and hurried back the way he'd come, heading for the stairwell that led belowdeck so he could stash the hose in his room.

A low, dark shape hurtled over the guardrail just in front of him.

Carlos squawked and flailed backward, more surprised by the sudden movement than anything. He fell hard on his side. The fuel line flew out of his hand and slid across the deck. He flung an arm out and felt his fingertips brush the rubber before it rolled off the edge of the ship. He heard the *ga-loop* sound as the ocean swallowed it.

He sat up fast. Reached for his gun. Scanned the shadows along the narrow gangway ahead of him for the shape that had vaulted over the side of the ship. It was so dark, and the thing had moved so fast, he didn't get a clear look at it. It had been short, maybe half his height, and hunched. An animal, maybe? Some sort of seabird?

Carlos looked over the railing, down at the rusted fishing boat. Its deck was dilapidated and silent, but it was the only place the shape could've come from.

That is, if he hadn't imagined it entirely.

No time to obsess over that or the lost hose. All he could do is take things one step at a time. Carlos hurried toward the sounds of the others just ahead.

5

Justin's head throbbed.

He thought it might be a hangover until he realized there was water pattering down on his face.

He opened his eyes and recognized the tiny control room of the *MishMasher*, but it looked different somehow. It took his aching head a minute to figure it out: everything was upside down. He lay in a heap on the ceiling, with the yacht's steering wheel jutting from the control bank above him. The only light came from red emergency beacons mounted on both walls, casting a ruddy glow down on him. Several inches of tepid saltwater had flooded the interior, and more trickled down every wall and dripped from the ceiling onto his head. Through the cracked glass window—now taking up the lower half of the wall in front of him—his view of deck and sky had been replaced by a murky, greenish-black world.

Memories surfaced to help him make sense of the situation. The crash. Being slammed into the control room wall, his head caroming off the window. The boat had capsized obviously, and he was now underwater. The crash must have slammed the control room door closed on its sliding track, sealing him in here with a bubble of oxygen; otherwise, he'd already be dead.

Might not be too late for that.

As if to confirm this, a groan of stressed metal and fiberglass sounded all around him.

He climbed to his feet in this space that was only a little bigger than a phone booth, using the steering wheel to help him stand, and probed at his head. There was a lump the size of a half baseball just above his right temple. He was still a little woozy, but even if he had a concussion, there were more pressing concerns.

The water in the control room was now up to his shins and rising fast. This booth wasn't constructed to be watertight. It would be completely swamped in minutes. And, as scary as that idea was, an even worse one came right on its heels.

Amber. Had she survived the crash? He had to get out of here to find her.

His only option was to pry the door open and swim for the surface. And if the ship were sinking, then the longer he waited, the longer that swim would be.

Justin grabbed the handle and pulled. The door wouldn't budge. Either the pressure difference was too great, or something in the door mechanism itself was broken. He hyperventilated, began to cough. Suddenly the room felt even smaller, the size of a coffin. One he would ride all the way to his final resting place on the ocean floor.

The only window was at his feet, the water in here close to covering it. In the black world beyond the glass, an even darker shadow flickered by.

Justin reared back his sneakered foot and kicked at the window. It was hard to get much force with the water as a cushion, but he thought he saw the cracks in the glass spread a little. He kept at it like a machine as the water level rose past his waist and headed for his chest.

In the middle of the operation, the red emergency lights winked out, plunging him into total darkness. He cried out, his voice ringing inside the tin can, and then went right back to kicking.

The glass shattered all at once. Justin felt the pressure change in his ears and had just enough time to grab a breath before a swell of chilly water shoved him against the wall. After the pressure equalized, he squeezed through the remains of the window and swam outward into the murk.

His eyes spun in their sockets, seeking input, but all this darkness was like going blind. He swam upward until he banged his head against the *MishMasher*'s upside-down deck, then felt along it until he reached the edge of the yacht.

Something huge blasted by him in the water, hard enough to create a wave of turbulence. Hard, scaly flesh brushed against his arm. He recoiled, heart pounding, then let go of the boat and kicked hard for the surface.

The trip through that pitch black void took an eternity. Every second, he expected to feel teeth chomping down on his leg. When he swam headlong into the forest of seaweed, he screamed out the last of his oxygen and then tore through the curtain of vegetation until he reached fresh air.

He submerged again almost immediately, too dizzy and exhausted to stay afloat. Justin flailed, his hands clutching at the air, and was relieved when they encountered a floating ring that took his weight. Only once he was supported across it and gasping for air did he open his eyes.

The ring was a life preserver. A rope was tied to it, and he followed it up to a ship floating right next to him. Someone above must be pulling the cord, because he was tugged forward like a hooked fish. The comparison was furthered when metal loops slid under his arms and his limp body was lifted from the water and dragged over the railing.

He was dropped on a solid surface. A blurry crowd of faces hovered over him, eyes peering from holes in knit ski masks.

"Amber," he wheezed. "Where's...Amber?"

"You ain't ever gonna see that bitch again if anything happened to our friend," a squeaky voice told him.

Justin tried to get up, and a booted foot forced him back flat. A pistol was jammed in his face.

"If he's here, then that means Rabid's over there with them," a new voice said. "So let's keep this *bastardo* handy in case we need to...*negotiate*."

6

At Eric's last dental appointment, his dentist told him his teeth were being worn down at an alarming rate, most likely from 'nocturnal grinding.' He custom-molded a clear plastic bit that Eric wore every night when he slept, but had done little to solve the problem.

If the dentist could see Eric's jaw working methodically as he swam toward the grungy houseboat, he might understand why.

His father. What the fuck was he going to tell his father? Not just about the boat; oh no, he had a feeling losing the *MishMasher* was some seriously small potatoes compared to making the delivery tomorrow. He swam with one hand for a moment and used the other to make sure the weird glass figurine was still in his pocket. There it was—damaged, missing a horn thanks to that meddling, nose-breaking bitch he'd brought along on this trip, and how was that for gratitude?—but at least it was still safe for the moment.

These guys with the guns had to be 'business rivals' of his father. They might want Eric for ransom or revenge, but more likely, they wanted this statue. He had to get it out of his hands in case he was captured, then convince them it went down with the ship.

Because somehow, someway, he would get out of this. Destiny demanded it. Dying at the hands of some goombahs like this was unthinkable. No way had the Man Upstairs written that into The Big Plan for Eric Renquist.

He approached the houseboat. The thing was a big, floating rectangular box, like a Winnebago on water, probably twice the size and length of the *MishMasher*; basically just one long cabin with an open sunporch jutting from the back above the engine propellers. A ladder fixed to the side allowed access to this open surface. He headed for it. As he got closer, he saw the thin layer of aluminum that served as an outer shell was stained and covered in a layer of moss, barnacles and other growths. Someone hadn't been keeping up their maintenance schedule.

"Hey! Anybody in there?" He was still getting used to the sound of his voice with his newly clogged nasal passages. "God-damn it, wake up! We need help!" There was no response, and no lights on in the cabin windows.

Eric grabbed the ladder bolted to the back, tried to pull himself up, but the rusted rungs broke off in his hands. He let loose a growl of frustration. Trying not to give himself tetanus on the jagged edges, he gripped as high up on the ladder as he could, where the metal still looked the cleanest, and used it as a boost to grab the lip of the porch, which rode a good three feet above the water. His arms were shaky, but he gathered the strength to pull himself up and lay exhausted and panting on his back, then began removing clumps of seaweed clinging to his t-shirt and shorts. The thin boat carpeting beneath him had rotted away in places, and was covered in accumulated mildew.

"Eric!"

He heard the garbled cry and leaned over the edge to look down at Cherrywine, treading water beside the houseboat. She held the remains of the ladder with one hand and reached out to him with the other. "Help me, I can't swim anymore!"

Eric hesitated. There was a voice speaking in his head, a voice he was barely even conscious of but that sounded a lot like his father, and it was telling him that he should let this girl drown, that it was a vitally important first step toward solving his current predicament, and all it would take is reaching down to hold her head below the surface for a few seconds—

"Eric, what're you doing?" Amber—just a few yards out and dragging the huge pirate right behind—cut into his thoughts with her shrill tone. Eric wasn't used to women talking to him like that. "Help her, for chrissake!"

He held out a hand. Cherrywine grabbed it, and he lifted her onto the porch in her sopping wet t-shirt and panties, which were now almost see-through. Even in the heat of the moment, he felt an erection pushing at the khaki material of his shorts. Nice to know at least one part of him was all-systems-go. She spent a few seconds coughing up seawater and then scooted away, out of reach, and watched him warily.

"What the hell's wrong with you?"

One hand clutched at her own throat. "Fuck you, you bastard," she said tearfully. "You know what you did."

What *he* did? *She* was the one that had snooped through his property, broken the statue, and then, when he'd confronted her, punched him right in the face and given him a kink in the nose that would take the country's best plastic surgeon to fix. That was what happened. *Right?*

Uh huh, the voice agreed. *And it'll stay that way, as long as she's not around to say otherwise.*

He waved a hand at her. "Whatever. I'm not playing games with you, you ungrateful bitch."

Amber reached the back of the boat. She made sure the pirate had a firm grip on the ladder, then grabbed Eric's offered hand, swung a leg up, and rolled onto the porch.

He gestured down at the other man flailing in the water. "I can't believe you saved this asshole."

The pirate looked up, lost his hold on the ladder, and found it agains just as he slipped under. He came up spluttering. Something about his face and all those tattoos rang bells in Eric's head. "I'm sorry mate, really I am! If you just get me outta here, I *swear* I won't give you no hassles!"

"Yeah? What about your friends?"

"I'll tell 'em to leave ya alone too!"

Eric laid down on his stomach on the edge of the porch, rested his chin on his hands, and smirked down at him. "And what if we decide to hold you hostage, huh? Will they care enough about a piece of shit like you to do what we say?"

"I don't know, do whatever you want, mate, just please, *help me!* My leg is bloody *killin* me!"

"Get him up, Eric!" Amber said behind him.

"How am I supposed to do that? Guy weighs a fucking ton!"

"We'll both do it." She joined him at the boat's edge. They reached down and each took one of the pirate's hands.

"Count of three. One...two..."

The water a few feet out from the boat parted. A monstrous shape breached the blanket of seaweed, something rough and angular. Eric saw jaws the length of a Volkswagen Beetle lined with crooked, triangular teeth just before the shape submerged again behind the pirate, leaving behind a cloud of pungent stench like sulfur.

The big man screamed in pain as his body was yanked taut, his upper half slanted at a diagonal and dangling above the water from where Eric and Amber gripped him. The unexpected force was so great, they almost tumbled in with him. Eric braced his knees on the deck and played tug-of-war as Amber did the same beside him. The water below frothed and churned. The pirate wailed as he was shaken back and forth, like a dog with a chew toy. Finally, he was jerked from their grasp. Eric leaned forward in time to see his large, tattooed hands disappear beneath the black ocean, then shoved away from the edge and fell back heavily on his ass.

"Did you...did you fucking see that?" he asked quietly.

"I saw it," Amber confirmed, still hunched over the side and staring downward.

"It fucking *ate* him." Something about this suddenly struck Eric as equal parts gruesomely fascinating and hysterically funny. "Grabbed him from below and...ate him."

"I said I saw it."

In her corner, Cherrywine covered her ears and sobbed quietly. "No, no, no, I don't wanna be here, I wanna go home!"

Eric ignored her. "Shit. I mean...*shit!* What the hell was it?"

"Calm down," Amber said without turning around. "It could've been a shark. The guy was bleeding badly and..." She trailed, sounding unconvinced by her own argument.

"Are you kidding me? Did you see the size of it? And it's skin? That was no fucking shark, it was more like an alligator the size of a bus!"

She didn't answer, just kept staring out over the water. He started to ask her if that thing was coming back, but then suddenly realized that wasn't what she was looking for.

"Justin?" he asked.

"No."

"Maybe...you know...that thing didn't get him." Eric tried to examine how the idea of his best friend being dead made him feel, and came up blank.

"So what, he drowned instead? Thanks, you're a real comfort."

There was silence for a moment, except for Cherrywine's sobbing and the lap of waves against the houseboat's hull.

Then that bright searchlight fell across them, and the amplified voice they'd heard earlier came crackling across the water from the direction of the pirate boat.

7

"EVERYBODY ALL RIGHT OVER THERE?" Lito winced at the sound of his voice through the bullhorn. The atmosphere out here—with all these empty, silent boats—was the kind you didn't want to disrupt, like shouting in a museum.

Or a graveyard.

He could see the distant figures on the back of the houseboat standing up to look in his direction, shielding their eyes from the light. A female voice drifted back to answer him. "*Go away and leave us alone!*"

"'FRAID I CAN'T DO THAT. WHERE'S OUR MAN?"

He sensed a moment of hesitation before she stammered, "*We...we don't...he's not here!*"

"BULLSHIT. I KNOW HE IS. LET ME TALK TO HIM."

"*No, really, he—!*"

She was cut off by a male voice; Lito recognized the dickhead from back at the port. "*Fuck you, you fucking scumbags! You sank my boat! You're gonna pay for that!*"

Carlos wandered up beside Lito and snickered. "Yo, tell 'im to send us a bill, homey."

Instead, Lito said, "IF ANY OF YOU ARE STILL ARMED, THROW YOUR WEAPONS IN THE WATER."

"*We're not doing jack shit, except get the people on this boat to radio for help!*"

"IF YOU CARE ABOUT YOUR FRIEND, I WOULD AD-VISE AGAINST THAT."

This shocked even the asshole into a few seconds of speech-lessness.

"*You got Justin?*"

"IF THAT'S HIS NAME."

"*No way! Prove it!*"

Lito waved two fingers over his shoulder. Jorge and Jericho

lifted the shirtless kid they'd fished out of the water to his feet. Lito held the bullhorn in front of his bruised face. "Talk."

"AMBER, DON'T LISTEN TO TH—!"

Lito jerked the horn away. "SATISFIED?"

"*What do you want from us?*" The girl again. "*Why are you doing this?*"

"YOU HOLD MY GUY, I HOLD YOURS. AND IF YOU CALL THE AUTHORITIES, THEN OUR ONLY CHOICE WILL BE TO RUN, AND TAKE THIS SCRAWNY *PENDEJO* WITH US. THINK ABOUT THAT BEFORE YOU DO ANYTHING RASH."

"*Please don't hurt him!*"

"THEN DON'T MAKE ME. WE'RE COMIN OVER THERE. I WANT YOU ALL TO STAY RIGHT WHERE YOU ARE. IF THERE REALLY IS ANYONE ELSE ON THAT BOAT, YOU BETTER GIVE THEM THE SAME MESSAGE."

Lito lowered the bullhorn and turned away, almost tripping over the other object they'd brought up with the white kid: a waterlogged, bloated textbook titled *Linguistic Relationships Through Time* that had gotten tangled in the life ring. He picked it up and then cocked a finger at Ray, standing by the wheelhouse door. "Get us in close."

Jorge yanked the white kid's arm up tight between his shoulder blades. 'Justin' uttered a short cry. "If they hurt Rabid, I swear you gonna pay, *cabrón*!"

Lito tossed the textbook to Mondo, who almost got bowled over as he caught it. "Take the kid downstairs and tie him up."

The cook answered him, speaking in the most solemn, respectful tone Lito had ever heard him use. "Cap'n, this out here…these other boats…I'm tellin ya, it just ain't right. I really think we oughta—"

"Not now. Do what I said." The last of Lito's patience ebbed. That heavy, burnt smell hanging over everything was giving him a headache, but a fresh breeze was finally clearing it out.

As the old man started to lead the kid away, Ray popped his head out of the wheelhouse. "Engines ain't startin."

"Jer, man, what the fuck, I thought you fixed 'em!"

"I did!" Jericho squeezed the back of his neck beneath the ski mask. "Who knows what de hell dis be?"

"Ah, *mierda*, not now!" Lito stood for a second with hands on his hips and closed his eyes. He had trouble thinking when he got this frustrated. The last self-help book he'd read had advised, in moments like these, to envision each exhale releasing a bit of tension until his head cleared, but something told him the author never intended for the technique to be used in the middle of a hijacking that had gone this far astray. "Okay, change of plan. Jericho, stay here, figure out what's wrong with the engines and do it *fast*. Keep in touch over the walkies. And let Mondo know to keep an eye on the kid and monitor the VHF for any chatter out here. The four of us are takin the other rowboat to get Rabid and the rest of those kids."

"Hey," Carlos said softly. "How 'bout I stay here to help with the engines?"

Jericho snorted. "What de hell you gonna help wit, boy? You t'ink pissin and moanin gonna fix dem?"

As impressed as he was that the kid had volunteered, Lito shook his head. "I need all hands, especially if we have to lug Rabid around. Jorge, bring your rifle. Everyone else, make sure you're packin somethin light, just in case. That guy over there thinks he's a real hardcase, so watch him like a hawk."

"And what if someone else *is* over there?" Ray asked. "We gonna start up our own prison colony or what?"

Lito glanced across the stretch of open water between them and the houseboat.

"We'll deal with that when we have to."

8

On the pirate's ship, Amber could see another rowboat being lowered over the side and into the water.

Eric grabbed her arm. "We gotta see if anybody's home on this barge!"

"They told us to stay here."

"Fuck that, we need to get away! Something tells me these guys ain't gonna listen when we tell them their buddy was just eaten by Godzilla!"

"But...they have Justin." She didn't know if him being in the hands of these scumbags was better or worse than the idea of him being dead. The way she'd treated him all day...it seemed so petty now. Just because she didn't want to spend the rest of her life with him, didn't mean she wanted this.

Eric moved toward the door on the houseboat's porch leading into the cabin. "It ain't gonna help him if we get caught too!" He reached down and grabbed Cherrywine's wrist, the way he had earlier before dragging her off to the bedroom. "Get up, goddamn it, let's go!"

"*NOO!*" the girl shrieked, flailing her body and battering at him until he let go. "*Leave me alone!*"

"Jesus, you crazy bitch!"

"Don't touch her!" Amber flew across the short length of deck and jumped between them. "Stay away from her, you maniac, I know what you did!"

"What're you two talking about? I didn't do anything! Look at my nose! *She* did that!"

"Yeah, and was that before or after you almost choked her to death?"

"*...huh?*"

"You think I'm blind, Eric? I see the bruises on her throat! You expect me to believe she did that to herself?"

"What? I didn't..." He paused with mouth hanging open, his eyes darting back and forth above his crooked, swollen nose, then leaned around her to look at Cherrywine. And, even though Amber believed deception and lying came factory standard in a guy like him, his confusion seemed genuine enough to make her falter.

"Screw you both then," he finally growled. "We don't have time for this." He spun around and ran into the dark cabin of the houseboat.

Amber knelt in front of Cherrywine. She moved limp, blond locks out of the other girl's face. "You okay?"

Cherrywine nodded. "There's something really wrong with him."

"I know. Back on his boat, did he…rape you?"

"He tried. So I broke his nose."

As she said it, Amber felt another surge of affection for her. "Good."

"But that's not what caused him to…" Cherrywine massaged her bruised throat and grimaced. Her voice was scratchy and hoarse. "He had this thing. Like a little statue. He thought I did something to it and just went nuts. Now he acts like he doesn't even remember."

"What happened to it? Do you think it was still on the yacht when it went down?"

"No, he put it in his pocket just before that big guy got on board."

Amber pointed across at their attackers' ship, where four men were climbing over the side and dropping into the metal bottom of the rowboat. "Stay here and yell when they get close. I've gotta see what he's doing." She started to get up, then turned back to the Cherrywine. "And stay away from the water. Just in case."

She went into the cabin and stood just inside the door for a few seconds, waiting for her eyes to adjust to the moonlight filtering through the streaked, filth-encrusted windows on either side.

The room in front of her was long and rectangular, and looked like a rather snug living room, circa 1980. The walls were paneled with fake wood grain, the floor tiled in a faded lime green. She could make out the shapes of plastic coated furniture, a couch and divan with gaudy, vintage upholstery, a recliner, and a small teak coffee table. A mini-kitchen stood to the left, with a refrigerator and short, wraparound bar.

Every horizontal surface held the thickest layer of gray dust she'd ever seen. Eric's barefoot tracks were visible in the grit on the floor, leading toward the far side of the room.

"Hello?" she asked, coughing a little at the staleness of the air. It smelled like the earthen basement beneath her grandmother's house in here. "Is anybody, uh, home?"

There were shelves along the front wall of the room, lined with seashells, kid's toys, and other knick-knacks. The top row was all framed pictures, most of them knocked over on their fronts or backs. Only one still remained upright on its prop, and she wiped away the dust to reveal a family photo of a smiling, olive-skinned man and woman in their 40's, maybe Middle Eastern or Indian, with a boy around ten and a girl maybe half that age crammed between them, all wearing the absolute chicest fashions the Reagan administration had to offer. The photo had been taken in this very room, while they sat on the couch only a few feet behind her.

So what had happened to this grinning quartet?

Maybe they went for a little swim, and ended up just like your friend the pirate back there.

She turned to go after Eric, but something on the coffee table caught her eye this time. A collection of magazines was spread across the surface beneath the sprawl of dust. Amber picked one up and blew sediment from the cover. It was an issue of People Magazine with Prince on the cover, wearing his signature purple jacket and frilly cuff ruffles.

The issue date was November 19, 1984.

If this was right, if these people weren't old periodical hoarders and it wasn't all some incredible hoax (and god, she really wanted to believe that it was, especially the men with guns, something cooked up by Eric to fuck with them), then close to thirty years had passed since the family in the photograph had sat in this room.

All of Eric's stupid Bermuda Triangle stories tried to run through her head at once.

She dropped the magazine and hurried out of the room, following Eric's footprints. Past the living area was a short hallway lined with closet space, clothes still on the hangars, and the top of a staircase that led below deck into pitch black, where she figured the bedrooms must be. Beyond that was the door to the houseboat's control room, with a curtain across it. She peered through the inch wide gap where the curtain met the wall.

On the other side was a space that looked like the driver's compartment of an RV, with two deep captain's chairs and a slanted windshield overlooking the water. In the near distance, the hulking outlines of other dark ships were visible, but she didn't take time to study them. Eric sat in the chair on the left with his head under the long console, working frantically. After a few seconds, he reached into his pocket, pulled out some long, thin object that she couldn't quite see in the dim light, and jammed it up into the space beneath the steering wheel.

She slid aside the curtain. Eric came up so fast, he banged the back of his head against the edge of the console. "OW! Christ, don't do that!"

"Can you get this thing going?" she asked.

"Not a chance."

"What about calling for help?"

"Both the radio and the engines run off the main power, but the entire electrical system's rotted out. Everything in here is dead." His choice of words seemed to make him falter. He swallowed thickly as he looked around the room, his face ghostly pale in the moonlight coming through the windshield. All except his nose, which was so red and swollen it could've guided Santa's sleigh. "I think this boat's been here a *really* long time."

"I know. So what's it doing here?" She pointed through the window, at the outlines of the other ships floating in front of them. "What are they *all* doing here?"

"Oh my god." He jumped up from the chair and moved to lean over the console so he could peer through the glass. "I didn't even see them…"

While he was distracted, she eased into the seat he'd vacated and felt around under the dash. Her hand encountered a cool, smooth cylinder tangled in the ancient wires beneath. The size and shape was actually pretty close to that of her vibrator back home. She freed it and shoved the object in the cargo pocket of her own shorts just as he turned around.

"They're derelicts. Just like the stories. We just stumbled upon the biggest motherfucking find in history!" He sounded ecstatic at the idea; the Bermuda Triangle skeptic who wanted to be proven wrong. "Do you remember the name on the side of this tin can?"

"I think it said '*Holy Mackerel*'."

"*Holy Mackerel, Holy Mackerel…*" His fingers drummed the houseboat's wide steering wheel. "I don't remember that name from any of the books."

"Look, it doesn't matter if Jimmy Hoffa and the Lindbergh baby are on board this thing, it isn't going to help us! Those pirates will be here any second! We have to figure out what to—"

From the far end of the deserted, time-ravaged houseboat, Cherrywine screamed.

9

As the rowboat glided through the water toward the moonlit sunporch where Cherrywine huddled, she wished with all her might that she was back at the hotel in Nassau, or in her shitty apartment back home, or even at the strip club, shoving her tits into a grabby, elderly gentleman's face for a few bucks. Anything but this royally fucked-up situation her Prince Charming had led her in to.

She could almost see the eyes of the men in the oncoming boat, the rest of their faces hidden under their masks. The craft had stopped about halfway across, and was turning in a lazy circle while they appeared to have an argument. As angry as she was at Eric for what he did (and scared too; that blankness that had stolen over his face and infected his eyes haunted her even now), Cherrywine had no problem believing these people would do far worse. She was just getting ready to yell for Amber when a scrabbling noise above drew her attention.

Perched on the edge of the houseboat's roof across from her was a large bird. She couldn't see any real details, but she thought it was the kind that had the big pouch under its bill for scooping up fish, like the bird in one of her all-time favorite movies, *Finding Nemo*. A stork? No...a pelican.

Something about it wasn't quite right. As it sat on the roof, turning its head back and forth on its long neck to watch her from one eye and then the other, she tried to figure out what it was.

The bird opened its slender bill and gave a half-squawk, half-shriek so horrible it struck her as almost obscene. She caught a whiff of something acrid, a stench both rotten and burnt. It opened its wings and flapped at the air awkwardly, as though trying to remember how to fly, then lurched forward and fell straight off the roof, faceplanting on the deck in front of her. The bird lay in a crumpled pile of stinky feathers.

"Oh, you poor thing!" Cherrywine cried. She couldn't stand to see animals in pain, and the thought of comforting another creature instantly took her limited attention span off the task at hand. She scooted forward, intending to gather it up in her arms, smell or no smell. Before she could, its head lifted to look at her.

Cherrywine screamed.

The thing was an absolute nightmare. Its feathers—the few remaining patches of them—were mangy and covered in a dark blue slime. Even worse, the flesh revealed by the bald spots was discolored and almost...*runny*, like melting candle wax. It fixed her with rheumy, bloodshot eyes and gave another of those awful caws through a beak that, she now saw, was cracked and covered with blackened holes.

The freakish pelican rose jerkily to its feet—reminding her of a malfunctioning robot in its stiff, shuddering movements—and launched at her.

Cherrywine flung an arm over her face out of instinct. Her forearm connected with greasy, hardened flesh. Its bill clacked shut beside her ear. She shoved it away and scooted back toward the end of the sunporch, sobbing.

The thing scrabbled at the deck on its gnarled, webbed feet, regained its balance, and came in for another attack. She flung her bare legs up, managing to brace her feet against the tattered remains of its flapping wings. It stretched its long neck between her legs in a grotesque parody of every orally-inept boyfriend she'd ever had and snapped at her face over and over again, missing by mere inches. Over its thrusting head, she saw Eric run out of the cabin.

"*What the fuck is* that?" Eric backpedaled, throwing himself flat against the wall.

Amber came out behind him, but wasted no time with words. She leaned through the cabin door and reemerged with an armload of framed pictures. She chucked them like Frisbees, the first one smashing off the deck to Cherrywine's right, but the next hitting the pelican right in its bald rump. It left off the attack and wheeled around, then gave a lopsided bounce into the air, open maw aimed at Amber's throat.

A booming gunshot rang out.

The bird exploded in a spray of blue feathers.

10

Lito and Ray sat on the front bench of the rowboat while Jorge and Carlos rowed behind them, the latter grumbling about forced labor. As their destination drew closer, Lito used binoculars to scan the water to the west and then passed them to Ray.

"I count at least five others, besides the pontoon and the houseboat. Looks like a few more little fishing boats, a couple of sail-boats, and another yacht. Too dark to see if there are any more past that." Something about the silent shapes drifting out there reminded him of ancient burials at sea, the deceased placed aboard miniature crafts and left to drift on the open ocean for all eternity.

Or maybe he just had Vikings on the brain.

Ray said, "Nope, there's something *big* farther out." Lito peered through the binocs again, with Ray directing where to point them. "You can't get any sense of it, you can just see where the horizon-line is broken."

Lito strained his eyes and finally spotted it, the barely percep-tible juncture of dark sky against darker sea broken by something enormous riding the water. Judging by the length and distance, whatever it was had to be close to a thousand feet long. "I see it. What do you think they're all doin here?"

The other man shrugged sheepishly. "I didn't wanna be the one to say it, but...this *is* the Bermuda Triangle."

"*Jesus H. Christo*," Lito groaned. "Don't feed me that, Ray. We been sailin the Sargasso our whole lives and never seen shit out here. *Bermuda Triangle*. That's for tourists."

"Hey, you want explanations, that's the only one I got."

They were all silent as this information digested.

"So what we gonna do, Cap'n? After we get Rabid back, I mean," Jorge inquired between pants. He worked his stick arms twice as hard on the oars to keep up with Carlos. Every time the paddles rose, they were covered in a mucky film of seaweed.

Lito sensed Ray watching him from beneath his mask, waiting for the answer that had been rolling around in his head all along. "If all these ships are derelict...that means they're up for grabs. We lost the yacht, but maybe there's somethin even better. I say we get these kids taken care of and have a look around."

Ray held up his wristwatch and tapped the face. "That bein the case, it's close to eleven now. Which means we got seven or eight hours to work until we're out here in broad daylight."

"Who cares?" Carlos said. "If they're derelict, it's all legit. We ain't gotta hide nuttin."

"Except the American citizen we got tied up on our boat. Oh, and the three more about to join him."

"So fuckin kill 'em."

Lito looked over his shoulder. Only the kid's eyes and mouth were left uncovered by the holes in the ski mask, not enough for him to gauge how serious he was. "We're not doin that."

Carlos let go of his oar. Jorge pumped for another few strokes before realizing he was alone, spinning them in a half circle. "Why the fuck not?" Carlos demanded. "We wanted their yacht, but that ain't gonna happen now. 'Less you plannin on sellin them or some shit, these muhfuckahs ain't worth nuttin ta us. So just get rid of 'em."

Lito raised a hand, wanting to wring his neck, but calmed himself enough to grab the boy's shoulder. "Nothin's changed. We're not killin 'em if we don't have to."

Carlos shoved his arm away. "Damn Lito, I thought we was pirates. You know, as in criminals? Those stupid-ass chink books made you into a chump."

Lito felt his cheek muscle twitch beneath the knit material. "Row the goddamn boat, Carlos."

"Make me. Better yet...get back here and do it yo'self."

This time it was Ray that reached back, gathering of a handful of the boy's jersey in one fist. "What'd you say? You forget who you're talkin to, you *puto* mongrel?"

"Get yo' hand off me, homey!"

Both of them reared back, ready to go at it, but a scream from the houseboat stopped them before the first punch could be thrown.

Lito pried his second-in-command away from the boy. "Get us over there. Now."

By the time they docked against the other vessel, Lito could see the pelican on the porch as it attacked the blonde. He snatched up his shotgun and waited for the water to calm so he could take a shot, then blew the thing out of the air when it went for the other girl.

The three white kids all stood frozen, mouths hanging open as they watched Lito and the others climb on board.

11

"Okay, you three. Let's have a chat."

Amber, Eric and Cherrywine sat side-by-side on the houseboat's dusty couch, where they'd been for the last five minutes. One of the hijackers (presumably the leader, a guy who looked dressed for a luau aside from the ski mask over his head) instructed them to stay here and not move while he talked to someone on a crackling walkie-talkie. Amber caught only part of the conversation; the person on the other end wanted to know what the gunfire had been about. Now he turned to them while two of the others waited by the door to the sunporch and the fourth—a little pipsqueak—stood over them from behind the couch with a huge rifle.

"*Are...are you gonna kill us?*" Cherrywine bawled, with tears streaming down her face. Amber put an arm around her. It was the question on all of their minds, but still, she wished it hadn't been voiced.

"Maybe." Hawaiian Shirt grabbed the leather recliner and dragged it around to the opposite side of the coffee table to face them, ignoring Cherrywine's renewed sobs. He put a flashlight down in the center of the table with its beam facing the ceiling so it cast the entire room in a weak glow, then plopped down in the chair so hard a cloud of dust poofed up around him. He laid a revolver casually across his lap. "Depends on the answers to my questions. And how fast I get 'em." Amber detected traces of a Spanish accent, an airy, almost regal dialect that made her think of swashbucklers and nobility.

"What do you wanna know?" she asked cautiously. She seemed to be the only one willing to speak. Cherrywine continued to cry into her hands while, to Amber's right, Eric sat with his arms crossed on the other end of the sofa, glaring at their captors. He was obviously still convinced these guys were here for him, but they didn't seem to treat him any differently.

"First of all...you know somethin about these derelicts?"

Amber squinted. "Huh?"

"This boat and all the others abandoned out here."

"Yeah, I understand what you meant. Why would we know anything about them?"

"When you ran, you led us here. Was that on purpose?"

"We were just trying to get away from you. If we knew they were here, why were *we* the ones that crashed into them?"

His fingers steepled and flexed. "A good point, I admit, but I prefer to leave no stone unturned. Just to make sure we understand one another...you're not here for the Dominican? You got nothin to do with him?"

"Honestly...I have no clue what you're talking about."

He nodded slowly. She knew she should still be terrified of these people, just as she had been back on the *MishMasher*, when her imagination was conjuring bloodthirsty psychotics, but now that she was actually in the same room with them, something about this one's demeanor—not to mention his wardrobe—just didn't instill the emotion. He was too calm, his voice too rational, and his eyes were clear and intelligent inside his mask. Even his death threats sounded forced. Either that, or Stockholm Syndrome was setting in already. "Okay then. Tell me what happened to our man. And don't feed me any bullshit about him not bein here, because I saw four people head to this boat with my own eyes. What did you do, drown him?"

"No, I *saved* him!" Amber said indignantly. "I dragged him all the way over here. We tried to help him on board and this... this *thing!*...came up out of the water and pulled him under."

"You lyin cunt!" the skinny man behind them spat. Unlike their host, the accent attached to his squeaky voice was so syrupy that the last word came out a long-Oed 'coe-nt.' Cherrywine jumped.

The man in the recliner snapped his fingers, then resumed the interrogation. "What do you mean, what kinda 'thing?'"

"I don't know, I barely saw it."

"Was it a shark?"

She ground her teeth in frustration, but she really couldn't blame him; she'd tried that rationalization herself. "This thing was too big to be a shark. It had disgusting skin, too. Almost leathery."

"Uh huh. And tell me, just how much weed did you kids blaze through tonight? Although, if you're hallucinatin that bad, I gotta believe you laced it with somethin."

"It's true!" Cherrywine pulled her palms away from her face long enough to add. "It was a monster, just like the one that attacked me!"

"Monster?" He frowned. "What, that pelican?"

Amber threw her hands up. "Don't tell me we imagined that, you saw it yourself!"

"What I saw was a diseased bird, so I put it out of its misery. It was probably more scared of you than you were of it."

"That thing didn't look scared."

He lifted a shoulder. "Maybe, but the point is, it wasn't Freddy fuckin Krueger either."

She clenched her jaw. "Whether you believe us or not, we don't have your man. We tried to help him, even after everything he did. I can't tell you anything more than that, so do what you want."

Hawaiian Shirt squeezed the arms of the recliner a few times before pointing at the small man behind the couch, and then twisting around to a pirate beside the door wearing a Tampa Bay Rays jersey. "You two, check the entire boat for him, top to bottom. If there's anyone else here, bring them out to join the party."

They nodded and hurried down the hall toward the front of the houseboat, the one from the door pulling a pistol. Beside Amber, Eric tensed up, craning his neck to watch the pair as they headed toward the driver's compartment.

Don't worry, she thought. *They're not gonna find your little toy in there.*

After the two men were gone, their leader crossed his legs and went back to studying them. His gaze lingered on Cherrywine until she pulled down her shirt as far as it would go over her legs. Out of all them, Amber was the most dressed, and the only one wearing shoes, even if they were just slip-on sandals. His eyes finally settled back on Amber's face. "Explain to me this: why were you havin to drag our man?"

"He was hurt. Shot in the leg."

"Who shot 'im?"

Amber turned her head to the right to glance at Eric, still slouched in his seat.

"That's your cue, kid. You shoot my man?"

Eric snorted through the ruins of his nose. "Yeah, and if I had a gun now, I'd shoot all you fuckers, too."

Hawaiian Shirt's mouth stretched into a grin through the hole of his knit mask. He held up the revolver in his lap and gave it a shake. "Well, rich boy, I guess it's a good thing *we* got the guns then. Tell me, did my guy do that to your nose?"

"Yeah, right. That big pussy was crying for his momma before he died."

"Eric…" Amber mumbled.

But the other man didn't seem offended. He shrugged and said, "I wouldn't say that in front of the small guy that just left. He's a little touchy about the subject."

"Why, they fags?" Eric smirked, but the expression dropped from his face fast. "Would you just get to the point already? You obviously know who I am, so what do you want?"

"Kid…maybe you're the center of the universe where you come from, but that don't mean the rest of the world carries your picture around in our wallets."

Eric stared at him in awe. "Unbelievable. You're telling me you really are just a bunch of lowlife pirates?"

"Sorry if we didn't meet your expectations. We'll try to look more like Johnny Depp next time."

"And you don't have any idea who my father is?"

"Nope. Don't care."

"You will when he hunts you down and puts your balls in a meatgrinder."

"*Shut up, Eric*," Amber hissed through clenched teeth.

Hawaiian Shirt turned in his chair to look at the man still by the door. Both of them chuckled. "Thanks for the warning, but we'll take our chances with Daddy Warbucks. What is he, a stock broker? Accountant, maybe?"

"You wish." Eric sat forward with a savage grin of his own. "And you may not know who I am, but I sure as fuck know who *you* are. See, I recognized your big, dumb friend with the tattoos. Next time you scout a mark, you probably shouldn't get close enough for them to notice you, retard."

It took this a second to sink in for Amber, but once she remembered the rough-looking men from back at the restaurant, everything fell into place.

The pirate just shrugged again, completely unflappable, and said, "Well...I guess these aren't doin much good then, huh?" He reached up and peeled off the ski mask to reveal a rugged Latin face, with high cheekbones and a buzz of jet black hair. The man at the door opened his mouth as if to protest, then closed it and took off his own mask. He was a bit heftier, and had a black ponytail.

"Look," Amber said, "we answered all your questions. Now you tell us, is Justin really okay?"

"He's fine. He's back on our ship bein treated to a steak dinner."

"So what *are* you gonna do with us?"

"Haven't decided yet. Mostly depends on you."

"We're not going to tell anybody about this, I promise. And we don't even have anything for you to steal. You can just let us go. Leave us right here on this boat, if you want."

The pirate settled into the recliner. "Tell me, *gringa*...with all the ghouls and goblins around, are you *sure* you want us to do that?"

12

Carlos and Jorge cleared the front of the houseboat first, checking the hall closets and all the way to the forward driving compartment. At some point, Jorge began to mutter in Spanish, "Rabid, where you at man, you gotta be here somewhere..."

Carlos let himself grin in the darkness. If those white kids had really offed the big tattooed inbred, they'd done him a favor. The whole side of his face still burned where the fucker hit him.

But, as usual, time was running out. Once Jericho discovered the missing fuel line, it was all over for Carlos. Lito was a dick, but he wasn't stupid. Surely he'd know who to blame for the sabotage, and it might not even be a stretch for him to figure out why.

Real question was...what would their newly zen captain do about it? There had to be a limit to his patience.

The only place left to search on the houseboat was below deck. The stairs in the hallway disappeared into pitch black after a few steps. A charred stench drifted up to assault their nostrils. He and Jorge pulled out flashlights, lifted their masks over their eyes, and started down.

"Rabid!" Jorge called down softly. "You down here, man?"

"You heard what those kids said, homey. Rabid's fuckin dead. Got ate by a sea monster or some shit."

"I don't believe that. Rabid can't be dead. And if he is...I'm gonna take care of those *pendejo* shitheads, no matter what Lito says."

"Why you care anyway, man? You act like you in love with Rabid. Shit, you practically wash his dick for 'im."

They'd reached the bottom of the stairs, and Jorge wheeled around. Dude was a full foot shorter than him, so he had to look up at Carlos as he snarled, "Shut the fuck up. Rabid's been takin care of me for years, and unlike some whiny little *putos*, I actually 'preciate when someone's watchin my back."

"Yo, what the fuck's that supposed ta mean?"

"Figure it out, *ese*." Jorge turned and walked down a hall in the lower level that led back toward the stern of the boat, where that pungent odor got worse. Two doors stood open on the left and one far down on the right. The skinny Cuban leaned in each one as he came to it—first a kid's bedroom with tiny bunkbeds and then a small bathroom—and waved his flashlight around the interior. "You think you tough, talkin all that shit Carlos, but you don't know jack about bein a real man."

"You know...you right," Carlos agreed, coming down the hall behind him. "I just need ta step up and be a man." As Jorge reached the last door and looked inside, Carlos raised his pistol and placed the barrel tip just an inch away from the back of his shaved skull. Lito and Ray, standing somewhere above their heads, would hear the gunshot, but Carlos would find a way to deal with them and then get back over to the *Steel Runner* to finish up.

Yeah, and if you start the party now, who's gonna get the ship fixed up so you can get it outta here?

"*Madre de dios*," Jorge whispered, breaking into his deliberation.

Carlos looked over his shoulder. The bedroom beyond the door was adequately lit by their flashlights to show the same shitty retro décor and scrim of dust as the space upstairs, but the white bedspread was covered in old, rust-colored stains. Dried blood reached to every corner of the bed, and more had been splashed on the surrounding beige carpet and bulkhead walls. The smell in here—like a closed-in barbecue where burnt hair and overcooked meat were on the menu—was thick enough to gag on.

Jorge walked into the room, covering his nose with his gun hand and shining his flashlight around in awe. Carlos let the pistol drop back to his side and followed. Bile collected in the back of his throat, but he swallowed it down.

"Whachoo think happened here, man?"

"Don't know. But yo, somebody got whacked, that's for sure. Maybe a couple of somebodies."

Carlos studied the stains. From their patterns—some of them reaching as high as the ceiling—it almost looked like a geyser of blood had gone off in the middle of the room, a volcanic eruption of gore.

But there were no bodies.

He would never admit it, but this place creeped him out. He was actually kind of glad he hadn't killed Jorge now, so he didn't have to be alone in this room.

And, as he looked around, he noticed something in the corner that struck him as even stranger.

"Check that out, homey." He moved his flashlight beam to the corner, where a common, everyday, potted houseplant sat, long stems jutting up proudly to display a thick growth of broad, flat leaves.

"So what, dude? It's a plant."

"Yeah...but why the fuck is it still alive, if it's been down here all this time with no sun or water?" In fact, not only was the plant still kicking, its leaves looked vibrantly green and healthy, almost glowing.

No, not green. Now that he drew closer, he saw that the color of the plant was actually closer to a deep aquamarine.

A fucking *blue* plant. Sounded like something you'd find in the rain forest.

Jorge shrugged, which didn't surprise Carlos. The guy wouldn't have the mental capacity to wipe his ass if the order didn't come from above. "I dunno, it's probably one of those, like, camel plants or whatever."

"*Camel plants?*"

"Yeah, you know. The ones that only need water, like, every ten years or somethin. Like a camel. I seen it on the nature channel once."

Carlos snickered. "I don't know 'bout no camel plants, but that shit looks like somethin my moms woulda had in her garden. The kind that died if they didn't get water *every* day." He could actually remember his mother's little garden quite well, one of the last lingering memories he'd retained, even when her face had melted from his memory. But he didn't think any of her plants had been blue.

From down the hall, Ray's voice shouted, "Guys, get back up here!"

"C'mon," Jorge said, hurrying past him and back into the hall. "Mondo was right, this place is spooky as hell."

Carlos went too, forcing himself not to run to catch up. As he reached the door, he glanced back, swinging his flashlight wildly through the bloodstained bedroom, and saw something he would later convince himself he must've imagined, but only once he reached the safety of the upper level.

The leaves of the houseplant seemed to be straining on their long stems, reaching out to him as he left.

13

Lito took Ray over to the door when he returned from calling down to the lower deck and whispered, "You believe any of it?"

"About Loch Ness eating Rabid?" Ray glanced at their three captives, sitting in a row on the couch across the room. The blonde still had her head down, and the rich boy with the cocky mouth had his eyes fixed on the wall as he shook his head and muttered to himself, but the one in the middle, the brunette with the pixie-short hair, was watching the two of them while they talked with obvious interest. "Not a fuckin chance. But then again, I don't believe they're lyin."

"Wow, that helps."

"I don't know what to tell you, Lito. I can only say that wherever Rabid is, he prob'ly ain't vertical, if you catch my drift."

"I was afraid you'd say that." Lito shrugged, unsure how to feel about the idea of the big bruiser's demise. He'd never gotten to know the man, had used him only as muscle and intimidation, but he was still a member of the crew. "In that case, we're just wastin our time here. Jorge's gonna be pissed, but if we wanna find out what's up with these other boats, we need to get movin."

"Now that you mention it..." Ray twirled a finger toward the ceiling to indicate the houseboat. "What do you make of this place? If we're excludin the Triangle as an explanation—"

"Which we definitely are."

"—and not even gettin into the other ships we saw, then walk me through the steps that end up with a houseboat this nice goin derelict. What, the owner comes out here alone, has a heart attack, falls in the water?"

"Or has to ditch for some reason."

"Why would anyone ditch a craft that's still seaworthy?"

"Don't know, Ray. That's why I said 'for some reason.' Anyway, he—or *she*, or *they*—ain't here, and that's all I care about. Might not be the yacht we were after, but a tub like this has gotta be worth a few grand if we tow it in, even if it's just scrap." He grinned. "Now imagine we start makin trips back and forth, takin one or even two of these boats back to the mainland..."

Ray looked over his shoulder and then leaned closer. "Yeah, but ain't you the least bit freaked out, Lito? That was a *Viking* ship those kids ran into. We all saw it. And there's a quarter-inch of dust on everything in this room. You know how long it takes to build up a quarter-inch of dust on the open ocean?"

"There's an explanation, Ray. Has to be. Don't get your panties all bunched."

"Oh yeah. I remember when Confucius gave that advice."

"It was Buddha, asshole."

Jorge entered from the opposite side of the living room with Carlos. "Hey, we not wearin masks anymore or what?"

"They know who we are. You find anything down there?"

"A helluva lotta blood," Carlos answered. "But it's been there a *loooooong* time."

Lito ignored the look that Ray shot him and stood still for a moment, thinking, but came up with zilch. This situation had him completely stymied.

He found himself looking at the brunette girl again. The blonde was extremely fuckable, no doubt, the kind of girl you would gladly take home from the bar and consider yourself blessed by the god of one-night stands, but there was just something far more interesting about the brunette.

Starting with the fact that she wasn't sniveling and bawling her eyes out like most women would in her position. What was she, 22? 23? College girl, no doubt; her eyes had a quick-witted gleam.

"Find somethin to tie their hands with," he said. "And get them in the rowboat."

"No, please, you don't have to do this," she told him.

"Look, *gringa*...what's your name?"

"...Amber."

"Okay Amber, we don't have any intention of hurtin you if you don't make us. Trust me on that."

"Why should we?"

"Because you don't have a choice. For now, you're gonna have to cooperate and come back to our ship."

She leaned forward on the sofa, the beam from his flashlight turning her face into a valley of shadows. "If we try to leave in that rowboat...and that thing comes back..."

"We made it over here and nothin happened to us."

"Yeah well, maybe it was just full from eating your other man."

"Fuck that, nobody's tying me up!" The guy with the broken nose—Lito thought Amber had called him Eric—started to get off the couch. Jorge jumped in front of him and drove his rifle butt into the white boy's stomach. He grunted and fell back on the couch, then growled through his teeth, "You are one dead wetback, fuckhead."

"If he tries that again, shoot 'im in the leg." Lito unclipped the radio from his belt, held the TALK button, and said, "Jer, how's the engine lookin?"

No response. He stepped through the door and back out onto the sunporch with Ray, then looked toward the *Steel Runner* before broadcasting again. "Jericho, you there?"

On the deck of their ship, several flashes of light popped in rapid succession, accompanied by the unmistakable crack of distant gunfire.

4

THE VOICE OF THE DEEP

SUGAR AND SPICE AND NOTHING NICE

BLUE

ERIC TAKES A POWDER

1

Justin stumbled down a set of stairs in the dark, feeling like a beaten piñata. The masked hijacker who'd been called 'Mondo' by one of the others limped along right behind him, keeping a pistol jammed between his shoulder blades. When they reached the bottom, the man flicked a switch which turned on an unshaded bulb dangling overhead, revealing a dingy communal area-slash-kitchen. A folding table was set up in the middle, playing cards and poker chips spread across it. A mangy pitbull lay on its side on the filthy floor beneath. It opened one eye to watch them.

"Stop right there, young 'un." Mondo came around in front of him, and Justin was surprised to see he was holding one of Amber's textbooks in his free hand. He set the heavy tome on the table, then kept the gun on Justin as he moved across the room, leaned through a hatch, and came back with a plain, dark blue t-shirt. He tossed this at Justin, whose half-dead reflexes let it whap against his chest and then fall onto the floor.

"Put that on," the man growled. "No reason I gots ta do ya the indignity of sittin around half-nekkid."

Justin bent, got the shirt, and pulled it over his head, something in his back throbbing when he raised his arms to put them through the sleeves. He felt like his whole body had been fed through a woodchipper, and the welt on his head was making him dizzy. While he dressed, Mondo grabbed a metal chair from the table, turned it to face the stairs, and ordered Justin to sit.

He hesitated. Once he allowed himself to be tied up, it was game over. Any hope he had of helping Amber and the others was gone. But what could he do; the guy had a gun.

After he sat, the man used nylon cord to bind Justin's ankles to the chair legs, then tied his wrists behind him and wrapped the rope around his chest and the chair back a few times for good measure. When Justin was secured, he put away the pistol, tucking it in the back of his waistband, then pulled off his ski mask. Justin expected someone along the lines of 50 Cent, but instead Mondo turned out to be a grizzled old black man that could've just come from the set of *Sanford and Son*.

"Hate wearin those things," he muttered. "'Sides, I'm too old ta care if some poh-leese artist wants to draw my pretty face."

Mondo limped to the refrigerator in the corner and retrieved a bottle of ice cold water, then held it to Justin's lips while he drank.

"T-thanks," Justin murmured. He'd been struggling to keep his head from lolling on his neck, but the water cleared some of the cobwebs from his brain.

The old guy bent over him to examine the knot above his temple. "Ya feelin okay, boy? Dizzy?"

He nodded.

"Look like ya took a nasty bump, but long as ya eyes ain't rollin back, I think ya be fine as paint after some rest."

"My friends. Where are they?"

"Should be here soon. Crew's goin ta fetch 'em right now."

"They better not hurt them."

"Relax, boy. I been workin with Lito fer a while now, and trust me, if ya gotta get jacked by pirates, he's defin'ly tha cap'n ya want."

"Oh yeah, look at me, tied to a chair. I feel like I just won the lottery."

"Better than tha altern'tive."

"Which is?"

"A bullet in tha brain and a meal fer tha sharks."

Justin said nothing, just stared at the canvas tops of his shoes.

"Lissen, ya just sit tight down here, don't make a fuss, and this'll all be over soon. Ya want somethin to eat? Or maybe some weed?" He pulled a tightly rolled joint from his shirt pocket. "I got some of tha most mellow cann'bis you evah tried. I lace it with honey. Mmmm *mmm*, that shit hits tha spot! Happy ta share with ya."

"Uh...no thanks."

"Suit yaself."

Mondo walked around him one last time, making sure the ropes were tight. As he straightened from checking the ankle bindings, his arm brushed against Justin's shorts and felt the lump in his lower pocket. He reached inside.

"No, wait, please don't—!"

Mondo pulled out the ring case, flipped it open, and gave a low whistle of appreciation. "Now *that's* a pretty sight. Who tha lucky lady?"

"Amber. One of the girls your men are going after."

"She say yes yet?"

"She'd be wearing that if she did."

The pirate turned the diamond back and forth, admiring it in the light. "I'd guess this be worth 'bout...two grand? That in tha ballpark?"

"More like three. Please, *please* don't take that ring."

Mondo snapped the box closed and rolled it in his hand. "I 'as married once, ya know. Most beau'ful woman in the Caribe. Died of breast cancer just 'fore my thirty-fifth." He pushed the box back into Justin's pocket. "Considerin we came out here after yer boat, three grand don't seem like it's worth tha trouble. Just don't let none a tha others find out 'bout it."

Justin sighed with relief. "Thank you."

"Hollah if ya need anything. I gotta get out on deck ta keep an eye on all this crazy bidness. There's evil tidings afoot." With that strange pronouncement, he hobbled back upstairs.

The dog under the table raised its head, regarded Justin, gave a long, squeaky fart, then went back to sleep.

2

Jericho Trellis waited on the deck of the *Steel Runner* until Lito and the others made it over to the houseboat, then radioed on the walkies to find out what was up with all the shooting. The crack of the shotgun had rolled back across the water, bringing him to full attention, but he'd just about choked on laughter when Lito told him he'd taken down a crazed pelican. Then, after Mondo returned from tying up the white kid to monitor the VHF scanner, it was straight down to the maintenance room to find out why the engines weren't turning over.

He'd been a boat mechanic just about his entire life, helping out around his father's business as soon as he was old enough to hold a wrench. That experience, however, wasn't really needed in this case. Even a novice could've diagnosed the problem in seconds.

Jericho sat in the sweltering engine room, removed his ski mask, and stared at the empty couplings where the fuel line normally connected. *How* the hose could've disappeared was one question; *what they were going to do about it* was entirely another. He dredged his brain but came up with no workarounds.

Finally, after his dreadlocks were dripping with sweat, he gave up and climbed the ladder out. His head had just poked above deck when he heard the scampering of feet.

The maintenance hatch was in a narrow alley between the bulkhead leading downstairs, and the one that comprised the upper part of the cargo holds. A shadow flitted past the entrance several feet away, a short, small shape heading down the gangway toward the stern of the ship. Jericho whipped his flashlight up, but was too late to catch whatever it had been. He stayed frozen for a moment, waiting for it to return.

From around the corner, he heard a low, angry hiss, like a wet cat.

The sheen of sweat on his skin turned cold all at once.

Jericho crawled the rest of the way out of the maintenance hatch and got to his feet. He'd left his damn pistol back in the wheelhouse, but his trusty machete was strapped to his back as always. He reached over his shoulder and pulled it from its sheath, two feet of razor-sharp, gleaming steel, then eased to the edge of the alley. The pontoon boat was visible next to them through the guardrail, the shredded remains of a curtain flapping from a broken window in its cabin. Jericho held the flashlight with one hand and hefted the blade over his head with the other.

He psyched himself up and jumped around the corner.

The gangway leading toward the back of the boat was empty. He lowered the machete—

"Jer'cho?"

—and then brought it right back up again as he spun around to find Mondo standing on the deck behind him. Jericho managed to curb his reflexes just short of taking the old fuck's head off.

"Jesus, why you creepin 'round like dat?"

"Sorry." Mondo looked like he was on the edge of a coronary himself, eyes wide and mouth hanging open.

"You okay?"

"Yeah." He licked his lips. "C'mere a sec. There's sumthin I want ya ta hear."

They returned to the wheelhouse, where Mondo pointed to the portable VHF scanner. "I was skimmin channels...just like the Cap'n said...listenin fer chatter from them other boats...and I heard sumthin."

When he said nothing more, Jericho asked, "Yeah? What was it?"

"Jus'…jus' turn it on and hear fer y'self."

Jericho went to the scanner—a square box with a telephone handset mic attached by a cord, almost like a CB radio—and asked, "What channel?"

"Well…all of 'em."

He turned the scanner on, releasing a brief squawk of static through the speaker on top. After that, there was nothing but the hum of an open line.

"It was pretty faint," Mondo told him. "Ya might hafta turn it up."

"Or maybe all dat pot finally fucked up your brain."

"I tell ya, I heard it!" the old man snapped.

"Heard *what*? You haven't even…" And then a voice poured from the scanner, just as faint as he'd claimed. Jericho turned up the volume as far as it would go.

He was tempted, at first, to believe the line was distorted somehow, the transmission garbled or maybe even encrypted. But no; aside from being quiet, the channel had crystal clarity. It was the voice itself that was the problem.

The timbre was deep and rough, like listening to someone who'd been smoking for a century. The language it spoke was not English or Spanish, the only two Jericho would've recognized, but rather something more guttural. Each sound—*word?*—that it made seemed to crawl into his ear, jostling about in his head in a way that made him nauseated.

He reached toward the scanner, meaning to change the channel frequency.

"*What're you doin?*" Mondo cried out, horrified. "*Don't answer it!*"

"I'm not!" Besides the fact that he wouldn't be able to broadcast while the other party was already doing so, the very idea of pushing the transmit button and trying to answer that somehow obscene voice filled Jericho with dread. It would've been like that old urban legend about saying 'Bloody Mary' in the mirror five times; tempting fate, in other words. He spun the dial to switch channels and found the same voice broadcasting on each one.

The receiving range on a VHF scanner like this one, if a highly amped broadcast came from a tall transmitter or a high hillside, was, at most, sixty nautical miles. From ship-to-ship in crafts as small as the *Steel Runner*, it was more like five.

Unless there was a freighter passing somewhere close by, that meant this transmission had to be coming from one of the derelicts.

As Jericho mulled that over, the speaker on the radio stopped abruptly, and the line was given back to open silence.

"It's the Voice of the Deep," Mondo said solemnly.

"Huh? What're you talkin 'bout now?"

"My grandfather. He was a voodoo priest on Saint Thomas, long befo' the white man came and startin buildin hotels on the island. I ever tell ya that, Jer'cho?"

"I don't remember."

"Well, he was, and he used ta tell me stories about the Voice of the Deep. An angry, vengeful creature that uses the ocean for its own whims. Not a god, not a demon, but sumthin in between."

Uneasy silence reigned after he finished speaking. Usually the old fart's stories were easy to pass off. Now though, Jericho could feel gooseflesh walking across both arms.

Before they could say anything else, the white kid began to yell from downstairs.

"I'll go see what he wants," Mondo said. He walked out of the wheelhouse, leaving Jericho alone with the scanner.

He quickly switched the device off before that voice could speak again.

3

As soon as he was alone, Justin heaved at his bindings. The ropes were loose enough not to chafe, but still far too tight to slip out. Struggling got him nowhere except exhausted. But using his feet, he found he could move the chair in half-inch increments.

On the kitchen counter sat a block of cooking knives. He worked his way around the table toward them at an agonizingly slow pace while the dog watched. After what felt like two hours of work but was surely no more than ten minutes, he was covered in sweat and barely three feet from where he'd started. He sagged in the chair and rested his chin against his sternum.

Footsteps on the stairs brought him around. Justin raised his head and tried to think up an excuse for his new position in the room. "Sir, I gotta take a leak so—"

The words hung in his throat.

The figure descending toward him was not Mondo. It was barely four feet tall, and looked like it might once have been a little girl around five years old, dressed in the tattered remains of a tiny pair of Levi's and a short sleeve, flowery blouse. And probably of some eastern ethnicity, judging from the dark tint of her skin.

Or what little skin she had left.

Most of her flesh looked runny and wet, almost gelatinous, and covered in oozing pustules. Her head, in particular, was horrible to look at. It was lumpy with tumorous growths, and only a few clumps of long hair remained on her diseased scalp. The skin of her face sagged in flaps and lumps like it was in the process of sloughing off, resulting in a hideous mask that had sealed over her right eye and left icicles of flesh dangling from her misshapen nose. It reminded him of the sick kids they used on TV to get you to donate money for disease research or burn wards, except they always found the cutest ones possible for those ads. This tiny little girl made him want to retch. She stood hunched on the next-to-last riser of the staircase, one shoulder swollen so much it almost reached her ear, small hands flexing slowly at her side as she looked around dazedly. When her remaining eye passed over Justin, she fixed him in a glassy stare.

Under the table, the dog rolled over on its stomach and growled.

"Um, hello?" Justin said tentatively. She may look like hell, but he didn't care who she was or what was wrong with her, especially if she could get him out of this. "Can you...can you help me?"

The girl's cracked lips peeled back, revealing blackened, gummy teeth. She threw her head back and shrieked at the ceiling. The sound was pure fury. She leapt off the last stair and ran at him full out, arms outstretched.

"Hey, stop! What're you doing?"

She was two feet away when the pitbull came flying out from under the table, knocking the whole thing over. Poker chips and empty beer bottles flew in all directions, along with Amber's textbook. The dog jumped at her with a shrill bark, the fifty-pound girl colliding with the sixty-pound canine to produce a meaty thud. The girl was knocked flat to the floor on her back.

The dog waded in to attack, latching on to her forearm just below the elbow. Justin watched in stunned horror as it shook its powerful head back and forth, mauling the appendage. Her boiled skin seemed to disintegrate beneath the canine's teeth. But instead of blood, a bright blue, almost phosphorescent liquid spilled from the sides of the dog's muzzle and poured across the floor.

A pungent, eye-watering stench singed the hair in Justin's nose.

The pitbull deflated at the first taste of the goo. It let go and backpedaled, whimpering and gagging. Before it could get out of range, the girl whipped out a hand, grabbed its lower jaw, and wrenched. The dog's head split across the middle as the two parts of its muzzle separated. Its limp body fell to the floor, and the girl looked up at Justin and hissed.

"Jesus Christ, help! Mondo, *help*!"

She came at him, hunched and ghoulish.

He struggled again in the chair, this time hurling himself side-to-side hard enough to lift the legs off the ground. The girl reached him, such a tiny figure but so much stronger than she looked. She grabbed his hair and yanked him toward her. Her stink enveloped him. Justin glimpsed her melted features coming at his face, teeth bared.

He threw all his weight toward her, tipping the chair. For a moment, he was suspended by his hair where she gripped it, but then it ripped out by the roots. Her fingernails dragged across his chest as he fell, shredding his borrowed shirt and the flesh beneath. His veins filled with fire as he hit the floor hard on his shoulder and writhed.

For a split second, his eyesight was blotted out by a cobalt blur, as if a neon flashbulb had gone off in his face.

"What's all this ruckus, boy?" Around the legs of the girl, Justin saw Mondo come down the steps. The old man took in the situation. His face bloomed with panic as he shouted up the stairs, "*Jer'cho! G'down here!*"

The girl spun and flew at him. Her appearance must've repulsed Mondo just as much, because he wasted no time pulling his pistol. He got off two shaky shots into the bulkhead before she was on him, climbing his torso with the agility of a monkey. Clinging to his jacket, she darted forward, sank her teeth into his throat, and tore it out. Blood sprayed across the room in an arc, making it all the way to the poker table. He flailed at the girl as she continued to take bites out of him.

Then Mondo—the man who was once married to the most beautiful girl in the Caribbean—collapsed at the base of the stairs with his eyes still open and staring at nothing. The girl leapt away as he fell.

Justin thrashed on the floor, but he was still bound tight. His chest burned where the insane little bitch had scratched him. She was coming back a third time, skittering toward him on hands and knees like an animal. Blue drool that looked like the stuff from the inside of a glow stick leaked out the sides of her mouth. He lay helpless as she fell upon him.

Another gunshot rang through the ship. The top of the girl's head sheared away. She slumped over Justin.

A second black man with dreadlocks past his shoulders stood on the stairs, holding Mondo's pistol. As Justin watched, he bent over and voided his last meal onto his shoes.

4

"Say again Jericho?"

His mechanic's voice was broken by poor reception, but even so, Lito could hear the panic in it. "I said he's fuckin dead, *mon!* Mondo's dead!"

Lito looked up from the walkie. They'd tied the white kids up with strips from the clothes in the front closets of the houseboat and had been in the process of loading them into the rowboat when he'd finally gotten a response from the *Steel Runner*. Now everyone stopped and stared at him, Ray frozen with one foot in the rowboat and one still on the sunporch. Lito stepped to the far side to escape his audience and lowered his voice. "What do you mean? *How?*"

"Some crazy, fucked-up little girl bit his t'roat out! She killed Cheech too!"

"Did you say a little *girl?*"

"Oh god. God, I shot her, Cap'n. I shot her right in de head, but I didn't have no choice! Dere was somet'in wrong wit her, she was sick or somet'in!"

"Jer, man, chill out, you're...you're not makin any sense!" Lito felt some panic of his own coming on. If he understood correctly, Jericho was not only telling him that he'd lost a second crewman, but that someone else—and not just anyone else, but a fucking *child*—had also been murdered on board their boat. That raised a hell of a lot more questions than it answered, but it also meant a long prison stretch would start looking good compared to the death sentence they'd get if they were brought in now.

And you're discussing it over an open line.

"Hey, maybe we oughta cool it with the urder-may talk," he said.

"Den just get over here and see for yourself!"

"All right, we're on our way. You figure out what's wrong with the engines?"

Jericho gave a laugh so hysterical it almost sounded like a sob over the static-heavy walkie. "Yeah, I solved dat mystery! You gonna love dis one!"

"What?"

"Better I show you when you get back. Hurry de hell up!"

Lito clipped the radio back to his shorts, aware that everyone's eyes were still on him. Jorge and Carlos were already in the rowboat, with Eric and the blonde trussed up on the seat in front of them. While Ray held the mooring, Lito offered his hand to Amber to help her down into the boat.

"No thanks," she told him. She stepped past him and plopped down on the end of the bench next to the blonde.

Jorge was first to break the uneasy silence. "Cap'n... did he just say Mondo's dead?"

Lito stepped in after Amber and took a seat at the front, facing the rest of the group. His lips felt numb as he said, "I think so. Ray, I'm sorry...he said Cheech was killed too."

Ray took the news with only a nod as he released their line and shoved them off from the houseboat. "Who did it?"

"I don't know. I don't understand exactly what happened. But from now on, everybody stays together until we figure out what's goin on."

Carlos leaned over the side of the boat to look at him. "Yo Lito, what'd he say about them engines?"

"I think he's got it figured out. Don't worry, if anybody can get us ready to roll, it's Jericho."

But Carlos *did* look worried. In fact, he looked almost sick with fear, and the emotion was utterly alien on his usually cocky face. He seemed to notice Lito watching him, wiped his expression clean, and threw himself into the oars. No matter how much trouble Carlos gave him, how much shit he talked, he was still just a 19-year-old kid. Lito hadn't seen his first dead body till he was almost 22, and even that was just a crewman that had been attacked by some rich old coot with a shock stick while they were plundering his yacht.

They were in motion a few seconds later, Jorge and Carlos grunting as they turned the boat and rowed back toward the *Steel Runner*. The wind had picked up out of the southeast, ushering those dark clouds closer to them. They held lightning deep in their hearts, visible as white flickers alternating between sections of the sky. The ocean was calm for now, but Lito suspected it wouldn't stay that way for long.

He looked around at their prisoners. The blonde stared at the aluminum floor, Eric at the shrouded hulks of the ships in the distance. Only Amber—sitting across from Lito with her tied hands clasped in her lap, their knees almost touching—met his eyes in the dark. "What about Justin? Is he still all right?"

"My man didn't mention, but I'm sure he's fine." He sized her up, waiting for her gaze to move away, but she met him with just as much intensity. "He your boyfriend?"

Lito couldn't be sure, but he thought there was a moment's hesitation before she finally answered, "Yeah."

"Well…we'll have you back to him in a minute."

The rowboat moved on through the still night.

5

The below-deck area of the *Steel Runner* reminded Lito of the slaughterhouse floor he'd worked at when he was 17: chunks of scattered gore, various corpses propped everywhere, and a sticky, partially-coagulated layer of blood underfoot. Even Jericho, sitting on the edge of the card table with his feet pulled up, had the same shellshocked, dejected look in his eye as the men who stayed in such a job for too long. That look was the main reason Lito had walked off the line fifteen years ago and joined up with Brewster.

What he wouldn't give to be back there covered in bovine intestines right now.

Mondo lay at the base of the stairs, a ragged hole in the side of his neck and blood down his shirt like spilled wine. Unlike with Rabid, Lito had considered the man a friend, and it stung to see him sprawled out so carelessly, like those cattle after their skulls had been bashed in. Cheech's body was just to the old man's left. The pitbull's head looked distorted, as if his jaw was attached with a hinge that went the wrong way. Across the room, almost in the corner, Amber's boyfriend sat tied to one of their chairs, a parody of a child undergoing punishment. Sweat-drenched hair hung in his face. And, in the middle of all this carnage…

"Jesus H. Christ." Ray crossed himself like the good little Catholic he'd been raised.

If Lito had believed in God, the sight of the tiny girl lying on her stomach with her brains exposed might've made him echo the sentiment. "Jericho…what the hell did you do?"

"*It wadn't me fault!*" the Bahamian cried. "She was batshit crazy!"

"She's fuckin five-years-old! You couldn't've held her down?"

"You didn't see her! She'd already killed Mondo and Cheech and was goin for de boy! What was I supposed to do?"

"You're tellin me she killed a grown man and almost tore that dog's head off with her *bare hands*? I call bullshit on that one, Jer."

"I don't care what you say, Lito, it's true. Dere was somet'in wrong wit her. Her face, *mon*…you shoulda seen her face…"

The girl lay on her stomach, with her small butt slightly pooched in the air. Lito put his foot against the shoulder of her tattered blouse and gently rolled her over. She hardly weighed anything. A wave of acridness like singed hair rolled across them as her disgusting features were exposed. "Ugh. I thought little girls were supposed to be made of sugar and spice and everything nice."

Ray peered over his shoulder, holding his nose. "What's that blue stuff?"

For the first time, Lito realized the dark blood puddles under her injuries had a tint to them the color of midday sky. "*Christo*, where'd she even come from?"

Jericho snorted before answering. When Lito glanced over, he was dabbing at his eyes with his fingertips. "I got no idea. I heard de yellin and she was here when I came down."

"We have to get her off the ship. Right now. If we were to get boarded by the cops..."

"Uh, Lito?" Ray discreetly pointed a finger at the white kid. "Lack of a body ain't gonna matter when there's a nice little witness gift-wrapped in the corner."

"Shit." He shrugged. "Well, if he's a witness, he might as well be *our* witness."

Lito walked over and stood in front of the chair. "Hey, kid. You're Justin, right?" He gave no response, just stared at the floor in front of him. Probably in shock. Lito knelt and waved a hand in his face. "Hey, look at me."

Justin blinked and raised his head. His eyes were clear, but his breathing seemed husky, almost labored. Beads of sweat rolled down his skin to soak his t-shirt collar. Lito noticed the front of the garment was torn, the cloth around it bloody.

"You all right?"

"I don't...feel so good. Where's Amber?"

"She's upstairs with your other two friends. Everybody's fine and they'll stay that way as long as you cooperate. Now, tell me what happened. Where'd that girl come from?"

"Don't know. She just...came down the stairs."

"Did she say anything?"

The kid took deep, shuddering gulps of air and talked in a rush between each one. "No. Just...screamed and ran at me. Killed the dog...then the other guy."

"You're a real help, kid." Lito stood and turned to Jericho, who was still sniffling. Ray had disappeared into one of the bunk rooms. "She sure as shit wasn't on board when we left! And don't tell me she was swimming out here, goddamn it!"

"Ain't it obvious?" Ray emerged with an arm load of sheets and began laying them out on the floor in the areas that weren't covered in blood. "She came from one of the derelicts. Maybe that pontoon boat we've been rubbing against for the past half hour."

Lito grimaced. He couldn't believe he'd missed the answer that was staring him in the face. He needed just a few minutes to clear out his head so he could think, but there wasn't time. "Okay, fine. Let's just get her wrapped up with some weight and toss her overboard. Mondo too."

"*No, you can't do dat!*" Jericho jumped off the table and stood with his hands held out in fists. "We can't just dump her for de sharks, she's just a little girl!"

"Yeah, a *dead* little girl! And we'll all be joinin her if anyone finds her body on board this ship! Trust me, the jury ain't gonna care if she looked like a G. I. Joe after you burn it with a lighter." He instantly regretted the quip.

And felt even worse when Jericho covered his face and began to sob outright, big, choked snorts. Lito had never seen the man cry. "I didn't mean to do it. I didn't have no choice..."

Lito laid a hand on his shoulder. "Jericho, it's not your fault. Not if it happened like you say. Nobody's blamin you. But we gotta get this situation taken care of while we still can. We're alone out here for now, but who knows how long that's gonna last?"

Jericho sobs cut off. He lowered his hands. "Oh god. With everyt'in else goin on, I completely forgot." He ran up the stairs, out of the galley, leaving Ray and Lito to stare at one another. Without speaking a word, Lito helped him move the body of the girl onto one of the sheets while the comatose white kid sagged in the corner. They had just packaged her up into a tidy bundle of blue-soaked cloth and were about to start on Mondo when Jericho came bounding back into the room with the VHF scanner. "We heard somet'in before... Well, just listen."

They did, long enough to get an earful, then Lito said, "Turn that shit off. It's givin me the willies."

"Sounds like two bears in mating season," Ray added. It was far too tame—too *normal*—a comparison, for that growling voice. Lito could practically feel the words crawling on his skin.

Jericho complied, silencing the speaker. "Mondo found it. He called it 'de Voice of de Deep,' or some of his voodoo nonsense. It's broadcastin on every channel."

"That means one of these derelicts you wanted to tow ain't so *derelict* after all." Ray hunkered on the floor next to his dog's corpse and looked up. "So we leave now. Right?"

Lito didn't answer.

"*Right?*"

"This could be comin from anywhere," he said finally. "Could be a stray signal. Somethin we're pickin out of the atmosphere from some radio tower in Bumfuck, Idaho. Hell, for all we know, it could be some guy talkin on his cell phone in China."

Ray sighed. "Lito...it's time to pull anchor and get the fuck outta here. We can take these white kids with us and dump them off wherever you want, but let's just get rid of the bodies and go before somethin even worse happens."

"I second dat," Jericho whispered.

Lito looked from one to the other. "I admit guys, this situation has gotten extremely FUBAR'd. I hate that we lost Rabid and Mondo. But runnin away and forfeitin whatever might be out here isn't gonna bring 'em back. So let's take a quick cruise through the neighborhood on our way out, see if anything looks choice."

"Well, dat brings us to our engine problem." Jericho swiped at his eyes again. "It seems our fuel line has disappeared."

"Disappeared? What, did it fall off or somethin?"

Jericho rolled his brown eyes. "No, Lito, it didn't fall off."

"Then what...?" He frowned. "Are you tellin me the engines were *sabotaged*?"

"I'm tellin you a vital piece is missin, and dat someone who knew what dey were doin had to've taken it."

"But who? And why?"

Ray folded his arms across his chest and stood up. "The why is pretty clear. We're not supposed to leave. As for who..." He moved his foot and tapped the tied bundle of sheets containing the dead girl.

Jericho shook his head vehemently. "No way she coulda done dat."

"You sayin a kid couldn't uncouple a hose?" Ray argued.

"No, I'm sayin *dat* kid couldn't do it. If she even knew how to tie her shoe anymore, I'd be surprised."

"Okay, maybe so, but just her bein here at all proves that we've been severely infiltrated. If she got on board, then who else—or *what else*—did?"

Lito had been pacing in front of the card table, but the cracking sound of the drying blood on the floor sucking at his shoe soles was making him sick. He stopped and stared at Ray. "Are you sayin there could be more like her?"

Ray shrugged. "What I'm sayin is that we got no fuckin idea what's goin on around here, or what to expect next. What we *do* got is a lotta derelict ships with their crews unaccounted for. And now some goddamn spooky voice on the long range is broadcastin God-knows-what from God-knows-where."

Lito felt cold suddenly. "We gotta search the *Runner*, top to bottom. Make sure we don't have any more stowaways. Jer, what are our options here?"

"*Options?*" Jericho barked laughter. "Our *options* are sit here dead in de water, find a new fuel line, or use de radio to call for help. When we can find an open channel, dat is."

"And not only would we be rollin the dice to see who shows up to rescue us," Ray added, plopping down in one of the chairs, "we'd also be alerting whoever's behind that broadcast that we're here."

"What about the pontoon boat? Could you get a hose from that?"

"Dat's a little outboard engine; I need an industrial grade fuel line that fits all de modifications I've made. But if I could get dat t'ing or maybe de houseboat up and runnin, we could at least use one of dem to get our asses outta here."

"And abandon the *Steel Runner*? I don't think so. *That* I'm not even gonna consider. You two keep an eye on the kid and get as much of this cleaned up as you can. Just...bury the bodies in the back of the cargo holds for now and we'll decide what to do with 'em later. I'm gonna get Carlos and Jorge to help search the ship." Lito took a few steps toward the stairs and then stopped. An object on the floor beyond Cheech's body caught his eye: the linguistic textbook they'd brought up from the yacht wreckage. He bent and picked it up, then said over his shoulder, "Wait, scratch that. Cut the kid loose. I got an idea."

6

"Hey, girlie. Hey. I'm talkin to you, *chica*."

Amber set her jaw and asked, "Yeah?"

"Not *you*, dyke," the skinny pirate—she thought she'd heard him called 'Jorge'—spat. "That little blonde *puta* next to you."

After climbing from the rowboat onto the pirates' scow (a process that involved them getting hooked under the shoulders and dragged over the side like trout) the man named Lito had gone below deck with his pony-tailed right-hand man, leaving the two younger guys to guard them. Jorge reclined against the railing with a cigarette jutting from his lips, while Carlos—shaggy hair and barely more than a teenager—paced further up. There was a nervous energy around that one, like the kids she saw in the library at school, studying at three in the morning the day before finals.

Amber, Cherrywine, and Eric sat on the deck up against the boat's wheelhouse, a steel cord threaded through the bindings on their hands and then through eyelets embedded in the wall, giving them freedom to move but not escape. The lights in the wheelhouse threw long squares of yellow light across the rubberized deck in front of them.

Amber looked at Cherrywine, sitting on her knees and pulling her long pajama t-shirt down so it formed a tent around her legs. The strengthening breeze kept blowing her long hair into her face. "Just ignore him," Amber told her.

"Hey girlie," Jorge pressed. His voice had the squeaky timbre of a cartoon chipmunk, which didn't help his seduction. "You got a nice ass, baby."

"I'm...I'm not interested," Cherrywine told him.

He flicked two fingers in her direction. "You like it rough, huh? I can do that." Cherrywine put her hands to the marks on her throat, her face clouding over.

"Leave her alone," Amber said.

"Just tryin to give her a chance to get with a *real* man."

"Why, are there some around that don't have the body of a fifth grader?"

Eric gave a loud, concentrated, "*HA!*"

Jorge flashed his teeth around the cigarette. "Don't be jealous, honey. You'll get your turn. You *all* will, for what you did to Rabid. I'm 'onna see to that, *pinche puta*."

He turned, flicked the cigarette out onto the water, and then slid up the rail away from them, giving them the first privacy they'd had since being brought on board.

Eric leaned closer to Amber and whispered, "We gotta get away from these guys."

"If you have a way to do that, I'm all ears."

"We get our hands untied and then, as soon as we can grab Justin, we should just…just…you know…"

"What?" Amber rolled her eyes. "Make a run for it? We're in the middle of the ocean."

"If we can just jump overboard, maybe we can swim back to the *Holy Mackerel*."

"I don't wanna go back in the water," Cherrywine said in a small, hoarse voice.

"Me neither," Amber agreed, "considering we saw a man get eaten by something out there."

"All right, all right, yeah, maybe that's not the best idea, but we can still overpower them and try to take *this* ship."

"They outnumber us, and they're armed."

"*Well, we can't just go with them!*" Eric snarled. "I have to get free and get back over to that houseboat!"

"Why? If the engines and the radio are out, then what's so important over there?"

Amber tried to make the question sound as pointed as possible, hoping it would get him to offer some explanation about the object currently taking up residence in her pocket, the one he'd been so eager to get rid of when he thought these guys were business associates of his mob boss father.

But Eric just shook his head and looked away. "Forget it. If you're not gonna help, I'll do it on my own."

She grabbed his shirt and pulled him back, hard enough to tear the collar. They were almost nose-to-broken-nose. "Don't you do a goddamn thing to get any of us hurt. That guy Lito has played straight with us so far, so let's just cooperate and see what happens."

He grinned as he removed her bound hands, the superior expression he usually wore, but there was a dangerous edge to it this time that startled her. Cherrywine's assertion on the houseboat zipped through Amber's consciousness, about something being broken in the upstairs kingdom of Prince Charming. But of course there was; she only had to look at that necklace of bruises around their companion's throat to know that. "You can stay here and suck his dick all you want, Amber. I'm gonna do what's best for me."

"Big surprise," she muttered.

Cherrywine hugged herself. "Please stop. I can't take this anymore…"

There was movement from the direction of the stairs on the other side of the wheelhouse. Justin staggered around the corner, face bruised and swollen, supported by Lito. He stumbled when he caught sight of Amber, fell to his knees, and practically dove headfirst into her lap.

"Justin?" She cupped his cheeks. "Jesus, he's burning up! Justin, what's wrong?"

Eric scooted closer. "Oh yeah, these guys are fantastic Amber, I wanna use them as my travel agents next time!"

"Not them. They didn't do this." Justin sucked in air and coughed it right back out, then shivered against her. "There was a girl…"

Amber leaned in to catch the rest of his words. She noticed the front of his shirt was torn and bloody. She held the cloth open to look inside.

A ragged wound stretched across the front of his chest, not deep but still oozing blood. The flesh at the edges looked dark.

"What happened to him?" Amber demanded. "You said he was all right!"

"Extenuatin circumstances." Lito held up a large, square object. She recognized one of her textbooks even though the cover was damp and badly shriveled. "I need to know, whose is this?"

Eric, Amber, and Cherrywine took turns exchanging glances.

"I don't have all day. Whose?"

"Mine," Amber admitted.

"You're studyin this? How good are you?"

She frowned. "Define 'good'."

"You know a bunch of languages and shit?"

"I...no, not really. I know about languages in general. Structure, form, that sort of thing."

The pirate chewed the inside of his lip, then shrugged. "Have to do." He pulled a knife from a sheath on his belt and moved toward her. Cherrywine gasped and Amber stiffened until they saw he was only sawing through her wrist bindings. "Come with me."

She slid out from under Justin, easing him back on the deck, but he sat up and grabbed at her leg as she stood. "Where are you taking her?"

"Relax hotshot, I'll bring her right back. You three sit tight and don't move. I'll be watchin."

Lito wrapped a hand around Amber's upper arm and led her away. He waved over Jorge and Carlos, who followed them just around the corner of the wheelhouse. Lito let go of Amber long enough to step away and talk to them in hushed whispers. She caught something about 'checking the entire ship' just before the two younger men raced away past them, heading toward the rear with their guns drawn.

"In here." Lito held open the wheelhouse door. She stepped inside ahead of him. The rectangular space was more modern than she would've guessed for an old ship like this, with upgraded, surely aftermarket electronic equipment and readouts installed in the dash around the wheel and throttle controls. Cherrywine and Eric were bound just underneath the front window, so Lito was able to keep an eye on them as he'd said.

"What do you want from me?" she asked. Despite what she'd just told Eric about cooperating with this man, she couldn't help but be suspicious. If he made the slightest move to take out his dick, she was going to do her best to remove it for him.

He watched her for a long moment but ultimately decided to ignore her question. "I'm sorry about your boyfriend. We didn't do that to him, I promise you."

"Okay. Who did?"

"Someone else. One of my men died tryin to protect him. Believe it or not, we have no interest in hurtin any of you."

"Tell that to the scrawny guy outside."

"I will. But for now, I brought your boyfriend back to you as promised."

His insistence at pointing out this fact made her understand that Justin had been returned to her as a sort of peace offering, to get her to go along with whatever he wanted. The manipulation made her angry.

Lito moved to the window and looked down on Justin and the others, coming uncomfortably close to her in the process. She caught a whiff of his scent—a clean natural musk, no trace of cologne or deodorant—and took several involuntary half-steps back to maintain the distance between their bodies. He didn't seem to notice as he took several long, measured breaths with his eyes closed, then asked, "What about the other guy? Eric? If my guy didn't do that to his nose, then did it happen in the crash?"

"If you must know, Cherrywine did it to him."

He grunted laughter. "I'm likin you girls more all the time."

"Glad we could amuse you. Now why'd you bring me here?"

He reached for a square, metal box sitting on the counter along the back wall and flipped a switch on its side.

Five minutes later, Amber sat in the room's only chair, completely engrossed as she hunched over the radio speaker and strained to catch each syllable that drifted out.

"Well?" Lito perched behind her on the control dash, where he could watch the others and her at same time.

"I've...I've never heard anything like it," she said. That was an understatement; she didn't know if *anyone* had ever heard anything like this. "I'm tempted to say it's nonsense, but it has too much structure. You can't fake that, especially not at this speech rate. It's definitely a language of some sort."

"Yeah, but *what* language? Russian, maybe?"

She shook her head. "It's full of choppy cadences like Russian, but not nearly as phonetic. I couldn't spell out these syllables if I tried. I mean, I'm not even hearing anything I can trace back to any of the major world language families."

"You're gonna have to dumb that down for me, *gringa.*"

Amber bristled at the name—the connotation surrounding it was insult, but the way it rolled off his Latin tongue gave it the lilt of a pet name—but did her best to answer the question in layman terms. "All the languages on earth can be grouped into nine families, based on geology, distinctive traits, and certain common components. For a trained ear, it's not too hard to pick out which family a given language falls into, even if the owner of that ear isn't necessarily fluent or even familiar with the language in question. Now, keeping in mind, I'm no expert or anything, but *this*? It doesn't sound like any of them to me."

More so than that, it sounded...*ugly*, to be perfectly blunt about it. Every professor she'd ever had insisted that even the harshest languages in history held beauty in the right context, but she wasn't seeing it here. This was almost more animal than anything a set of human vocal cords could produce.

Lito interrupted her thoughts. "So you're sayin this is some kind of...what? Alien language?"

A haughty laugh escaped her at that. "I didn't say that."

"Well, if it's not from one of these earth families..."

"I just meant that it's fabricated. Unique. Someone completely made it up. Like...I don't know, Klingon."

"Not to get technical, but Klingons *are* aliens."

She stared at him as he favored her with a lopsided grin.

"Anything else concrete you can give me?"

"Well, it isn't live. This is definitely a recording."

His heavy brow drew together. "How can you tell that?"

"It plays every two minutes exactly, with a thirty second break in between each cycle. And every broadcast is exactly the same."

"Yeah, but how do you know for sure? I can't hear anything

in that garbage."

"I memorized the phonemes at the beginning and end of each cycle to see if they matched up. They do. Whatever this is, it's automated. Maybe a distress call or something. Although why someone would broadcast it in a made-up language is beyond me."

"Okay. Well, I appreciate you taking a look." He slid off the dash and beckoned. "Let's get you back out there. Lots more to do, and the night is still young."

7

"C-can you see her?" Justin asked. He lay flat on his back, with his eyes closed. The world seemed too bright every time he opened them, even in the middle of the night. He felt like he had a case of the flu, and the wound in his chest burned with a constant, even heat, as if he were being roasted alive.

Eric rose up enough to peer in the wheelhouse window. Because of his awkward angle, hands still tied to the boat, a sudden gust of wind almost blew him over. The night's temperature had dropped several degrees since their time aboard the *MishMasher*. Distant thunder muttered every few seconds from the horizon off the port side of the boat. "Yeah, he's got her in there listening to something."

"The signal. They're having her listen t-to that signal."

"What signal?"

"Some voice on their radio scanner. Creepiest thing I ever heard. Had them all freaked out."

Eric crouched again and held his bound hands over Justin's face. "Bro, you're free, see if you can untie my hands before one of them comes back!"

"No, we can't. It might make them mad."

"Just do it, man! You owe me after wrecking my dad's boat!"

"Don't blame that on me. If I hadn't gotten us out of there, we'd be—"

"We'd be, what? Fucking tied up like a dog to a parking meter? Thanks, glad you saved me from *that* experience!"

Justin shook his head. "I'm not doing anything that might get Amber hurt while she's in there with him."

Eric gave the wheelhouse wall a frustrated kick. How many times in his life had his royal highness been denied something he really wanted? Justin felt a sudden perverse glee at finally being the one to do the denying. "After what she did to you, you still care if she lives or dies? Don't be a fucking tool!"

"What are you talking about? What did she do to me?"

"Didn't you *pop the big question?*" Even with the high-pitched whine in his voice from his broken nose, Eric managed to make the prospect of marriage sound like syphilis.

"No, I never got the chance."

A smile spread across Eric's face so slowly, glacial ice could've beaten it in a race.

On the other side of Justin, Cherrywine said, "Don't, Eric. Don't be an asshole."

But that was what Eric excelled at: being an asshole. If they'd offered a course in it at school, he might've actually made the dean's list. Justin had always known it, he'd just figured he was immune to its effects.

And suddenly, he wasn't sure if he wanted to hear what his *best friend* had to say.

"Let me clue you in here, bro: Amber knew the whole time. About the ring and all of it. She told little miss whore over there she was gonna turn you down cold."

"I *hate* you," Cherrywine whispered, turning away from them both.

"The feeling's mutual," Eric told her. "And if you go spreading any more lies about me, my nose is gonna look pretty compared to what I do to you."

Justin lay still on the deck for a while, trying to figure out if he was more angry at Amber for doing this to him, or Eric for taking so much joy in telling him. He ultimately decided Eric, because he couldn't pretend he didn't know this was coming with Amber. She of the 4.0 GPA and him, who had switched majors four times in the last year and a half. Had he actually bought a ring? The whole thing suddenly seemed like a child's idea.

Eric nudged him. "So let's do this!"

Justin started to tell him to fuck off, but a cramp ripped through his stomach. The scratches across his chest felt like napalm. He moaned.

"You okay?" Eric asked, with as close to concern as he was capable. "What happened down there anyway? They cut you up?"

"No, t-there was a little girl. She attacked me. They...they had to shoot her."

"Woah...you're telling me these fucktards killed a *kid* on this boat?"

Before Justin could explain further, there were footsteps on the deck. The three pirates that had been downstairs with him strolled out onto the deck, pushing Amber ahead of them.

8

Lito had a hand in the small of Amber's back, guiding her back toward her friends. She had an athletic figure; he felt the muscles bunching as she walked, and couldn't stop his eyes from wandering south to her hips. He felt sleazy all of a sudden, and even more so when she pulled away from him with a glance back over her shoulder to catch him looking. She sat on the deck beside Justin just as Carlos and Jorge came running up the opposite gangway to join Lito, Ray, and Jericho.

"Whole ship is clean, Cap'n," Jorge reported. "We didn't see nobody."

"Yeah, and who were you looking for?" The taunting question came from Eric, still bound to the ship. His eyes flashed triumphantly in the dim light from the wheelhouse. "More kids to kill?"

Lito saw the look of alarm that crossed Amber's face. Maybe it had been a mistake to let them intermingle after all. He grimaced as he said, "That's not exactly true."

"Not what my boy here just told me. He says you're blowing kids away on this piece of shit."

"Look, we're not sure exactly what happened." He could already imagine saying something similar to a very hostile jury. "A little girl got onto our ship somehow. She was...sick or something. She killed one of my crew and did that to your friend. So we had to put her down."

"*Put her down?* What, like ol' Yeller?" Eric looked at Amber and hiked a thumb at Lito. "You hear that, your hero over here is murdering sick kids on this boat."

Lito tried not to falter at the use of the word 'hero.' "It's not like that. It was self-defense."

"Keep telling yourself that. Maybe next you wanna go to a burn ward and poison the Jello." Jorge hauled back a boot and kicked Eric in the hip. "*Fuck!* That hurt! Save the rough stuff for your tattooed boyfriend! Oh, that's right, he's fuckin dead."

"*Puta tu madre, cabronito!*" Jorge lunged for him.

"Stop! No more of that," Lito barked, pointing at Jorge, who froze with his hands in front of Eric's face. "Whatever else is goin on, these kids didn't off Rabid, so nobody harasses them. That's an order. As of right now, consider them our...guests."

"L-like at a hotel?" the blonde asked hopefully, through fresh tears.

Eric held his bound wrists in her face, reminding Lito of some old movie with a plantation slave in shackles. "Sure, they tie me up every time I stay at the Four Seasons, you stupid bitch."

"*Jesus Christo*, what is your deal, you pampered little brat?" Lito felt the last of his self-control slip. "Don't talk to her like that!"

"Gimme a break. You gonna defend this whore's honor now?"

"Look, I'm tryin to be civil here, but if you want, I can toss your ass down in our cargo hold and leave you in the dark to rot!"

"Was she Indian?" Amber's voice was so quiet, Lito barely heard her.

"Who?"

"The little girl. Was she Indian, or maybe Middle Eastern?"

From Lito's right, Jericho tensed. "Yeah, I t'ink so. How'd you know dat?"

"Because she was on that houseboat with her family at some point. I saw her picture. If what you're saying is true—"

"It *is* true!" Jericho sounded wildly defensive. "Ask your boyfriend! Or better yet, come downstairs and see for yourself!"

"I'm not doubting you, I'm just saying, where's she been all this time? And how can she possibly still be a little girl when that boat's been out here for almost three decades?"

A silence grew on the deck that Lito rushed to fill. "We can all agree somethin ain't kosher out here, but there ain't no way that boat or any of these others have been out here for thirty years. *Someone* woulda found them by now. This is one of the heaviest trafficked waterways in the world."

"I don't want to debate with you. And I don't care about what's going on. I just want to know what your plans are for us."

"Well, I was gonna take you into Bermuda and drop you off at the closest port—"

"No, we can't leave yet!" Eric, again. *Dios*, this was one *bastardo* that thought everyone lived to hear his opinions. This time though, he sounded panicked.

"Why do *you* wanna stay so bad, rich boy?"

The kid hesitated for a second, eyes flicking back and forth like a trapped animal, the first break in that condescending façade the higher tax brackets had perfected so well. "You know that yacht you morons caused us to sink? Well, it's somewhere below us, and there's a lotta shit on it my father will probably want back."

There was a loud, hacking cough as Justin squirmed and finally sat up. "D-don't be stupid, Eric. Your dad will understand."

"If you think that, bro, then you don't know my dad."

"But we gotta get outta here. Get s-somewhere safe. And I think I need a doctor…"

Lito cut in. "Look, all of this is moot. We can't go anywhere. We're havin some engine problems."

"What kinda problems?" Carlos had wandered away from the rest of the group, and stood rigid at the far end of the deck with his hands held behind him.

"Someone—maybe the girl, maybe someone else—sabotaged us. No idea why, but the bottom line is, we need parts, so…we're gonna have to go scavenge them."

Jorge interpreted his meaning first. "What, from those other boats?"

"Yep. Just gotta pray we find what we need."

"I don't think that's such a good idea," Ray said softly, his first contribution to the proceedings.

"We don't have any choice."

"What about your radio?" Amber asked. "Can't you call someone?"

"Sure, we could send out a mayday in the thirty seconds that the lines aren't bein tied up by that other signal. Only problem is, if we manage to contact anyone at all, it'll probably be the Coast Guard. And, as you can imagine, that's not so good for us."

"Look, if you just let us go, we won't say anything. Will we?" Cherrywine and Justin nodded their agreement, while Eric leaned back against the wheelhouse and rolled his eyes.

"You won't have to. They'll know who we are." Lito put a finger to his upper lip. "Tell you what, though. I *can* be diplomatic."

He grabbed the knife from the sheath on his belt again and sawed through Eric and Cherrywine's bindings.

"Everybody gets a vote, even you four," Lito said, straightening up. "Majority rules. As for my crew, feel free to be honest.

Those that wanna try our luck with the radio, raise a hand."

Only three went up: Amber, Cherrywine, and Justin's shaking arm. They all looked at Eric.

"What? I'm not gonna play this fucker's games. You really think these criminals are gonna call the cops and get carted off to prison for the rest of their lives if we vote for it?"

Lito ignored him. "And those that wanna try to get ourselves outta this?"

He put his own hand up along with most of his crew. Ray was the only one that abstained, shaking his head as he looked skyward. Luckily, it was still enough to swing the vote. "Okay, no more debate. You four sit tight and we'll find clothes and shoes for those that need them."

"Why do we need—?" Amber blanched. "You're taking us with you?"

"Of course. I'm down two men. I can't spare the manpower to guard you here."

"If we're really your guests and not your prisoners, you wouldn't need to guard us."

He sighed. "I meant, for your protection. Better we not split up."

Lito turned and walked around the corner, heading below deck. Ray followed him into the gangway, waiting till they were out of earshot to speak.

"You tricked them into goin along with your little treasure hunt. You know that, right?"

"It's either this or call for help, Ray."

"Or abandon the *Steel Runner* and try to find another way out."

"Really? *That's* your vote? We already lost the yacht, now you wanna leave with even less than we came into this thing?" Lito put a hand on the railing beside him and squeezed that comforting metal. "This ship is all we own in the world, Ray. We leave it and...shit, we'll be panhandling on the streets wherever we wash up within a week. Not to mention, if Jericho can't get an engine working in one of these other rust buckets, we're right back to square one anyway."

"It's just real convenient that doin things this way also lets you go pokin around out there." Ray crossed his arms. "And we can't drag these white kids around if we go, they're dead weight."

Lito sighed. "You're really fuckin up my inner peace here, Ray. I need Jericho with me, and I don't trust Carlos and Jorge enough to leave them behind. So do you wanna stay here on guard duty? Alone?"

The other man thought about that. "No."

"Okay then. Round up every flashlight, gun and bullet we have on board and get them in the rowboat."

"Hey!" The voice belonged to Carlos. They turned in time to see him chasing Eric onto the narrow stretch of deck behind them. The white boy skidded to a stop.

"Listen." He wheezed through his swollen nose. "We got off on the wrong foot earlier. I can pay you, okay? My father can pay you...whatever you want."

"Oh yeah?" Lito asked. "And just what's the going rate for an obnoxious, spoiled *cabron* and the rest of the gang from the Abercrombie catalog?"

"Who gives a fuck about them? I'm talking about *me*."

Lito chuckled. "That's very mercenary of you, but ransom isn't really our thing. Even if it was, what do you expect me to do? We still have to fix our engines."

"All I'm asking you to do is leave me here when you go. On that houseboat, maybe. Then call someone when you get away and tell them where I am. *Not* the police though." He swallowed uneasily. "I mean, I can give you a number to call."

"And where exactly does our payment come in? You gonna run by the ATM first?"

Eric's mouth fell open, his tongue working soundlessly within. "I can...mail you a check, or something..."

Ray snickered.

Lito leaned closer to the kid. "Your money can't solve every problem in life, rich boy."

"You're making a goddamn mistake," Eric snarled.

Before Lito could tell him how little he cared, the night sky blazed with blue light.

9

As Eric got up and chased after Lito, Amber leaned forward to put a hand against Justin's clammy forehead. He jerked away, scooting out of reach along the wheelhouse wall, and sat stiff and shivering.

"Woah, what's wrong?" she asked.

"Nothing," he snapped. "Just...leave me alone."

Amber frowned. Beside him, she noticed Cherrywine kept her eyes rooted to the deck. "Am I the only one not in on the joke here?"

"It's nothing," he said again.

Amber looked between them. From the odd sense of guilt coming off them, she couldn't help wondering if maybe these two actually *had* gotten up to some hanky-panky while she was in the wheelhouse with Lito. "I just wanted to see how you felt."

"Like my insides are f-filled with kerosene and someone lit a match." All at once, the rigidness left his body and he slumped against the wall. His shivering stopped. He seemed to soften as he said, "I don't know, it comes and goes. Maybe the cut's infected. Are you two okay? They didn't hurt you, or..."

She shook her head quickly. "These guys might not be as bad as I thought." She glanced over her shoulder at Jorge, who had retreated to the far end of the deck so he could watch them and look around the corner at wherever Carlos had chased Eric. "Then again, if they're really shooting children..."

"It wasn't like that." Justin squeezed his eyes shut. "I saw the whole thing, and he wasn't lying. This girl...it's like she wasn't even human anymore. You know that guy with the ponytail? He's scared there could be more like her. We can't let them drag us out there into the middle of those ships."

Amber gnawed at her bottom lip. That disembodied voice from the radio echoed in her ears. "I don't see that we have a choice."

As she said this, a glaringly bright light bathed them from above. They turned their faces upward. The sky in front of the ship flashed with a vivid, almost neon-blue light, turning the stars into a field of hanging sapphires. The effect was beautiful, like an explosion of fireworks. Except with fireworks, you expected noise and heat on your face, but this phenomenon was eerily silent. Charred ozone hit her nostrils again. The roots of every hair on her body bristled as static electricity coursed over her, causing the fillings in her teeth to buzz.

And, even though its color was cool and inviting, like pool water on a hot summer day, there was also something entirely unnatural about it. Some primitive sliver of her core cringed away, so much so that she felt sick again.

Then it ended, not all at once, but dying down to a mutter somewhere on the horizon.

The night—so quiet on the ocean without the honk of car horns or even just the chirp of crickets—stretched on into infinity.

Lito came running back onto the deck, shoving Eric ahead of him. "Did you see that? What was it?"

Jorge pointed at the dark horizon. "It came from somewhere out there!"

Next to Amber, Justin whispered in a dreamy, distracted tone, "God, it was so pretty…"

The pirates started for the bow, but stopped when a hollow *bong* sounded below their feet like the clapper of some gigantic church bell, accompanied by a tremor that ran through the deck. All nine people jumped. Another deep gong came right after the first, and this time the entire ship lurched. Cherrywine shrieked and jumped across Justin, into Amber's lap.

Lito broke for the starboard side of the boat. More of the noises came now, one right after another, each jolt causing the boat to rock. Ray and Carlos joined him at the railing and looked over. A second later, Carlos exclaimed, "Yo, what the hell are *those?*"

Lito turned and jabbed a finger at Amber. "You. Get over here."

She looked around at the others—Cherrywine and Eric looked at her in confusion, but Justin was still staring at the sky where those flickers of light had come from—then stood slowly and went to stand in front of Lito.

"Now you tell me, and think *really* careful," the pirate said, moving aside and ushering her to the railing with a hand on her neck. "Are those your goddamn sea monsters?"

The fishing vessel had drifted away from their ship, leaving a wide canal running between them. Amber squinted at the black water below. There was a disturbance down there, a flurry of splashing movement, and it took her eyes several minutes to pick out what was causing it.

An army of rigid fins carved through the dark water, glistening triangles of all sizes that parted the mat of seaweed in front of them. They darted at the hull of the ship all along the starboard side, making a beeline that ended with them colliding against the metal hull to produce that reverberating gong. Then they about-faced, swam out several yards, and sped back to do it all over again. It was like some perverse version of Sea World, where Shamu was trained to ram himself against the wall rather than jump through a hoop.

"No," she answered Lito. "I already told you. I know the difference between a shark and…whatever we saw."

"Good god almighty," Jericho exclaimed, from farther down the railing. He lifted a shaking hand toward one fin that towered over the others by a good two feet. Amber could make out the rounded back of the thing it was attached to when it breached above the water just before slamming into the ship. "Dat's a great white, *mon*. You ever hear of dem t'ings comin so far south?"

"Sharks don't do that." Ray shook his head vehemently. "They don't attack ships for no reason like that."

Carlos leaned out over the railing as several of the thrashing figures below jumped up and hit the boat in unison, tipping them the other direction, and sending Amber's stomach into a tailspin. The smallest of the trio left a dark smear as it fell back into the water and floated belly-up. "They're bashin their brains out on the side of the boat! Yo, that's fucked up, man!"

"No." Lito watched a few more strikes then glanced over his shoulder, past the prow. "They're tryin to push us. Toward the other ships."

He reached back and pulled the revolver from the back of his pants. Amber flinched at the sight of it.

"Relax, this isn't for you." He twirled a finger in the air at his crew. "Kill every last one of these things."

The others pulled out pistols and opened fire over the bulwark. Jorge ran over and added his semiautomatic rifle to the chaos, each bullet a burst of ruddy light. The water churned below, and, just before Amber covered her ears, she thought she heard garbled mewls drifting up between the shots. She closed her eyes and waited for it to end.

When she finally peeked, Lito and Ray were using boathooks to snag one of the dead sharks under its fins. The water was littered with smooth, oblong bodies bobbing on the surface. The pirates lifted their catch and hauled it over the railing, then allowed the creature to fall to the deck on its stomach with a wet *plop*.

"Jesus, that thing smells like *mierda*!" Jorge exclaimed.

"Stay back," Lito ordered. "Don't anybody touch it."

An unnecessary command; Amber didn't think she could be paid enough to lay a finger on the putrid, disgusting hunk of flesh still wriggling in front of her. The others gathered around in a football huddle, squatting and holding their noses, and even Cherrywine drifted forward to peer over Amber's shoulder.

The shark was a lean creature, maybe six feet from tip-of-tail to rounded snout, just above a mouthful of razor teeth. Amber had never seen one without a pane of glass to separate them from her. It was in bad shape from their attack: bullet-riddled, missing hunks of flesh, its dorsal fin as tattered as a battlefield flag. But even besides this damage, she could tell that its rubbery skin was distorted, covered with ripples and cracked valleys and open, rotten-looking sores, just like the pelican. Ray played the beam of a flashlight down its glistening form.

The liquid dribbling from its wounds was a viscous, shimmery blue, more like oil than blood.

"What's wrong with it?" Jorge whispered.

"It's just like de girl," Jericho answered, voice tinged with disgust.

Ray exchanged a glance with Lito. "You think its some kinda pollution, maybe? Somethin in the water?"

"Fuck that, man!" Jorge said. "That's some kinda disease, like a flesh eatin virus!"

Beside Amber, Justin stifled a cough.

"Oh god, that's what happened to them." Cherrywine backed away, holding up her hands as if to ward off an attacker.

"Happened to who?" Amber asked.

"The people from those other boats. Don't you see? It's like the story Eric told us about that man, the one the government took away. All these people, they got sick and their skin started melting off, just like *that* thing." Each word she said was more shrill than the one before it. Her manicured fingers stole up to grip the long, blond hair above either ear, like a B-movie scream queen. "Are we gonna catch that? *Are we all gonna look like that?*"

Jericho frantically rubbed his palms against the legs of his shorts. "Oh shit, I touched dat little girl!"

"Hey." Lito's calm voice cut through the growing panic in the rest of the group. He was hunkered down right in front of the shark, his face just a foot or so from its maw of tangled teeth. "Everybody, just chill out and take a look at this."

He grabbed one of the boathooks and used it as a lever to roll the shark onto its side, revealing the blackened remains of its long belly.

Looking like one of her professors, Lito used the boathook to point at a gaping cavity in the flesh just below the shark's open jaw. At first, Amber thought it was an exceptionally big exit wound from one of their gunshots, but then she saw the jagged bits of blue bone sticking out around the edges and she understood.

It was a second mouth.

No more than a rudimentary hole buried below the first, ringed with bluish teeth, like the gullet of a lamprey.

"*That*, is a mutation," Lito declared. "When we were fishing him out, I saw another one down there with a second dorsal fin, and another with no eyes. And the girl had the same bluish tint to her blood. It's all connected, but last I checked, there ain't no disease on earth that spontaneously mutates you. And there sure ain't one that keeps you young for thirty years, or every Hollywood actress would be tryin to catch it."

"Then we're back to somethin bein in the water," Ray said.

"We swam in there," Amber said quietly.

"And when you start growing extra limbs, then we'll worry about you." Lito straightened and faced them from the other side of the shark. "My point is, we don't know anything for sure, so let's just cut the hysterics."

They all went back to contemplating the double-mouthed shark in silence until Carlos finally raised his head and looked around at the group. "Yo, where's the other one?"

The question confused Amber until she realized the deck behind them was empty.

Eric was gone.

10

"Looks like all he grabbed was a pair of Jericho's shoes from downstairs," Ray reported. "No guns, no flashlights, nothin. Just took the rowboat and ran while he could."

"*Hijo de puto! Idiota!*" Lito brought a fist down on the *Steel Runner*'s prow. Black rage consumed him, the kind that all his books and meditation were supposed to be saving him from, but at least this was directed inward rather than outward. "My fault for not keepin his ass hogtied!"

"In that case, we should lock down the other three again."

Lito simmered a second before answering. "What's the point? They can't go anywhere now unless they wanna swim. No, that other cocksucker was the problem. I say good riddance."

Ray shrugged and looked away, but not before Lito caught the look on his face.

"What?"

"I'm not blind, *amigo*. You think showin a little goodwill is gonna get you in with that high class, bookworm, *gringa* piece of ass? The blonde maybe, she seems desperate enough, but the brunette? *Jorge's* got better chances, and his idea of romance is a roofie and a ball gag."

"Ray…I got no fuckin idea what you're talkin about."

"Uh huh. So what's the plan?"

"Depends. What did Jericho say about the pontoon?" After discovering the last rowboat had been stolen, they'd roped the fishing boat and hauled it closer, then lowered the mechanic aboard to see if the vessel was serviceable.

"Engine on that thing's shot. Says he'd have a better chance at fixin the jet skis."

"Fine. Then we transfer everybody over and row the damn thing."

"We can't do that."

"We sure as hell can. One man on each side with long poles as oars. Be like a gondola ride. We don't got that far to go."

"But—"

"What other choice we got, Ray? We need to get to those ships." Lito flipped the switch to turn on the searchlight, then swept the beam across the seaweed-strewn surface of the ocean in as wide an arc as it would reach. To the south, those crooked forks of lightning drew ever closer. "We don't got a lotta time either. That storm'll be on us in an hour or two, and that rich *pendejo* has a head start. He's probably out there lookin for a radio that works on one of these derelicts as we speak."

"I don't know 'bout that. He didn't seem too eager to be rescued."

"You noticed that too, huh?" Lito turned back off the searchlight, then leaned one elbow on the guardrail. "He couldn'ta got too far. We'll look for him along the way. But let's take the VHF and keep monitoring, just in case."

Ray lowered his voice and switched to Spanish. There was no real need; Jericho had taken the white kids belowdeck to find some clothes, and Carlos and Jorge were gathering the last of their weapons and ammo. For the time being, they were alone on the deck of their ship. "What about everything else, Lito? The voice on the scanner...the sharks and the girl...that weird blue light..."

"I saw it before," Lito said.

"What're you talkin about?"

"That blue light. I saw it right before we sent Rabid over to board their yacht. It was just flickers on the horizon then. We're a lot closer now."

Ray's mouth twitched in anger. "When the fuck were you gonna tell me about it?"

"Right now, obviously."

"We shouldn'ta made a move on those white kids if there was even a chance anyone else was out here."

"Well, we did. At the time, it didn't seem too important."

"No, of course not. Because Lito Porto was ready to play pirate, so nothin else mattered. Now we're stuck out here just waitin to be picked up by any patrol boat that wanders by. You know, if that white boy dies from whatever that little bitch gave him, that shit is on us."

"He's not gonna die."

Ray tugged on the back of his ponytail hard enough to give himself a facelift. "I just want you to say you're takin this situation at least a little seriously."

"I'm takin the situation very seriously, Ray."

"Then make me feel better. Tell me what happens if we don't find a fuel line out there. Or if someone boards the *Runner* while we're gone on your little fishing trip and finds Mondo and that girl rottin in the holds?"

"If that happens, Ray," Lito said, leaning back against the guardrail, "we're no more fucked than we are right now."

11

Eric stayed crouched in the bottom of the rowboat for another ten minutes after the deck of the pirate ship cleared. He'd headed out into pitch darkness after his escape, far beyond the range of the searchlight. The damn seaweed had fought him every step of the way, like it was trying to keep him from leaving. From way out here, he could see the pirates, but they had no hope of picking him out against the black expanse of the sea.

The much smaller fishing boat began to move away, past the *Holy Mackerel* and on toward the other derelicts. He couldn't hear an engine, so he figured they were rowing the damn thing. In a way, he was weirdly jealous; they were setting out to explore the collection of derelicts that, he had no doubt, the Bermuda Triangle had spewed forth from some hellish pit at its center.

A once-in-a-lifetime opportunity.

But now wasn't the time. His head felt too muddled, as if there were more people than just him taking up space in it, and there was only room to concentrate on so much.

His destiny; that was the only thing that mattered. Now that the pirates were out of sight, and the night had descended into a deep silence broken only by the grumble of thunder, Eric could consider his next move.

I'll tell you your next move. That voice again, emphasizing words just the way his father would. Never had it spoken to him this much before, and never so loudly. It was as though it had been locked up behind a door in his head, and something finally sprang the lock. *You* need *to get that fucking statue back, and then make sure that blonde* bimbo *won't be around to tell people you tried to* squeeze *her neck like a tube of toothpaste.*

"What are you talking about?" Eric asked aloud, acutely aware he was talking to himself. Beads of sweat jumped out across his forehead. "I didn't do that."

You did though. Somewhere in that junkyard you call a brain, you know *you* did. *She saw behind the* mask, *Eric, saw you for what you* really *are, and now that bitch Amber knows too. Maybe even Justin. So you need to* clean *up all your messes before you even start* thinking *about escape.*

"But they're...they're with the pirates...they're as good as dead anyway..."

YOU GODDAMN JACKASS! The words in his head were so loud, Eric pitched backward like he'd been physically slapped, sprawling across the benches and rocking the rowboat. *You saw Amber and that* wetback *captain of theirs making* googoo *eyes at each other! Those two little* whores *are gonna blow every* spic *on that boat and get dropped off at the closest five-star resort! Then, even if you get your* dumb *ass outta here, they're gonna have the cops waiting for you when you get back! So grow up and stop* MAKING EXCUSES!

"O-okay," Eric whimpered, lying in a fetal ball on the bottom of the boat. "Just tell me what you want me to do."

The voice didn't answer. Instead, he heard the steady thrum of an engine growing louder in the distance.

Eric uncurled, sat up, and peeped over the rim of the rowboat. He looked to the southeast, toward the gathering squall. Somewhere in that direction lay the tiny island they'd left just a few hours before, but much closer than that was a small craft skimming the waves, heading right toward him. He waited till it got close enough to be sure it wasn't a patrol boat before standing up and waving his arms.

"*Hey! Hey, come over here!*"

The boat—a slick little speedster with a flaming paint job—made a final course correction toward him and cut its engines. As it coasted toward the rowboat, a halogen flashlight beam hit Eric in the face, blinding him. He raised a hand and barked, "Jesus, do you mind?"

A heavily-accented voice asked, "Whatchoo doin way out heyah, *bredda*?"

"My friends and I were taken prisoner by this group of pirates, but I got away! Listen, you gotta help me, I need a ride to this houseboat over here and then to the closest port! I can pay you whatever you want!"

"Oh really now?"

The light clicked off, and Eric could finally see the occupants of the speedboat by moonlight. Three black men sat with submachine guns pointed at him, while a fourth—a guy with a mohawk of dreadlocks down the middle of his scalp—stood on the bow, scratching the shaved part of his head with the barrel of a pistol.

"We cyan talk *aaaall* 'bout payment latah, white boy, but first..." He leaned forward, displaying a mouthful of gold that seemed to float in the middle of his dark face. "How 'bout you climb aboard and tell us which way dem pirates went?"

5

THE FINAL FATE OF THE RING

A FLOATING GRAVEYARD

BIDWELL'S FLASHLIGHT

ERIC GETS A TOUR

1

"*Those fucking gringo pinche puto pendejos,*" Jorge muttered, for what must've been the thousandth time since they boarded the fishing boat. Carlos rolled his eyes. The gawky little Cuban added an additional insult each time. "This is all their fault. And I don't care what the Cap'n says, I'm gonna get a little revenge for Rabid the first chance I get."

The fishing boat was just a big, rectangular aluminum raft on top of two barrel pontoons, two feet of clearance beneath and a narrow fiberglass shack running up the middle. Carlos stood at one rear corner of the vessel and Jorge at the other, both of them rowing with extra oars from the *Steel Runner* lashed to boathooks to form long handles, like they were goddamn Huck Finn floating down the Mississippi. Carlos hated that book in school, but he could remember him and his homies—Diego Palacios among them—laughing their heads off whenever that Twain dude wrote 'Nigger Jim.' The going was slow, and their standing positions were so precarious that if they didn't brace their legs just right during the backpaddle, the resistance of the water against the oars could easily cause them to fall into the ocean.

And, after seeing that deformed shark, Carlos had decided the ocean was the last place he wanted to go.

"Homey, I agree with you and shit, those muhfuckahs is bad news, but do you think you could...you know...just shut the fuck up?" Carlos stopped paddling long enough to glance over his shoulder. "We got worse problems than those white kids anyway, like the *Cap'n* leadin us out here to the middle of nowhere."

"Ain't got no other choice, *mon.*" Jericho spoke so quietly between them—with his head jammed under the hood of one the old jet skis parked on folding skids at the boat's stern—that Carlos had trouble hearing him. The deck around the mechanic was covered with the bags of tools, weapons, and gas cans they'd brought from the *Runner*, and, on the fishing bench that ran the width of the rickety vessel, the VHF scanner started up again, speaking low in its garbled tongue. That creepy-ass voice had been drifting from the speakers every couple of minutes since they'd left, and it never got any easier to listen to.

"He had plenty of choices. Anything besides draggin us out here."

"We voted, idiot. Your hand was up just like everybody else's."

"I just didn't wanna call the pigs for front door pickup. I didn't vote to row your asses around all night." He pointed at the scanner. "And turn that shit off! If you can't understand what the muhfuckah's sayin, then listenin to it for an hour ain't gonna help!"

Jericho pulled his head out from under the hood and turned the scanner down, but not off. His face was nothing but shadows, while his eyes were as big and round and bright as the nearly full moon overhead. "De signal's gettin clearer, which means we gettin closer to de source."

"Yeah, and what if the person sendin it is like that little girl you killed?"

"I didn't kill her," Jericho snapped.

"Yo, I'm pretty sure when you put a gun to the bitch's head and blew her brains out, it didn't send her to Disneyland." Carlos waited to see if that would get a response—his face still stung where Rabid had smacked the shit out of him, and he'd love to pass the beating on to this beach trash mechanic—but Jericho just stiffened momentarily and then went back to work on the jet ski's engine. After a couple of seconds, Carlos thought he heard the man sniffle. What a pussy.

He wanted to feel triumph, but a sudden overwhelming sense of urgency turned his blood to acid. There was no time to sit here jawing with these assholes. He'd been telling himself that he couldn't make a move until the Steel Runner was mobile again, but now that felt like another excuse, a way to delay what needed to be done. He couldn't afford to keep waiting for the perfect opportunity, not when every second took them farther away.

Carlos pushed his paddle through the water again to keep their coasting momentum going, and asked Jericho, "So you really can't just rig somethin up back on the ship? You know, just to get us goin?"

"If I had de right parts, I could prob'ly do somet'in. But you know, Ray's t'eory was dat somebody like de little girl took dat fuel line. But de more I t'ink about it, de less sense it makes. If dere was someone else on de *Steel Runner*, den where'd dey go?"

"Well, whatevah," Carlos said quickly. The words sounded much too guilty to his own ears. "I'm just gettin tired of rowin this thing, is all I'm sayin."

"Yeah, well, you best get used to it, cause if we can't fix de Runner, you gonna be rowin a loooot more."

Carlos turned away, meaning to put his back into the rowing, and felt something move against the end of his oar, startling him so bad he almost let go of the pole. He yanked a flashlight from his pocket and shone it down at the water beside the boat.

At first he expected more shark fins (or even the monster the white kids kept talking about), but there was nothing, just the carpet of seaweed surging gently on the ocean currents.

And yet...

He knelt on the edge of the boat, leaning closer to hold the flashlight just a foot or so above the surface of the water.

The seaweed was moving all right, but the undulations didn't have anything to do with the water. As he watched, slimy tendrils rose from the water and slid along the rusted side of the pontoon, as though caressing the metal. In the harsh beam of the flashlight, they were the blue-green color of the plant on the houseboat, the one whose narrow stems had reached for him like a baby toward its mother. It was like some blue dye had been injected into them.

The color was so vivid, the seaweed almost seemed to glow.

Carlos felt sure that if he fell in the water, those tendrils would wrap around him tight. Cover his mouth to keep him from screaming. Drag him below the surface.

He shuddered and thought about pointing his discovery out to the others, but decided against it.

Maybe there was a way to use this.

2

Justin couldn't stop thinking about that blue light.

He kept seeing it flash in his mind's eye, that strange, somehow delicate shade of teal, the same color that had popped behind his eyelids when the little girl flayed open his chest with her filthy, ragged fingernails. Something about that light, pulsing across the night sky like explosions in heaven, had made him want to jump in the water and start swimming till he found wherever it was coming from, till he could bathe in that color and let it wash away all his troubles and cares. Even now, as he sat with Amber and Cherrywine at the front of the old pontoon boat, listening to the lap of water and the soft murmur of the radio from the opposite end, he found himself gazing into the sky to the west every few minutes, waiting for that light to begin its entrancing dance again.

But instead, the sky only darkened as more clouds roiled across the moon, reminding him of a bubbling cauldron. The stars were blotted out one by one; the night deepened until it became something alive and dangerous. In the distance, the other derelicts drew closer, shrouded, skeletal shapes floating in the gloom.

As part of their newly acquired 'guest' status, they'd been allowed to roam freely about the boat with minimal supervision. Which was horseshit of the first degree; if they were 'guests' here, then that made Guantanamo Bay the newest four-star resort. Justin suspected the real reason was because the pirates knew there simply wasn't anywhere for them to go.

He huddled with his arms around his chest, trying not to shiver or cough, while Amber sat cross-legged and stared into her lap. When he wasn't waiting for the blue light, Justin watched her instead, wondering what she was thinking. Behind them, Cherrywine fiddled with the laces of the tennis shoes the pirate captain had given her, along with a pair of baggy jeans that didn't fit but at least covered her bare legs.

"He left us." Cherrywine sniffled and tried to tame her long hair as the wind whipped at it. It took Justin a second to realize she meant Eric. "I can't believe he just...left us."

"Why would you *not* believe that?" Amber demanded. In the distance, a sharp crack of thunder split the night. The storm wasn't here yet, but it was coming on fast. "The guy's a selfish, borderline-sociopathic asshole. Think about what he did to you!"

"I know, he's horrible, it's just...he didn't even *try* to help us."

"Yeah, because guys that are willing to crush your trachea are usually more than happy to risk their lives for you." A pained look crossed the other girl's face, at which Amber softened and said, "I'm sorry, Cherrywine. I didn't mean to joke about it. As soon as we get back, we're...we're going to the cops so you can press charges."

"What are you t-talking about?" Justin shivered and sat up straighter. "I mean...'press charges?' What for?"

"Justin...look at her throat."

"If he did that, it had to be an accident." Justin realized how stupid he sounded, like a wife making excuses for the abusive husband.

"It was *not*!" Cherrywine argued.

"Look, I've known him since elementary school, and, I admit, he can be a little rough around the edges. But he's not gonna leave us like this. He'll find a way to get help."

Amber shook her head in disgust. "Why are you so blind when it comes to him? Wake up and get it through your head: he's not going to help anyone but himself."

She was right. Justin knew that, like he knew that Cherrywine probably wasn't the first of Eric's sexual conquests to receive some unwanted bruises. But, right now, he was just too pissed off at Amber to concede any point.

He looked away, muttering, "You're probably right. I guess *I'm* obviously not the greatest judge of character."

"What does that mean?"

When he didn't answer, Cherrywine said uncomfortably, "Uh, Amber? He...kinda...knows."

"Knows what?"

"What you said on the beach. I told Eric and Eric told him. I'm so, so sorry."

Amber was quiet for a long moment. "Justin?"

"I don't wanna talk about it."

"Listen, I found the ring in your bag last night and..."

He spun around on the deck to face her. "So it's true. You were, what? Just waiting for me to ask so you could say no?"

"I...you just...you caught me a little off guard, I wasn't expecting to have to deal with something as serious as a marriage proposal on this trip! I'm a little preoccupied with graduating right now!"

From the back of the boat, they heard one of the pirates—it sounded like Jorge—say, "Uh oh, someone didn't get the deep dick last night." There was muffled laughter.

Justin lowered his voice and asked, "Is this about that internship? I told you I would go with you!"

Amber groaned and covered her face. "We are being held captive by pirates while they go exploring a bunch of ghost ships. For god's sake, do we have to do this right now?"

He jammed a hand into the pocket of his shorts and pulled out the velvet-covered box that started this whole thing. Justin pulled the lid open and flashed the diamond at her. "Just tell me, do you want to marry me or not?"

"Don't force me like this, it's not fair."

"Quit stalling and answer the question."

"Then no, goddamn it, I don't! Are you happy, is that what you wanted?"

Justin cocked his arm back and threw the box as far out over the water as he could, regretting it the instant it left his hand. He could see its arc against the sky, but lost sight just before it hit the water.

"That was fucking childish," she said.

He opened his mouth to answer, and a massive cramp ripped through his guts, accompanied by a wash of fire across his chest. He moaned and lay back, curling up on his side.

He felt Amber crawl up next to him. "What is it, what's wrong?"

"Nothing, go aw—" He was in too much pain to finish. Justin squeezed his eyes shut, but the darkness behind them was threaded with a soft neon blue.

"Would you stop? We can deal with our problems later, but just let me help you." She forced him to uncurl and laid a hand on his forehead. "Your fever feels worse. Let me see those scratches."

His t-shirt was damp with sweat. She lifted the end to look at his chest, but said nothing.

"Is it bad? Let me see."

"No. Just lay still." Amber stood. "I'll be right back."

As she walked toward the door of the cabin where the captain and his ponytailed right-hand man had disappeared after they all got on board this piece of floating garbage, Cherrywine asked, "Where are you going?"

"To make this captain of theirs listen to reason."

3

Was it awful that the first emotion Amber felt when the ring hit the water was relief?

It was like when her father used to put her to bed, and open up the closet door to show her a distinct lack of monsters. The boogeyman's gone, it can't hurt you anymore. She could imagine part of herself sinking with the diamond, maybe one of those fly's eye versions she used to imagine, one that had said yes and married Justin and been the happy little homemaker.

So, relieved that it was over and she didn't have to hide anymore...yes. Still worried about Justin...also yes. The flesh around his scratches had turned a necrotic shade of black, and the network of veins around it was visible beneath the skin, a dark web spreading up toward his neck.

She pushed open the door to the cabin without knocking. Its hinges squalled as a rain of dust and rusted metal flakes drifted down. The space beyond was narrow and cramped. A tiny kitchenette full of cupboards sat just inside the door, which then opened up into living quarters the size of a family tent, with hammock-style bunks that folded down from the walls. Broken dishes, old food wrappers and other garbage was spread across a carpeted floor that was spongy with water damage and giving off the cloying scent of mildew. The conditions looked worse than a prison cell; she couldn't imagine taking to the open ocean on this junkheap even when it was brand new.

Old, rust-colored stains painted the floor and walls in irregular patterns. In the far corner, an adult-sized skeleton lay wedged between the end of one bunk and the back wall, dressed in a few shredded scraps of cloth. Not a stitch of flesh remained on it, and the bones were so old, they'd taken on a dingy, waxen look. The skull grinned up at her, jaw askew as though caught in a perpetual moment of surprise.

Lito and Ray crouched in the middle of the living space as they dug through the layer of garbage on the floor. An electric lantern they'd brought from their ship sat on an old folding stool in the middle of the room.

"Looking for something to steal?" she asked.

Lito glanced up. "Tryin to find out who our friend in the corner is."

"Oh. Any luck?"

"Near as we can tell, his name was Robert Watts of Wilmington, North Carolina. Found a gas station receipt that says he left port sometime around June 3 of '97." He lifted his chin toward the huddled skeleton, with its wide, shocked look of surprise. "Somethin tells me that's about the last time him and this boat were ever seen."

"Can you tell how he...?"

"What, died? Sorry, I left my forensics kit back on the boat." One side of his mouth pulled up into that smarmy grin as his sidekick chuckled.

"I just meant, was he like the shark and the little girl?"

"Not that I can tell. But then again, we don't even know that the problem with the shark was the same thing that was wrong with the girl in the first place."

Amber was quiet a second while she thought about that. "Can I talk to you? Um, privately?"

"I was just leavin." Ray climbed to his feet and had a rapid exchange with Lito in Spanish, obviously to keep her from hearing.

The only problem with this being, her degree plan called for her to learn at least two foreign languages, so she was fluent in both Spanish and German.

"*I'll leave you alone with your girlfriend here*," Ray told him.

Lito's eyes cut over to her. "*Would you knock that shit off?*"

"*Only if you admit your little schoolboy crush.*"

"*I'm a sucker for a perfect ass. So sue me.*"

Ray grunted and switched back to English as he squeezed past Amber on his way out of the cabin, and she pretended not to notice as he checked her out from behind. "I'll let you know when we get close to the other boats."

Other boats. Amber had been trying hard not to think about where they were headed. The idea of more abandoned ships—more pictures of missing families, more forgotten rooms covered with decades of accumulated dust—frightened her.

Of course, the thought they might *not* be abandoned terrified her even more.

Lito pushed up from the floor and perched on the edge of one of the bunks, then motioned to the other one. "Wanted to have a word with you, too. Take a seat."

She stepped carefully through the flotsam—jumping far over the remains of Mr. Watts's shinbones—and took a seat on the narrow bunk across from Lito. The netting sagged on its frame, causing her to sink down until her chin was almost on her knees, so she struggled back up and balanced on the edge. They stared at one another from a few yards away. The light from the lantern turned the scruff on his dark face into a beard of shadows.

"So, *gringa*, what can I do for you?"

"It's Justin."

"Your boyfriend? That's still what we're callin him, right? Doesn't sound like he got upgraded to fiancé quite yet."

She licked a bead of sweat from her upper lip. "You heard all that?"

"*Florida* heard all that. You two might wanna consider a marriage counselor before you take the plunge."

"That's not any of your...can we just...?"

He held up a hand. "Sorry, sorry. Start over. What about him?"

"He's getting worse."

"I know." He bent over, pulled a small plastic first aid kit out from under the bunk, and slid it to her. It clattered against the skeleton's dusty hip bone. "I found some antibiotics and aspirin for him. Expired for about a decade, but maybe they'll still help."

"But if he's got whatever this little girl had—"

"Okay, again, it can't be a disease. No disease could be responsible for everything we've seen. He probably got some blood infection from the wound. We'll get him help as soon as possible."

Amber thought briefly about the man from Eric's story, the one that had come back from the Bermuda Triangle with a disease so awful, the government made him disappear. "And what if that's not soon enough?"

Lito ran a hand back and forth through the short bristles of hair on the back of his head, took another of those slow, deliberate breaths, and said nothing.

"You realize how stupid this is, don't you? Going to these other ships, after everything that's happened?" She nudged Mr. Watts with the toe of her sneaker, causing a rattle that reminded her of hard raindrops against a windowpane. "You don't think he ended up like that from natural causes, do you?"

"We don't have much of a choice. We either find the parts we need, or try to get all the way back to the east coast on this thing. It's about three-hundred miles ahead of us. You think your boyfriend will last that long?"

"You *did* have a choice, though. You could've tried calling for help. You still could."

"And me and my men would've spent the rest of our lives in a cell the size of this room. But hey, so long as you white kids are happy, right?"

She frowned and let her voice frost over. "That's not really fair. We wouldn't even be in this situation if it weren't for you."

"Listen, we can point fingers all night, but it ain't gonna help. We need a solution, and that's what we're lookin for."

"Is that really it? Or are you hoping you'll find something out here besides boat parts?"

A series of creases raced across his forehead. "You think you know so much about us, don't you?"

"You're not fooling me," she said. "Sure, you've been decent to us now that things have gotten weird, but that doesn't mean I've forgotten you're all just criminals. In the end, I can't trust a thing you say."

Now there was outright anger on his boyish face, and she wondered if she'd gone too far. "You want honesty? Yeah, I admit, I wanna scavenge these derelicts, but that don't mean I'm heartless. I lost two men already, and I'm gonna have to live with that long after you've gone back to your mansions and your cars and your life of endless parties."

"*Mansions?*" She broke eye contact with him for the first time, and looked at the wall. An odd sense of embarrassment crept over her, as if she should be ashamed to have been on that yacht. "Sounds like you're the one with the preconceived notions."

"Four loudmouth, twenty-year-old yuppies on a boat worth more than everything I've ever owned in my life? I see your kind all the time."

"Yeah, when you're robbing them." She swiped at the moisture accumulating at the corners of her eyes. She'd never met anyone so infuriating in her life. "So tell me this: would you have killed us? If we hadn't cooperated, or even if everything had gone according to plan and you'd taken our boat? Made us walk the plank, or something?"

"No," he answered, without the slightest hesitation. "I just don't appreciate you judgin me."

"Yeah, well...ditto. And for the record, you're the first person to use the word 'yuppie' since 1989."

"But pirates makin people walk the plank is all good, huh? You prob'ly expected me to have an eye patch and a hook hand."

She shrugged. "Or at least look like a young Cary Elwes."

He raised an eyebrow. "You're a strange one, *gringa*."

"Yeah, that's what they tell me." An awkward silence fell between them, and she rushed to fill it. "What did you want to talk to me about?"

His demeanor darkened as he shifted uncomfortably. "I just wanted to make sure we all had our facts straight, in case we do run into the cops. About that girl—"

"Relax," she interrupted. "Justin told us your mechanic saved his life. If we run into the police, we'll tell them that."

"Okay. Thanks. Probably won't help with the hijacking and kidnapping, but at least it's one less thing to worry about. And my crew has plenty of those at the moment."

"Like this 'Dominican' person?"

Surprise spread across his face. "How did you—?"

"You mentioned the name back on the *Mackerel*, remember? You thought we knew something about it."

"Right, right." He shrugged. "That's just a drug dealer who wants us dead."

"Classy. I can see how that would happen a lot with you guys." They sat for a minute, looking at one another in the lamp light, but this time the quiet was nice. "I better give these to Justin." She grabbed the first aid kit and wiggled, trying to climb out of the creaking bunk. He stood and offered a hand. As he pulled her up, there was a heavy clunk on the floor between their feet. She looked down to see that the glass statuette had fallen out of her cargo pocket. She'd almost forgotten about it.

"What's this?" He picked it up, and she got her first good look at the figurine. An ugly thing, leering like some ancient totem pole. Lito ran a thumb across the tiny devil's broken horn.

"Beats me. Belonged to Eric. He tried to hide it back on the houseboat."

"Got that valuable antique look." Sudden understanding came into his eyes. "Might this be the reason he was so eager to stick around out here?"

"Yeah, I think so. Probably belongs to his father."

"Who is this guy anyway?"

"Some kind of Philly mob boss."

Lito gave her a sharp look. "No shit?"

"That's what Justin told me. I had no idea before tonight."

He tried to hand the statue back, but she pushed it toward him, her palm brushing his fingers in the process. "Keep it."

Lito raised a dark eyebrow.

"I know it's not a yacht or anything, but maybe it'll cut some of your losses. Serves the dipshit right for abandoning us."

He seemed on the verge of saying more, but the door opened and Ray stuck his head in. "Lito...get out here and take a look at this."

4

There were more ships out here than they'd thought. *Lots* more.

Lito figured they'd only been able to count the closest ones in the dark from a distance, but now that they were approaching the frontier, he could see that vessels of all sizes floated in this loose grouping. How far they strung out on either side along this anonymous stretch of the Sargasso—or even how deep they went ahead—was impossible to tell, but the prospect of sailing into their midst struck a primal chord in Lito's head akin to entering a skeletal, leafless, autumn forest in the middle of the night.

"I don't wanna go in there," Cherrywine whimpered. She cowered behind Amber, peering over her shoulder as they closed in. No one answered her.

Carlos and Jorge steered their pontoon raft into a narrow corridor lined with derelicts haphazardly drifting in all directions, with barely fifteen yards of clearance on either side. Lito spotted commercial fishing boats...schooners...more yachts, sailboats and pleasure ships of all sizes...a steamer that looked like something from the 1920's...and other, less identifiable crafts, including some small industrial freighters that towered above the others. He lost count somewhere in the forties, and still there was no end in sight. After a few minutes, they were so deep that the view behind them closed off, and every direction held only more derelicts. Most of them were in even worse shape than the houseboat—weatherbeaten and falling apart at the seams, a few of them no more than rusted-out husks—but some looked as shiny and new as the day they rolled off the assembly line.

Again Lito was struck by the idea that, even though they may look like ships, they were really coffins. Burials at sea.

"What is this place?" he asked aloud.

Ray crossed his arms as he watched a broken-down party yacht with the upper floor caved in slide by to their port. "A floatin graveyard," he whispered, reading Lito's mind. "There're more ships here than we could possibly search on our own."

They all stood at the periphery of their raft now, gazing in wonder at the forgotten vessels. Lito turned to Jericho and asked, "You see anything that would have what you need?"

"All depends on de fuel deliv'ry systems. Wouldn't know unless I took a look meself." The mechanic frowned. "But hoses rot fast, so we can pretty much count out some of dese dat look like dey been here since Jesus was a bitty baby in de manger."

"Not that long." Lito shook his head adamantly, wandering over to starboard where a mini-freighter drifted by, bearing a collection of barnacles on its hull so thick a person could climb them like a ladder. "Like I said before, there's no way these boats coulda been out here longer than a few months unanchored. Besides the fact that the tides woulda carried them apart, *someone* woulda stumbled onto 'em."

"Someone *did* stumble onto 'em, just like we did." Ray turned to him and swept a hand across the other boats. "How you think they all got here in the first place?"

Lito had a brief flash of the *Steel Runner* out here in fifty years, abandoned and left to rot. The image made him sick.

There were several gasps behind them. Lito spun around to find a huge wooden ship looming out of the dark, its long, pointed prow about to pass right over them. He pulled out his flashlight and said, "Slow us down some, guys. Bring us over there."

Jorge and Carlos manned the paddles to reverse their momentum until the edge of the pontoon bumped gently against the other boat. Lito moved around the deck toward the contact point and shined his flashlight along the side.

The vessel was old-world craftsmanship, like something his imagination would've conjured from the adventure-on-the-high-seas books he read as a kid, an all-wooden sailing sloop at least fifty yards long with a rigid, straight-backed stern riding high out of the water. The top of the bulwark rose at least five yards above their heads; taking its girth into consideration, there was probably enough room below deck for this boat to hold sixty men. Lito could see square portholes down its length, studded with blunt metal spikes all around. The fat, round barrels of cannons poked out from a few. It was in great shape too, not a barnacle in sight, still so fresh and new he could practically smell the varnish and laminate on the darkly-stained beams that formed the hull.

Lito turned his flashlight upward as far as the light would reach, following the shaft of the main mast, all the way to a huge cloth sail stretched between wooden timbers. It whipped and rippled in the strengthening wind, but the ship was turned the wrong direction for the sails to fill. He centered his light on the depiction in the middle.

A crude, blood red hourglass painted on a background of black canvas.

"That's a jolly roger," Ray said. His voice was full of awe.

"Nah uh." Carlos shook his head. "Everybody knows the jolly rogers was a skull and crossbones. What kinda pirate are you?"

"The bones were just one kind. A jolly roger represented death. And to people who lived in a time when disease or famine or war could wipe you out any minute, an hourglass pretty much said it all. Lito…" Ray paused to swallow, but looked like he had trouble getting his throat to work. "This is a pirate ship from the 17th…maybe 18th century at the latest."

Lito shook his head. "It's a replica. Something that floated away from a movie set or a museum. Has to be."

"Like that Viking boat those kids crashed into? That come from a movie too? Maybe *Erik the Red Gets Lost in the Bermuda Fucking Triangle?*"

"What Viking boat?" Amber asked.

"I told you to knock off that Triangle BS." Lito retrieved one of the bags they'd brought with them from the *Runner*, unzipped a flap, and brought out a tied bundle of heavy twine. "All right, you want an explanation, let's go have a look."

Ray shook his head. "I never said I needed an explanation."

Lito tossed one end of the rope over the prow and caught it when it came back down. "Okay, then I do."

"Why waste the time? I'm pretty sure this thing don't run on gasoline."

Lito didn't answer, but Amber snorted as he tied the rope to one of the docking eyelets on the pontoon boat, securing the two ships together. "He wants to see if this thing has any gold doubloons on board."

Ray slung an arm around Lito's shoulders and steered him away from the others. "That it? You wanna go treasure huntin?"

"We'll just go up and have a quick look around. If it's really what you say, then we can't afford to pass it up."

"Give me one of those paddles and watch me."

From the far side of the pontoon boat, Cherrywine gave an excited, "*Oh!*" The blonde clapped her hands and bounced up and down, jiggling her breasts. "This is just like the boat in Eric's story!"

"What is this story you keep talkin about?" Lito directed the question at Amber, hoping for a coherent answer.

"Eric told us about some guy that found a ship like this in 1970. He boarded it, got attacked by something, and escaped.

The story goes that when he got back he was sick, and the government put him into permanent quarantine."

"What did he get attacked by?" Carlos asked.

"He didn't see it. He dropped his flashlight and ran. And for some reason, Eric thinks that makes the story gospel truth." She looked from him to Lito. "Don't go on that ship."

"You scared?"

"Yes. But not because of some stupid story. We don't have time for this." She inclined her head toward Justin, standing in front of her.

Lito might've caved at that—he didn't want the white boy dying on their watch any more than Ray did—but the kid looked better, on his feet and with a little more color in his face, so maybe the situation wasn't as dire as they'd thought. "It'll take two minutes, I promise." He checked the revolver in the back of his waistband and gave the rope leading up to the deck of the sloop an experimental tug. "Ray, you're with me. Jericho's in charge down here. Everybody just sit tight and we'll be right back."

With that, he hoisted himself off the ground and began shimmying up the rope.

5

Amber watched first Lito and then Ray climb the rope and disappear over the side of the old boat (old in *style*, she had to remind herself, and not necessarily in *age*), trying to bring her blood temperature back from the boiling point that Lito's stunt had sent it to. The man viewed the world as nothing but one big joke for his own amusement, and, to make it worse, his sleeves had slid down as he climbed, revealing muscular biceps. She looked away, refusing to watch as they reached the top. The sounds of their heavy feet treading the wooden deck above were surprising crisp and clear.

After that, the group drifted apart. Amber approached Justin and held up the pills Lito had given her. "Some antibiotics, aspirin, and painkillers. Maybe they'll help."

He held out a hand and said nothing.

"Not here. Come inside the cabin to one of the bunks. Some of these could knock you out."

"And leave you alone with these guys? I don't think so."

"What?" Amber lowered both the medication and her jaw. "You honestly think I'd...*sleep* with one of these scumbags?"

He frowned in confusion. "To protect you. Both you *and* Cherrywine. We still have no idea what their plans are for us."

"Oh." She felt heat creep into her cheeks, and hoped the darkness hid it. "I don't think they're gonna do anything until they find these parts they need. We can take care of ourselves for a couple of hours. You've got to rest or you'll just get worse."

"Fine."

He allowed himself to be led into the cabin. Cherrywine followed, cringing when she caught sight of the skeleton in the corner. Amber gave Justin double the recommended dosage from the bottles, hoping there would still be enough active ingredients in the old pills. He stretched out on the bunk, and she spread an old wool blanket over him that smelled like fish.

"I'm sorry about throwing the ring," he said. "And buying it in the first place. It was stupid."

"Just get some sleep." She turned down the lantern to a low glow, then glanced at her watch. Almost twelve-thirty; hard to believe how far they'd come in a little over three hours. "We can talk about all that later."

He nodded, rolled over to face the wall, and fell asleep almost immediately.

On her way back out, she met Cherrywine in the kitchen and said, "I can't stay in this stinking room. Would you mind keeping an eye on him?"

"No problem. So...you told the truth, huh?"

"Yeah, and you were right. It was the best thing to do."

"It usually is. That's what I'm gonna do with Lito. Cross your fingers for me!"

Amber spun back around at the edge of the door. "Huh?"

"Lito. You know, their captain?"

"Yeah, I know who you mean, Cherry. What am I crossing my fingers for?"

Her eyes lit up with excitement as she grabbed Amber's shoulders. "Isn't he *cute*? And did you see the way he stood up for me back on their ship? I think he likes me! Maybe *he's* my Prince Charming!"

"More like Quasimodo," Amber said. There were too many high school flashbacks hitting her all at once. "They're pirates, Cherry. Criminals. Try to keep that in mind."

6

Raymundo Vargas had been raised by two of the most devout Catholic parents a boy could dream of murdering in their sleep.

The slightest transgressions had been catalogued by his mother, so his father could deliver long diatribes on the value of one's soul and the fires that awaited those who didn't appreciate them. The constant dogma had resulted in an absolute rejection of religion and everything it stood for, which was probably why Ray was now a wanted man in at least three countries.

But he'd never quite gotten rid of the habit of crossing himself when he got spooked, an almost subconscious response to fear.

And, as he and Lito reached the top of the sailing sloop, his hand began to make the furious circuit between forehead, chest, and shoulders.

The deck was clean though, as new as the rest of this relic from a much simpler time, the wood beneath his sneakers gleaming with fresh varnish. A moment of surreality passed over him as he craned his neck back to take in that dark sail again, with its blood red emblem. Everything looked so authentic—from the lanyards threaded through the side rigging, to the crow's nest high above their heads—that it was easier to believe they'd wandered onto some pirate-themed carnival ride, where the guides wore eye patches and said 'Avast ye mateys' every five seconds. As he and Lito crept across the deck, the other man peeled away and climbed the short staircase to the helm on its upraised platform, and went to stand behind a massive, spoked steering wheel whose top reached his neck.

"Check it out, Ray," he whispered in Spanish. "I'm Blackbeard."

Ray scowled at him. "Stop playin, fuckhead, or I swear I'm goin back."

"Yeah, but just think: if we'd lived two hundred years ago, this coulda been *our* ship!" A doofy, boyish grin spread across Lito's face. Ray understood. Hard to be a pirate if you didn't get excited about swashbucklers and sea battles as a kid, before you found out that the reality of early high-seas life was all scurvy and syphilis. He had to admit, he was more than a little curious at what might be on board, but that didn't stop his hand from continuing to sketch lowercase T's on his chest.

He continued on to a long rectangular hole cut into the deck and shone his flashlight inside. A simple wooden staircase led to the lower decks. Lito joined him a few seconds later.

"Why do I listen to you?" Ray mumbled. "Goddamn, I don't wanna do this."

Judging from the stiff way Lito stood as he searched the darkness down there, Ray suspected he didn't either. All that meditation he'd been trying to hide from the rest of the crew may have quelled the temper that used to get the better of him, but it hadn't done much for his stubborn streak. "One quick look around, just to see if there's anything worth takin back."

"You don't really think we're gonna find the lost treasure of Atlantis on this thing, do you?"

"We don't have to. If this thing is as authentic as you say, then it *is* the treasure. Hell, maybe we could even sail it back. Imagine the look on Dully's face if we pulled into port on this thing." He slapped at Ray's hand. "And stop crossin yourself, you look like a damn retard."

They pulled their pistols, held them in the opposite hand as their flashlights, which stopped Ray's rogue hand from its frantic blessing. Lito went first, easing down each step. Ray followed until he could crouch and look into the room below.

What he saw, by the beam of his flashlight, was a cramped galley with cafeteria-style seating at crude wooden tables and stools. Food was still laid out for whatever meals had once been prepared on this vessel. Ray sniffed, searching for signs of rot and decay, but the air was only musty. They took the rest of the stairs and walked through the tables. The boards under their feet were so new, they didn't even creak.

"Hey," Ray hissed. Their voices were much louder in the enclosed space. He picked up a potato the size of his fist from one of the plates and held it out. "This is still good. Not even a spot of mold."

Lito didn't seem too interested. He pointed further ahead. "Do you see that?"

"What?"

"That light."

Ray saw it now. The galley ended at a narrow doorway with a short hallway that would take them to the rest of the ship, most likely the crew bunks and holds. If there was anything of value on board, that's where it would be. But a light shone on the walls beyond the door, gleaming off the glossed and polished wood, and not the shifting orange glow of fire from a torch or lantern either, but the clean, white radiance of modern electrical illumination.

Lito jumped around the corner, and Ray took the opposite side, half-expecting shaded lights from a movie set, and a director screaming that they were blocking his shot, but instead, what they found on the floor was a flashlight not too different from the ones they held. It lay on its side, rolling back and forth ever so slightly with the rocking of the ship, and projecting a wide, bright circle on the wall. Lito picked it up and thumbed the switch a few times, turning the beam on and off.

"Your girl's story." Ray tapped the device's barrel. "She said that guy dropped his flashlight on the ship he boarded. Remember?"

"Yeah, but she also said it happened in 1970." Lito unscrewed the base and let two fat Duracell D's slide out into his hand. "How long you think batteries like this last in a turned-on flashlight, Ray?"

"Seven, eight hours, tops."

"Then how could this one have been sitting here for close to forty years?"

"I got a better one: how can this ship be as new as the day it was christened, and that houseboat has fifty years worth of dust built up on it?"

A ragged, drawn-out moan came from the opposite end of the hallway leading deeper into the ship.

7

As Amber left the cabin, she almost ran into Carlos and Jorge just on the other side, looking up at the wooden ship and speaking in hushed tones. Funny; she'd gotten the idea these two didn't like one another, but they looked thick as thieves now, in the most literal sense. They shut up in a hurry when they saw her, Jorge's eyes blazing while Carlos ogled her up and down. She'd wanted to wait out here for Lito to come back, but she couldn't do it around them.

"'Scuse me, fellas." She squeezed past and went down the side of the boat toward the stern, where Jericho was just closing up the hood on one of the jet skis. She knew very little about this one, but he seemed friendlier than the other two. At the moment, that's all she could ask for.

He swung his flashlight up when he heard her coming.

"You mind if I sit here?" She motioned to the scanner that was still playing softly. "I'd like to listen to that."

He shrugged and turned up the volume, and she sank down onto the padded plastic bench beside him.

That horrible voice. Uninflected, but urgent somehow. Deep and growling, almost chewing each individual syllable and spitting them out. Her imagination conjured an image of the mouth that could've spoken these strange, foreign words, something with long jaws full of too much slobber and wickedly sharp teeth.

"De Voice of de Deep," Jericho said.

The phrase startled her. "What?"

"Our cook, Mondo, dat's what he called it. Said it wasn't a god or a demon, but somet'in in between."

She felt the short hairs at the base of her neck prickle in the night wind blowing across the water. The Voice of the Deep. It was silly, more fly's eye, through-the-looking-glass fairy tales—but she was suddenly very claustrophobic again, trapped in the middle of the ocean.

"You supposed to be some kinda language genius, right?" he asked. "You got any idea what it's sayin?"

"I would need something to compare it to before I could even begin to decipher it. Let me ask though: did the Indian girl sound like this?"

He seemed to tense up; she remembered that the girl was a touchy subject for him. "Never heard her say a word. I don't t'ink she could speak. Whatever happened to her...she was barely human anymore."

Amber switched off the radio and had to admit that, as fascinated as she was by the language it spoke, she felt relieved when the voice went away. "Well, whoever that is, they're definitely trying to tell us something. Otherwise, why go through the trouble of broadcasting it over and over again?"

"Distress call. One of dese boats had a foreign crew and left dere mayday goin. Before...whatever happened to dem."

Amber nodded, not bothering to point out that this crew he was imagining would have to be pretty damn 'foreign' for her not to have any inkling on the origin of their language. "So you haven't tried using the radio at all since it started broadcasting?"

"Would *you* want to risk answerin whoever is sendin dat out?"

Amber said nothing. Some part of her would very much like to try speaking back to that voice, if only to try and garner more information. All of this was like pieces to a puzzle that didn't fit together: the Voice of the Deep, speaking in a language no one understood...a hundred or more derelict ships...dazzling blue lights in the sky...freakish people and animals all tinted the same color...

And did it even have anything to do with the Bermuda Triangle?

Jericho had turned to watch her. Now his eyes flicked past her shoulder, and he raised his flashlight. "Lito back?"

Amber turned to find Jorge standing several feet away, by the back wall of the cabin. "Not yet."

"Den whachoo want?"

Jorge's hand twitched, and a silver switchblade appeared as if by magic. The blade glinted in the light of Jericho's flashlight.

"To cut this bitch's throat," he said.

8

The pathetic moan startled Lito badly enough that the batteries to the amazing, never-run-down flashlight squirted through his fingers, clattering back to the floor and rolling away from him. He went after them, unwilling to let them go until the mystery was solved.

Something shuffled in the darkness down at the other end of the corridor, a shadow against shadows.

Ray grabbed his arm and pulled. "Still wanna try to sail this thing back?"

"Not so much." He decided to let the batteries go after all, and even dropped the empty flashlight. "Let's get the fuck outta here."

They turned and bolted back through the galley of the ship. When they reached the stairs leading up to the deck, Lito chanced a look over his shoulder.

The narrow hall was full of shapes hurrying after them, a legion of dark, groaning figures with outstretched hands. His own flashlight grazed across them in his panic, giving him a brief impression of twisted faces and snarling mouths. Lito raised his revolver and opened fire while they were bottlenecked. He heard a grunt of pain, and the leader stumbled back into the others. It didn't stop them for long.

"Move your ass, Porto!" Ray shouted from the top of the stairs.

Lito charged up toward him. By the time he got to the top, he could hear the stomp of feet ascending right on his ass. He was too terrified to look back again.

9

"Whachoo talkin 'bout, Jorge?" Jericho came forward, moving to stand in front of Amber.

Jorge's lips stretched back so he could talk through gritted teeth. "This bitch and her friends gotta die for what they did to Rabid. I owe him."

"Jesus, for the last time, we didn't hurt your friend!" Amber yelled around Jericho.

"*You lyin! I know you killed him!*"

Jericho spread his arms out protectively, like a kid playing Red Rover. "You ain't doin any such t'ing. Cap'n don't want dem hurt."

"I don't give a shit. In case you ain't noticed, the Cap'n lost his stomach for doin what needs to be done." Jorge held out the knife in a fencing stance. "Don't get in my way, Jericho. I ain't got no problem with you."

"If you t'ink I'm gonna let you do dis...den yeah, you do, *mon*. And if you wanna see who's got de biggest knife..." He reached for the machete strapped to his back.

Jorge took a swing without warning, slicing through the air with the knife. Jericho jumped back in the tight quarters, unable to get his own weapon, and bumped into Amber's knees just before sprawling across her. He regained his balance in time to dodge a jab from the blade. As soon as he was clear, Amber kicked out, planting a foot in Jorge's crotch and shoving. The skinny little guy screeched and fell back against the cabin wall, dropping the knife to clutch at his balls.

Jericho finally freed his machete and waded in. Jorge let go of his crushed testicles long enough to lay his hands on one of the boat paddles. He swung it up in a wide arc, smashing the mechanic across the face with the flat wooden spade. Jericho fell to the deck on his ass, dazed and bleeding from the forehead.

There were running footsteps just before Carlos and Cherry-wine came around the corner of the cabin. Amber didn't think the former looked very surprised, but the latter squealed, "What's happening?"

Throughout the fight, Amber had remained on the bench. Now she scrambled to her feet just as Jorge got up and retrieved the knife. He came at her, the tip of the blade questing through the air toward her like the tongue of a snake, but he stopped when several quick, muffled pops rolled across the night. They all looked toward the bow of the wooden ship, looming over them.

Lito and Ray appeared at the bulwark, dangled their feet over the edge, and somehow managed to slide down the rope anchoring them to the sloop together. "*Get the paddles, go, get us outta here!*" Lito yelled, as he sawed at the bindings with his knife.

A chorus of miserable moans drifted down after them.

10

When the first figure appeared at the railing above them, Carlos pointed his flashlight beam at it.

A heavyset man in a loose-fitting white blouse and baggy leggings—*pantaloons* was actually the word his mind threw out—stood looking down at them. Carlos hadn't seen the little girl that Jericho claimed had killed Mondo, but, based on the description, he figured this dude must have the same problem. His complexion was the consistency of Jello, like his skin was getting ready to ooze right off the bones. It reminded Carlos of the VHS box cover of an old, shitty superhero movie that his mom would never let him rent as a kid, a picture of some mutated, pop-eyed creature holding a janitor's mop. The man standing at the edge of the pirate sloop took a few seconds to register their presence, blinking stupidly in the light, but then his eyes sharpened and his mouth stretched into a snarl.

"*Puta de madre*," Jorge said in awe. They were all frozen, his switchblade still pointed at the girl. Carlos had pumped the Mexican up, convinced him this was his chance to deal with the white kids, hoping that him or someone else might get offed in the process. But of course, the *idiota* had fucked it up.

Lito ran by and slapped Carlos in the back of the head. "*Stop starin and get us outta here!*"

Carlos broke the trance and dove for the paddle that Jorge had dropped after smacking Jericho, but it was already too late.

The freak gave a wordless screech and flung himself over the side of the other ship like the setup for the world's most painful belly flop. He smashed into their deck in a facedown heap, the impact on the rickety vessel hard enough to lift the starboard pontoon completely out of the water.

The world tilted violently. Everyone on the deck tumbled into one another, scrambled to grab hold of something. One of the girls shrieked just before she fell into the water with a splash; the blonde, he thought. Carlos leapt for the rack of jet skis and clung to a handle to keep from catapulting after her. For a second, they hung suspended before the pontoon crashed back down.

On the edge of the boat, Jorge waved his arms in circles to keep his balance.

Carlos kicked the back of his leg.

Jorge's mouth was a round, shocked O as he fell backward into that ocean infested with moving, clutching seaweed.

11

Amber saw Cherrywine fall backward over the side of the raft, but was too busy clinging to the bench with one hand and holding on to the VHF scanner with the other to help. When the boat fell back onto the water, she ended up on her back, clutching the radio to her chest.

A few feet away, the thing that had landed in their midst—although perhaps 'landed' was too graceful a word—pulled itself upright. One of its arms dangled limply now, with a shard of bone jutting from the elbow, but it didn't seem to notice. It glanced around, confusion in its eyes, then scuttled forward on its knees like some demented homeless person begging for spare change. A constant stream of gibberish ran from its mouth as it slashed at her with one deformed claw of a hand.

Amber scooted backward, still holding the scanner. There was nowhere to run on the tiny deck of the pontoon boat. The mutated creature—a guy that looked like a pudgy extra from an Errol Flynn pirate film after being dipped in sulfuric acid—crawled after her. He surged forward, grabbed hold of Amber's throat, and pulled until she was inches away from the melted ruins of its face.

"*Huuuuuurtsssss...*" it groaned, the single word of English interspersed in its nonsensical burbling.

In its eyes, anguish flashed brightly, as though it were pleading for help.

Then it was gone, replaced by mindless fury. The hand on her throat squeezed as the creature's mouth darted forward to bite her with teeth stained the color of ripe blueberries.

Lito tackled the creature with one arm and threw it backwards onto the deck. He aimed his revolver and put three rounds into the thing's chest. Blue flowers blossomed on the stained blouse it wore, then it shuddered and lay still. Lito put a boot on its shoulder and rolled it into the water, then yelled over his shoulder, "*Paddle! Get us away from the ship!*" It was an unnecessary command; Ray and Carlos already had oars in the water and were maneuvering them away.

"Wait, Cherrywine's out there!" Amber put the scanner down and scrambled on hands and knees to the edge of the boat.

The blonde girl treaded water a few yards out, trying to catch up with them. Beyond her, Jorge sputtered and thrashed.

Amber held out a hand. "Swim! You gotta get out of the water!"

"I'm...trying!" Cherrywine sobbed. Her head slipped part of the way beneath the surface, and she flailed until she came back up. She kicked hard, as if she were fighting the water itself, but got nowhere. "I can't swim, the seaweed's dragging me down!"

"*HELP!*" Jorge squealed in absolute panic. He appeared to be having just as much trouble.

More growls came from above. Amber looked up. On the deck of the sloop, an entire horde of deformed men in pirate garb appeared at the bulwark, looking like the cast of some hellish play. They hissed and lurched against one another, then began tumbling over the side of the ship in a display of lemming single-mindedness. Their bodies plunged into the water with tremendous splashes, then they surfaced and dogpaddled awkwardly after the raft.

They reached Jorge first. Amber's last glimpse of the Hispanic man was amid a knot of limbs and grasping hands that began tearing him apart just before their numbers shoved him beneath the water. She had to admit, she wasn't sad to see him go.

Ray and Carlos paddled hard, trying to put some distance between them and the mob, but the boat seemed to barely be moving, like a car stuck in neutral. Even so, Cherrywine still trailed behind, her eyes huge as she tried to catch up. Amber stretched a hand out, but couldn't reach her. The mutant pirates seemed to be having no such trouble; they would be on her—and then them—in seconds.

"Here!" Lito snatched the oar from Ray's hands, then crouched at the edge of the boat next to Amber and stuck out the paddle. Cherrywine latched on, and he dragged her back onto the raft just before the wave of pirates reached the side of their pontoon.

At least twenty of them clutched at the port side, trying to claw their way onto the deck. Their combined weight was enough to drag down an entire corner and start the boat tilting all over again.

"*They're swampin us!*" Carlos pulled his oar out of the water and used it to beat at their attackers. The blows had little effect.

Jericho and Lito ran for their guns, grabbing the shotgun and Jorge's huge military rifle. They fired down into the crowd as they had with the sharks, but Amber could see they were being overrun. Several of the creatures wriggled over the side on their bellies and jumped to their feet, ready to attack. She and Cherrywine scooted away as one of them grabbed Lito's arm.

Blue light burst across the sky.

It was brighter than the lightning this time, as intense as a camera flashbulb, chasing away shadows as it painted the deck in harsh navy overtones. Static crackled all around them, visible as miniature arcs of electricity along the metal parts of the boat. Staring at the light made Amber dizzy and even sicker than last time, but it didn't have that effect on the freaks. They all froze in place, their prey forgotten, and turned their faces up to it. Lito carefully stepped away from the one that had hold of him, bringing the shotgun up in case it should change its mind, but it paid no attention. The ones on the deck stumbled toward the light, arms upraised like ancient villagers worshipping the sun. When they reached the end of the deck, they fell right back into the water. The whole group began to swim west with those awkward, flailing strokes, in the direction of the stuttering lights.

"Get us outta here," Lito repeated. "Before it stops."

Carlos and Ray went back to paddling. This time, the boat moved easily, putting distance between them and the freakish pirates.

12

The speedboat coasted through the haphazard maze of ships, its engine no more than a quiet sputter. Eric sat in one of the vinyl chairs at the rear, bound to the seat by duct tape, while one of the thugs refilled the boat's tanks with the extensive fuel reserves they'd brought. The renewed bondage should've had him fuming, but Eric found he hardly even cared as he gazed around in wonder at the silent, dark derelicts.

Of the ones that had their names displayed, perhaps one in ten he'd heard before, during his extensive reading on the subject. Some he actually recognized from their pictures, although a few of these were in such bad shape, he couldn't be sure. But it all pointed to one inescapable conclusion.

The Bermuda Triangle was *real*.

He'd wanted to believe his whole life. Now here he was, in the middle of every ship that had ever disappeared in this revered section of the Caribbean, provided with absolute proof that it wasn't all a hoax, wasn't all exaggeration or legend. It felt like part of the Big Plan, his destiny at last coming to fruition.

Eric couldn't remember feeling so giddy since the time when he was 12 and one of the girls who lived on his block—the daughter of some rich lawyer whose mansion put even the Renquist property to shame—had let him finger her down in the dry creek bed that ran behind their neighborhood.

Except she didn't let *you do squat*, the friendly new voice sharing space in his head purred. It was getting louder and clearer all the time, keeping him honest. *Remember? You held her down and almost jammed your whole fist up there. Made her squeal. Bitch probably didn't walk right for a month.*

He flinched as the new memory swam into focus to replace the old, like a blurry photograph overlaid by a fresher one, the sensations, the heat and violence of that moment, the excitement that had built in him as she screamed and pleaded. How could he ever have forgotten about that?

The Jamaican, who had introduced himself as 'Vishon' when he oversaw Eric's binding, swiveled his chair around. "You know anyt'ing 'bout all dis, *bomba claat*?"

Eric met his gaze with the straightest poker face he could manage. "No idea."

The other man sucked at his gold teeth as he regarded Eric. "I t'ink dat's a lie, li'l white boy. I t'ink you know quiiiiite a bit. You givin alla dese boats a myajor eye-fuckin."

"Think what you want." Eric shrugged. Or shrugged as much as he could while duct taped to a chair. "I can't tell you what any of them are doing here, which is what you really wanna know."

Vishon rocketed up from his chair and brought the heel of one booted foot up to smash the ball of Eric's knee joint. Shockwaves of pain ripped through him, but he bit down on the scream that wanted to accompany them. He would never give this fucker the satisfaction.

But those pirates are starting to look like pretty gracious hosts, huh?

"I'll be de judge of what I want to know, white boy. And if you don't tell I, I gonna be your executionah, too. Now...where did dey come from?"

"It's the fuckin Bermuda Triangle, dickhead!" Eric snarled. "Do I need to draw you a chart?"

Vishon took another look at the tombs around them. "No. Cyan't be."

"Oh really? Why not?"

"Because if alla dese ships had disappeared out here, da Triangle wouldn't be just a story anymore."

The response stopped Eric cold. Small pleasure crafts or old ships whose stories had been lost to history were one thing. But there were some seriously valuable freighters and commercial shippers out here that—no matter how old they looked—logic dictated couldn't have been missing more than fifty years. Ships that wouldn't have been written off as sunk or hijacked without an exhaustive and costly search by their owners. Their disappearances would've made national news, and yet he'd never heard of them.

The Jamaican was right; if this many boats had vanished in the Triangle, the Sargasso would've been abandoned as a naval pathway long ago, until someone could come up with an explanation.

Ahead of them, the sound of distant gunshots split the otherwise silent night.

Vishon grabbed Eric's shoulders. "Why did Porto and his crew come out here?"

"I told you, they need parts!"

"Den why did dey leave dere ship abandoned, wit'out even a single guard? Why does it sound like dey brought enough weapons to wyage a war?"

"Ask them! I escaped, remember? Jesus, I don't know why you're taking this out on me, I hate them as much as you do!"

Over his shoulder, the sky filled up with that unearthly blue light. All the men on the boat stared up at it and then quickly looked away, a couple of them holding their stomachs. Eric understood; something about it was utterly repulsive. Vishon released him so he could swivel and stand up.

When it ended a few seconds later, he asked, "I s'pose you don't know anyt'ing 'bout dat, eithah, li'l white boy?" Eric didn't answer, so he turned to the driver and said, "Run silent and find dem. I want to be up on dese *punaanies* before dey know what hit dem."

13

After she was certain they'd escaped the group of deformed pirates, Amber hurried into the cabin to check on Justin and found him still asleep. The expired medication must've still had a little kick after all. If she'd put him in the opposite bed, he would've been pitched out when the boat tipped, but here the intersection of wall and bunk must've kept him in place. She decided not to wake him, but instead grabbed another of the old, smelly blankets and carried it back outside.

Cherrywine sat huddled on the bench, soaking wet again and shivering. The others had stopped rowing, and all four men were gathered around her. Amber wrapped the blanket around her shoulders. "I couldn't move," she whimpered. "It was like the seaweed was trying to hold me back…"

Lito knelt and patted the knee of her baggy pants. "You okay?"

She surged forward and threw her arms around his neck. "Thankyouthankyou, you saved me!"

"Uh…you're welcome."

He returned the hug, glancing over her shoulder at Amber and giving her a shrug. Seeing the two of them like that, with her massive stripper breasts pressed against his broad chest, gave Amber a sudden, sharp pinch.

My, my, Ms. Dunley, is that jealousy I detect?

"Jer, you're bleedin, man," Ray said.

Jericho gently touched the gash across his forehead. "Compliments of Jorge, dat son of a bitch. After you two left, he tried to turn dis one into filet of white girl."

"Why?"

"Kept goin on 'bout revenge for Rabid. Good riddance, I say."

Amber stuck out her hand. "Thanks for helping me, by the way. You didn't have to do that."

He smiled sheepishly and accepted the handshake fast, like a young boy scared of cooties, then asked his captain, "What happened in dere?"

Lito finally managed to break free of Cherrywine's embrace and dug through the gear bags they'd brought with them. He came up with a box of ammunition and began refilling the cylinder of his revolver. "We didn't get very far. Those things just swarmed outta the lower decks when they heard us. Don't know what they were doin down there."

"They would've killed us all if not for that light," Amber said. "It was like they were attracted to it."

"Moths to a flame," Lito agreed, looking down at the place on his arm where he'd been grabbed. The skin was smooth and unbroken. Amber reached up to feel her own neck, recalling the slimy touch of the thing's palm.

"It made me feel like I was gonna barf," Cherrywine sniffled.

"Me too," Ray agreed. "Same thing last time."

Lito asked, "How long's it been since then? Couple of hours?"

"About that."

"Start timing. I wanna know how long it takes for the next one."

"You think there'll be a next one?"

Lito only nodded.

"Yo, what about those guys?" Carlos asked. "Was they really pirates, or maybe just wearin costumes or somethin?"

"I'm pretty sure they were just as authentic as the ship," Ray told him.

"Dat's two or t'ree hundred years." Jericho gave a low whistle of amazement. "Dat's a long time to just be sittin 'round out here."

Amber saw Ray shoot an uncomfortable look at Lito. "Tell them about the flashlight."

Lito grimaced and looked up from his reloading. "The one from Eric's story. I think we found it. Still turned on and running, like this guy from 1970 had just dropped it right before we strolled in."

"But it was more than that," Ray added. "The ship was clean, no dust, and there was food in the galley that was still good. Screw the seventies, it was more like it'd only been a few days since those buccaneers were out plunderin."

Amber sank down onto the bench with Cherrywine as she considered this newest piece of the puzzle. "How? How is that possible?"

Lito snapped the cylinder closed on his revolver. "I call a ban on anyone askin that question."

"Fuckin Bermuda Triangle," Ray muttered. "Always hated those stories growin up."

"What now, Cap'n?" Jericho asked quietly.

"We keep movin. Find a boat that has what you need, and do it fast."

"So we're all finished treasure hunting?" Amber asked.

Lito's expression was halfway between a grimace and a grin.

"Depends on the treasure, *gringa*."

THE BOYS FROM COMPANY C-12

DRUG DEALERS AND SEA MONSTERS

WHAT BECAME OF THE FAMILY WAY

LITO LOSES HIS COOL

1

The pontoon raft had grown quiet. Ray and Jericho took up a position at the front with binoculars, scouting for other ships that might have a compatible fuel line. Lito stuck to the back, helping Carlos with rowing duties. The girls retreated into the cabin.

They were completely enclosed by derelicts now; the ships stretched to the horizon in all directions, so densely packed they were almost a maze. Their course had become a meandering cruise through this minefield in whatever direction they could find an opening. With the wind picking up, it was a constant struggle to keep their distance from these other vessels.

And they *needed* to keep their distance. It might be his imagination, but he could swear that pale faces were watching them from a few windows as they passed, faces that were gone whenever he looked back again. With all the lightning overhead now, tossing shadows, it was hard to tell. But he had to operate under the assumption that all of these ships held more monsters, more crew that had been transformed into those things.

Lito glanced over at Carlos. He was quiet, bent into the oars. God, if this was getting to Lito so bad, he could only imagine what was going through the kid's head.

"I'm gonna get us outta this."

"Yeah, homey. Sure you are."

"You don't think so?"

"I dunno. Jorge and Rabid and Mondo thought you was Superman, and look where it got them."

That stung, but he didn't let it show on his face. "You know, that's exactly the sort of thing I'm talkin about. If you just dropped the attitude once in a while, life would probably go a lot easier for you."

"Yeah, well, you ain't gotta put up with it much longer. I'm out at the next port."

Lito forced himself to count to five before answering. "I promised your mom I'd—"

"Goddamn, would you shut up about my mom? I don't want you talkin 'bout my mom anymore, okay?"

"Fine." Lito pulled the oar from the water and tossed it on the deck next to the ingrate. "I gotta go check on the others. Keep us movin."

He made his way around the cabin, to the front of the boat, where Ray and Jericho stood scanning the night. "You seen anything worth tryin?"

"Too old." Jericho lowered the binoculars. A look passed between him and Ray that Lito couldn't read. "All too old or not de right engine."

"I've seen several ships the same size as the *Runner*. Some of 'em looked like they were in even better condition."

Ray said, "And any ship we try to scavenge could be crawlin with more of those things."

"Then we'll just have to kill 'em."

"We don't have the ammo. Another clip for the AR, a handful of shotgun shells, and whatever rounds everybody's got for their pistols."

"Then we'll figure somethin else out." Lito shrugged. "I know they're disgusting, but those things ain't invincible. They ain't even all that smart. They go down just like a regular person."

"See, that's another thing that's botherin me. The thing that everyone's thinkin but nobody's sayin." Ray pointed at the oily blue stain on the deck where Lito had killed the first of the mutants that attacked Amber. "They go down like regular people because, at some point, they *were* regular people. They didn't all start out with blue blood and melted skin. Whether it's a disease or too much fluoride in the water, *somethin* happened to make them this way. We should probably think long and hard about all that before we keep pokin around."

"And we're obviously gettin closer to whatever's broadcastin dat voice on de radio," Jericho added.

"Okay," Lito said, "I get it, I'm with you. Just find us another ship that's guaranteed to have what we need and we'll get outta here."

That look passed between them once more, something hesitant.

"What's up?"

Ray's brow wrinkled. "We figured out what the big one is. The thing we spotted earlier from the houseboat."

"And?"

"We're pretty sure...it's a cruise ship."

"Oh really? Carnival or Disney?"

"I'm not jokin."

"No goddamned way." Lito snatched the binoculars from Jericho and looked for himself. The enormous silhouette on the horizon—so much bigger than anything else they'd seen out here—was much clearer against the backdrop of lightning-filled clouds blowing in from the south, especially now that he knew what he was looking for. A lot of ships still lay between them, but he estimated they were probably closer to it than they were to the *Steel Runner* at this point. "That thing can't be another derelict. If an entire *cruise ship* had disappeared in the Bermuda Triangle, don't you think we'd know about it?"

"So now it *is* the Bermuda Triangle, huh?"

Lito rolled his eyes and said nothing.

"Dere's a smaller craft comin up on de left dat looks new," Jericho said. "If it don't have what we need, den dat cruise ship may be our last hope. Dey should have a fully stocked maintenance room, and even if de hoses are old, I can probably use dere equipment to rig somethin to get us by."

"Unless there's more of those things on board," Ray added.

"One problem at a time." Lito rubbed at his tired eyes. If things had gone according to plan, they would be most of the way back to port by now, and he'd be catching a nap on rich boy's yacht. "Let's check out this other boat."

2

Amber fell asleep on the floor of the cabin with the radio scanner playing next to her head, like some gruesome lullaby. Because she'd been the one to save it from flying overboard, Lito had said she might as well keep up with it. Once she'd been left alone, she fought the urge to send out a mayday between broadcasts. She tried to tell herself it was because she didn't like the idea of answering that growling monologue any more than the pirates did, but, if she were being honest, the real reason she didn't call for help was because she didn't want to betray Lito's trust.

Now, as she swam back to consciousness, with Cherrywine snoring loudly in one bunk, Justin moaning and thrashing in the other, and the skull of Mr. Watts grinning at her from a few feet away, the Voice of the Deep was even louder and clearer.

The academic side of her wanted to find a way to get an audio sample, to take back to school. A person could spend years studying something like this; it could be the modern day equivalent to cave drawings or the Phaistos disc, or even that Peruvian letter they'd discovered a few years back. Other linguists had made their entire careers from such finds. She realized she sounded like Lito, looking for treasure around every corner.

Maybe you oughta worry less about how famous it'll make you, and more about what it's trying to tell you.

She didn't know. As she'd told Jericho, without some sort of Rosetta stone, she had no hope of translating this.

Amber turned off the scanner and went to check on Justin. He was still asleep, but tossing back and forth. Heat rose from him like a stove burner. She thought again about Eric's story, about the man who'd contracted a disease in the Bermuda Triangle so dangerous, the government had made him disappear when he returned home. It sounded so phony and paranoid...and yet, the part about the flashlight had been true, hadn't it?

From outside, she heard Lito ask, "Is it some kinda mini-sub?"

"That's not submersible." Ray's voice. "Look, it has natural buoyancy. This thing was designed to ride *on* the water, not *under* it."

She crept out of the cabin. The deck rocked a little more than she remembered beneath her feet; the ocean was getting turbulent. Lito, Ray and Jericho stood at the right side of the boat, gazing into the night with weapons held ready.

Their boat was drifting up next to another strange craft. The vessel—about two-thirds the length of their pontoon raft but riding much lower in the water—gleamed in the flickers of lightning being thrown over their shoulders. It was all highly polished metal and shaped like a gigantic segmented bullet, with a blunt, tapered front end that rested just on top of the water. There was no place for any of the creatures to ambush them either; the exterior was free of outside decking and walkways, and only a single hatch on top for access to the interior. Its smooth surface was free of the rust and barnacles eating away at so many of the other derelicts, but it was marred by a few blackened scorch marks down one side and some extensive writing across its hull. If not for the huge metal propellers jutting from its rear, she wouldn't even have thought of it as a watercraft.

Ray let go of the shotgun barrel with one hand and pointed at the writing neatly stenciled along the upper curve of the hull. "Is that Japanese?"

"Vietnamese," she corrected. They turned to look at her as she walked over.

"So you know Vietnamese?" Lito asked.

"Again, I don't need to. The Vietnamese written language is one of the few Asian derivatives that uses Greek-based alphabetic letters like that, as opposed to the logographic *kanji* symbols you find with Japanese and Chinese writing."

They stared at her. "You mean those weird stick things?" Ray asked.

"Yes. Those 'weird stick things.'"

Lito gave her a sarcastic grin. "Okay, thanks, *gringa*. So it's Vietnamese. But what *is* it? I've never seen anything like it."

"Whatever it is, it's been t'rough hell and back." Jericho leaned out over the water to get a better look. "Dese look like explosive impacts, but dey didn't seem to've done a lotta damage. Gotta be one tough son-of-a-bitch."

Ray squatted. "And that looks like a projectile launch tube under the chin there. Maybe torpedoes."

"This is a *war machine*?" Lito looked incredulous as he tucked his pistol in the back of his waistband. He asked Jericho, "You think it would have your parts?"

"No fucking idea, *mon*. For all I know, dis t'ing could run on nuclear fission."

"Only one way to find out. Hey Carlos, get us in next to it!"

The raft maneuvered closer, until their pontoon rubbed against the strange craft's hull with a squall of tortured metal. At the same time, the skies opened up as promised, dropping a slow but steady drizzle. Jericho insisted Lito take one of their radios this time, which he sealed in a double layer of plastic baggies and slipped into a cargo pockets of his shorts. He stepped off the boat onto the shiny surface, then climbed up the curved, segmented body toward the hatch at the apex.

Before anyone could stop her—or before she could stop herself—Amber jumped from the edge of the raft to follow him.

The craft's metal body was slick beneath her tennis shoes from the rain. She stayed hunched low so the wind couldn't get a grip on her, and used her hands to keep balanced until she reached the area that leveled off at the peak. Lito waited for her there.

"What're you doin?" he asked.

"Hey, you're the one that dragged us along for this ride. I'd rather be involved and know what's going on instead of cowering inside."

Lito studied her, then closed both eyes and gave a few of those long inhales.

"Why do you keep doing that?" she asked.

He opened one eye. "A few cleansing breaths clears the mind so you can make more rational decisions."

"Riiiight. And what decision do you have to make?"

Lito pulled his revolver and held it out to her, handle first. On the pontoon boat, someone gave a short, outraged grunt. "I need you to cover me while I try to get this hatch open. Can you do that?"

Amber accepted the gun, tried to pull the hammer back like she'd seen in the movies, and ended up almost dropping the thing. "Piece of cake," she muttered.

"Just pull the trigger, Annie Oakley. You don't have to cock it."

She pointed the weapon downward while he hauled at the metal wheel jutting from the hatch. After a long minute of straining and grunting, he gave up, walked past her back to the bow, and called up to the others on the pontoon, "No good, this thing is locked from the inside."

"Then just come back," Ray told him. "We should've given this up a long time ago and gone back to the *Steel Runner*."

"Not yet. We go for the cruise ship."

"That is a stubborn, stupid idea, Lito."

"Duly noted. We're goin anyway."

"What if the rest of us don't want to?"

"Then you're gonna have to mutiny. The captain has spoken."

"I thought this was a democracy."

"Hey, we voted!"

"Not for this."

Amber had turned her back on the hatch to listen to this exchange, but realized her mistake when she heard the metallic scrape of hinges. She spun around, ready to fire the revolver at the hideous monstrosity she knew must be coming at her, and instead found herself staring down the barrel of a long, thin rifle poking out of the half-open portal.

3

Their names were Due Trung and Tuan Pho.

Both were young—their Asian features made it hard for Lito to guess their ages, but, judging by their skittish nature, he guessed even Carlos had a few months on them—and wearing sweat-stained military jumpsuits made of a shimmery brown material, the kind of getups fighter pilots wore in the cockpit.

Only after convincing the duo they meant no harm were the soldiers willing to put down their rifles—heavily-modified AK-47's—and introduce themselves. This part was so easy, Lito suspected they were relieved to have the company. They were obviously inexperienced soldiers, pressed into service at an early age. But they made Lito and Amber stand with their hands up on the outside of the craft while they waved a weird silver wand over them from the safety of the hatch. The device was connected to some sort of beeping PDA readout, and the two soldiers huddled over it intensely as they waited for results, the green backlight from the screen washing over their pale, round faces.

"What the hell are they doing?" Amber asked quietly.

"I have no idea," Lito answered.

Whatever the device told them, it seemed to satisfy. They let Lito bring Jericho onto their ship, where the process was repeated, then allowed all three of them to climb down the short ladder on the inside of the hatch.

The interior of their craft was cramped and muggy, the ceiling barely big enough to stand up in, and smelled like a poorly ventilated locker room. The walls looked like solid metal from the outside, but from within a narrow, transparent strip ran the length of each wall, seamlessly integrated into the design, which gave the crew a limited outside view. They had undoubtedly watched as the raft approached, and Lito and Amber climbed onto their ship.

There were four crew seats around the interior, each in front of a complicated-looking control terminal full of screens and control panels lined with buttons and switches. All of these were powered-down and dark except for some soft-hued lighting around the edges, enough to see by. Lito spotted the crusty remains of MRE packaged dinner tins piled in one corner, the bane of the enlisted man. Due and Tuan sat nervously in two of the chairs, watching them.

Lito leaned close enough to whisper in Jericho's ear. "Take a look around, see if there's anything we can use for the *Runner*."

The mechanic nodded and started to slip past a narrow bulkhead dividing the cockpit from the stern, where a tiny head the size of a closet with a metal toilet was visible, and other compartments further on. The soldier named Due stood up and shouted in Vietnamese while gesturing angrily. One hand went to the pistol holstered at his waist.

"Hey, hey, cool it! No need for that!" Lito put his hands back in the air. He considered taking them by force, but decided it might be better to play this tactfully; after all, they needed all the allies they could get. Carefully, he reached over and used two fingers to pull the revolver he'd given Amber out of the waistband of her shorts, and set it on one of the consoles. "See, boys? Friendly. He just needs to take a piss. You got a can in this place, right?"

There was no sign of comprehension on Due's pinched face,

but Tuan nodded after a second and gave a consenting wave. Jericho disappeared past the bulkhead, and Due plopped back down in his seat with a scowl.

Lito turned to Amber. "Talk to these guys. See what you can find out."

"I told you, I don't know Vietnamese."

"You know it a lot better than I do." He glanced over her shoulder at the young soldiers. "These are the first two normal people we've come across. If they know anything about what's goin on, or if they can tell us why they haven't caught whatever those other people did, it would be helpful, don't ya think?"

"Oh, so now it's a disease?"

"Disease, poison, took the brown acid, whatever. I wanna know what *they* know. The one on the right—Tuan?—he seems to understand a little English. See what you can get outta him."

"Fine. Just don't get used to ordering me around. I'm not one of your crew."

"Course you're not. Girls can't be pirates." He winked. "But you would look great with an eye patch."

Her brow stayed wrinkled, but Lito thought he caught the hint of a smile before she turned away.

She moved forward in the claustrophobic cockpit. The two Vietnamese boys watched her carefully. Amber knelt in front of them and introduced herself. "How long have you been here?"

Tuan furrowed his brow.

"Uh, how long?" She tapped her watch face. "Here?" She pointed at the floor.

The young man's face lit up. He held up a hand with all five fingers extended.

"Five...hours?"

He seemed to think about how to answer, then pointed at the pile of empty ration tins in the corner.

Lito got it after a second. "Five *days*? You've been out here for five *days*?"

"Days," he repeated, nodding.

"How'd you get here? Do you know why the people from these other ships are all messed up?"

"Don't confuse him," Amber chided. She swept a finger at the other ships visible through the narrow viewport. "Do you know anything about those?"

Tuan held his hands out, palms up.

"What happened to you? How did you come here?"

This time, he shot an uncomfortable glance at his compatriot. Due squinted his already narrow eyes as he tried to follow the conversation. Finally, Tuan shook his head.

"You can't tell me? You mean you don't know?"

Tuan grasped for words, then took his fingertips and made a show of clamping his lips shut.

"I think he means he *won't* tell you," Lito said. "If they're really Vietnamese military, then whatever they're doin here could be classified."

"You think they had something to do with the derelicts then?"

"Either that, or they're just as stuck as we are."

"Maybe they're terrorists." Amber turned to Tuan and asked, "Is that it? Are you here to attack America?"

"A-ttack...America?" the boy repeated. He looked genuinely puzzled. "No, no to...'a-ttack.' *Friend.* Asian Faction. Company C-12." This last bit sounded more memorized than translated to Lito, a crucial bit of English they'd been taught in case someone wanted name, rank, and serial number.

"You're a friend?" Amber asked. "I don't understand what you mean."

Due interrupted in rapid Vietnamese, jabbing a finger at them. Tuan shook his head emphatically, negating whatever he'd been told, then grabbed the other soldier's hand and pushed it down. Due jerked away from him and said something recognizable as a curse in any language, then threw a hand up and spun around in his chair. He flung his head down against the console and wrapped his arms over it, like a kid throwing a tantrum.

Tuan ran a hand over his dark, bristly hair and gave them an embarrassed frown. Lito was getting the idea this levelheaded kid was the only reason they hadn't been shot the minute they stepped foot on their vessel. These two were stressed to the breaking point, but the difference was, Tuan was willing to trust them if it meant a chance at help.

"What are you doin here?" Lito repeated.

The young soldier searched for words, then put his palms together and moved them apart, while making a sound like an explosion. Then he pantomimed firing a gun.

"Fight?" Amber prompted. "Battle?"

"War?" Lito offered.

Tuan nodded eagerly. "War! Help war! America!"

"What fuckin war is *Vietnam* helpin to fight in Caribbean waters?"

The young soldier gaped at him, and Lito suspected it wasn't because of a language gap this time. When he spoke, it was as though talking to a child. "War. *War. Biiig* war."

Amber looked up at Lito and shrugged helplessly. "Do you have any idea what he's talking about?"

"Not a clue. Doesn't make a damned bit of sense."

Lito was set to continue the line of questioning, but Jericho came up behind him and laid a hand on his shoulder. "Lito...talk to you a sec?"

Lito nodded and told Amber, "See what else you can get."

The two of them stepped out of earshot toward the back of the cockpit. "What's up?"

"I took a look at dere engine. What I *t'ought* was dere engine. Dis ship...I ain't never seen anyt'ing like it."

"So they don't have a fuel line?"

"You kidding? I was prob'ly closer when I said nuclear fission." Jericho leaned even closer to him and whispered, "We need to figure out who de hell dese guys are."

"They're kinda tight-lipped, and I don't know how much time we have for an interrogation, Jer." Lito stood still for a moment. "Tell me this though: you think this thing could be worth somethin?"

Jericho snorted. "I don't know how Vietnam got dere hands on a ship like dis, but de technology ain't common. De design alone has got to be worth millions to de right country."

Lito nodded. "Let's keep this between us for the time being."

4

Amber had participated in a study on non-verbal communication her junior year as part of a course requirement, where the participants had been forced to convey complex ideas without any vocalization. The experience was designed for situations exactly like this, where two individuals from radically different backgrounds had a language barrier between them. And, although she never expected to use it in a situation as odd as this one, she did find that the more she spoke with Tuan, the easier she found it to grasp his meanings. It also helped that he seemed to already have some English exposure. Their exchange became an intermingled soup of shared vocabulary and improvised sign language that she translated for the other two.

After ten more minutes, she was able to piece together their story: there were originally four soldiers manning this craft, which had taken damage in whatever fight they'd been involved in. Dead in the water, they'd floated into the midst of the derelicts while waiting for extraction. Here the story got fuzzy, but as she understood it, the sky had flashed blue to the west, and 'day had turned to night.' She had to ask him about this part twice, thinking at first he meant it the other way around, that the flash was so bright it had *seemed* like daylight, but he was absolutely adamant that the sun was out before the flash, and afterward, it was moonlight and stars. His only explanation was that they had lost consciousness, except none of them could recall waking up, or any sort of gap in their thought stream. That had been five days ago.

"What about their superiors?" Lito asked. "They must have a radio on this thing. They heard from anyone?"

Tuan cringed at this question and mumbled something in Vietnamese. Beside him, Due lifted his head from his arms and looked up fearfully.

"What? What'd I say?"

Tuan reached out to his control console, flicked a switch beside a built-in microphone jutting up from the plastic, and the entire cabin was filled with the Voice of the Deep, spouting its gibberish through speakers hidden somewhere around them. Tuan shivered.

"Damn. Forgot about that," Lito said.

"Yes," Amber told Tuan. "We know, we heard it, too. We don't know what it's saying."

As the current transmission stopped, lapsing into one of the thirty second gaps of radio silence, the Vietnamese soldier leaned to the microphone and held down a button.

Amber realized too late that he was about to attempt broadcasting.

"No, don't!" Jericho shouted behind her. The terror in his voice sent a tingle of fear across her scalp.

Tuan spoke a quick, simple sentence in Vietnamese into the microphone, sending his voice over the airwaves. Amber imagined it floating up and away, to be intercepted by whoever was broadcasting that other cryptic, monotonous spiel. She held her breath, waiting to see what would happen.

When Tuan let go of the button and relinquished control of the channel, there was a metallic click, followed by a low tone. The broadcast started up again, but this time it was one single, repeated syllable. And, even though she still didn't understand what it was saying, Amber could at least identify the language now.

It was deadpan, perfectly unaccented Vietnamese.

From the other chair, Due pressed palms over his ears and squeezed his eyes shut, forcing tears down the sides of his nose.

The word played a few times before Amber whispered, "What did you say, Tuan?"

Anticipating her question, he struggled to find the words. "Ask name."

Amber opened her mouth, let out a rasp, and had to swallow before she could try again. That one word repeating over and over again—in a recognizable language now, but so cold and emotionless—was somehow worse than the other. She realized she was terrified to speak too loud, lest it somehow hear her over the speakers. "And what is it saying back?"

"'Leave,'" he translated. "Say…'Leave. Leave.'"

They listened to it for a full minute, then the tone came again, and the original broadcast resumed. Tuan turned off the speakers, and everyone seemed to deflate as the tension left them.

Amber twisted around to look at Lito and Jericho. "What does it mean?"

"I was just about to ask you the same thing," Lito said. "That voice…it didn't just sound like a recording that time, it sounded like a damn robot."

"And it spoke dere language." Jericho gestured at the soldiers. "Does dat mean it has somet'in to do wit dese two?"

"Not necessarily." Amber rubbed at her temples. "It only spoke Vietnamese in response to him. If whatever is broadcasting this is truly automated, then maybe it just took in what he said, decoded it, then spoke back to him."

"Is there some computer program that'll do that?" Lito asked. "Understand any language and use it to answer you?"

"Not *any* language. There are spoken translators you can buy that understand the big ones—English, Spanish, French—but they're far from reliable. Plus, it would take massive computational storage space to be able to house every language on the planet." She held up a hand. "But we need to be very clear here. That thing didn't answer him at all. Chances are, it probably didn't understand *what* he said, just what language he said it in. Then it sent out a preprogrammed response that matched the verbal patterns. That would account for the simplicity; it probably has a very limited vocabulary, just enough to get across its message."

Lito looked over her head at Tuan, who was desperately trying to follow their conversation. "Kid, that's obviously not the first time you've tried that. Has it ever said anything else?"

Amber had to work to translate the question enough for him to understand, but the young soldier eventually shook his head.

"It's a warning," Amber said.

"Or a threat," Jericho added.

Lito's jaw clenched. "Or it could be somebody with somethin to hide, so they're tryin to scare people off by flashin lights in the sky and makin spooky voices on the radio, like a goddamn Scooby Doo villain."

"We have to try it ourselves," Amber said. "In English. See if it answers us."

"No, can't let you do that. Anyone else within range could pick up the broadcast. The less radio presence we have, the better."

Amber felt her fingernails biting into her palms as she said, "Enough with your goddamn anti-authority bullshit. We are *way* beyond the fact that you guys are pirates. This is our best chance at finding out what the hell is going on around here."

The two of them locked eyes, like matador and bull.

The tension was broken when Ray's voice spoke from Lito's pocket. "You guys copy? Everything okay in there?"

Lito glared at her a moment longer, then pulled the radio out. He left the device in its protective bags while he spoke. "We're fine."

"Water's gettin pretty choppy out here. This storm's gonna be on us any second, and it's lookin more and more like a doozy."

Amber had been so engrossed in her conversation with Tuan, she hadn't realized how much the vessel was now rolling from side to side, a slow, gentle pendulum motion, like being inside a giant bassinet.

"We'll be out in a sec." Lito put the radio back up and turned to her. "We can play detective on our own scanner when we get back. Finish this up. I wanna know what happened to their other crewmen, and if they know anything about those blue flashes."

"Blue!" Tuan came alive all of a sudden, swiveling in his chair to sift through piles of paper print-outs on the desk. He started handing several of these to Amber, documents packed densely with Vietnamese writing and complicated graphs, then pointed out the viewport to the west and waved the strange handheld device they'd used earlier. "Blue, blue!"

"I don't understand." She held up the sheaf of papers. "What does this have to do with the blue flashes?"

Tuan thought for a second, then grabbed another piece of paper and bent over it with a pen. He scribbled for a few seconds and then handed this new slip over to her.

It was a quick drawing of three flat-topped cones arranged in a triangle, all pointing inward to a circle in the middle. She recognized the crude pictogram immediately.

The international symbol for radiation.

5

The end of their story came quickly to Amber, although it made such little sense, she preferred to believe the meaning had been lost in translation.

The flash that turned day to night (*big*, Tuan insisted about this one, much brighter than what Amber and the others had been seeing) had also set off alarms all over their ship. One of their crewmates had been outside when it happened, standing on the hull to keep an eye on the derelicts, and became violently ill over the next day. Fearing that their enemy had used a new weapon in whatever battle they were fighting, they'd locked themselves inside their ship for two days, eating their food stores and trying to restore power to their craft while their crewmate went downhill fast.

"It was radiation poisoning, wasn't it?" Lito asked quietly.

Tuan nodded.

"Oh shit," Jericho moaned.

"What?" Amber demanded. "What does that mean?"

"Don't you get it? The sickness, the mutations...one of dese ships is carryin radioactive cargo, and it's fryin everything dat comes t'rough here!"

"I don't know if that's it at all," Lito said.

"Course it is, *mon*! Goddamn it, the little soldier boys have been protected on dis ship, but who knows how much exposure we've had!"

Tuan jabbered at them and held up the PDA device with the short, silver wand attached.

Lito said, "We're okay, Jer. I think that thing must be some kinda Geiger counter. They were testin us earlier, seein if we'd been exposed. Since they let us on board, I guess that means we haven't."

"So the blue flashes we've seen, like the one that just went off a little bit ago...they're *not* radioactive?" Amber asked.

Tuan shook his head emphatically.

"Maybe it was a nuclear bomb den," Jericho said. "Someone coulda set one off miles from here, and we're gettin de fallout."

"No new-clee-are," Tuan said, sounding very sure even as he pronounced the last word in heavily-accented imitation. He reached out and tapped the packet of graphs he'd given Amber. "Computer...no say new-clee-are. Other. No name."

"Finish your story," Lito told him. "What happened to the other soldiers?"

While they awaited rescue, they'd heard screeches and moans from the other boats that drifted by, and something big had slithered around beneath their vessel, bashing at the underside of their hull before finally giving up and going away. During each of these incidents, the radiation detectors had gone off. Then, as their crewmate got sicker, *he* began to set off the detectors. He had a fever, screamed and thrashed violently, and they'd been forced to quarantine him to his bunk as best they could. From the way Tuan described him, it seemed to Amber they were scared of the man. When the others became convinced they'd been abandoned by their superiors, one of the crewmen commandeered a small sailboat that floated close enough to lasso. He took the sick one and left to find help. That had been three days ago, and they'd never returned. Since that time, the sky had flashed brightly three other times, with the smaller bursts in between. Tuan held his stomach and stuck out his tongue as he attempted to convey this, miming a bellyache.

"So the small flashes make you queasy, like what we felt before, but it's only the bright ones that are dangerous," Lito said. "Tuan, how often do these things happen?"

The response was translated through Amber after some effort: the time period between the bright flashes were completely random—the shortest about eight hours, the longest close to two days—but they were always separated by four of the lesser bursts.

"Dat's not so bad. We've only seen two of dem so far."

"Three," Lito corrected. "I saw one from a distance, before we ever found the first derelicts. Is that right, Tuan, there have been three so far in this set?" The soldier nodded. "Which means we're pretty damn deep into this thing."

Amber cleared her throat of the spit that had suddenly flooded it. "Can...can radiation poisoning be passed on though? Through a scratch?"

"No. It also doesn't turn you into a burnt-up psychopath that doesn't age. It makes you sick and kills you, or, if the dosage is low enough, it turns your unborn kids into freaks. Period."

Jericho shook his head. "But Lito, what you're talking about is nuclear radiation. And he said dat's not what dis is."

Lito shrugged as coolly as some of the guys in Amber's dorm when answering about which kegger they were going to Friday night, and she marveled at how anyone could be so nonchalant after everything they'd just heard. "Well, unless this mysterious new radiation also conjures up brand-spankin new pirate ships with the original crew still aboard, I don't think it's as simple as that."

"Don't forget sea monsters," Amber said softly. She'd meant it as a lame joke, a way to ease the building tension, but once the words were out, they had the opposite effect.

Tuan had given them some much needed answers, but still, the puzzle wasn't looking any easier to put together.

"Lito, look." There was a pleading tone to Jericho's voice. "If we're still out here when one of dese flashes hits, den we're all dead. If dis tin can of dere's has some kinda shieldin, we need to get everyone aboard right now, and den start tryin to call for help."

"We'd barely have room to breathe with all of us on board this thing. Besides, if that storm gets bad and starts rollin this thing over, the inside'll be like a washin machine." Lito's dark eyebrows shot up. "But we could leave Amber and her friends here, and the rest of us could use one of Tuan's detectors while we search the other ships for a hose. If they work like he said, then anything that's been affected by the radiation won't be able to sneak up on us."

Amber stood up for the first time since she started talking with Tuan, the muscles in her legs flaring briefly. "You're not gonna leave us here!"

"Why not? It might get a little bumpy, but at least you won't drown. You can stay here and play with the radio all you want."

"And what happens if you don't come back? We'll be just as bad off as they are."

"We'll come back for you," Lito said. "I promise."

"Help?" Tuan asked, pointing at himself. At this, Due spun

around and grabbed angrily at him. Tuan planted a hand on his face and shoved him away, reminding Amber of the type of feuds she'd seen her friends' brothers engage in. Tuan repeated, "Help you?"

Amber told Lito, "They'll die if they stay here. I think he knows it. We're their best shot at getting out of this."

"Sure, we can use all the help we can get to search. And a few extra guns wouldn't hurt." Lito hunkered down. "Tell you what...if we can get our boat working, we'll even tow their ship outta here with us."

She gave him an impressed look. "You would do that?"

"Of course. Can't leave these friends of America stranded out here, now can we?"

Amber made sure Tuan understood. The poor kid just looked relieved to have someone else in charge. He and Due had another rapid, angry exchange.

"We don't have time for an argument, boys. We gotta get our gear and the rest of the group transferred over here and then get a move on."

Due seemed to relent. It took the two soldiers less than a minute to gather up their belongings—mostly their rifles, spare ammunition, and two of the handheld radiation detectors, which Tuan tucked in the pockets of his jumpsuit. After retrieving their own guns, Jericho climbed the ladder up through the hatch, followed by Lito. Amber went also, to help move Justin over. As her head emerged from the hatch, she saw the raindrops had gotten fatter and denser. The pontoon boat still sat at the bottom of the slope that formed the nose of Tuan and Due's ship.

Lito helped her out onto the top of their slick craft, gripping her wrist, but when the boat gave a lurch to the side, she stumbled. His other hand flailed before grabbing her ass to stop her from falling back down the ladder. It lingered there just a second too long after she'd found her footing, cupping one cheek.

"You know, I probably should've told you," she said. "I don't speak Vietnamese, but I *am* fluent in *Español*."

She watched the look of horror that came over his face as he first recalled his conversation with Ray earlier, and then realized where his hand was, before snatching it away. Nice to know there was something that could throw him off his smug, unflappable game.

They moved aside to make room for Tuan. He stood astride his vessel and sucked in a lungful of cool night air, then turned his face up to the rain and stretched, the rifle dangling around his neck by a strap. The look of contentment on his face made it clear he was thankful to be free of the enclosed space.

His partner started to crawl through the hatch behind him, but made it only halfway when a line of bullets ripped open his chest.

6

Lito heard the gunshots, but couldn't at first tell them apart from the sharp cracks of thunder in the clouds above them. It was only after Due cried out and then tumbled over the curved side of the ship that he realized they were under fire. The Asian kid performed an awkward somersault, leaving a smear of blood on the slick hull that the rain quickly washed away. There was a splash as he fell into the water.

"*Hit the deck!*" Lito shouted, although there was very little deck to hit up here, and no cover whatsoever. He grabbed Amber and pulled her down until they lay stretched out on their stomachs. Tuan and Jericho did likewise on the far side of the open hatch. The rain fell harder against their backs, beating a staccato *ting-ting-ting* against the metal.

"*Where's it comin from?*" Jericho shouted.

Lito didn't have an answer until he heard an engine rev somewhere off to their left. He raised his head. The clouds had blotted out the moonlight, so at first his eyes could pick out nothing against the backdrop of the midnight ocean. Then a flash of lightning revealed a speedboat cruising through the choppy waters about twenty yards away.

Automatic gunfire rang out as the craft strafed. Bullets spanged off the hardened hull of the Vietnamese vessel, producing winks of light but leaving no mark on the steel.

Ray shouted something from the deck of the pontoon, but it was lost under the growing noise of storm and gunfire. Lito could see him and Carlos taking shelter behind the cabin. Cherrywine's screams drifted out through the open door.

"*Stay back!*" Lito shouted at them. "*See if you can draw some fire!*"

They got the idea, edging around the cabin to shoot from the corner. The speedboat swerved and sped up, then focused its attention on the pontoon raft. As soon as the sleek craft pulled away, Lito got to his knees, pulled out his revolver and fired every round in the cylinder at their attackers. At this range and in these conditions, he might as well have been shooting spit wads.

Tuan walked on his knees until he took a position beside Lito and then opened fire with his huge AK. The chain of shots from the big machine gun was deafening, but not even they had much effect. The speedboat circled the two crafts, weaving among the other derelicts, forcing Ray and Carlos to circle the cabin to avoid exposure. They disappeared around the far side just as the exterior was peppered with shots.

The occupants of the speedboat—whoever they were—had the advantage: as long as they stayed in motion, they could just keep firing from all sides until Lito and the others were dead.

From the deck of the pontoon, someone cried out in pain.

The thought of Carlos getting shot—the boy Lito had promised to keep out of situations exactly like this—was bad, but the idea that it might be Ray sent a flood of desperate adrenaline through him.

Lito put the empty revolver in Amber's hand, then rolled over next to Jericho and yelled, "*Did you fix those jet skis?*"

The mechanic looked at him in confusion. "*I hadn't tested dem or anyt'ing, but I t'ink so! I put in some of de gas we brought, but de fuel systems still need to be flushed!*"

"*Gimme your pistol!*"

Jericho held the weapon out hesitantly. "*What are you doin?*"

Lito yanked the gun away from him. "*Get as far from here as possible, in case they come back!*"

"*And go where? If one of dese flashes hits while we're outside dis ship, we're dead!*"

"*We won't be here long enough for that to happen! Get to that cruise ship and find what you need for the* Runner! *I'll meet you there!*"

Lito leapt to his feet, charged down the length of the Vietnamese warship, and jumped onto the deck of the pontoon raft.

He didn't waste time checking on the others, just ran for the metal ramps at the back and the jet skis parked on them. The speedboat would be circling around to his side any second, and then they would have a clear angle on him. He unfolded the ramp—the rusted hinges tried to stick, but he forced them—then hopped on the seat and kicked off, sliding backward down into the rough seas.

The jet ski was a short, lean craft with stubby handlebars and a long seat made of badly cracked vinyl. The key dangled from the ignition where Jericho had left it while making repairs. Lito twisted them and the engine started up with a high-pitched whine. It had been years since he'd ridden one of these, but it all came back as he throttled up and steered around the far side of the pontoon raft. He passed right in front of the speedboat's bow as it came around for another pass, and Lito threw a few shots over his shoulder to get their attention.

When he was sure they were giving chase, he poured on the speed and fled into the maze of derelict ships.

7

"*What is he doing?*" Amber demanded. She rose up in time to see Lito shoot away on the jet ski into the curtain of rain. She felt a searing moment of panic to see him go. The speedboat made a tight U-turn and sped after him, disappearing between two other ships.

"*Givin us a chance to get away, so let's not waste it!*" Jericho stood. "*Move!*"

Amber regained her feet along with Tuan, who stopped to peer over the ship's side. Due floated face-down amid the seaweed, the waves tossing his body against the hull. Tuan glanced at Amber, his face anguished. She expected him to stay behind as she and Jericho fled down the ramp of the vessel's nose, but he eventually followed. The three of them climbed aboard the pontoon raft. The rain was getting worse, pounding at them now, rattling against the deck and soaking their clothes as the wind howled.

Cherrywine poked her head out of the cabin. "*What happened?*"

"*Someone shot at us!*" Amber had to yell to make herself heard over the growing storm. "*Are you and Justin okay?*"

"*Yeah! What should I do?*"

"*Just don't come out!*" Amber told her, then turned to Tuan and motioned at the door. "*Stay here, in case they come back! Okay?*" The young soldier nodded curtly and stepped aside, taking a sentry post in the doorway.

Amber and Jericho moved on down the gangway toward the opposite side of the boat. Ahead of them, Carlos knelt beside Ray, who was stretched out on the deck. Blood poured down the man's side, mingling with the rainwater collecting on the deck. She dropped to her knees and lifted up his shirttail, used it as a cover against the rain so she could see beneath.

A small, round hole dimpled his side, just above the hip. A steady stream of dark maroon gushed out. Ray's face was drawn up in a painful grimace, but his hand moved across his chest in a continuous circuit, up and down and back and forth. It took her a second to realize he was sketching the sign of the cross.

"*Is it bad?*" Jericho asked, skidding to a stop behind her. "*Can you do anyt'ing for him?*"

"*I don't know, I'm not a nurse either!*" She put her hands over the gunshot wound and pressed, putting all her weight on her arms. Blood seeped between her fingers.

"*Who the fuck were those* pendejos?" Carlos yelled.

"*No idea! But we need to get out of here before dey come back.*" Jericho grabbed the young man's arm and pulled him to his feet. "*Help me row!*"

"*Where we goin?*"

"*The cruise ship!*" Amber's declaration was almost drowned out by a roll of thunder that shook the heavens. She looked up from Ray. "*We have to head toward the cruise ship! To meet Lito!*"

"*No fuckin way, lady! Since when do you give orders around here?*"

"*We gotta go!*" Jericho nodded but didn't look happy about it. "*If dis storm gets bad, den we gotta find some shelter fast! Dat cruise ship might be de safest t'ing around!*" He picked up one of the oar paddles and held it out. "*Help me, goddamn it!*"

Carlos accepted the paddle and went with him. They disappeared around the corner, toward the back of the raft, and Amber turned to Ray. He stopped crossing himself long enough to grab her upper arm.

"Where's Lito?" His voice was so quiet she had to lean in to hear him.

"He led them away. Lie still now. I don't know how bad this is yet."

"D-Dominican," he uttered. "Has to be…"

His eyes rolled back and his hand dropped away from her as he slipped into unconsciousness. Amber continued applying pressure as their raft began to move.

8

Lito had the advantage on the jet ski. Not for speed; the boat behind him was an 8-cylinder beast, would overtake him in a heartbeat on a long stretch of open water. But here, amid the twisted tangle of drifting derelicts, maneuverability was much more important.

He wove through them, taking tight corners whenever possible, trying to stay out of the range of the mystery guests' gunfire but not gain so much ground that they gave up chase. He could look over his shoulder and make out several figures back there, shooting wildly from the speedboat every time they had him in sight for a few seconds.

But he dared not look for too long. The abandoned ships in this area—a few pleasure crafts but mostly bigger, industrial vessels—were densely packed, jostling and crashing against each other as the waves tossed them back and forth like toys in a rambunctious child's bathwater. One narrow canal between an old steamer and a cargo ship disappeared as he tried to enter, the two huge boats slamming together like titanic anvils, forcing him to divert. Lito skimmed over increasingly bigger waves that popped him several feet in the air. Visibility was horrible; he slit his eyes against the wind and rain and watched for openings to escape.

And then, after leading them for what he figured was a good ten minutes, he came around the bow of a schooner listing so badly its broken mast almost touched the water, made a hard right, and the towering wall of a mini-freighter loomed immediately in front of him. Its hull stretched out to either side, blocking his path.

Lito was forced to throttle down to avoid smashing into it headlong. He yanked the handles of the jet ski back the other direction, leaning into the turn, then gunned it. The speedboat roared around the corner beside him. For a moment, the two crafts raced side-by-side down the length of the freighter. A flash of lightning revealed the surprised faces of the occupants, black men in shorts and neoprene shirts.

He let go of the jet ski handle with one hand, raised Jericho's pistol, and fired blindly into their midst before they could mow him down.

A scream sounded over the howl of the wind. The boat swerved left away from him, clipping the prow of a broken-down yawl hard enough to peel paint from their hull, and then came roaring back, intent on crushing him into paste against the freighter. All Lito could do was brace for the impact.

Above them, the storm-choked sky flashed with almost blinding blue light.

9

Eric thrashed in his bindings at the back of the speedboat when the shooting started. His abductors had all but forgotten he existed as soon as they caught sight of the pirates, so now was his best chance to get free. Not only so he could start working on his escape, but mostly so he wouldn't drown strapped to a seat if the Jamaican flipped the boat.

It wouldn't be hard to do; the waves bounced and rattled the craft harder with each passing second as they chased after the jet ski. A few of the bigger whitecaps formed impromptu ramps that tossed them into the air, like stunt boats in a water exhibition, then allowed them to crash back down hard enough to jar his broken nose and send a fresh throb of pain through his head. The ocean was getting rough so fast, Eric wasn't even sure they could've ridden this mess out aboard the *MishMasher*.

A terrible image popped into his head as he wriggled in his seat and gulped at what little air he could get from the rain driving into his face: the *Holy Mackerel*, that dust-filled old houseboat, sinking beneath the angry waves, taking his father's fucked-up little statue with it. No sir, that wasn't in the cards; he wouldn't *let* it be. He had to find a way to get back there.

The duct tape binding him to the speedboat's vinyl seat came loose in ripping chunks. He struggled harder and peeled himself away, then, once his arms were free, tore the rest from his clothes. The four gorillas sitting in front of him were all so intent on firing their automatic weapons at the jet ski, they still didn't notice. Eric couldn't see which one of the pirates was riding that thing, but—to give credit where it was due—the guy had some serious moves.

The speedboat slewed violently side-to-side as Vishon took corners at unsafe speeds to pursue their target, forcing all the passengers to cling to their seats with one hand. Eric did the same while trying to decide what to do with his newfound freedom. He was, after all, still in a boat with four heavily-armed men, which didn't change his situation much. He could probably jump out without them seeing, but even if the storm didn't drown him, he did *not* intend to be the next course on the menu for whatever had eaten Mr. Tattoos.

They came around a sailboat and suddenly the jet ski was right beside them. Eric looked over and caught sight of that dipshit pirate captain, the tail of his Hawaiian-print shirt flapping in the wind. The goons, caught unaware by his sudden appearance, all scrambled to bring their machine guns up.

Lito raised a pistol and started shooting. Eric saw the thug closest to him take several bullets to the chest and neck. He tumbled sideways out of his seat, flopping bonelessly into the bottom of the boat. His uzi bounced from his hand and landed squarely between Eric's feet in the water collecting in the floorwell. Before he could snatch it up, Vishon yanked the wheel away from the jet ski, bashing the end of another ship hard enough to toss the passengers to the floor along with the dead man. They swerved back in the opposite direction, lining up their prow to ram the jet ski from the side.

Eric raised up to watch, interested to see what this would look like.

The blue flashes started up again, reflecting off the clouds this time, so bright his vision shorted out as if a flashbulb had gone off in his face. His stomach lurched. He threw an arm over his eyes and heard the other men in the boat shouting. When the light stopped a few seconds later, and his vision cleared again, Eric saw the speedboat had gone wide of their target. Vishon and his two remaining goons rubbed at their eyes, one of them gagging. To their portside, Lito leaned forward over the handlebars of the jet ski and throttled into the night.

The submachine pistol was still on the floor. Eric snatched it up and got to his feet. One of his captors caught sight of him and tried to swing his own weapon around. Eric beat him to the trigger. The small gun in his hand purred, the recoil tossing shots in an arc, but they ripped through the other man hard enough to pitch him backwards over the edge and into the water.

Savage glee filled Eric. The world pulsed red in tempo with his beating heart.

Vishon and his last cohort turned to him, fury on their faces. Eric tried to bring his weapon back down to take aim again, but the crafty Jamaican spun the wheel fast enough to slew them around nearly 180 degrees in the rough waters. Eric stumbled back, the sidewall of the boat striking behind his knees. He dropped the gun in an attempt to catch hold of something, but would've fallen out anyway if the other man hadn't lunged forward and grabbed him by the collar of his shirt.

A fist drove into his stomach hard enough to deflate his lungs. Eric fell to his hands and knees and was kicked in the side, forcing him over on his back next to the body of the other black man. He lay there, blinking away rain, a booted foot on his chest to hold him down, and stared up at the Jamaican.

"I'm gonna spit on your corpse," Eric wheezed, when air finally reentered his lungs. "A great big fuckin loogie."

"*We see 'bout dat, white boy!*" Vishon shook his head, like a dog, his mohawk of dreadlocks wagging. He turned back to the controls and revved up the engine again. "*Aftah we catch Porto!*"

10

Ray had an exit wound on his back just above the swell of his hip, which Amber took as a good sign; at least the bullet wasn't still in him. When she'd done all she could to stop the bleeding, she had Jericho help her lift the man up and carry him inside the cabin and out of the storm. Probably wasn't wise to move him, but the pontoon raft had begun to bounce and roll as the storm worsened—one side or the other flipping up so high at times, it left their stomachs behind when it plummeted again, like the best rollercoasters—and she was afraid he might be dumped off the edge. He was unconscious as they laid him gently in the unoccupied bunk across from Justin, who watched them with glittery, fever-bright eyes. Their new Vietnamese companion still stood guard in the doorway, feet braced against either jamb to keep steady, while Cherrywine clung to the cabinets in the kitchen and uttered a tiny shriek every time a wave tossed them.

Amber set about securing Ray and Justin to their bunks with the leftover rope, ignoring Justin's pale skin and sunken eyes as she tied straps across his chest to keep him in place. One problem at a time, that was the best she could manage.

Carlos bolted through the door, pushing Tuan aside. "I can't row in this shit anymore!"

Amber finished with Justin, then turned to Jericho. "Where's the walkie-talkie?"

The mechanic frowned at her. "What for?"

"Because Lito took one, remember? If he still has it..."

He hurried to the bag of equipment they'd brought and dug out the second radio. "Lito, *mon*, you dere?"

She watched as he tried a few more times, committing to

memory which buttons he pressed. There was no response.

Her heart fell. It must've shown on her face too, because Jericho said, "It doesn't mean anyt'ing. If he's still on de run, he can't hear it."

She wondered how likely that was. How long had he been gone? Fifteen minutes? If the speedboat hadn't caught him by now, this storm would. Amber bit her lip as Jericho turned away, her eyes prickling with the damp heat of impending tears, and became suddenly aware that Justin was still staring at her, searching her face intently.

"Tuan," she said quietly. "Can I see one of your detectors?" She had to pantomime to get him to understand.

The young soldier pulled out one of the PDA units and turned it on, indicated with a few gestures how to use it, then handed it over. She made her way across the rocking floor to Justin's side and held the metal wand in front of his face.

"What is that thing?" he asked, coughing.

"It's...like a thermometer." She pressed the button on the side to begin taking a reading. "Just lay back for a second, okay?"

At first, nothing happened, and she realized she had no idea what to expect from the device in the first place. But then, on the tiny screen, there was movement. Lines and graphs and a string of numbers that she didn't understand. The unit gave off a slow series of clicks.

"Why's it doin that?" Carlos asked. "Yo, what's that mean?"

"Nothing," she answered quickly. "It doesn't mean anything."

"Tell dem de truth," Jericho said. "Dey got a right to know."

"Know what?" Justin tried to sit up, but the ropes she'd tied across his chest held him back.

"It means you got some kinda radiation poisoning. Dat's what's causing all dis."

Justin's eyes bulged. "Oh my god, I'm gonna look like that little girl?"

"*No*," Amber reassured him forcefully, then turned to glare at

Jericho. "Tuan never said the radiation turned his crewman into onto one of those things, only that it made him sick!"

"Don't fool yourself, girl." Jericho had a guilty look on his face, as if he hated having to say this to her. "Dat detector says he's got it. So for our own safety...we gotta tie him up, so he can't give it to de rest of us."

"Yo, fuck that man, let's just kick him off the boat!" Carlos shouted.

"You're not gonna touch him!"

Amber felt a hand curl around her wrist and looked back; Justin had slipped an arm free from the ropes and clutched at her gently. "They're right," he said. "If there's even a chance I have whatever those other people do, you need to get as far away from me as possible. Either that, or..." He watched her eyes and swallowed, but it seemed to take effort.

"What, *kill you*? Jesus Christ, has everyone gone..."

The argument was interrupted as the detector in her hand began to click faster, the lines on the screen scrunching into thick, steep hills.

"Uh, why's it doing that?" she asked.

Something slammed against the underside of their raft. The carpeted aluminum floor directly under Amber's feet bulged upward a few inches, permanently dented. As she jumped off the little mound, Cherrywine screamed.

Everyone else backed away, eyes rooted to the cabin floor.

The entire room bucked up on its side without warning.

Amber tumbled across the steeply canted floor of the cabin, friction burns from the cheap carpeting blazing across her bare legs and arms. The electric lantern crashed against something and broke, plunging them into darkness. She caught only jumbled, quick glimpses of the others falling also just before she slammed into the base of the wall next to Ray's bunk, her elbow striking someone in the face and several other bodies landing on top of her hard enough to crush the air from her lungs. Loose objects plunked down all around them. Shouts and groans floated up; Cherrywine's keening shrieks rose above them all. Amber braced herself in case the pontoon boat flipped over completely, but the opposite side of the room fell after only a few seconds.

Something in the bottom of the boat gave a sickly creak as their raft righted itself, then everyone began yelling at once.

"Turn a light on!" Cherrywine's voice pleaded.

"I told you it was gettin bad out there!" Carlos called out.

"Dat wadn't no wave, somet'in tipped us!"

The radiation detector was still going haywire. A flashlight came on at last, and Amber found herself face-to-face with the grinning skull of Mr. Watts. She shoved it away as everyone untangled. Once she could stand and made sure nothing was broken, she checked on Ray and Justin and found them both still in their bunks thanks to her homemade seat belts.

Jericho freed the machete from the sheathe on his back. He ran for the cabin door, with Amber right behind him.

Outside, the night was a maelstrom. The wind tore at them. Skirls of freezing rain had her drenched and shivering in seconds. Waves slammed the boat from side-to-side, still growing in size. Lightning—of the plain white variety—turned the whole world into a slow-motion strobe light. The few derelicts still visible around them reminded her of rodeo cowboys trying to ride an angry bull as the seas tossed them. She held the detector's wand in the air and pointed it in different directions until she found that the left side of the boat gave the most reaction.

Something long, flat and scaly slid over the pontoon, working its way onto the boat beside them. It was a few yards long, several feet wide, but mere inches thick, and it took her only half a second to realize it was a gigantic, aquatic flipper. She suddenly imagined an enormous dolphin swimming beside the boat, using this diseased appendage to feel along the deck.

Except this dolphin wanted to eat them, like it had the tattooed pirate.

This was their sea monster, returning for another meal. It had shaken the vending machine, and now it wanted to see what snacks had fallen out.

"*There!*" she shouted, her voice barely audible to her own ears. Jericho spotted the monstrous appendage and brought the machete whistling down at it. The weapon left a long, dark gash in the scaly hide.

The flipper pulled away so hard, the boat rocked heavily. They grabbed on to the captain's chair at the front to keep their balance. From beyond the raft came a deep, bass moan that Amber felt in her bones more than she heard, a sound as mournful as whale song.

"*What de hell is dat?*"

A dark shape breached the rough water in front of them, a bald, leathery dome as big as the roof of a Volkswagen. Two baleful greenish-yellow eyes like dinner plates glared at them, above a set of jaws at least seven feet long, three wide, and full of crooked, dagger teeth.

Eric was right; it really *was* a crocodile the size of a bus. It had to be the largest living creature she'd ever seen.

Watching it as it watched them, she felt the first frayed ends of her sanity start to pull loose. She could rationalize everything else that had happened to them, keep panic away by viewing all of it as one big problem a professor had placed in front of her, a puzzle that had to be solved, but this behemoth's presence couldn't be explained by radiation poisoning...

Jericho held the machete up, as if in challenge, an almost laughable gesture. Its jaws swung open, and the next flash of lightning revealed a scarred, blackened gullet.

From the west, the sky burst into shades of brilliant powder blue. Amber closed her eyes, but the unearthly light seemed to blaze right through the lids, worm its way into her brain until she thought she would vomit. When it stopped, she saw the gigantic creature pull back, looking toward where the light had been, and dive beneath the frothing waves once more.

Tuan exited the cabin and stood behind them.

"Dat was number four, right?" Jericho asked him, holding up fingers to get the number across.

Tuan nodded. "Next...*big*."

"How long we got?"

He tapped his watch, then held up first two fingers, then three, then shrugged.

"He doesn't know," Amber interpreted. "Two or three hours, maybe."

"Den let's get off dis damn raft before dat t'ing comes back."

11

The light was so bright this time, Lito thought for sure it must be the 'big flash' Tuan had warned them about, the one that had turned day to night, or whatever he'd been talking about. A queasy cramp ripped through his stomach. Lito's vision cleared just in time for him to avoid scraping the jet ski against the freighter. He twisted around on the seat to look behind him. The speedboat had drifted past, missing him entirely. His attackers must've been just as walloped by the blue burst. Damn thing had saved him from being creamed.

And if it really is radioactive, maybe you can all go shopping for dentures together after your teeth fall out.

Lito realized his hand was empty; he'd lost the pistol at some point. If there was no fight, he'd have to rely on flight. He throttled up the jet ski and blasted away. Now was his best chance to lose them, while they were still recovering. Once he was sure he'd gotten clear, he could double back and try to find the others.

Ahead was a rough corridor formed by the freighter on his right and an ongoing line of smaller ships to his left, all of them packed so tight there was barely room to squeeze between. They crashed into each other as they rose and fell, some of them hard enough to scrape hulls and groan against one another. To his left, a nice-sized fishing boat was crushed as a heavy steel cutter rolled over on top of it.

Lito followed the corridor and jumped a wave that swept under him, feeling like Evel Knieval, and landed hard enough to jar his tailbone and nearly flip him over the handlebars. These were no conditions to be riding a craft like this in. Jagged whitecaps stabbed upward from the ocean surface, crashing together like cymbals. If one of them came at him from the wrong direction, he'd be swept right off this thing.

As it turned out, he didn't have to worry about it for long.

The canal took a sharp right turn, and he entered an expanse of open water filled with boats bobbing as randomly as driftwood on a stream. The tiny, thrumming jet ski engine between his legs began to sputter. His speed dropped. Within seconds, he was sitting dead in the water.

Lito twisted the key again. The gas gauge needle was still at the halfway mark, so he had to assume the peppy little junker had finally given up the ghost, or that he'd used the only unspoiled gas Jericho had put in the tank.

Water washed over him, rocking the whole craft onto its side. He dug his heels in and rode the seat until it righted. He had to get off this thing. Between the gunmen and the growing squall, he was entirely too vulnerable just sitting here.

The waves pushed him steadily toward the stern of a two-story craft ahead, a huge, older-model yacht even bigger than Eric's vessel. Something about its paint job looked odd. When the sky overhead lit up with another burst of crooked lightning followed by an angry drum solo of thunder, he realized why: the entire vessel was covered with dark, rope-like vines that had completely overrun the deck, some of them as thick as his wrist.

Dread uncoiled in the pit of his stomach.

No choice. When the next wave tossed him up, Lito jumped from the seat of the jet ski and dogpaddled toward the boat. Something bobbed up to the surface of the water beside him. He almost screamed—Amber and her goddamn sea monster stories had gotten to him a little more than he realized—before recognizing the walkie-talkie, in its waterproof plastic bags. He grabbed it before it could get away.

The water was too rough to stay afloat in, and the seaweed clinging to him only made it worse. They felt like tiny fingers skittering against his skin as the ocean tossed him. He rode each crest as it lifted, and was finally slammed against the hull of the yacht by a sudden surge. Panic seized him as he clawed at the slick side of the boat for purchase. The undertow tried to suck him beneath, but he managed to grab one of the thick vines growing down from the boat.

Lito shimmied up them one agonizing inch at a time, expecting the greenery to tear lose at any second, but they held his weight. They were slimy to the touch even with the rain on them. The whole yacht rocked back and forth as he climbed. Nausea bubbled through his stomach; it was years since he'd been seasick. He concentrated only on hauling himself up until he tumbled over the bulwark and sprawled on the overgrown rear deck, shivering and exhausted.

During a brief lull between wind gusts, he heard the throaty growl of an engine. He crawled back to the edge to peer over.

The speedboat chugged toward him. A powerful halogen flashlight first picked out his overturned jet ski, then lit up the back of the yacht. Lito ducked again before they could spot him.

The front half of the yacht was all one big cabin. Ahead, the rear wall had been made of glass at some point, but most of the panes were busted out now. Dark vines curled around the doorframes and spilled out onto the deck in all directions.

Lito got to his feet, striving to keep his balance as the floor beneath him tilted at nearly 45 degree angles, first one way and then another. He made his way into the black cabin just as the speedboat arrived behind him.

12

By the time Vishon docked at the yacht's stern, the waves were bouncing them so high Eric's butt lost contact with the speedboat seat. They'd thrown the body of the dead man overboard, where it was quickly claimed by the angry sea. The wind was a constant shriek now, blowing through the net of decrepit ships with enough velocity to knock them off their feet if they weren't careful. The last remaining lackey managed to catch the guardrail with some nylon boat rope and drew them in close.

The yacht's name was stenciled across its wide stern and, even though it was partially obscured by a mass of creeping vines, Eric could still make out the words.

The Family Way.

Why did he know that name? One of his books? And then it came to him, as brilliantly as one of the lightning bolts tearing up the sky above them: the squinty bartender and his sob story. Something about a missing son and pregnant daughter-in-law. The entrance to the cabin waited just on the other side of the short rear deck, gloomy and overgrown.

His balls shriveled at the thought of going in there.

Vishon seemed just as hesitant as he killed the engine and stuffed the speedboat keys in an inside pocket of his windbreaker. He and the other thug studied the yacht as rain washed down their faces. Finally, the Jamaican raised a hand and pointed toward the cabin. "*Porto gotta be in dere! Go on and find 'im!*"

The other man—big, with broad shoulders and cantaloupe biceps—shook his head like a child refusing to look under the bed. "*No way Boss, I ain't goin in there!*"

"*It just be some plants! Now get in dere and bring me 'is 'ead!*"

The thug cast another fearful glance at the other boat as waves slammed against them. "*I don't wanna go alone!*"

"*You fuckin* punanny!" Vishon slapped him across the top of his bald head, then turned and yanked Eric to his feet by the collar of his shirt. He leaned close enough for Eric to get a good look at his gold-capped incisors and shouted, "*Go on rich boy, you get to go first! And if you try to run from I...*" The barrel of his uzi dug into Eric's ribcage. "*You gonna get whatever Porto does, ransom or no!*"

He shoved him forward. Eric waited for a lull between waves and then hoisted himself up and over the guardrail of the yacht, falling sideways and giving his hip a painful bruise when the deck pitched to the right. He stayed down until the other two climbed aboard and dragged him up, then pushed him ahead of them through the shattered back wall of the cabin, like villagers offering a sacrifice to a hungry god.

13

The interior of the yacht cabin was more like a South American jungle than manmade living quarters: dark, muggy and full of vegetation. The strange, gooey vines grew across every surface, dangled from the ceiling, wrapped around the furniture and fixtures.

Lito couldn't decide which was creepier: this place or the abandoned houseboat with its layer of dust.

But at least he didn't have to wait for his eyes to adjust to the darkness; in here, the leafy plants gave off a cool, blue glow, casting just enough light for him to see without distorting his vision. It was like being inside some cave from *National Geographic*, a place with fluorescent lichen on the stone walls, except there was something almost sickly about this light. This whole radioactive theory was looking more and more plausible.

Lito had no idea where he was going, except away from the gunmen. If nothing else, maybe he could find a place to hole up for a last stand. He made his way quickly through the interior, wishing he had Jericho's machete but settling for his hunting knife to slash at the iridescent vines that got in his way.

From the rear deck, the cabin opened up into a spacious living room with lumps of plant-covered furniture scattered around. A few chairs were overturned, and one recliner was turned around to face the corner, but Lito was able to make his away across a long, open space up the middle without tripping. He was cold, wet, and shivering, and the sound of the storm followed him from one end of the boat to the other. The yacht continued to rock from side-to-side; long, slow yaws that first pitched him at one wall and then the other. Each tilt caused an avalanche of loose bric-a-brac and shifting furniture he was forced to dodge. He leaned with the yaws to keep his balance, but one unexpected tilt when he reached the front of the room tossed him up against a glass bulkhead obscured by plants as thick as his forearm, a see-through wall sectioning off the communal space from the galley. A large crack skewed across the glass from his impact, but it held. He pushed away from the bulkhead and went through the gap that served as a doorway just a few steps further down.

The galley on the other side had a gas-fed range and full-size electric refrigerator. On the far side was a doorway leading to the lower quarters, but it was choked with more plants. They grew around the doorframe in all directions, layer upon layer of glowing, tangled vines, like slimy electrical cables. Whatever had spawned these freakish growths must've come from down there. In his head, Lito imagined a few ferns or an ivy, some small houseplant kept by the lady of the boat, grown rampant in her absence, aided by the bursts of radiation. He hacked at them frantically, wanting to move further into the boat to hide from his pursuers.

One of them twitched beneath his palm, a small but deliberate movement.

Lito stumbled away, giving a yip of surprise. The vines in front of him jittered against one another angrily, producing a sound like a rattler's tail. The juices from the ones he'd sliced dripped onto the floor, forming a neon puddle. Its mutilated end curled up, as though looking at him.

He spun around and bolted back out of the room, but ran into a large black man with a submachine pistol coming from the other direction.

They startled each other, rebounding away. The other man tried to get his gun up. Lito slashed out with the knife and cut him across the forearm. The gun dropped to the floor as he clutched the wound.

Lito reared back to strike again, meaning to stab him in the chest and end this as fast as possible but lost his balance as he and the boat tilted in opposite directions. He stumbled back, arms pinwheeling. His attacker took the advantage by grabbing his wrist and sucker-punching him in the face.

The blow caused a starburst of pain across his vision. His legs noodled. This guy was a bruiser, not quite Rabid's size, but he had a good thirty or forty pounds on Lito, all of it muscle. He wrenched the wrist he held up behind Lito's back, forcing him to let the knife fall, then smashed him face-first into the glass bulkhead. This time when they collided, the wall shattered. Lito plunged straight through in a hail of tinkling shards.

He fell in a heap on the other side, bleeding from a dozen small wounds. Whatever fight he had left was gone. He tried to stand, but the guy was on him in a heartbeat, driving the steel toe of one boot into his side. Lito squawked and fell over, clutching his throbbing torso. The rocking of the boat combined with the swirling darkness behind his eyelids served to reinforce his nausea.

"Well, well, Porto. Dis been a long time comin. You t'ink you was gonna run fohevah?" The words had a much more syrupy Caribbean accent than Jericho's.

Lito opened his eyes. The bruiser stood over him, one hand on his bleeding wrist, but the voice had come from deeper back in the room. By the queasy glow of the vines, Lito could see another silhouette, one with a mohawk of limp dreadlocks. And, in a weird enough twist that Lito thought he might be hallucinating, in front of this guy was—

"Richie Rich? Zat you?" Lito gave a chuckle that made his ribs ache. "Jesus, you must keep goons on retainer to get these guys here so fast."

Eric held up his hands. "Not that I don't love seeing you get your ass kicked, but I got nothing to do with these dickheads."

"Shut up, botha you." The owner of the first voice stepped forward, holding on to the thick vines growing along the wall to keep his balance, and Lito recognized Vishon the Vicious. The man squatted in front of Lito. "Da Dominicyan sends his regards, *bomba claat.*"

"Christ. *That's* what this is about?" Lito coughed. Pain lanced up his side. "All the shit that coulda killed me in the last five hours, and I end up at the mercy of Santiago's shithead brigade?"

Vishon smiled and reached out to smack his cheek several times. "Lesson numbah one, pirate: keep dat tongue in yo' mouth or I snatch it out." He straightened and ordered his cohort, "Pat 'im down. Might as well take what we cyan get foh dis job."

The bruiser pushed Lito flat to the floor with one foot, then ran a hand down each side of his body. Lito's ragged leather wallet was back on the *Steel Runner*, and the radio was in his back pocket, so there was nothing for them to take. Yet the man's hand stopped at the cargo pocket of his faded shorts anyway, reached inside and drew out an oblong object that, at first glance, Lito couldn't remember being in there.

"What the *hell*?" They all turned to Eric, whose eyes bulged so much from his skull as he took in the statue, they gave his broken nose a run for its money. "How did...? You fucking lowlife, you took that off the houseboat?"

"Nope. Amber did."

"Oh, that cunt whore! That's *mine*!"

"Actually, I think it's mine. She gave it to me. Finders keepers, and whatnot."

The bruiser passed the ugly little statue over to Vishon, who looked it up and down. "De way you two arguin, I guess dis t'ing worth a few coins."

"Listen man, I *need* that." Eric held out his hands, wobbling for balance as the deck swayed. "These assholes stole it from me, so you gotta give it back."

"I don't got to do not'ing, white boy."

"*Just give it to me!*" Eric sounded shrill and desperate. "I can pay you whatever you want!"

"Watch out," Lito told Vishon from the floor. "This kid loves to pay with credit he don't have."

"*Shut the fuck up, scumbag!*"

"*'Ey!*" The Jamaican said sharply. "We cyan 'andle bizness latah." He slipped the figure into an inner pocket of his jacket. Eric's eyes followed it with the eagerness of a hungry dog watching a T-bone.

"Boss, can we just finish this?" The bruiser looked around uncomfortably. "This place is givin me the fuckin creeps. And that light earlier..."

"You talkin 'bout the blue flash?" Lito asked. "Yeah, you know what that was, *cabron*? Your first taste of radiation poisonin."

He gaped. "Whattaya mean, 'radiation poisonin?'"

"One of these ships out here's leakin plutonium or somethin. We'll prob'ly all be dead in a few hours."

The bruiser's eyes flicked around in wide circles, as though he might actually be able to see the deadly radiation creeping up on him. "You're fuckin with me."

"Nope. 'Fraid not. That's why all the derelicts are out here. And what do you think's up with these plants? It's just like in the old black-and-white horror movies. Everything glows and gets gigantic."

"Oh Jesus, Boss!" The thug stepped away from the vines, moving to a clear spot in the middle of the room. "We gotta get to a hospital!"

"'Im's lyin, you chickenshit. 'Ere." Vishon tossed him a key-ring. "Go start da boat and take da white boy wit you. If we all gonna be dead in a few hours, we better catch up wit da rest of his crew. Make sure 'is boy finish dem off."

Lito frowned. "My boy?"

Vishon's grin was wickedly sharp this time. "Degas? You little cabin boy? 'Im made a deal wit da Dominicyan. 'Im take care of you pathetic assholes, bring in dat shitty boat of yours, and all be forgiven."

"No."

"How you t'ink we knew where to find you? 'Im bring back yo' head, 'im even gets a new job runnin product." Vishon laughed, jiggling his mop of dreadlocks, then winked. "Maybe we help out wit dat one."

"Carlos. Shit." Lito closed his eyes and thought about the boy's 'business' in town earlier today. Jesus, he'd known the kid was miserable, but a betrayal like this seemed beyond even him.

"Don' be too mad at 'im." The Jamaican leveled off his Uzi at Lito's chest. "If da deed ain't done by da time we get back to 'im, dat li'l *batty* boy'll be keepin you comp'ny in 'ell."

"Can you just get this over with? I forgot how much I hate listenin to you mouthy fuckin dreads."

Vishon pulled the trigger.

14

A tingle of excitement built in Eric as he realized Vishon was about to kill Lito. His head whirled with fragmented images: his father, kicking the shit out of rival 'businessmen' in the warehouse by the river...the big tattooed guy getting dragged beneath the water...firing the uzi and killing one of the thugs...

He found himself wishing it were him taking out the pirate scumbag. Preferably with his bare hands.

The Jamaican's finger tightened on the uzi's trigger.

But, as he opened fire, a dark shadow whickered through the air, latched onto his forearm, and jerked the gun off target. A trail of bullets ripped across the yacht's ceiling.

"De *fuck*?" Vishon stood with his arm suspended in the air, a fat length of florescent blue vine wrapped around his wrist and stretched taut to the ceiling. He tried to yank free, raised his other hand to pry at the plant, but another glowing loop uncoiled from the wall and whipped around his midsection. It dragged him backward as they watched, pinning him against the bulkhead.

"*'Elp me!*" he screeched.

The whole room came to life.

Vines whipped the air, peeling away from the walls and rearing up from the floor like snakes, their glow pulsating as they twitched and spasmed. The other thug swatted at them like a man going after mosquitoes. A horde ensnared his legs and jerked his feet out from under him. He hit the ground squarely on his chin, leaving a spatter of blood and a single tooth that rolled away on the canted floor.

Eric felt several of the tendrils slither across his own chest. He flung them off and squirmed away before they could get a grip. He tried to run, but misjudged the current slant of the deck. He fell, landing in front of a recliner that was turned to face the corner.

As he looked up, the chair creaked around to face him.

Eric saw what was in it...and screamed.

15

When the vines came to life, Lito thought of the angry quaking from the other room, a dry rattle like corn stalks rasping against each other. By the time he'd come to terms with the fact that he hadn't been shot, the entire cabin of the yacht was overrun with waving, neon tendrils, like glow sticks at a rave, every surface squirming and wriggling. Most of them seemed preoccupied with the others at the moment. He jumped to his feet amid the chaos, staying hunched and low, and tried to figure out what the hell to do.

The keys, he thought. *You better get those keys if you want off this deathtrap.* Some part of him, at least, was still cool and collected enough to form a plan. All that meditation must be paying off.

Lito turned to the bruiser on the ground, unconscious or dead. The keys to the speedboat were still clutched in one palm. He knelt, plucked them out, and dropped them in his shirt pocket just as the plants tugged the man's body away, reeling it in toward the galley and, he suspected, that doorway leading below deck, where the growth had been thickest. The thought of those vines parting to allow their victim passage into the infested bowels of the yacht sent a violent shiver up Lito's spine.

The boat shifted on the turbulent waters again, causing the flood of objects to tumble and slide toward the opposite wall. He saw his knife among the flotsam this time and snatched it up.

Vishon was still shouting from where the vines held him to the wall, like a fly in a giant spider's web. Now Eric's voice joined him, and Lito turned to see what the rich kid's problem was while he slashed at the few plants coming at him.

The recliner held in the corner by a net of vines had been freed as they came to life, and now it spun to reveal its sole occupant. One of the charred mutants struggled up out of it, a gaunt, balding woman much worse off than any they'd seen, with half her face sloughing off and a tiny third arm growing from a lump on one of her shoulder blades.

And a grossly swollen belly. She was pregnant to ridiculous proportions, a distended globe hanging off the front of her emaciated frame.

Eric crouched in front her, staring upward, face slack with terror. He tried to back away, crawling on hands and knees, but the vines finally succeeded in hooking him. Several strong stalks lifted him completely off the floor and slammed him against the bulkhead next to the broken glass windows at the rear of the cabin.

The pregnant creature lost interest in Eric when she caught sight of Vishon. She took halting, jerky steps toward him with all three arms upraised, like some hellish marionette. He screamed and wailed as she reached him, pleading for help, but only until she grabbed hold of his face and clawed most of it off. What was left when she finished was just muscle and bone, with one eyeball dangling from its socket. Vishon the Vicious twitched and gurgled for a few seconds before going limp in the embrace of the vines.

She made a ninety degree turn and came at Lito next, as he stood horrified in the middle of the room. Most of her clothes had rotted off, leaving the huge lump of her stomach exposed. The skin there, unlike the rest of her sagging flesh, was blackened and bruised-looking, stretched so tight it looked like plastic. As he watched her approach, the shape of tiny hands were visible, pressing against its surface from within.

Lito couldn't move. He truly believed these things hadn't been anything close to human in a long time, but something in his moral code just wouldn't let him fight a pregnant woman.

He broke his paralysis just before she lunged, raising one foot and kicking her squarely in that bulging mass of hard flesh. The skin shredded as she flailed backward, releasing a flood of foul-smelling guts and a hideous, squirming monstrosity about the size of a full-grown beagle. The deformed infant hit the floor, shot him a reproachful look, and hissed.

Lito turned to flee. This was a nightmare, worse than anything he could imagine. His cool was gone, and if he didn't find calmer waters to drop a mental anchor in, then no amount of deep breathing or searching his inner chakra would be able to put him back together.

As he ran for the shattered glass at the back of the cabin, fending off the last few loose vines as they came at him, Eric yelled, "*Hey, help me! Don't you fucking leave me, asshole!*"

Lito was in such a blind panic, he almost ran right by the kid, but stopped short of stepping back out into the rain. He hacked at the vines holding Eric in a blind panic, somehow managing not to cut the younger man, and glanced over his shoulder as he worked. The woman lay on the floor, unmoving, but the freakish baby crawled toward them on stubby limbs. In seconds, Eric was free.

"*Let's go!*" Lito tried to pull him outside, but he jerked away.

"*Not yet!*"

Eric crossed the room quickly, leaping over the infant—it held up one stubby, gnarled fist to grab at him—and the remains of its mother. He went for Vishon where the vines still held him in their luminescent embrace, reached into his jacket, and pulled out the statue.

Then he took the time to perform a massive snort that shook his upper body, and spat a huge wad of phlegm into the dead man's mangled face before running back toward Lito.

Together, they sprinted out onto the rear deck of the yacht. The storm was in full swing, but that was the least of Lito's worries. A few of the vines had stretched over onto the speedboat, and Lito cut them away before jumping down. The smaller vessel rocked and jumped with each wave that crashed over it. The damn thing could break apart in weather this bad. If it got any rougher, there was no way they could survive on it.

But it was either take their chances on the speedboat, or try to ride out the storm on the yacht.

He found that decision very easy to make.

"*Go, get us outta here!*" Eric demanded. He plopped down into a seat and held on as the craft was slammed against the yacht's stern.

Lito jammed the keys in the ignition, started the engine, and throttled up. He had to cup a hand over his eyes just to be able to see as he navigated through the narrow canals formed by the other derelicts. The ocean had become a living, undulating carpet, the smaller whitecaps joining together in the heart of the storm to form long, rolling waves that continued to grow in height. Finally, when he had them back out in less clogged waters, Lito turned to the west and pushed the engines as fast as they would go.

The sky was far too dark to see the silhouette of the cruise ship any more, but he knew it was out there somewhere ahead, waiting to gobble them all up.

7

ALL ABOARD

ERIC ON A LEASH

WHAT THE CALENDAR SAID

CHERRYWINE RUNS

1

The pontoon raft was at the mercy of the storm as the swells grew worse; rowing the vessel wasn't even an option.

Most of the group took shelter in the cabin. Cherrywine made herself useful by tending to Justin and Ray, while Carlos worked frantically to bail out the water that seemed to be flooding them from all directions. It was a pointless task, considering every time he opened a window to dump out a bucket, even more water blew in. Most of them had puked already, the violent rocking of the boat inducing a nausea from which there was no escape. The best they could do at this point was hold on and hope they didn't capsize or get dashed against one of the derelicts.

And that the monster didn't return. Amber and Jericho had agreed not to tell the others what they'd seen, since there was little they could do about it.

So she braced herself in the shack's doorway, where she could see outside. The sheer violence of the squall both amazed and terrified her. The wind's howl was punctuated every few seconds by fierce thunderclaps, and gigantic waves crashed over the front deck now, one second attached to the ocean surface, the next shattering across their bow like a crystal vase, spraying a torrent of briny, frothy, seaweed-ridden water. Jericho and Tuan clung to the captain's chair and control console out there, to keep from being washed overboard.

But the sea beyond the front of the ship—cast in muted, bare-bulb overtones with every frantic fork of lightning—was empty. Before surrendering to the storm, they'd exited the main mass of derelicts on their way to the cruise ship, rowing into the first patch of open water they'd seen since leaving the *Steel Runner*. They'd tried to maintain a course toward the towering shadow, their only hope for survival, but now...she had no idea where they were.

Out on the deck, Jericho suddenly raised a hand and pointed. He shouted something she couldn't hear over the roar of the storm.

She looked past him, straining to see into the night. All at once, the maelstrom of darkness and rain parted in front of them, and the cruise ship loomed out of the tempest. It sat diagonal across their path, the blocky rear end pointed at them. The vessel was far larger than any other ship they'd encountered, dwarfing their small raft like a pebble in the face of a mountain. She had to crane her head back to take in its entirety, the wall of the hull stretching seven or eight stories over their heads and dimpled with rows of round portholes, and several open levels stacked on top of one another beyond that.

Lightning gave them a brief, dirty sort of daylight. In it, she could make out huge patches of rust that had overtaken the ship's exterior. Where once there had been gleaming white, now there was only a dark maroon. The cancer was so bad in some spots it had eaten holes straight through the metal. A steel girder was visible through a massive hole near the front, like a rib bone poking through the skin of a rotted animal carcass.

A weathered name was still visible across the ruined hull: *The Atlantic Queen*.

And below that, *Ozuna Sun Cruise Lines*.

Where in God's name had it come from?

Jericho gestured frantically to Tuan. Amber let go of the door and lurched out into the storm. She made it out to them and found a grip on the captain's chair just as a wave swept across the deck. Amber recalled some water amusement park she'd been to as a girl, where she'd waited in heady anticipation on a bridge overpass for one of the rides to come hurtling down a steel track and pass beneath them, throwing up a tsunami as it splashed down, a watery avalanche hard enough to shove them back a few steps. Oh, how she'd giggled and even waited for the next car to come so she could experience it again, but this wave wasn't fun like that; the force of it sent her muscles into a state of shock, like slamming into a brick wall. Or having the brick wall slam into *you*.

She spat out a mouthful of salt water and shouted, "*What's going on?*"

"*We have to board dat t'ing, or we're dead!*"

"*How? Climb up the side?*"

Again, Jericho pointed, this time toward the stern of the enormous craft. When she squinted, Amber could make out a long, sloping ramp connected to the back of the cruise ship, leading up to a gaping, square entrance in the hull that looked like a cave.

"*Small craft launch!*" Jericho told her. "*De bay door's open! De current is carryin us dat way, so we'll try to steer toward it! Get everybody ready to go!*"

Jericho and Tuan stayed at the wheel, leaning on one side to try and keep the pontoon's rudder pointed the right direction, while she ran back inside.

Minutes later, the front of the raft slammed up onto the ramp, the pontoons squealing against the metal.

"*Go!*" Jericho yelled. "*Dis won't hold forever!*"

They stormed the cruise ship like soldiers at Normandy. Carlos was first off; he leapt from the pontoon boat as soon as it touched down, then scrambled up the ramp without looking back. Tuan came right behind him, but he waited to catch Cherrywine in his arms when she jumped down, then carried her up like Tarzan.

Jericho dragged Ray in a makeshift travois they'd created from one of the cabin's bunks; the man was still unconscious, but he awoke and cried out when the back end of the sling slammed against the ramp.

Amber came last with Justin, who insisted he could make it on his own. They were forced to leave most of the pirates' equipment, but she hefted Jericho's bag of tools and the VHF scanner as they ran for the edge together.

No sooner had their feet left the deck of the raft then the waves ripped the vessel away from its tenuous mooring. Amber looked over her shoulder and watched as the raft got pulled away into the night, where she soon lost sight of it.

2

They wearily climbed the ramp that Jericho had called a 'small craft launch' and entered the room at the top. Amber understood what the place was for as soon as she got a look at the dank interior in the beams of their flashlights. It was no more than a rectangular metal room with a clerk counter in the corner, the walls lined with recreational conveyances like paddleboats, one- and two-man kayaks, jet skis—big, name-brand SeaDoos this time—and even a few small speedboats on wheeled trailers to get them down to the water, all meant for patrons to rent and launch from the ramp behind them whenever the cruise ship was docked. They were in bad shape, metal parts rusted, covered in mildew and rot, cracks webbed across their plastic parts. A sign mounted on the wall behind the rental desk gave prices, but it was so faded, she could barely make out the letters.

The wind blew in through the open bay door, creating a chilly draft that goose pimpled their wet skin, but at least its roar was dampened enough to give their eardrums a much-needed rest. The group collapsed in the middle of the floor, exhausted. Justin straddled one of the Sea-Doos like it was a kid's ride outside the grocery store, while Cherrywine sprawled across Tuan's lap. He gave an uncomfortable glance around, as though unsure what to make of her. Carlos crawled into the narrow space between two kayaks, where they heard him retching. Amber still felt a little queasy herself, but it helped being on the cruise ship. The massive craft rode so heavy in the water, it would take hurricane levels of turbulence before they would feel it as badly as they had on the pontoon.

She lay still and tried not to think about the pounding behind her eyeballs, watching Justin as he leaned over to rest his head on the handlebars of the beaten jet ski. It made her think of Lito for a second, jetting away like some action movie hero with the speedboat on his tail, and a curious ache pressed on her guts from the inside.

After a few minutes of silence, she reached into the knapsack of supplies and pulled out the battered walkie-talkie. "Lito, are you there?" she asked. "If you can hear us, we made it to the cruise ship. We're on board now."

"Lady, Lito's fuckin dead!" Carlos told her. He stood up, wiping his lips with the back of one wrist, and made his way drunkenly to the top of the ramp. Rain blew in the wide bay door at an almost horizontal angle. He stood in the spray, looking down the ramp.

"We don't know that for sure."

"Whatever. Don't see why *you* give a shit." He flung a hand out toward the sea. "Great! Just fuckin great! The raft's gone! Now we're stuck here!" His voice rang against the high, metal walls of the room.

"Only choice." Jericho turned over onto his back and rubbed at his temples, kneading the flesh in little circles. "Couldn't have survived out dere much longer. We got to ride out de storm here, give Lito a chance to catch up."

Carlos snorted. "Yo, did you not just hear me, fuckhead? Lito. Is. *Dead!* Whoever those muhfuckahs were in the speedboat, they smoked his ass by now! We gotta—!"

"Shut your goddamn mouth." Ray's voice was surprisingly strong and clear from where he sat propped against a rust-eaten paddleboat. The gunshot in his side must've broken open again in the charge to get off the pontoon boat; the makeshift bandages Amber had tied around his bare waist were rapidly turning crimson. She forced herself up and went to examine it while he spoke. "Lito ain't dead. And even if he was, that puts *me* in charge, so I'm the one that's gonna be issuin orders around here, not you."

Carlos turned away, shaking his head and muttering something about 'what a great fuckin job he was doing,' and stumbled over Tuan's outstretched legs. "And yo, who the hell is this chinky shithead anyway, starin at me with his slant eyes? We the fuckin dog pound now, takin in strays and shit? Bad enough we still haven't hogtied the sick guy over there!"

Amber realized she hadn't introduced the young Vietnamese man to the others; they'd been running non-stop since the second he came on board. "His name's Tuan. He's…a soldier." She tucked her wet bangs behind her ear and used a flashlight to check Ray's gunshot wound. It looked clotted, the fresh bleeding no more than a trickle. Her only medical training was a CPR class she'd taken at school her sophomore year, but she figured if the man wasn't dead or in shock by now, then the bullet hadn't hit anything vital. "He offered to help us if we'll tow his ship out of here when we leave." She gave a tentative glance up at Ray's face. "Lito agreed."

"Well, he's more of a gentleman than the rest of you." Cherrywine sat up and threw her arms around the collar of Tuan's stained jumpsuit. A look of confusion crossed his pale, round face before he gave a wide grin and hugged her back, his hands resting just above her hips. "Thanks for helping me back there… uh, Private? Is that right, sweetie?"

Amber gave her a tired smile. "He doesn't speak English, Cherry."

The stripper grabbed one of Tuan's hands and held it to the chest of her borrowed t-shirt, right between her huge breasts. "Then maybe I can thank him some other way."

Jericho grunted. "Maybe you can also t'ank him for gettin us in dat mess in de first place."

"What are you talking about?"

"T'ink 'bout it. Dose guys wit de guns showed up when we boarded deir boat."

Amber tied a new bandage around Ray made from strips of her own shirt sleeves and scooted back. "Tell them. Tell them what you told me, right after you were shot."

Ray regarded her with bloodshot eyes and then said to the others, "They weren't shootin at our new friend over there. They were after us, like they have been for the past five months."

Carlos whirled around at the edge of the ramp so fast his feet almost went out from under him on the slick floor. "The Dominican? Yo, you sayin those bitches were *Santiago's* men?"

"Only thing that makes sense. And before you ask, I don't know how they found us out here, unless they followed us all the way from Prince George."

"Aw, shhhhit," Jericho hissed.

"Can't be," Carlos mumbled. His eyes latched onto the floor, but they were glassy and faraway suddenly, pupils bouncing around like they planned to escape from his head. He sidled away from the door, circling as far around the outer edge of the room as possible, stopping only after he'd reached the rental desk.

"Look," Amber said, jumping in before someone else could take control of the conversation, "I think there are things far more important we need to discuss right now then whatever drug dealers are after you guys."

Ray asked, "Like what?"

"Everything that we learned from Tuan." She gave them a brief rundown of the conversation about Tuan's ship. "The reason all the people and animals around here are mutating is because of radiation exposure."

"From what?"

"They don't know, they just picked it up on their instruments. They survived inside their ship for the past five days because it's shielded, and they've seen a pattern. After every fourth flash of blue in the sky, some kind of...of radiation wave hits all of these ships. And that last one...that was number four."

"Blue..." Justin muttered, from his seat on the jet ski. They all turned to look at him, but he didn't raise his head. "Beautiful..."

"So we just left their boat?" Cherrywine asked. "It could've, like, protected us from this...radiation, or whatever...and we just *left*?"

"Storm woulda killed us if we'd stayed on dat t'ing," Jericho muttered. "I see dat now. But we only got a couple of hours at most before dis next wave of radiation hits..."

"So let's fuckin go!" Carlos yelled from the far side of the room. He waved his arms in panicked circles. "Yo, we gotta go, right *now*! Let's just...find the parts and get back to the ship!"

"Just a minute, there's something else," Amber said. "Back on Tuan's ship, he tried broadcasting to the voice on the radio. And it answered him, in Vietnamese, told him to leave. I wanna try it on your scanner in English and see if we get a different response."

"Who the fuck cares? If it's sayin for us to leave, then let's do it!"

"But this could be important!"

Ray told her, "We don't got time for science experiments. We make ourselves scarce first, in case that speedboat comes back. Then we start looking for the fuel hose and another way off this ship, so we're ready to roll if...*when* Lito gets here. Jer, you said you needed a maintenance room, right? Where would that be?"

"You got me. Dis ship is huge. We need a schematic map. Dat means de bridge."

"Then the bridge is where we're headed."

"Okay, *c'mon*!" Carlos urged.

"Hold up," Jericho told him, sounding irritated. "How're we supposed to get dere, Ray? We got two people who can't walk—"

"I can walk," Justin said softly.

"Even so." Jericho lowered his voice, "you know how many of dose t'ings could be on dis ship?"

"We have the detectors, remember?" Amber dug the device she'd used before out of the equipment bag. "They'll warn us."

"Yeah, and what good is dat gonna do if we're trapped on dis ship with whatever dey warn us about?"

Ray shook his head. "I don't give a shit about that. Lito is comin, and we're not gonna tell him all we did was sit around with our thumbs jammed up our asses while we waited. Now let's move."

They all nodded and began clambering up. Amber was so exhausted and sore she could barely move, but she forced her muscles to keep working. Jericho went about handing out weapons and the remaining ammunition, like a dreadlocked Santa Claus. He shot her a questioning look when she held out her hand, until she pulled Lito's revolver from the back of her shorts and brandished it. He debated with himself for another second and then gave her a little cardboard box half-filled with bullets. She figured out how to open the cylinder herself, and refilled each of the six chambers.

While they worked with Ray's makeshift stretcher, she went and sat down behind Justin on the jet ski's saddle seat.

"We don't have to do this, you know. You can stay here if you're not up to it. I'll even stay with you."

Justin sat up and turned halfway around to sit sideways on the long seat. "I'm feeling better, actually."

He didn't look it. His skin was sallow and pale, chest working like a bellows.

"You need to rest," she told him. "Once we make it to this bridge, you've got to lie back down."

"Amber, I may not have much longer—"

"Don't say that, we're gonna—"

"*Shut up and let me finish*," he snapped, in a tone he'd never used with her. "If I'm gonna die—or turn into one of those things—all I want is to know that you're safe. So I have to ask... what the hell are you doing?"

The question—softly spoken but with an air of bewildered disgust—surprised her. "What do you mean?"

"With this Asian guy on our side, we outnumber these pirates now. One of them is even shot. We can get away from them. So why are you going along with what they say like we're all best friends, and calling their captain on the radio? Hell, they even gave you a *gun*."

"Justin…we…we need them, all right? If we're gonna survive, we all have to stick together." The words came out like an excuse. It was embarrassing to admit, but she'd all but forgotten that just a few hours ago, these people had taken them prisoner.

He shook his head. "I heard you and Cherrywine talking back on the raft. You actually like that Lito guy, don't you? Don't deny it, I can tell. Jesus, I think everybody can." He held up a shaking hand. "I don't care about that—well, I do, but I don't want it to seem like this is some jealousy thing. I just want you to consider what's gonna happen if we make it out of this. You think they're just gonna let us go? This may be our only chance to get away from them. We can find a way back to the Asian guy's ship on our own, and lock ourselves in. Or you and Cherrywine can go in by yourselves and lock me out, if you want."

Amber listened to everything he had to say, her tongue sitting dead in her mouth. She felt ashamed and embarrassed, but also a little scared.

Because she'd noticed something while Justin was talking.

His irises had a faint blue ring around them, a smear across the whites that almost seemed to glow.

Justin reached out and gripped her shoulders, squeezing painfully. "I'm gonna protect you from them, no matter what. I won't let them or anybody else hurt you."

Ray saved her from having to answer by calling out, "Let's go!"

She and Justin made their way to the only door leading out of the small craft launch bay and into the interior of the cruise ship.

3

Lito could barely see as he piloted the speedboat into the driving rain, which was why he almost missed the cruise ship in the dark. They hadn't seen another derelict for a good ten minutes; he was beginning to think they'd driven right out of the grouping, gotten lost in the storm, when a sudden wave swelled in front of the boat before he could turn. They hit the inclined plane of water on their port side at close to fifty miles an hour.

"*HANG ON!*" he yelled to Eric.

The uneven ramp popped them completely out of the water in a lazy corkscrew. The boat slewed onto its starboard side in midair. Lito clung to the steering wheel. For a second it seemed as though the boat might tumble over all the way, dumping them out and surely snapping their necks in the process, but then itevened out and came down hard. Both he and Eric were thrown forward by the impact, falling to the floor. Another wave crashed over on top of them, filling the boat with salt water and seaweed.

"*Get some of this bailed out!*"

"*With what, my goddamn hands?*"

"*Just do it! We gotta keep movin!*" It seemed like the squall had reached its zenith, the water starting to calm, but Lito figured it was still more than enough to drown them.

He slid back into the driver's seat. The engine sputtered as it spun them around in a weak circle. According to the compass, their bow was turned to the north now.

Eric leaned over his shoulder and pointed along the sharp wedge of the speedboat's front end. "*What is that?*"

At first, Lito could see nothing in the swirling murk of the storm...but then his eyes picked it out, a slightly lighter shade against the darkness. A pulsing glow in a very familiar shade of blue. It looked like a lighthouse flame, coming from almost dead ahead.

Weren't there old ghost stories about that, too? Blue flames on the Sargasso, another part of the Bermuda Triangle legend? Or did that have something to do with swamps?

He throttled up and headed toward it, at a reduced speed. He couldn't tell if they were getting any closer. That sickly light—a few shades darker than the iridescent vines back on the yacht, but the exact color of the flashes in the sky—looked like the neon glow of Vegas on the horizon from miles away. It was so bright he had to wonder why they hadn't seen it before the storm, either from the *Steel Runner* or the field of derelicts, but a few seconds later he had his answer, when the huge shadow of the cruise ship's port side appeared off to the east. They had somehow circled all the way around the big bastard in the storm. From the opposite side, its enormous silhouette would've completely hidden the strange beacon away.

For a long moment, he kept their course locked between the glow and the ship, trying to decide between the two. He knew they needed to get to the cruise liner and find the others (*if they'd even made it this far, which was a big if on that rattletrap pontoon*), but he suddenly *really* wanted to see what that light was all about. He wasn't drawn to it, as those mutant pirates had been—in fact, it made him feel a little green around the gills just looking at it—but intuition told him whatever answers were to be had about this whole mess would be found out there.

The question is, do you actually want *them?*

Before he could answer that, Eric slapped him across the face, hard enough to rattle his teeth. "*What are you doing, dickhead! Wake up and get us outta the storm!*"

That decided him. That, and Carlos. There was no time to go exploring; he had to save Ray and Jericho (*and Amber, don't forget her*) from Carlos before he made his move. The boy had probably only waited this long because he was trying to secure a ride out of here first.

Lito coaxed a little more speed from the Jamaican's boat,

turning away from the blue glow. The gas needle on the gauges behind the wheel read less than a quarter of a tank, but that would still get them back to the *Steel Runner*. Now they just needed a way to get on board the cruise ship.

As they got closer, he spotted the solution. The entire liner was rust-eaten and rotting away. Huge chunks of steel siding were missing, including one long ragged section at the waterline that had penetrated all the way through the double hull just about midship, forming a neat little cove in the side of the boat between two girders of its massive frame. It probably led into a sealed bulkhead or else the entire ship might've sunk by now, but if they could get the door open...

Lito aimed for this. He slowed their speed. Even with the waves tossing them, he was able to maneuver the boat through the hole in the cruise ship's hull. Something metal squealed against the underside of the boat, and they had to duck their heads under the maroon-colored upper edge of the hole, but in the end, the speedboat fit into the space as neatly as a gun in a holster. The wind and rain were blocked, and the walls even kept the worst of the waves away. Lito stood, shrugged out of his shirt without unbuttoning, and wrung as much water out as he could while he checked out the place.

The light from outside was just sufficient to see that the room was part of the maintenance corridors deep in the bowels of the ship, filled with rusty pipes and barnacle-encrusted machinery.

He wondered briefly how long it would take for a vessel of this size to reach such a deteriorated condition on the open seas, to the point where the hull—a slab of metal several feet thick—had been eaten straight through. Thirty years? Forty? Even longer?

Cruise liners of this magnitude had only been built in the last decade.

It was the exact opposite of the flashlight conundrum; instead of something that hadn't logically aged enough, it was something that had aged more than was even possible.

The interior area was sealed, just as he figured. A catwalk led up to a heavy, watertight, steel door with a wheel release in the center. Lito dabbed at some of the worse of the cuts from his plunge through the glass bulkhead, then pulled his shirt back on over his head and did a quick inspection of the speedboat, pocketing the ignition keys. In a storage area under the back bench, he found enough gas reserves to get this boat pretty much anywhere on the eastern seaboard, a waterproof flashlight still in its original packaging, and a fully loaded Walther PPK. Kind of a weird choice for guys that had been carrying submachine guns, but maybe it was a backup piece. After cutting open the flashlight with his knife and popping in the batteries that had come with it, he pulled out the radio he'd been carrying this whole time, removed it from its waterproof bag, and switched it on. "Guys, you read me? Jericho? Ray? Anybody?"

"They're dead," Eric said from behind him. He'd settled down in the leather captain's chair. "All dead. Storm had to've killed 'em all." It was stated as a fact, without the slightest bit of concern. You'd never know the asshole was talking about people that were supposed to be his friends.

"Doesn't mean anything. On a ship this big, they could be out of range. Or it could be all the steel blocking the signal."

"Okay, let's talk about this ship, since we're on the topic. No cruise ship has ever disappeared in the Bermuda Triangle; trust me, I would know. So how the hell is it here?"

"You're preachin to the choir. I've already covered this with people I like a lot more than you. Now get up, we need to find a way to get inside."

Eric snorted and went about inspecting his fingernails. "Man, fuuuuck *that*. You may've dragged me all the way out here, but this is where I get off the insane train. There's not a thing I need bad enough to set foot off this boat."

Lito held up the pistol. "I'm not askin you, rich boy. I need your help."

Eric gave the gun a passing glance, smirked, and shook his head sadly before going back to his manicure. "You know, your days of bossing me around at gunpoint are pretty much over, *Captain.* You're not gonna use that. And even if you were, I'd rather get shot than be torn apart by one of those freaks, or eaten by goddamn plants. I mean, after what we just saw, do you *really* wanna risk going into a dark ship that's been sitting here for God-knows-how-long?" He shivered, but it looked somehow forced to Lito, as if he were doing what he knew was expected of a normal person in a situation like this. The curious thought occurred to him that this was *exactly* what this young, rich gringo wanted, to see more of the wonders of the Bermuda Triangle, but only if his own life weren't on the line, if he could view the monstrosities from a detached distance like they were no more than characters on a movie screen.

Lito stuck the gun in his waistband. "I don't suppose you're at all familiar with the concept of karma, are you?"

"Oh, what, the guy that robs people on the high seas for a living is gonna try to guilt me?" Eric shook his head and leaned back to prop his legs and bare feet on the dashboard. The position caused the little glass statuette to jut from the side of his back pocket. "I'm not getting killed for you, or Justin, or anybody. I'm gonna wait right here until the storm blows over, and then I'm finding a way to leave, with or without you. Deal with it."

Lito lunged forward and wrenched the figurine from his shorts.

"You son of a bitch!" Eric spun in the chair and made to leap at him, but stopped cold when Lito extended his arm and held the narrow glass figure over the rough water beyond the cruise ship's hull. *"OH MY GOD, STOP, WHAT THE FUCK'RE YOU DOING?"*

"Puttin you on a leash."

"Be careful, do NOT drop that!" Eric fell against one of the seats and clasped his hands like a kid in Sunday school. Lito had to admit, it was satisfying to see the *pendejo* grovel.

"I don't know what this thing is rich boy, but I know you seem more concerned with losin it than anything else in your life. So I got a deal for you. You stop actin like a spoiled brat, help me save my crew and your friends from Carlos, and you can have this back."

Eric gave him a black look. His eyes were shiny with hatred. "That's mine. It belongs to *me*. And I shouldn't have to help you stop a mutiny by your own people to get it back. That's your problem, shithead."

Lito opened his hand, allowing the glass figure to drop, and then snapped it closed again, barely catching the statue's head. Eric gasped. "It's either roll over and play fetch on command, or this thing goes to Davey Jones's locker right now. Your choice."

For a second, it seemed the little cunt might keep arguing, but then a faraway look crept into his face, like he was listening to distant music. A grin—wistful and supremely creepy—twitched at the edges of his mouth.

"You okay, rich boy?"

Eric focused again, as though shaking off a daydream. "I'm fine. Lead the way, fucko."

"Well...okay then." Lito slipped the statue back into his own pocket on the leg of his khakis, buttoning the flap over it. "And if you try to get it back before we're through, I'll bash it to pieces."

Eric didn't answer, just stood aside to let him pass. Lito stepped out onto the flooded catwalk. The water came up to his hips and the whole structure creaked under his weight as he waded up to the stairs and then climbed to the bulkhead door to examine it with the flashlight. He gave the wheel in the middle a few experimental tugs, but it was rusted too much to turn.

His unwilling accomplice splashed up beside him. "Were you telling the truth to those assholes earlier? About the radiation?"

Lito reared back and kicked at the flat, metal crossbar that held the door closed. Red flakes rained down in the beam of his flashlight, and the thing snapped after the second time his boot hit it. "Yes and no. We met a couple of military boys out here after you ran off. They told us those blue bursts are some kinda weird radiation. The next one that hits is gonna be bad. We figure that's what's causin everyone around here to look..." A brief mental flash of the pregnant creature, and the horrors contained in its belly. "You know."

Eric rolled his eyes. "And yet you still wanna go wandering around this ship instead of getting our asses out of here? Sure hope the pussy's worth it when you start growing a second head."

"Hey," Lito growled. "Don't talk about Amber that way."

"Amber?" Eric snorted. "I was talking about your friend with the ponytail. But if you think you can pry that ice queen's legs apart any better than Justin could, be my guest."

"So glad I have your blessing. Now gimme a hand with this."

With the two of them putting their shoulders to the door and straining, they were able to shove it open enough to slip through. Stagnant, brackish water poured out onto their feet from the other side, falling through the metal grating to the open ocean and the hood of the speedboat.

"Jesus, that fucking stinks!" Eric pinched his nose closed.

Lito waded into the flood and found a partially submerged maintenance corridor on the other side. He shone his flashlight down it, but it only reached a few yards before the tunnel turned a corner to the right.

"Where to?"

Lito pointed. "Down there. We have to find a way to get to the top of this ship."

4

Tuan and Jericho carried Ray through the dark bowels of the *Atlantic Queen* on his bunk stretcher, reinforced with metal kayak paddles. He said he could try walking, but they forced him to stay immobile. Cherrywine, Justin and Amber stuck close to them, hauling the last of the gear, Cherrywine with the electric lantern, which cast a weak circle of light around them like a shield. Amber clutched Lito's revolver in one hand and the radiation detector in the other. The device gave off no readings except when she pointed the wand too close to Justin, and she was careful to keep it away. Carlos took up the rear, following like a sulky child, occasionally bounding forward to hurry them up. The Hispanic kid had suddenly become a cheerleader for urging them along on their mission.

The exit from the launch bay led out to a wide, two-story mall concourse running up the middle of the ship. The place had to've been opulent once upon a time, a huge shopping plaza designed to serve the tourists' every need, but with no lights or people—not to mention the drip of distant water—it felt more like they were spelunking in a vast cave. There were several broad parallel avenues laid out like city blocks under a high, arched ceiling, and lined with defunct stores, gift shops, eateries, and even a few small casinos, their front windows filled with dusty slot machines that glittered when the lamplight fell on them. Amber was able to read some of the faded names over their entrances. Even though she recognized the familiar logos of Gucci and Starbucks, the establishments were so old and dilapidated, they reminded her of the tomb of some ancient Egyptian pharaoh, uncovered by an archeologist. They had to watch each step also; the decay and corrosion in here was so bad, it had eaten straight through the tile and the steel deck below in places, leaving gaping black pits to the levels below. Amber got an image in her head of the *Atlantic Queen* as one gigantic block of Swiss cheese.

Besides what time had done to this place, it looked like a stampede had come through here. Or maybe even a war. Glass storefronts were shattered, doorways filled with wreckage—overturned tables, chairs, racks of goods and products, broken exercise equipment from a day spa—that spilled out into the walkway under their feet. A few of them were fire-gutted, nothing left but blackened, charred interiors.

And there were bodies also, lying randomly in the rubble or stretched across the tile floor, so shrunken and desiccated they looked more like skeletal rag dolls than human beings. Their condition made it impossible to tell how they died. In a place like this, you expected the air to be heavy with the smell of rot and decay, but it had no scent, as though everything organic—everything capable of stinking—had long since withered away.

The dust more than made up for it though. If it had been bad aboard the houseboat, it was absolutely *epidemic* here, a quarter-foot deep layer of micro-fine sediment that billowed up around each of their footsteps in lazy slow-motion eddies, reminding Amber somehow of an astronaut stepping on the moon surface. It followed them in a cloud like Pig Pen from the Peanuts strip, causing them all to cough and wipe at their watering eyes. Amber's allergies, usually bad in the winter, kicked up until she was sneezing every few minutes.

Otherwise, the cruise ship was oppressively silent, and they did little to break it.

"It's just like in that movie I saw," Cherrywine said finally. Her voice, barely more than a whisper, was still uncomfortably loud in the stillness. Amber suppressed the urge to tell her to shut up.

"How long you t'ink it's been?" Jericho asked over his shoulder, straining with the effort of carrying the front end of Ray's stretcher. "How long has dis t'ing been floating out here, waiting for us to find it?"

"Judgin by the corrosion for a ship this big...fifty years," Ray answered. "Maybe a hundred. Who knows?"

"Really? Cause, I'm not a history major, but I don't think they were buying iPads around the turn of the century." Amber waved the detector at the sleek metal-and-glass front of an Apple store, the emblem above the door smeared with grime.

"Not only dat, but I been around Caribbean ports me whole life, and I ain't never heard of no 'Ozuna Sun Cruise Lines.'"

"You think the government might be covering it up? Not telling us about all the ships that really disappear in the Bermuda Triangle?"

"If this ship was full of people when it ended up out here, there's no way anyone could keep it quiet," Ray said. "Course, if it was full of people, where are they all now?"

At the foot of the stretcher, Tuan stumbled, tripping over the corpse of a child on the floor curled into a fetal ball, and almost dropped his end.

Ray hissed in pain as he was jostled. "Let's take a break."

They lowered him gently to the floor, unsettling a cloud of dust. The others sank down around him, all except for Carlos, who caught up to them and cried, "Yo, what are you doin, get up, we gotta keep movin!"

"We're goin as fast as we can, but if we don't rest, we'll crash out."

"We don't got time! Those guys, they could...!"

"The ones from the speedboat?" Ray asked. "Who gives a shit about them, they won't be able to find us even if they do get on board. I'm more worried about this radiation."

Carlos's jaw flapped a few times. His dark face was tinged with frustration in the lantern light. "Yeah, yeah, the radiation, that too! So let's hurry and find the fuckin hose!"

Ray sat up on the ground, wincing with a hand on his side. "If you're so eager, why don't you scout ahead and start lookin for some way to get us topside? The sooner we get to the bridge, the sooner we get outta here."

Carlos stood there a moment longer and threw a look over his shoulder, as if he expected one of the men from the boat—or perhaps far worse—to be creeping up on him. Both ends of the concourse faded into soupy darkness; it was possible the world no longer existed outside their bubble of light. He snatched a flashlight from Tuan's pocket, picked up the shotgun from the bag on the floor, and hurried away. His footsteps bounced around the empty mall for another thirty seconds before fading away.

"I've never seen that worthless brat be in a hurry for anything." Ray snagged the walkie and attempted another broadcast to Lito in hushed tones, but received no response.

"Maybe he got de right idea." Jericho looked at the ground between his crossed legs. "You know I wanna wait for Lito just as much as you do, but we running outta time."

"When we get to the top, we'll be able to see the entire area. If there's no sign of 'im...then you guys can look for a way off the ship, and I'll wait to see if he shows."

Uneasy silence fell over them until Amber finally said, "As long as we're resting...I wanna try broadcasting on the scanner."

"Jesus, you don't give up, do you?" Ray sighed. "Fine. Do it. At this point, I think I'd welcome a nice Coast Guard cutter."

Amber set aside the radiation detector—making sure the device was still taking a reading on the surrounding area—and dug the scanner equipment out of the bag she'd been lugging on her back. This time, when she turned it on, the Voice of the Deep was so loud, it might have been someone shouting right next to her. The gibbering echoed off the high ceiling above the upper level of the mall, and bounced between the abandoned stores. Beside her, Justin cringed, and Cherrywine buried her face in Tuan's chest.

"Turn it down!" Ray hissed.

"We're practically right on top of dat signal," Jericho said. "I wouldn't be surprised if it was comin from right here, on dis ship."

Amber found the button on the scanner that allowed a broadcast and waited until the current transmission ended. Now that she was here, on the cusp of actually answering that hideous voice, all of her willpower was draining away. She had to remind herself that Tuan had already done it several times.

Finally, when the radio speaker fell silent, she leaned down to the mic and said, "Hello? Can you understand me?"

As before, there was a click followed by the melodic tone. She almost expected to hear the single Vietnamese word again, but instead the voice that answered this time was in English, so emotionless it couldn't even be classified as male or female.

"WARNING, DANGER," it squawked, and, even though she had turned the volume low, once again the speakers blared so loud it made everyone jump. "WARNING, DANGER. ALL... RECEIVERS... ENGINE... FAILURE... BREACH... CRITICAL... LEAVE... AREA... UNSAFE." The message started to repeat, that jerking pause between each word, as if it were having to stop to think about which one went next.

"Turn it off," Cherrywine pleaded. "Please, turn it off, it's horrible!"

"Just a second," Amber said. After the English message repeated three times, and the line was open once more, she leaned to the microphone and asked the question in Spanish. "*Hola? Puede me entiendes?*"

Click, beep, like an old answering machine message starting up, then, "PELIGRO. DESAPARECE...AHORA."

"What did it say?" Jericho asked.

"Pretty much the same thing, 'Warning, leave now.'"

"No, it's more informal than that," Ray argued. "It's closer to, 'Danger, go away now.'"

Amber waited until her turn to transmit came, and this time gave the inquiry in the only other language she knew.

"What are you speakin now?"

"German."

The click and beep came, but this time, there was only silence afterward. Amber turned the scanner back off and chewed on her thumbnail as she thought. The quiet of the deserted cruise ship seemed to rush back in from all sides.

"I don't understand," Cherrywine complained. "What's any of that mean?"

"Does it matter?" Ray shifted on the stretcher. "Does it really matter what this thing is sayin or why it's sayin it? It's not tellin us anything we didn't already know."

"It proves that whoever is broadcasting isn't hostile," Amber said. "They're trying to warn people about the radiation. And whatever setup they have is capable of taking in our transmissions, determining the language, and then answering in kind."

"Yeah, but why is de return message different in every language?" Jericho asked. "It said more in English den it did in Spanish, and way more den in Vietnamese. And it didn't even answer you dat last time."

"Because I don't think these are pre-recorded messages at all. At least, not in each language. The fact that the sentence construction is so awkward makes me believe that the original message is being translated live, for our benefit. This computer—or whatever it is—is using what it has at its disposal."

"I'm not gettin you," Ray said.

Amber rolled onto her knees, gnawing her lip as she tried to think of a way to explain this theory, which she was almost positive had to be right. "One of the biggest pushes in linguistics programs is to develop an interface that can actually learn a language as it's exposed to it. In other words, the more you talk to the computer, the more it's able to speak back."

"Like Furbies!" Cherrywine exclaimed.

Amber threw a jubilant arm around her neck, pulled the girl to her, and planted a smacking kiss on the top of her blonde crown. Cherrywine squealed in delight. "Yes, just like Furbies! If this automated broadcast is like that, then it's going to have a larger vocabulary with whatever language it's had the most exposure to, which, in this part of the world, would obviously be English and then Spanish. For all we know, Tuan might've been the first Vietnamese person it ever had contact with. It might've even picked up the word 'leave' from him, and then parroted it back to warn him. And it didn't answer me in German this time, but if I keep speaking to it, it might." She grinned. "The applications for something like this are...well, priceless."

"Okay, before we start plannin to win first place in this year's science fair," Ray said, "I have to repeat, we already know we need to get the hell outta here ASAP. It's not exactly a revelation."

"Well maybe this is."

The words came from Justin, hunkered at the edge of the lamplight. They all turned to look at him. He held Lito's revolver out with one shaking hand, and Amber realized she'd put the weapon down on the ground when they sat to rest.

"None of you move," he said, then coughed into his other fist. "We're getting out of here right now."

5

Carlos sprinted up the middle of the dark mall until a stitch in his side forced him to stop. He bent overwith his chin nearly touching his knees, and sucked at the humid, dust-filled air. The particles coated his tongue, caused him to cough, but he barely noticed. He felt too anxious. Too desperate to get those other fuckheads moving again.

Because, if Ray was right, and those really were the Dominican's men in the speedboat, then there had been a time limit on the drug lord's gracious offer, one he didn't bother to make clear in their meeting. That, or maybe he hadn't trusted Carlos in the first place. And really, why should he? Carlos hadn't exactly done a bang-up job so far. Three of the *Steel Runner*'s crew were dead (four if you counted Lito in that group, and, god, Carlos certainly hoped he was rid of the man, even if it meant not having his head to present to Santiago), but he could only claim indirect responsibility for one of them. Anger warmed his cheeks at the thought of failing this test, followed by an even more acidic flush of sorrow at missing out on the opportunity.

There is *a third option, muhfuckah*, a sly voice in his head purred. *That Santiago was playin you for a fool from the beginnin.*

He forced himself upright and started running again. The only obstacle in his way was the missing fuel hose, and what a stupid fucking idea that had been. He needed Jericho alive now, to work his magic and either find a replacement or rig up something to get the *Runner* moving, and once that happened, Carlos could finish off the rest of them, including the white kids, and find a way off this ship. He just hoped it would still be in enough time for Santiago to have mercy on him.

Ahead, the concourse opened up into a huge lobby in the belly of the cruise ship, with an ornate chandelier suspended over his head, from which most of the glass had long ago fallen. Far above, he could see an arching skylight that stretched across the entire ceiling. When the ship had been new, this lobby would've been filled with sunlight during the day, and anyone standing where he was now would have had a fantastic view of sky or stars. Now, it was so crusted over, all he could see were the last distant pulses of lightning the storm had to offer. A bank of elevators stretched around the lobby in a semicircle, but they weren't going to carry anyone to the top of the ship anytime soon.

A door to the far left bore a drawing of a stairwell. He hurried to it, jerked it open...

And froze.

The dark stairwell beyond was littered with bodies, stretched out across the steps, and lying over and across one another in the floor at his feet. Carlos *thought* they were bodies, anyway. They weren't dried-out husks like the corpses they'd seen—or even those spongy, melted-looking things the pirates had become—but deformed shapes so twisted he couldn't tell where one ended and the next began.

All of them emitted a cool, blue glow, as if their leathery skin was made of neon.

They lit up the entire stairwell. In the glow, he could see chests rising and falling in easy, gentle rhythms. The goddamn things were *asleep*, like bears hibernating in a den deep in the woods.

Carlos backed up slowly. Every muscle in his body felt as taut as tripwire. When the door he'd just flung open started to swing closed again, the rusted hinges gave an angry squall.

In the stairwell, there was movement. A few heads rose up from the pile of bodies, fastening on to Carlos with eyes that pulsed so brightly with blue light, they were like staring into car headlights. One of them gave a strangled, raspy cry, and that it was all it took to wake up the entire brood.

Carlos spun and ran.

6

Justin was sick.

There was no fooling himself any more. He could feel the disease or radiation or whatever it was working through his guts like a snake, changing him, remaking him. Soon, it would turn him into a creature like that little girl, so he could haunt these derelict ships for all eternity.

But he'd come to terms with that. He could even live—or die—knowing that Amber didn't love him.

What he *couldn't* stand—what he could not tolerate for even another second—was the idea that these lowlifes might get her out of this, only to rape and kill her like they'd probably planned in the first place. Amber may've forgotten what they were, but he hadn't. He would make sure she was safe if it was the last thing he did.

And then, before he could surrender to the siren song of those blue flashes, the ones that now seemed to be inside his head, he would put this gun in his mouth and pull the trigger.

But first things first. He attempted to steady the weapon he'd taken with both hands, but the barrel still wavered wildly between the two remaining pirates. Sweat trickled down his face, and he wiped it on his shoulder. "Show me your hands!"

From the opposite side of the lantern, Ray asked, "What the hell are you doin, kid?"

"*Don't move!*" Justin shouted. "I mean it!" He got to his feet, wobbling unsteadily. The darkness crouching beyond the lamplight seemed tinged with midnight blue to his dizzy eyes. "I will shoot you if you make me!"

"Justin, put the gun down!" Amber begged. "They're not gonna hurt us, don't do this!"

"Bring that flashlight and get up," he told her, without taking his eyes from Ray and Jericho. He continued backing away, toward the nearest mall avenue, and beckoned. "You too, Cherrywine. Your new boyfriend can even come, if he wants. But we're leaving these two here and finding a way off this ship on our own."

"No, we are *not!*" Amber argued. "We will die if we split up, don't you see that?"

"Listen to her," Ray said. "We need you as much as you need us."

"That's bullshit! You're just...just t-trying to confuse me!" Justin paused to cough. A vein in his forehead pulsed fire in tempo with his heartbeat. He *did* feel confused, fuzzy-headed.

And angry. So angry, and he wasn't even sure why.

Justin darted forward, grabbed Amber by the wrist, and hauled her up. "Move! *Now!*"

Cherrywine made a move to rise. "Amber, what do we do?"

"Just stay there, stay with Ray!"

"Do what you want, but we're going!" Justin tugged Amber along, toward the next row of stores, where they could turn the corner and be out of sight. Then they would be safe. Cherrywine and Tuan made no move to follow. What was wrong with these people? To the pirates, he shouted, "Don't try to follow us!"

"Amber, we'll find you," Ray called back.

Justin started to rage at the audacity—them making *him* out to be the villain!—but the little electronic gadget Amber had left on the ground began to emit a fast clicking noise.

7

The cruise ship's maintenance tunnels were a dank, corroded maze. Lito and Eric followed them more or less randomly, avoiding holes, taking ladders or stairs whenever possible, going whichever direction would lead them up. It was claustrophobically hot down here, and Lito wondered what they would do if their only flashlight went out. Eventually they found a hatch leading up to a space that was more of a hallway than the pipe-and-electrical-conduit corridors that took up the very bottom decks of the ship. He shone his light on a door just a few yards away marked 'SECURITY OFFICE A.'

Lito crawled out onto the floor and then offered a hand to help Eric up. The rich prick brushed it off, pulled himself up, and then leaned against the wall to rest. He'd sulked the entire time, following without speaking. Not that the silence hadn't been appreciated, since every time he opened his mouth, Lito wanted to punch him.

He tried the walkie again, got nothing but static. They were just some amateur models he'd picked up at Radio Shack a few years back, not designed to transmit through the heavy steel bulkheads of a ship like this.

Either that, or Eric's right, and everybody else is dead.

"Let's keep movin," he said. "That next wave of radiation is comin."

They approached the door of the security room, an office that had once housed whatever passed for law enforcement aboard this ship, flabby rent-a-cops charged with escorting drunk passengers back to their staterooms. Lito handed Eric the flashlight and said, "Hold this a sec."

As he figured, the metal door was locked. He put his shoulder to it one time, and almost ended up falling straight to the floor when the rusty lock shattered into pieces. Eric snickered.

"You ever get tired of bein a douchebag?" Lito asked irritably.

"You ever get tired of being a fuckup?"

"I don't think you know me well enough to make that call, *gringo*."

"Oh yeah? Tell me, what exactly have you accomplished to-night? Besides losing *my* ship, losing *your* ship, losing your crew, and ending up here while you wait to get fried?"

Lito couldn't argue with that, so instead he stepped through the broken door.

On the other side was a plain office with only one cluttered desk, and several lockers with a duty roster posted beside them. One of the lockers was a metal-screened gun cabinet stocked with nine-millimeter pistols and riot shotguns. Lito figured he could break the lock with some muscle, but there probably wasn't much point; the weapons inside were long past their prime after so much time in the sea air.

A thick glass door offered another exit to the left. It was caked with dust, but when Lito wiped it off, he found 'PORTSIDE SE-CURITY CORRIDOR' stenciled on the glass.

"I think we're headin the right direction," he said. "We're finally gettin to the passenger areas."

The flashlight beam swung away from him.

"Hey," Eric said. "Take a look at this."

He turned to find the younger man bent over the desk. He'd put the flashlight down so that its beam fell across a dusty ceramic paperweight in the shape of a Christmas tree. Lito moved around behind the desk, shoving aside an office chair whose leather seat cushions were dry and cracked open. He figured this was some ruse to get back the statuette, but then Lito spotted what was written along the base of the tree.

Merry Christmas, 2027.

"What the hell...?" He picked the paperweight up and turned it over in his hands. There was no writing anywhere else on the object besides the ever-present MADE IN CHINA stamp on the bottom. "What does it mean?" he asked.

"The same thing *this* means." Eric slapped a hand against a wall calendar dangling next to the desk. It was turned to the month of December, and it claimed, in bright digits striped to look like a candy cane, that the year was 2027. The theme of the calendar must've been something to do with cars, but the picture above the weekly grid was of a sporty little car called the 'Chrysler Dumala,' which looked like some hybrid muscle car.

Lito felt the conscious, thinking portions of his brain try to shut down. "No. No, it's impossible."

"Impossible? Shit, this is the first fucking thing about all this that actually makes sense." Eric's eyes gleamed in the darkness on the other side of the desk. "It kept bothering me, how all these ships could've gone missing in the Triangle and I'd never heard of any of them." He grinned wickedly. "Well, we've never heard about any cruise liner disappearing because it *hasn't happened yet.*"

8

Amber didn't struggle as Justin pulled her away. She couldn't risk one of the others getting shot, as hard as it was to imagine Justin opening fire like a desperate criminal. But this wasn't him. This fever was affecting his judgment, she was sure of it. So she would wait until they were away from the others, then try to reason with him.

But all that ended when the radiation detector she'd left on the ground went berserk.

And then a shout echoed to them from up the mall. The beam of a flashlight bobbed into view.

"*They're comin!*" Carlos's voice drifted toward them in the heavy air. He came running out of the darkness, tripped over debris, and fell into the circle of lamplight. "*They're goddamn everywhere!*"

Amber heard their screeches first, dry and raspy hoots. A cloud of stirred dust floated toward them, but in its heart was a gallery of blue glows, as though a collective of fireflies was buzzing toward them. The effect was almost pretty.

Then they got close enough for the glows to sharpen and resolve into individual shapes, and she understood.

From somewhere behind her, Cherrywine screamed.

Unlike the pirates aboard the old wooden sailing ship, the creatures coming for them now held only the most tenuous resemblance to human beings. They were hunched, ghoulish nightmares, too disfigured to even be able to discern sex, scurrying awkwardly on crooked limbs joined to their torsos in the wrong places, dolls that had been anatomically rearranged by a hyperactive child. Arms sprouted from waists, legs had become cloven clubs, spines were twisted into grotesque curves, heads had migrated to various other locations, and they had a multitude of extra appendages that made her sick to look at. All of them glowing, their melted, leathery skin casting an aqua light and their eyes—those that still had them—shining like twin blue suns. And, in a final touch of horrid parody, some of them still wore the remains of their vacation clothes, bright floral prints stretched and shredded by the deformed shapes of their owners.

This is what happens, Amber thought in horror. *This is what happens when you get exposed to a hundred years' worth of this radiation.*

"*Run!*" Justin barked. He dragged her away from the others as the creatures swarmed down on them. Amber heard gunshots behind them, another of Cherrywine's high-pitched screams, and then Justin pulled her around a corner and they were running in the opposite direction.

But the things came from everywhere now, as if the whole ship were waking up. One of them scuttled out of an aisle just ahead, a thing with so many appendages sticking out of its body, it looked more like a giant spider. Justin shot it twice. It spilled neon blue blood on the ground as it tumbled over backward and writhed. Justin took the next corner, leading her into the farthest avenue, where the line of stores met the ship's inner walls.

Amber stopped and yanked free of his grasp. She had to find a way back to the others. She could still hear their gunshots, the big blast of the shotgun and the repeated fire from the rifle, so they had to be alive. But every direction was blocked as more of the glowing things came lurching up the concourse.

There was no way out. They were going to die.

"*Amber, over here!*" Justin stood in the doorway of a little knick-knack souvenir shop, pulling at the rolldown security shutter from the inside. She ran in with him. Together, they got the rusted shutter yanked down. From somewhere out in the mall, the booming sounds of gunfire continued.

The metal grating slammed into the floor, and a second later the creatures were at the other side, rattling the mesh, reaching through the wide slats to swipe at them. Amber and Justin leapt away from their gnarled, grasping fingers. The shutter wasn't even locked in place, but these things were too stupid to try lifting it. Even so, with all that weight against the ancient barrier, she didn't think it would last long.

Amber had somehow managed to hang on to her flashlight amid all the chaos, but the mutated people outside cast such a bright light, she didn't need it. She turned in a circle, examining the rest of the convenience store.

The rectangular space was small, just a few overturned rows of ancient candy bars and shattered soda coolers, with a cash register kiosk against the back wall beside a heavy bulkhead door. She hurried over and tried to open it, but the metal was bolted solid and she saw no way to release the latches from this side.

When she turned back, Justin was on the floor.

9

The situation turned to shit before Ray could scarcely comprehend what was happening.

Carlos ran up and fell panting into their midst, and on his

heels was a wave of glowing monstrosities that reminded Ray of the horrors from that old Kurt Russell flick, where the people devolved into all sorts of random, crazy-as-fuck abominations. There were hundreds of them, enough that their screeches and moans filled the cruise ship's mall with a constant, hellish squall. Most of them couldn't move very fast on whatever disfigured limbs they used for ambulation, but they would still be all over them in seconds.

Ray forced himself up from the stretcher, ignoring the throb in his side. No time to be injured anymore. Jericho snatched the rifle from the ground, took a wide-legged stance, and opened fire into the oncoming horde. Ray took aim with his pistol, unconsciously moving deeper into the lamplight, as if it's pure illumination could shield them. The bullets struck the freaks at the front of the pack, spilling geysers of blue blood that filled the mall with a tangy stench. They went down, but there were three to replace every one that fell.

"*We can't hold dem!*" Jericho cried out.

"*Need some help!*" Ray shouted. Defending their position was useless, he knew it, but he wanted to stave off the inevitable as long as possible.

Because once they started running, there would be no end to it until they were all dead.

Carlos was back on his feet, pumping the shotgun like mad. The Vietnamese kid joined in with his AK, spraying fire in sweeping arcs, the muzzle flashes coming in shutterflash bursts. His bullets mowed down a large portion of the creatures, but the rest just stumbled over their fallen brethren and kept coming as he pulled fresh clips from his jumpsuit to reload. Ray used the opportunity to throw all the gear he could in one of the backpacks, including the radiation detector and walkie, then slung it over his shoulders. Something wet trickled along his thigh during the operation. He looked down to find blood flowing freely from his gunshot wound, reopened once more.

Behind them, Cherrywine shrieked and took off running into the darkness, away from the approaching horde.

"*Come back!*" Ray yelled after her. "*We have to stay together!*"

But that was proving impossible. The creatures came from other directions now, running, limping, bounding, and crawling; creeping out from the stores to their left and right and falling from the second level above to smash against the floor. A flabby, balding man with a stunted leg, a jawbone that showed through the waxy flesh dangling from his cheek, and a tumorous lump like an extra head growing from his breast (but still wearing the sun visor and Bermuda shorts he'd probably bought specifically for this trip through paradise) reached their small camp first and leapt at Ray, forcing him back against Tuan. He shot it in the face, but a flood of the things swept in and cut him and the soldier off from Jericho and Carlos. Through the glowing crowd of mangled limbs, he saw the other two crewmembers forced in the opposite direction.

"*C'mon!*" Ray slapped the Asian kid in the shoulder to get his attention. "*We gotta get out before they surround us!*"

He pressed a hand over the bloody hole in his side and the two of them fled in the direction Amber and Justin had disappeared, firing at anything that got in their way.

10

Carlos made sure to keep Jericho by his side as they backed away. If these things killed the others, that was a bonus, but he needed the mechanic alive. It wasn't easy; Jericho had grabbed his bag of tools just before they'd been forced to retreat, and it was slowing him down. They inched their way along the new path, firing at the creatures as they bottlenecked in the cross aisle.

"*Wait, what about de others?*"

"*Who fuckin cares, let those bitches die!*" Carlos checked over his shoulder to make sure nothing was sneaking up on them, and spotted a recessed door set into the wall between shops. He turned his flashlight on it and, under the layer of dust and grime, made out the word 'MAINTENANCE.'

"*In there, go!*" Carlos left off the fight and sprinted for the door. It was locked, but he pointed the shotgun at the knob and blasted the lock, then held it open for Jericho. The dreadlocked moron hesitated, then plunged into the narrow, dark hallway with Carlos on his tail.

11

Lito was still trying to process the magnitude of what Eric had just shown him when a string of muted thuds came from the direction of the glass door, short and fast explosions that reverberated through the ship's structure like fireworks in a tin can. He hopped off the desk and hurried over.

The door wasn't locked, but he had to push hard to break the seal of grime and dust around the jamb. There was just enough residual glare from the flashlight to see the security hallway beyond had a series of watertight bulkhead doors along the right side. The passage must've been for the ship police to get across decks quickly. When he stuck his head out, he could hear the thuds distinctly, just on the other side of the wall, and what sounded like a scream.

"Those're gunshots!" he said, pulling back inside. "It's gotta be them, we have to—"

He never saw the ceramic paperweight coming. The only reason it didn't cave in his skull was because he was still in motion, and Eric misjudged his swing. As it was, the heavy base of the Christmas tree from the future glanced off Lito's temple, causing a burst of twinkling stars across his vision. Lito fell back against the door, which swung open under his weight and dumped him into the hallway beyond.

Eric was on him in a heartbeat, straddling his chest and arms and snarling in his face as he raised the paperweight over his head. The flashlight on the desk behind him threw light over his shoulder. He looked crazed, his face transformed from his usual smarmy, my-shit-don't-stink smirk, eyes as empty as abandoned mineshafts in their shadow-covered pits. Lito yanked one hand out from under the guy's knee and grabbed an elbow to keep the paperweight from coming down.

"Give it *back* to me," Eric muttered. Even though Lito could see his mouth moving, the voice sounded older, huskier. "It's *mine*, you can't *stop* me, I will *fulfill* my destiny, and fucking kill *anyone* that gets in my way…"

Jesus, the kid wasn't just an asshole; he was stone-cold *nuts*.

The Walther Lito had taken off the speedboat was in the back of his waistband; he could feel it digging into his spine. And the statue—the one thing that might be capable of controlling this maniac—was out of reach in the pocket of his shorts. No help there. So instead, as Eric pulled his arms higher to free them, Lito bucked upward with all of his might, turning his hips to toss the other man off.

Eric hit the floor and bounced back up, growling so fiercely his lips were dotted with flecks of foamy spit, like a rabid dog. Lito managed to sit up and pull the little pistol from the back of his pants. He had already decided that he wouldn't pause, wouldn't give the lunatic a chance, he would just plug him and be done with it.

The kid must've known his intent, too. He scrambled backward, into the security office, narrowly avoiding a shot that spanged off the metal wall where his head had been. Lito crawled after him, entering the office in time to see Eric hurtling through the broken door they'd come through. By the time Lito could get to his feet, grab the flashlight, and peek around into the corridor, the kid was at the hatch leading back into the bowels of the ship.

He glanced over his shoulder as Lito trained the light on him, a look of purest hate made downright terrifying by those dead, empty eyes. Then he leapt into the opening in the floor, disappearing all at once.

Lito ran after him. When he reached the lip of the hatch, he fired two quick shots down, then carefully leaned over, afraid the kid would come shooting back out and grab him like a movie monster in the last reel.

The tunnel below was empty. Lito moved the flashlight around and then shouted, "Yeah, keep runnin, you crazy dickhead! I'm gonna smash your fuckin action figure!"

He wouldn't, not really, but let the kid think that. What Lito really wanted was to go after him and finish this, but if the others were in trouble, he had no time. Those shots might've been Carlos making his move. Besides, Eric was in the pitch-black underbelly of the ship now, without even a light, and perhaps that was a far worse punishment than death.

Lito closed the hatch, spun the wheel to seal it, and ran back toward the security corridor.

12

The disfigured tourists piled up on the other side of the metal shutter, howling in animal frustration as they rattled the barrier. Already it was bowed in the middle, and more rusted slats snapped under their relentless fists.

But Amber didn't have time to worry about that.

She rushed around the check-out counter to where Justin flopped against the filthy tile, in the throes of a violent seizure.

"*Justin!*" She yelled his name as she slid into the floor beside him. He had dropped the revolver as he collapsed, and she swept it up and stuck it back in her waistband almost without thinking, then cradled his head before his thrashing could crack it open on the tile. She trained the flashlight on his face, and saw his eyes were rolled up to the whites. Blue-flecked foam poured from both sides of his mouth.

His eyelids fluttered as the irises—still ringed in blue—floated back into place.

They focused on her, but there was no recognition in them.

Justin's mouth stretched open in a feral snarl.

Amber jumped away just as he swiped out at her, his fingernails missing her by inches. One slash, and she knew she would end up no better off than him. Justin scrambled up, his back hunched so much his shoulders were almost level with his ears, and advanced on her. She backed away across the store as the glowing creatures beyond the threshold continued to screech their outrage and tear at the metal shutter. It was almost ridiculous; they wanted in here, and right now she would almost rather be out there with them.

"*Stop!*" she pleaded, as Justin stalked after her. "*Justin, it's me!*" He gave no sign that he heard her, let alone understood.

She came up against the back wall. Amber pulled the revolver out and aimed it dead center at his pale forehead, but it was a half-hearted gesture. She couldn't do it. She'd already broken his heart tonight; taking his life—such as it was—was more leeway than her morals would allow her.

"I'm sorry," she whispered. He reached her, grabbed her shoulders, opened his mouth wide to tear into her throat. His face was twisted with rage, and, she thought, a deep, remorseful sort of sadness. "I never meant to hurt you."

There was a creaking squall to her left as the sealed hatch swung open, and Lito Porto's head poked through.

13

Lito followed the shouts from the security corridor, found the door they were coming from, then took in the situation in a heartbeat. He grabbed the back of Justin's shirt, ripped him away from Amber, and slung the boy away like a bouncer tossing a drunk. He flew across the store, coming to rest against the base of the steel shutter. The ghouls trying to bust through from the other side ignored him completely.

That was enough for Lito.

He pointed the Walther at the young man, ready to put him

out of his misery.

"*No, don't!*" Amber's voice was desperate. He glanced at her. "Please don't kill him!"

No time to debate. As Justin picked himself up, the steel gate broke along one side, letting in a tide of people even more hideous and misshappen than the pregnant one had been. They tripped over one another in their haste to attack. Justin was swallowed up by their ranks.

Lito and Amber rushed through the hatch he'd just opened. He tried to slam it back shut, but several gleaming blue arms snaked through, keeping the metal from sealing. They shoved against it, almost flinging him away, but he leaned on the door and pushed against their weight.

"Careful, don't let them scratch you!" Amber appeared at his side, helping him hold the hatch shut. The flailing limbs sticking through the crack stank like burnt, rotted meat. "I thought you were dead!"

"Me too! Where're Ray and the others?"

"Out there somewhere! We got separated!"

There was no way they'd be able to close the door again. They were steadily losing inches as the crush of bodies piled up on the other side.

"Go on!" Lito told her. "Up the hall! I'll buy you as much time as I can!"

Amber shook her head. "You don't get to play hero twice! On the count of three, we go together!"

She counted it down, and they jumped away from the door and ran. Behind them, the hatch clanged open. Snarls and screeches filled the empty passage. Lito threw a few blind shots over his shoulder, considered trying to make a stand, but there was just too many of them. He and Amber charged up the corridor with both their flashlights gleaming against the floor and walls.

Ahead, the hall turned to the left. They careened around the corner and skidded to a stop.

The deck ended in a ragged line just a few steps ahead. The flooring had corroded straight through, the cancer in its bowels slowly eating its way upward, leaving a black pit several yards long just in front of the door at the end of the hall. Amber shone her flashlight into it, but Lito could see no bottom, just random jutting pipes, and a few slabs of rusted metal.

"We gotta jump," he said.

"I can't make that!"

"Yes, you can. I'll go first so I can catch you."

Before he could talk himself out of it, Lito backed up for a running start, charged at the hole, and leapt across. In midair, reaching for the other side, the thought crossed his mind that this was a lot easier than it looked; he was going to hurdle right over the entire pit as nimbly as a gazelle.

Then the jagged edge of the metal deck on the far side struck him in the stomach and knocked all that optimism out of him.

He fell backward, sliding into the hole, scrabbling at the remains of the corridor floor, but there was nothing to grab, no place to get a grip...

Just before he dropped, a hand latched onto his wrist. He looked up into Ray's face. Tuan stood just behind him, holding the door open.

"You made it," his second-in-command said through clenched teeth.

"You know me, I never miss a party."

"Save it, shithead. This is kinda tearin apart the gunshot wound I got savin your ass last time."

He and Tuan pulled hard enough for Lito to swing a leg up onto the deck. By now, the howls of the tourists were echoing around them against the cold steel walls. They would be coming around the corner any second.

Amber came next, and they caught her easily. No sooner had she gotten on her feet than the crush of fiends rounded the corner and began tumbling off the edge without even slowing, their phosphorescent bodies visible as sparks of light as they fell into the pit. They seemed to get the idea after a few seconds and stopped pushing, just stood on the far side and roared with frustration.

"Where's Cherrywine?" Amber asked Ray.

"I don't know. She ran and I couldn't follow."

"Then we have to find her!"

"I wouldn't even know where to start. There's hundreds of those things out there, and she didn't have a gun or even a flashlight…"

"No. Goddamn it, *no*." Amber shook her head and then burst into tears for the first time all night. She threw her arms around Lito and sagged against him.

He held her until Ray finally said, "There's a stairwell outside. I think it'll take us topside, but we better hurry. A whole platoon of them split off to follow me and Tuan, and I don't know if we lost 'em."

They filed out of the security corridor, sealing the hatch behind them to block out the cries of the damned.

14

Cherrywine had to wipe sweaty strands of hair out of her eyes as she pelted through the dark mall. The creatures chasing her gave off enough of a glow for her to see where she was going. She could hear them back there, slavering at her heels, but didn't stop to look back as she climbed a set of stairs leading to the upper level.

As she sprinted through darkness, she realized it might've been a bad idea to leave the others. She was no good in a fight, wouldn't have known what to do with a gun if she had one, but one of the few activities that held her interest in high school—which seemed so long ago when she was taking off her clothes and jiggling her ass against the erect penises of strangers for money—was running. She'd always been able to run like the wind.

And when she'd seen the army of horrible nightmares charging at them, it was all she could think to do. So she just put her head down, pumped her arms, ignored the awkward shoes on her feet, and said a prayer of thanks they weren't her stripper pumps.

The upper story of the mall took a sudden turn. She followed it, and the wall of the cruise ship loomed on her left. She let her fingers brush along it as she ran to help keep herself oriented. When debris popped up, appearing suddenly out of the murk, she hurdled the messes rather than try to go around. That bobbling blue light at her back was giving her a headache.

The line of stores cut off abruptly at the edge of her vision ahead. When she got closer, she understood why: the entire upper floor of the mall and the ancient deck below had collapsed into a chasm so wide she couldn't even see across it.

Behind her, one of the creatures gave a triumphant howl.

A sliver of ledge no more than six inches wide clung to the wall beside her, nothing more than a shelf of rusted, sheared-off steel. Cherrywine eased out onto it, sliding the soles of her borrowed shoes along it and flattening herself against the wall. She worked her way out an inch at a time, trying not to look down at the yawning darkness in front of her.

The creatures reached the edge of the pit. Several tumbled over the edge into the abyss. A few tried to crawl out after her on the narrow ledge, but with their awkward bodies and twisted limbs, they were too uncoordinated, and ended up falling after their freakish brethren. The rest stood at the edge, hissing and squalling in futile rage as she escaped, like a pack of hunting dogs braying at a treed raccoon.

She'd outsmarted them. She'd never outsmarted anyone in her life. A nervous giggle escaped her.

Cherrywine kept moving. The farther she got from the creatures' glow, the more total the darkness around her became. Soon she was in the middle of a void so black it made her eyeballs ache. Fear almost caused her to freeze up, but she focused on moving her feet along the ledge with one hand stretched out along the wall in front of her.

It was this hand that first encountered the metal bar, the only deviation in the smooth steel bulkhead. She felt along until she realized it was a ladder, bolted to the wall, for what purpose she had no idea. Cherrywine stepped onto its rungs, praying it would hold her weight, and climbed downward.

The descent seemed to take hours. The only proof she was getting anywhere came when that blue glow reappeared below her, bleeding into the darkness. She almost stopped climbing until she realized it came from the bodies of the fallen mutants. They lay crushed and broken among the wreckage at the bottom of the pit, surrounded by glowing puddles of irradiated blood, enough to create a world of eerie blue glow down here. She reached the bottom and stepped off the ladder, then stood uncertainly as she tried to decide what to do next.

Tears pricked her eyes. Cherrywine swiped at them angrily. She just had to keep moving, find Amber and the others. And be ready to run.

The bottom of the pit was a junkyard, with mounds of debris piled everywhere. She picked her way through the crushed remains of shops, decking, and rusted pipes, and almost bumped into a figure that stepped out from behind a huge slab of steel.

She leapt back with a short scream. In the faint blue light, she recognized Eric, standing ramrod straight in front of her, eyes staring dead ahead above his crushed nose.

"E-Eric?" she asked. She was so relieved to see anyone that had a normal arm and leg count, she didn't even care that it was him. "Is that really you?"

He didn't answer, just cocked his head to one side as though listening to something.

"How'd you get here? We thought you'd left to get help and—"

Eric seemed to notice her for the first time, but his eyes were glassy and empty. She remembered that look, the one he'd given her while he was throttling the life out of her back aboard the yacht.

"I won't let you stop it," he said simply.

Cherrywine swallowed. "What do you mean? Stop what?"

He smiled at her, but there was nothing friendly about it; it was cold and indifferent and as empty as his eyes. Maybe it always had been, and she wondered why she didn't see it when he'd first walked into the strip club and given her an extra fifty bucks for a handjob in the champagne room.

"The Big Plan, of course," he said simply. "My destiny."

Intuition told Cherrywine it was time to run again. She wheeled around, but he grabbed her, his fingers sinking into her arm. The fight that had swept over her on the houseboat reared up again, and she kicked out blindly, the toe of her boot thudding against his shin. He grunted and stumbled backward, tripping over debris, but his grip never let up. Eric went over backward, dragging Cherrywine with him.

"*Let go!*" she screamed. They rolled through the wreckage, her using her free hand to slap at him. His breathing roughened, and she realized she could feel his erection against her leg again.

Her fingers found the hot lump of his nose. She wrenched.

Eric bellowed in pain, the cry echoing against the cold steel around them. Cherrywine ripped free of his grasp, got to her feet, and took off running.

She heard him scrambling up, the clumsy crash of his footsteps, but when she looked back, she found that he was falling behind. He might be in good shape, but spending six hours a day on a stripper pole in positions that would tax a yoga master had her body operating at its peak. Cherrywine leapt over obstacles, while Eric blundered through them.

And then she skidded to a stop at the edge of another precipice.

The deck ended again in front of her, the unearthly glow revealing a drop through twisted wreckage. Somewhere at the bottom, she could hear the crash of the ocean.

Eric stood behind her. She turned to face him. He grabbed her again, but this time, his arms slid around her waist, drawing her close, and he pressed his lips to hers, a more gentle kiss than she would've thought him capable of. Eternal optimism had plagued Cherrywine throughout her life, and, even now, she allowed herself to hope that everything would be all right.

When they parted, he whispered, "I won't let any of you stop me."

He put a hand on her stomach and shoved. Cherrywine felt herself tilting backward, over the edge, but she refused to give him the satisfaction of hearing her scream.

She fell only a short distance before striking a jutting shard of metal. Something in her arm snapped, with a brief flare of pain like the striking of a match, but before she could worry about that, she was falling again, tumbling through darkness, smashing into other obstructions along the way.

By the time she hit the water below, Cherrywine was nothing but torn skin and broken bones.

15

Justin stood amid the other mutated tourists, but he was oblivious of them. His thoughts were a blue-hued blur, his entire identity erased by the boiling agony in his veins. He wanted to rend, wanted to tear something apart with his bare hands, but only one image could get through the jumble of his brain.

A girl. One with short, dark hair. He felt like he knew her name once, but couldn't remember it now. He wanted to find her. To kill her. Or was it kiss her? He couldn't remember.

But he knew where she was going. Up. To the higher areas of this place. He would go there too. It took incredible effort for him to stay focused on this goal as he made his way back into the dark mall concourse.

The other creatures followed him.

CHANGING CHANNELS

FULL TRANSLATION

THE EXCHANGE

ERIC'S DESTINY FULFILLED

1

"That piece of shit," Ray growled. "Oh, that son of a whore."

Lito grunted with the effort of helping him up the stairs. "I knew his mom, and she was no whore. That woman would be ashamed of her kid."

"If it turns out he's the one that sabotaged the *Steel Runner* and got us into this mess, I swear, I'll kill him before the Dominican ever gets a chance! Shit, I told you, Lito, I fuckin *told* you that kid was bad news!"

"I know, I just didn't think he'd be capable of something like this."

They had gone up fifteen flights of stairs by Lito's count, with Ray leaning on him heavily. Tuan led the way with his AK-47 and a flashlight, and Amber came close on their heels, testing the air with the radiation detector to ensure they didn't get ambushed by more mutants. All the landings they passed seemed to lead to passenger room floors, the last place they wanted to go. So they kept moving toward the upper decks, and Lito used the opportunity to fill them in on what had happened since he'd left.

Except for one thing.

"I'm sorry about Carlos," Amber said, "but honestly, I'm more worried about Eric being on this ship."

Lito mulled that for a second. "Me too, actually."

"That rich *gringo*?" Ray grunted, either in pain or disbelief. "Who gives a shit about that *bastardo*?"

"Easy for you to say. You didn't see him when he attacked me. Like he turned into a robot. He's totally lost it."

"I saw it, too." Amber admitted. "Back on that houseboat. Plus, he tried to strangle..." She stopped just short of saying the blonde girl's name.

Lito wouldn't feel bad no matter what happened to Eric—that fucker deserved whatever he got—but, as Amber had reminded him once already, the fate of the other white kids was his responsibility. "We'll look for her. Justin too, if you want. But there's one other thing you need to know. And you're probably not gonna like it."

Ray tripped over debris on the dark stairs, then hissed in pain and stopped to hold his side. Lito let him sit down to rest. "I don't think it can get any worse."

"I'll put it this way: the radiation could be the least of our problems."

"So tell us already."

"I will, but first..." He turned to Tuan, who had taken up a post at the next staircase landing to guard the door. Lito had gotten a hunch at some point since he and Eric parted ways, an idea that grew in the back of his head, and now it was time to see if he was right. "Tuan," he asked, "what year is it?"

Ray and Amber waited with curious expressions as he got the idea across as best he could to the soldier. As Tuan began to understand the question, he squinted in confusion and held up fingers to answer.

2143.

Lito nodded. It was so obvious now, he couldn't believe they hadn't thought to ask before.

"Wait, what's he mean?" Ray demanded. "I don't understand."

Lito told them what he'd been holding back, about the calendar in the security office somewhere below, from the year 2027.

"*Dios, dios, dios,*" Ray chanted. "Are you tellin me…Tuan's from the *future?*"

Lito shot another glance up at the Vietnamese youth, who was trying hard to follow the conversation. "I don't think he realizes that, so let's not freak him out just yet. But yeah, I think he and those other soldiers got caught up in whatever's happenin here, their ship protected them from the radiation, but they still ended up here with the rest of the derelicts."

"It all makes sense." Amber crouched on the stairs below and looked up at Lito. "That's how so many of these ships from centuries ago can look brand new, and why the newer models are so ancient. They haven't been just sitting out here since they disappeared, they've been…what? Jumping through time?"

"I think so. That would explain the flashlight back on the pirate ship. It was still running because the fucker had probably just come from 1970, just a few hours before."

"Fuck the flashlight," Ray said. "You know what this is? It's the answer to the goddamn Bermuda Triangle. Every boat, every plane that's ever disappeared out here—that ever *will* disappear—they just got…blipped to a different time, like changin the fuckin TV channel or somethin. And the people on them turned into those things."

"Might be the answer," Lito agreed, "but it still ain't the cause."

"Is it random?" Amber wondered aloud. "Or is there a pattern? I mean, why here, why now?"

"Before we get all wrapped up in the Hardy Boys Solve the Mystery of the Sargasso, here's my point. Remember what Tuan said, about the bright flash turnin day to night? If that was, like Ray put it, the channel bein changed, then that means the radiation has somethin to do with this, and the next time one of those flashes hits, all these ships are gonna jump again. And, for those boys and girls playin the home version of our game, if we're all still here when it happens…"

"We're goin wherever they go," Ray finished for him. "All right, I'm terrified. What are we gonna do then? We still need a way outta here."

Lito jabbed a finger upward. "First, we get to the top deck, out in the open. I wanna see where we are."

2

The top of the staircase ended at a wide set of double doors that had all but fallen off their hinges. Moonlight filtered in around the edges, and when they pushed through, the four of them found themselves outside once more. The storm had passed, leaving the sky without a trace of clouds. The glittering palette of stars and the orange haze of daybreak to the east were so comforting it made Amber realize that she'd never truly expected to see them again. She stood for a moment and sucked in lungfuls of fresh oxygen, heavenly after the stale, musty air in the lower decks of the cruise ship.

Then she thought of Justin and Cherrywine, still down there in that darkness, and an unbearable sadness hit her so hard, it was almost a physical weight, stooping her shoulders and making each foot weigh a ton.

They were at the top of the *Atlantic Queen*, on the football-field-sized party deck, where the deformed things downstairs had once sunbathed themselves. Now the deck chairs were gone, and the huge swimming pool was empty except for several feet of scummy water at the bottom. The full-size lifeboats had probably been somewhere on the lower decks, but smaller, emergency versions were lashed to the upper deck in recessed rows along both sides of the ship, covered in rotting canvas and tucked under a partial ledge where they wouldn't make the passengers nervous. From way up here, close to twenty stories above the ocean's surface, they had an almost 360 degree, unobstructed view of the surrounding sea. The angle, coupled with the coming sunrise, let them take in the entire region for the first time.

"We're smack-fuckin-dab in the middle of it all," Ray muttered.

He was right. The water immediately around the cruise ship was clear for a good distance, forming that empty space they'd sailed through in the storm, but beyond that the band of derelict ships stretched for several miles in every direction, clustered around the cruise ship like those rings of debris that encircled Saturn. There were hundreds of crafts. The perspective from up here reminded Amber of being at the top of a tall skyscraper and looking down at a sleeping city.

Lito ran over to the port side railing. "Down there."

They followed, and Amber looked over the side of the ship. It was a dizzying sheer drop to the calm ocean. "See that huge hole in the side of the ship?" Lito said. "That's where we docked the speedboat. There's enough gas in it to get us outta here."

Amber saw where he meant, but then her eyes were drawn up, to something a few hundred yards out from the cruise ship. She brought up one hand to shield her eyes. "Hey, what is that?"

In the ring of empty water below them was a pulsing aquamarine light so fierce she couldn't look directly at it. It was the queasy color of the sky flashes, but more concentrated, localized. She instantly felt that disoriented nausea again.

"Is that a buoy?" Ray asked. Right after the question came a disgusting belch. He looked away from the light quickly.

"It helps if you don't look directly at it." Lito put a hand in front of his face and squinted through the fingers to cut the glare. "Whatever it is, I saw it in the storm when we came in."

The glow ebbed and grew, ebbed and grew, in rhythmic cycles, like some kind of phosphorescent beating heart, and even when it was at its weakest, when the eye could almost penetrate through the light, Amber still couldn't get any sense of what was beneath. She closed her eyes before stomach acid could work its way up her esophagus.

"That's it, isn't it?" Ray asked. "Whatever's causin all this."

Lito didn't answer. He broke off the examination and pointed toward a rectangular structure on the bow of the cruise ship, on the other side of a rusted metal security fence. "That's gotta be the bridge. Stay here, I'll look for a ship schematic."

He took the radiation detector and hurried away, waving the tiny, silver wand in front of him like a kid with a toy sword, then kicked his way through the gate in the fence. Tuan, Ray, and Amber waited for him, not speaking and trying not to look at the glow. She would've given anything for the VHF scanner, but it wasn't in the rucksack of items Ray had managed to grab. Lito returned five minutes later, carrying a tube of laminated paper.

"What're we doin?" Ray demanded.

"You're gettin off this ship, right now. All of you."

"Sounds good. So what the hell're *you* doin?"

Lito held up the tube. "I'm goin to the maintenance room."

"Goddamn, would you let it go? That fuel hose can kiss my—!"

"This ain't about the *Runner*," he interrupted. "I'm gonna look for the others. If they're still alive, Jericho and Carlos would've gone to the maintenance room, so I'll start there. Along the way, I'll look for Cherrywine and…" He glanced at Amber. "…and Justin, too. Maybe we can still get him some help."

Ray shook his head adamantly. "You weren't down there with us, you don't know what it's like. This ship is infested with those things."

"Yeah, but they're all down in the lower decks, and I don't think they're smart enough to find their way out. We haven't had one hit on the detector on our way up here, and I didn't see any of them in the maintenance corridors."

"But that's not the point, Lito. We don't have time, unless you wanna end up like them."

"I don't, and I don't want Jericho or anybody else to, either. Not even Carlos deserves that." Lito set his scruffy jaw. "With this map, I can cut down the starboard side of the ship and be there in twenty minutes."

"Fine, then I'm goin with you."

"Get the fuck real, Ray. I had to carry your ass up the stairs as it was."

Ray snorted, looking from Lito to Amber, and flung a hand out at her. "You're the one he's got the hots for, you try talkin some sense into him."

Amber's cheeks burned, but she told Lito, "You didn't carry *me* up the stairs, asshole. If you're staying to look for the others, then so am I."

"That's not exactly what I meant," Ray grumbled.

"I can't worry about you while I do this." Lito stepped closer and slipped an arm around her waist. Her knees actually went weak. She thought that only happened in the romance novels.

Are you shitting me? You're falling for a pirate with a heart of gold; for all you know, this could actually be *a romance novel.*

"All right, all that stupidity aside," Ray interjected, "how do you expect us to get off the ship anyway? Call a taxi?"

Lito stepped away from Amber. On their own recognizance, her fingers held on to the tail of his shirt for just a split second before letting go. He patted one of the lifeboats. "I'm gonna lower you down right next to the speedboat. You jump onboard, and drive it outta here."

"We're not leaving you," she blurted.

"And I'm not askin you too. Just get away from the ship, where you're safe. Circle if you have to. I'll find the others, bring them back up here where the reception is better, and give you a call on the walkie." When neither of them said anything, he raised his eyebrows. "The longer we argue, the less time we have."

"If you're not gonna listen to reason, fine, let's do it," Ray agreed.

The two of them inspected the rigging and handcrank pulleys for lowering the lifeboats, to find the one most serviceable. The cables were steel, rusted badly, but Lito said they would hold. He and Tuan pushed one out over the water, where it dangled on the other side of the railing, twenty stories in the air.

They helped Ray aboard first, then Amber. The fiberglass boat swayed but seemed sturdy. When Tuan's turn came, he shook his head and saluted Lito.

"Guess he's comin with me?"

"I think he had a thing for Cherrywine. Just take him with you, so at least someone is watching your back."

Lito returned the salute. "All right, glad to have you, soldier."

Amber and Ray took only the revolver, and Tuan's other radiation detector. Lito handed her the speedboat keys last of all. She looked up at him and said, "If you...if you *do* see Justin..."

"I'll bring him back."

"That wasn't what I was gonna say. It's just...I can't stand the idea of him stuck on this boat, ending up like one of those things. I should've let you..." She couldn't finish.

He nodded. "I'll make it painless."

Amber started to sit down, but he leaned over the railing and grasped her upper arm. She closed her eyes, turned her face upward, and waited for his lips to touch hers.

"What are you doin?" he asked.

She opened her eyes to find him staring at her with his head cocked to the side. Hot embarrassment burned across her skin. "Oh...oh, I thought...you were..."

"Keep it in your pants, *gringa*," he said, flashing that too-charming grin. Then it fell away, and he growled, "Forty minutes. Don't give me any longer. And if that thing shows any sign it's about to blow...just cut and run. Don't even look back."

She nodded, then settled down on the seat opposite Ray. A few seconds later they were being lowered smoothly down the side of the *Atlantic Queen*. After several feet though, they came to a stop, and Lito yelled out above them, "*Hey, catch!*"

Amber looked up and managed to snag something oblong and heavy before it crashed onto the floor of the boat. Her hands recognized the smooth glass surface of Eric's hideous statue before she'd even looked at it.

"I'm gonna want that back!"

She grinned and stuffed the figure back into her pocket as they dropped away toward the sea.

3

Carlos and Jericho fled blindly through the corridors of the ship until they were sure they'd lost the mob. After that, Jericho made him stop so they could decide what to do next.

They had two flashlights, Jericho's tool bag and machete, the shotgun, and the AR, all of which had about ten shots between them.

"We'll never make it back out dat way," Jericho wheezed.

"We don't gotta go that way. Let's just find the hose and—"

"*Fuck de hose! Everybody else is dead! We're lost, and we're gonna die on dis ship! Don't you see dat?*"

"We ain't lost." Carlos aimed his flashlight at a sign mounted on the wall. They were covered in dust, but the writing underneath was still visible. "Chief Maintenance and Parts, that's what you need, right?"

"Well...yeah..."

"All right, we go there, find the shit, then get up topside and catch a ride back to the *Steel Runner*. Yo, easy as shit, homey."

Jericho said nothing, seemed to calm down. It was a new sensation for Carlos to have people listening to his orders for a change; he could get used to that, when he had his own crew. For now, he just had to keep this chickenshit moving. He led the way down through the corridors, following the signs until he reached a swinging door leading into a shop that looked like an auto garage. Parts and tools were scattered across the bare concrete floor, and there were shelves lining nearly every wall, with marked bins sitting side-by-side.

"Okay, do your thing."

"'My *thing*?'" Jericho laid the shotgun on a metal shop table and walked over to the bins. He used his flashlight to scan through the tags on each, then grabbed out a fistful of coiled hoses that looked like limp snakes. "You see dese, idiot? Dey're rotted through! I'd have to find a metal pipe and den try to solder it to fit de gaskets!"

Carlos gritted his teeth. "Back on the raft, you said you could rig something up. Can you do it, or not?"

"Dere's tings trying to kill us!"

Carlos held up the automatic rifle and pointed it at him. "That ain't what I asked."

Jericho studied him for a long moment. He must've seen something in Carlos' face, because his next words were, "It was you. You sabotaged de *Runner*."

"That's right." Carlos pulled the shotgun out of his reach. "Now get to work muhfuckah, or I'm gonna use those ugly ass dreadlocks for target practice."

4

The lifeboat leaked. Water seeped up through the cracked fiberglass almost as soon as Amber and Ray touched down on the ocean surface. They hurried to get it released from the cables, and Amber used the plastic oars to maneuver them to the gaping hole in the *Atlantic Queen*'s side.

"Is it there?" Lito's voice crackled on the walkie.

"It's here," she confirmed. The speedboat's huge chrome-plated engine caught their flashlight beams and reflected them into blinding starbursts.

"All right, we're goin. I'll keep tryin you when we're on our way back."

She helped Ray transfer over to the other craft just before the lifeboat capsized and sank. It took Amber a few minutes to figure out the speedboat's controls, then she started up the engine and backed out of the little artificial cove, scraping the sides against the jagged edges of the cruise liner's hull.

Ray stretched out across the padded bench at the rear with the walkie on his bandaged stomach. "Just take us out a few hundred yards and we'll wait."

"Screw that," Amber said. "There's still a sea monster out here that could flip us right out of this thing." She throttled up, spinning the steering wheel to turn them around.

"Then where are you goin?"

"To find out why the hell all this is happening."

"Oh shit." Ray's head popped up to watch as she steered the speedboat toward that sickly, pulsing blue light.

5

Lito waited until he saw the speedboat emerge and roar away, then signaled to Tuan. They pelted across the long deck, toward a stairwell entrance beside the bridge that, according to the schematics he'd found, would lead them down through the engineering levels of the ship. Ten minutes later, they were once more charging through lightless corridors, but making better time than he'd figured. Tuan used one of his fancy Geiger counters to take readings as they went, leaving his machine gun to dangle on its strap against his back.

"*Chinga*. Shoulda kissed her," Lito mumbled. Tuan gave him a puzzled look. The kid was a more pleasant traveling companion than Eric. "Let that be a lesson, my man: always kiss the girl. It may be your last chance."

Tuan shrugged in confusion, then went back to studying the detector screen again as they walked.

"Ya know, it's kinda nice to have someone around that can't understand a word you say." Lito's voice echoed a long way in the deserted corridor. He considered shutting up—at the rate they were moving, they could come up on more of the creatures before either of them had a chance to react—but as long as the detector was silent, a little conversation, even one-sided, might put them at ease. "Course, it's also probably good that you got no idea you're about a century and a half in the past right now. I have no idea what's gonna happen to you when we get outta this, but I promise I won't let 'em lock you up in a lab somewhere." He snorted. "Like anyone's gonna believe all this anyway. We'll just be more Triangle lunatics."

They came to a juncture. Most of the hallways in this part of the ship were labeled—they undoubedly saw more traffic than the dank maintenance tunnels where he and Eric had boarded—but Lito still needed to check the schematic to get his bearings. They were nearing the engineering offices. He and Tuan started down a long hallway with no other doors, and a vented ceiling from which most of the metal panels were either missing or rusted through, revealing a narrow crawlspace of pipes and ductwork. Withered, skeletal legs dangled from one of the open sections, as though the person had tried to cram themselves into the tight space to escape. They gave the dead appendages a wide berth.

For the first time, Lito wondered what it must've been like on this ship when everything went to hell. The panic and crazed fear would've created chaos. Had the passengers mutated all at once, or had some of them changed before the others and then started killing the rest? Had they seen the derelicts? Or were there even any derelicts to see? This *Atlantic Queen* might've been one of the first vessels collected by the Bermuda Triangle, nearly 14 years from now.

An even bigger idea hit him. If they got away, they could stop this from happening, warn the cruise line company, or even the passengers. They could save all these people from their horrible fate. He'd always loved sci-fi stuff as a kid, so he understood the disastrous concept of paradoxes, but he didn't know if his conscience would allow this maritime disaster to happen if he could prevent it.

"So Tuan," Lito said as they walked. He suddenly wondered what else it might be possible to change in the future. "Tell me more about this war of yours."

"Biiiig war," the soldier repeated in his limited English. And he had that tone again, as if Lito should know all of this.

"I know, I know, it's a big war, but just humor me, kid. Tell me who America's fightin this time. Korea? Some turban head in the Middle East? The Germans again?"

The nationalities were the only part Tuan seemed to comprehend. He sighed in exasperation and slipped the detector in his jumpsuit pocket long enough to make a fist with one hand and whap it into the palm of the other, then gave what sounded like another recitation. "All to stand. All to fight. All world. *Together.*"

"The whole world, huh?" Lito stopped to look at him. "Well if the whole world is joinin together and holdin hands for a change, then who the hell're you up against?"

The younger man swallowed, his narrow eyes stretching open to their fullest in the middle of his round face, and whispered, "*Filament.*"

The word meant nothing to Lito, but the reverence with which the other man said it gave him chills. "And this...*Filament*...the war with them started in 2143?"

Tuan didn't get this one. Lito thought the numerals were the problem again. He wrote '2143' in the dust along the corridor wall, and, when that still didn't work, he conveyed his meaning with individual tick marks, spelling out each number as 'II I IIII III'.

"Start?" Tuan asked. He shook his head. "First battle..." He proceeded to write the year out in hashes, using slashes for zeros, until he'd written, 'II / / IIIIIII'.

"Wait, 2007?" Lito frowned, sure there was still a misunderstanding.

Tuan raised an eyebrow, then made the same exploding gesture and noise that he had earlier. "Tokyo. No more."

Was he trying to say that the city had been destroyed six years ago? "Um, hate to break it to you, Tuan ol' buddy, but you got some bad intel. Tokyo is just fi—"

The radiation detector in Tuan's pocket went haywire, clicking and squawking like an angry chicken.

Lito raised the Walther and looked both ways up and down the hall. "Where's it comin from?"

Tuan waved the wand around in circles frantically. "All! All places! Close!"

"Huh?" Lito pointed his flashlight down the hallway ahead of them, able to see all the way to where it dead ended at a T junction. Nothing. He pointed it behind them, and found the path just as empty. "I don't see anything, man!"

And then the first bulbous, squirming ship rat dropped from the ceiling vents onto Tuan.

6

The seaweed glowed brighter the closer Amber and Ray got to the beacon of light on the water's surface, becoming a cool blue carpet beneath the speedboat. Tiny tendrils stretched skyward and reached for them as they passed, reminding Amber of fanatical concertgoers grabbing at a musician on stage. Of course the vegetation would've been exposed to the radiation also; she didn't know why she hadn't thought of it before, connected it to Cherrywine's claims that it held her back, or even the feeling Amber had herself that the plants were pawing at her after the yacht crash. Perhaps it was even the reason the seaweed was so abundant in the Bermuda Triangle, and why, as Eric had told them, early sailors feared it. When the radiance became too bright too look at, she concentrated on their destination.

They'd circled the beacon several times at a good distance before approaching. Whatever it was, it appeared to be only a little larger than the speedboat. The closer they got, the more they could see through the shifting mask of pulsating, sparkling light that seemed to emanate from somewhere on top. Ray tested the air heavily with the radiation detector as she eased forward, keeping the boat throttle just a hair above neutral.

He shook his head. No dangerous readings, but they both still felt like someone had tied their guts into knots every time they looked at it dead on.

She found what she thought was the boat's radio scanner, turned it on. The broadcast was crystal clear now, but with a whine of electrical interference, like a cell phone held up next to a speaker. She moved the boat even closer.

When they got within ten yards, they entered a narrow shadow where the light was blocked, and she could see the object clearly.

It was a craft, but it looked even more futuristic than Tuan's boat. Dull, copper-colored metal reflected none of the early morning sunrays and even seemed to absorb the beams of their flashlights. The main section was as rectangular as a giant refrigerator box, with a rounded cone on one end that she took to be the front, and two blunted wings attached to either side; all-in-all, a functional, ugly design. It looked brand new, not a barnacle or spot of rust on it.

A squat cylinder perched on top of the vessel, and it was from this that the blue light poured, like a spotlight at the premiere of a Hollywood movie. Since it faced upward, only a sliver of the radiance was visible to them. The angle eliminated the nausea, but the glare was so fierce, she was afraid it would give her flash burns on her retinas. The roots of her hair bristled from electricity in the air, but still the radiation detector was silent.

"The Deep," she whispered, hardly aware she'd spoken out loud.

"What'd you say?" Ray asked.

"The Deep," she repeated. "We've been hearing this thing's voice on the scanner all night. It's been talking to us."

But it was more than that. It was her Rosetta Stone. She was sure of it.

Amber directed the speedboat alongside one of its stubby wings as best she could.

"What're you doin?" Ray asked, panic in his voice.

"Going inside." She pointed at a round portal visible in the side of the vessel's body, just above the wing. "I didn't come all this way to admire it. If there's answer's to be had, I want them."

"Answers are overrated, college girl."

She sighed. "Look, this thing isn't dangerous. It's been trying to warn people. Anyway, you don't have to come. It's probably better if you lie still."

"The hell I'm not. Lito will do a lot worse than shoot me if I let you get killed."

He struggled up from the rear seats and helped her tie off the boat to the edge of the wing. The water below them, choked with seaweed, looked like a glowing soup. The leafy growths around the base of the ship clung to its sides, straining upward, as though attempting to climb toward the light from the dish on top. She was careful not to touch them as she stepped over onto the new vessel.

Amber expected the strange metal to be slick, but instead it yielded subtly beneath her weight, providing traction for her shoes.

She gave a few experimental bounces. "It's like being on a trampoline." She knelt and brushed her fingertips across the surface, found it slightly warmer than the air and vibrating.

Ray climbed on behind her with the revolver and the walkie-talkie. "This thing wasn't designed for the water. It ain't a boat."

Amber had been thinking the same, but hadn't wanted to say it. She walked toward the circular entrance, no more than a seam in the metal. A strange calm descended over her, equal parts exhaustion and curiosity. She had to know. *Needed* to know.

When she touched the brown metal with her fingers, it irised open, the door seeming to melt into the walls. A whoosh of compressed air blew across her.

She saw what was on the other side...and screamed.

7

Tuan slapped at the mass of hairless, glowing flesh on his shoulder. Lito saw it surge forward and sink its crooked teeth into the young man's neck, peeling away a hunk of flesh the size of a dime.

"Goddamn it!" Lito raised the Walther, putting the barrel right up against the animal's putrid, melted side, and pulled the trigger. The rat exploded, splattering the corridor walls with its luminescent blood.

But there were more, they were everywhere now, dropping from the narrow crawlspace above and streaming out of more vents along the sides of the hallway to cover the floor. Lito had always heard that cruise liners like this were home to thousands of vermin, and here was the proof.

"Run!" Lito pounded down the hallway, dodging as many of the glowing rats on the floor as possible and stomping on those he couldn't. One fell from the ceiling and managed to catch hold of his shirt, but he knocked it away before it could climb.

Behind him, Tuan opened fire. Machine gun bullets whined and ricocheted. Lito looked back to see him shooting at the floor as the rats closed in on him. "Tuan, don't! Just keep moving!"

They were climbing his legs. Ripping at his jumpsuit with their misshapen claws and teeth to draw blood in tiny wounds, surely injecting their strange radiation poisoning. Lito saw several tear a hole in the fabric near his crotch and slip inside. The soldier began to scream and flail, firing wildly, the bullets somehow missing Lito. As the little beasts swarmed up his body and onto his head, Tuan crumpled to the floor.

The rats split up, a huge contingent surging toward Lito in a half-foot deep wave.

8

Jericho stood hunched over the work bench, using a soldering gun from his tool bag to refit the ends of a metal pipe he'd found on the ground. Carlos straddled a bench to the right, with the rifle across his lap and the shotgun against the wall behind him, using the tip of Jericho's machete to clean under his fingernails.

"You muhfuckahs thought you was so funny," the kid said. "Always doggin me, Rabid slappin me across the face, alla you laughin at me. Even you, Jericho. Well, who's laughin now?"

"Lito took you in," Jericho said, without looking up from his work. "When nobody else wanted you, he took you in, made you part of dis crew."

"Yo, I didn't ask him to. You think I wanna spend the rest of my life like you assholes, scroungin around on that boat, robbin people for just enough cash to get by? Fuck no, I'm gonna be somebody."

"And you t'ink betrayin us and throwin in wit de Dominican is the way to do dat? You are one sad little shit."

"Yo, whatevah. How much longer till that thing's ready?"

The correct answer to that question was 'never.' There was no way to know if this pipe was even long enough to bridge the gap in the engine left by the missing fuel hose, but Carlos hadn't been interested in hearing that. The Steel Runner was stuck, Jericho saw that now, and there was no getting out of this for any of them.

"It's finished," he lied. "Come take a look."

The kid pushed up from the bench, laid the machete on the end of the table, and walked over with the rifle. Jericho waited until he got close enough, then tossed the pipe directly at his face. It hit him in the forehead, drawing blood. "Oh, you fuckin—!"

Carlos swung the rifle up. Jericho launched across the distance between them.

9

Carlos meant to kill him, just...fuck the *Runner* and Santiago and his dream of being a drug smuggling sea captain, none of it was enough to quell his blind rage as he prepared to blow this island nigger away without a moment's hesitation, but the bastard was on him before he could get the rifle up. Jericho grabbed the AR and wrenched, trying to rip the weapon out of his grasp. When that didn't work, he brought a knee up into Carlos' stomach hard enough to make his eyes water. The pain only served to feed his fury.

He let go of the rifle with one hand and bashed Jericho in the side of the head as hard as he could, aiming for the lump by his ear that Jorge had given him. The heel of his palm came away bloody. The mechanic's head rocked to the side, his grip loosening just long enough for Carlos to pull away.

But there was still no time to get the long weapon swung around in time to fire. Jericho dove for the table to retrieve his machete, then sliced outward in a blind arc. It was everything Carlos could do to block the sharp edge with the butt of the rifle.

Jericho came at him like the killer in a slasher flick, swinging the machete in short, overhead swipes, driving Carlos back against the wall. The rifle was his only shield as he thrust it out in front of him to keep the man away.

And then one of the mechanic's frantic blows sliced down the back of Carlos's left hand where it gripped the AR.

Carlos howled. The sound startled Jericho enough to make him pause, and Carlos used the opportunity to smash the rifle butt across his face.

The mechanic crashed to the floor with a groan and crawled away. Carlos tried to get the rifle into position to shoot him, but when he attempted to hold the barrel with his left hand, it slipped from his grasp and fell to the concrete.

His damn fingers wouldn't close. He turned the hand over to look at the back, where Jericho's last blow with the machete had landed, and found that he'd been skinned all the way from the second knuckles of each finger, nearly to his wrist. This stretch of his arm was nothing but mangled tissue now with a few gleaming white bones sticking out, like a cross-section drawing of the human body for an anatomy class. A river of blood coursed down his arm and spattered on the floor.

Whattaya know, he thought in amazement. *I got bottlecapped after all.*

Jericho was several feet away, still on hands and knees. Carlos figured he was trying to escape, but then spotted the shotgun against the bench and understood.

Rather than manipulate the gun with his crippled appendage, he used his good hand to snatch up the rusted length of pipe from the floor. He walked over and kicked Jericho in the side once, twice, and on the third, the man was finally smart enough to get the idea and flop over on his back.

Carlos straddled his legs, his mangled hand leaking blood onto the other man's shirt.

"Yo, when you see Lito in hell, tell 'em I said hello."

He rammed the end of the pipe down into the soft part of Jericho's stomach, just below the ribcage, then leaned over to look at the man's face. This was the first time Carlos had ever killed someone in cold blood. Jericho's eyes were wide, his mouth twisted in pain, but he wasn't quite dead yet. It might take a while, but Carlos was prepared to wait. He had nowhere else to go.

The swinging door slammed open behind him, and he twisted around to see Lito come pounding into the room.

10

Amber's scream was small and flat on the open water. She backpedaled, bumping into Ray.

On the other side of the entrance was a shallow alcove. A form had been scrunched in the corner against the inside of the door, curled up in a ball, and it flopped halfway out onto the wing when the round portal opened.

"Hold on, it's okay, don't freak out," Ray told her, keeping one hand on her so she didn't topple backward into the water. It didn't make her feel much better that he was using his other to sketch a cross on his chest again. "Whatever it is, it's dead. Been dead a long time, from the looks of it."

She forced herself to move forward again, training her flashlight on the form lying across the threshold. The creature was small, barely larger than a toddler. If it was another mutant, she had no idea what it was before radiation deformed it. The closest comparison she could draw was to a squid. It had multiple tentacles growing from its underside in a gnarled tangle, and a puffy, bloated head that sported a host of antennae and mandibles like those of an ant. A ring of glassy, flat, disc-like indentions stared at her, like the glassy eyes of a doll. Its skin was shrunken and shriveled, a bland, no-color gray, but she thought this was from decay rather than natural pigmentation.

Amber prodded it with the flashlight. The flesh had looked rubbery when it flopped out onto the wing, but now it crumbled beneath the slight pressure. A crack ran up and down its main mass, and then the entire form seemed to collapse in on itself like a punctured soufflé. It disintegrated as she watched, becoming no more than a pile of ash and dust that the sea breeze scattered.

"It mummified," she told Ray over her shoulder. "That happens to people buried in ancient tombs when they're exposed to fresh air for the first time."

"Yeah? And how long does that take?"

"A few thousand years, at least."

"That's all, huh?"

Stepping over the powdery remains, Amber entered the tiny ship. Before she could shine her light around, clean, white illumination blazed overhead. She blinked at the brightness until her eyes adjusted.

The floor, walls and ceiling in here were smooth, featureless white, made of a glossy substance that almost resembled marble. There were no switches or dials or gauges, no way at all that she could see to control this craft, just those plain, clinical surfaces. She couldn't even see where the light was coming from. The effect created an optical illusion that the landscape stretched to infinity on all sides, giving her a small flutter of panic; Amber had to touch the walls to confirm they were still there. In actual physical terms, the space was so cramped it made Tuan's ship look like a suite at the Four Seasons. She could reach out and put her palms flat on both sides of the narrow enclosure at the same time.

But underneath the panels, she could hear noises all around them. Small pings and whirrings, like the sounds of machinery starting, or computers booting.

"We woke it up." Ray slid into the ship behind her and leaned against the wall, holding his injured side. "*Dios*, I hope that's a good thing."

At the front of the narrow room was a structure—the only object in this otherwise sterile room—that looked to Amber like a giant, black spice rack. It was a huge bowl on top of a narrow central column, which had ringlets on all sides running down its length. She had to stare at it for a few more seconds before she understood.

It was a chair, just not a chair meant for human anatomy.

Somehow, looking at this structure—specifically designed for the creature at the door, so it could perch on the bowl and slide its tentacles through the holsters on the side to secure itself—brought the undeniable truth crashing down.

"Cherrywine was right all along," she said softly. "This is a spaceship. And that thing over there was its pilot." She couldn't quite bring herself to say, or even think, the word pressing at the back of her lips, the one she and Lito had joked about just a few hours before.

The shorter wall in front of the chair suddenly lit up in a display screen. It was only a blue background, with a narrow white band across the bottom and a series of strange symbols scrolling quickly above it. The sight of them thrilled her; yet another discovery that could easily make her famous. She tried to get a sense of them, even commit them to memory, but the alien (there, she'd thought it, no going back now) characters moved too fast. So instead, she took in the screen as a whole, tried to understand what message it was conveying rather than decipher the specifics.

The band at the bottom was growing, she now saw, slowly crawling from right to left across the screen. Every few seconds, it would jump forward, eating up a little more area. It had a foot or so left before it would reach all the way across.

The answer to this, at least, was glaringly obvious.

A completion bar. She was looking at a computer completion bar meant to countdown the time to a certain event, like a program loading. *Nice to know even technology throughout the universe works on Microsoft principles*, she thought.

From hidden speakers somewhere overhead, the Voice of the Deep began to play. The man from Lito's crew that had come up with this name probably hadn't known just how apt it was. This *was* a voice from the deep, just not deep in the ocean. Amber found it easy to imagine the harsh language being spoken by the mandibles that formed the dead creature's mouth.

Something above her clicked. Before she could move, a short pole flipped down from the ceiling in front of her face, phasing right through the surface as if it were no more substantial than smoke. A bulb at the end shone a short burst of green light the color of emerald directly into her left eye. She felt a tickle somewhere far back in her skull, like a feather moving against her scalp, but before she could even blink or jerk away, the pole disappeared back into the ceiling.

"You okay?" Ray asked, starting toward her.

She waved him back. "Yeah. I'm fine."

"What the hell did it do?"

The recording of the alien language cut off, and the tone they'd heard before on the scanner sounded, the one that preceded a translation.

"I think it just took some language lessons directly from my head."

All around them, a calm voice began to speak in perfect English.

11

The squealing of the ship rats wasn't quite as bad as the baby on the yacht, but it still sounded thunderous in the enclosed corridors. The disgusting creatures were nipping at his heels when Lito spotted the swinging door to the engineering room ahead. He plunged through, then forced the door shut. There was no way to lock it, so he once again settled for putting his back against it as the rats piled up against the other side and clawed at the doorplate. The click of their claws was like rain falling on sheet metal.

It was only then that he swung his flashlight over and saw Carlos squatting on the floor on top of Jericho, who had a metal stake stuck through his chest like a new age vampire. His friend pawed weakly at the younger man's face.

"Get off him, you little fuck. Right now."

Carlos looked like a guilty teenager caught sneaking out of the house in the flashlight's glare. He and Jericho were both covered in blood. "It...it ain't like that! It was an accident..." His eyes flicked to the shotgun just a few feet away as he spewed excuses. Lito knew he would have a similar accident if he let the boy get the upper hand for even a second.

He leveled the Walther at Carlos as the tinny shrieks from outside got louder. The door jumped and shuddered behind him. "Save it. Your friends in the speedboat told me all about what you've been up to. Now get over here and help me."

Carlos pushed up from Jericho, who went limp on the ground.

He approached cautiously, cradling one hand that bled profusely. "Yo man, what's out there?"

"You don't wanna know. Find something to hold this door."

Carlos grabbed several heavy chairs and dragged them over. Even their weight wasn't enough; the door shoved open a few inches and several plump, misshapen rodent heads squeezed through, hissing. Carlos yelped and jumped away as Lito crushed them with the toe of his boot.

"I need *you* to hold it then!"

"Uh uh, man, no way!"

Lito fired the gun, putting a bullet in the bulkhead wall beside the boy. "Don't make me ask again."

They traded spots. Lito went to Jericho, who was taking big, panicked gulps of air on the floor.

"It's all right," Lito whispered, "we're gonna get outta here, buddy. Ray's waitin for us, and we're goin to California just like you wanted, okay?" He couldn't tell if the man heard him or not, but decided not to remove the length of pipe from his chest. He went around and slipped his hands under Jericho's arms, and started to pull him toward the room's only other exit, another water tight hatch. Lito had no idea where it led, but at least it would put a solid door between them and the vermin.

"Wait, what about me?" Carlos yelled.

For a second, Lito was tempted to leave him. He deserved no better. Everything that had happened to them was his fault.

But he couldn't. The boy might not think of him as a father, but Lito was the closest thing he had.

"Let me get Jericho out, then we'll make a run for it!"

He pulled his mechanic to safety on the other side of the hatch, into a long room along the starboard side of the ship, with portholes that allowed in the strengthening sunlight in dusty shafts. Back in the other room, he picked up the shotgun and yelled, "Go and don't look back!"

Carlos bolted away from the door. It swung open, letting in

the tide of glowing rats. Lito pumped the remaining shells in the shotgun at them, slaughtering them wholesale, but it did little to stop the flow. When the weapon ran out, he flipped it over and used the butt like a hockey stick, sweeping the floor back and forth, flinging rats in all directions.

He saw the hatch swinging shut from the corner of his eye. Carlos was trying to seal him in. Lito jammed the shotgun through the slot before it could close, then rammed his shoulder against the steel as hard as he could. He heard a grunt of pain as the edge of the door swung back into Carlos, then jumped through and sealed the hatch before any of the beasts slipped through.

Jericho lay on the floor where Lito left him, unmoving. Blood had stopped oozing from the pipe in his chest. When Lito knelt down to check, he could find no pulse. He looked up at Carlos, standing sheepishly a few feet away.

"You murdering shit," Lito snarled. There would be no meditation, no calming techniques that could stop the rage boiling through him. He grabbed the boy and punched him across the jaw, hard enough to make the bones in his hand hurt. The kid's legs failed, dropping him to the ground, but Lito followed him down, still putting knuckles to his face. Lito's own father had cut loose on him a few times like this, and maybe the man had the right idea after all.

He might have kept going, might have caved in the boy's face, but after the fifth or sixth hit, something crashed against the back of Lito's head hard enough to put the lights out.

12

Carlos's vision had tripled at some point during the beating, but he was still able to make out the shadow that peeled away from the wall and smashed Lito unconscious. The figure jumped on the captain, going through his pockets while it muttered, "Where is it, goddamn it, *where is it?* You gave it to *her*, didn't you, you wetback fuck?"

"Who...w-who...?" Carlos stammered.

The figure turned. In the watery sunlight from the portholes, he was finally able to make out the face of the rich white *gringo* from the yacht.

"You're Carlos, right? We didn't get a chance to talk before, but from what I hear, we got a lot in common." He pulled an object out of Lito's shorts and held it up. Carlos recognized the walkie-talkies from their ship.

Eric grinned, the expression ghoulish in the weak light. "In fact...I think you and I just became best friends."

13

"*This is a warning to all sentient species of planet designation E68239, capable of receiving low-yield transmissions,*" the voice said over the ship's speakers in that sexless, robotic drone. As Amber had suspected, whatever scan the spacecraft had just performed on her had fully translated the message, or probably gotten as close as the two languages would allow. Her capacity for awe had been so numbed by everything else that happened tonight, she wasn't even curious about the amazing technology, but just content to listen to the solved mystery. "*Please be advised, you have entered a dangerous quarantine zone. My ship has suffered cataclysmic engine failure in the form of a core breach. Repair attempts have been unsuccessful. I have no choice but to set the core to automatically vent radiation at critical levels, or risk a detonation that could destroy a full quarter of your world. Be warned: these releases can cause temporal and dimensional displacement of anything within a five mile radius.*"

At this, Ray grunted and opened his mouth to speak, but Amber silenced him with a finger to her lips.

"*Scans indicate my vessel's particular isotope signature is not native to this planet, so this radiation is also expected to have devastating molecular effects to all carbon-based life forms. For preventative measures, I am directing my ship to display a visible spectrum which should simultaneously attract any irradiated specimens while repelling those unaffected, in order to prevent the spread of infection. I will also begin continual broadcast of this transmission with an adaptive language cipher to attempt communication with any replies. This should continue for at least the half-life of my ship's core—approximately fifty-thousand of your planet's revolutions—or until my craft's systems degrade too much to continue the venting procedure, in which case, an explosion is probable. I regret that I was not able to do more. Please leave the affected area immediately, or get to safe containment within adequate radiation shielding."*

The voice cut off. Another bong sounded, and the message began to repeat in full Spanish.

"Oh god, it learned every language I knew," Amber said. Then, on a hunch, she called out, "Stop the broadcast, please!"

The ship's speakers went silent.

"Uh, I think I caught about one out of every five words of that," Ray said, "but it sounded to me like a goddamned intergalactic apology letter."

"It's a tower of thorns," Amber muttered.

"Huh?"

"Tower of thorns. It's a language barrier problem that the scientists who deal with nuclear waste are having. They bury the stuff in the ground, where it needs to stay for ten thousand years until it's safe again. The only problem is, how do you mark it so that future generations will know it's dangerous? Language changes so fast and so drastically, you can't be sure any sign or symbol would still be in use. The best solution they can think of is to put up some menacing structure, like a tower of thorns." She touched the strange chair in the middle of the room, suddenly feeling a kinship with the creature that had sat in it. "That broadcast...and the lights in the sky...those were its tower of thorns. It was doing the best it could to warn people to stay out of the Bermuda Triangle, but I have a feeling all it's doing is just attracting more and more ships."

"Nothing brings in human beings like curiosity," Ray agreed.

"At least it's fully translated into three languages now. If this 'adaptive language cipher' works, than anyone else who attempts to answer the broadcast will get the full message."

Ray slid down the wall until he was sitting, leaving a smear of blood against the gleaming white surface. "I get most of it. The energy that powers this thing, just like we figured, it's drivin everything apeshit: people, animals, plants, even the damn seaweed. And the more doses you get, the worse off you are. But what do you think it meant by all that 'temporal and dimensional displacement' talk?'"

"It means whatever weird radiation this thing produces isn't just tearing holes in time, like Lito thought." She shook her head and gnawed at her bottom lip. "That's the real reason there are more ship out there than have ever disappeared in the Sargasso. They're not just from the past or the future. As insane as it sound...I think they're from *different dimensions*, too."

"Woah...that's gettin a bit heavy for me."

"Fly's eyes," she said slowly, tasting the phrase as if it was the first time. "That cruise ship? It might not even be from our future, it might be from the future of a completely different Earth. Tuan, too. This ship has been bouncing through time and space for god-knows-how long, and dragging everything that stumbles through the area with it. It must've visited—or *will visit*—our world a few times in the past, enough to start the legend of the Triangle, but it could've been doing the same thing in these other dimensions."

"So 1970 on our world for a few hours, then a couple of days in the Middle Ages on some other world?"

"No pattern, no purpose," Amber confirmed, answering her own question from earlier. She couldn't stop thinking about the diamond in that ring, the one that was now somewhere on the ocean floor. And the game she'd played as a child, the one with multiple versions of herself. If she was right, this ship had been to places where there might actually be other Ambers.

Ray whistled. "Jesus, this thing is just throwin out a fishin net and seein what trash it can haul in."

"More like a spider's web. And all these people—along with us—are caught in it." She blanched at the image. "We have to get clear of that five-mile radius before the next pressure release hits."

"We could just stay here, or go back to Tuan's ship. The broadcast said we could shield ourselves."

Amber shook her head. "That's a last resort. You said it yourself before. Even if we escape the radiation, we're going wherever this thing goes next. And that's a one-way trip."

"Well, it sure would be nice if the pile of dust in the corner had told us how long we have."

Amber's jaw fell open. She turned slowly, and pointed at the bar on the display screen, with the scrolling numbers above it. There was just a scant six or seven inches left till it would reach the far left side. "How much you wanna bet that's the venting program?" She raised her voice. "Um, hey, computer? Would you please translate the front...screen to English?"

Her clumsy command must have been sufficient, because the alien characters became familiar numerals. It was indeed a timer, with incremental columns for seconds, minutes, and hours.

There were 18 minutes remaining, and the seconds were ticking down as they watched.

"Call Lito," she said. "Tell them they have to get out. *Now.*"

He raised the walkie-talkie to his lips and said, "Lito, you copy? Answer me right now if you can hear me, goddamn it."

"He's indisposed at the moment," a voice purred from the device. "But you can talk to me. This is the one with the ponytail, right? *El Capitan*'s right-hand man? Is Amber there too, or is she too busy sucking your cock to come to the phone?"

"Shit. That's Eric." Amber motioned for the radio, and Ray handed it over. "What did you do with them, you bastard?"

"You mean your little boyfriend here? He's fine, and he'll stay fine as long as you do what I say." Eric gave his mean-spirited chuckle. "Déjà vu, huh? This seems to be happening to you a lot tonight, but with different guys. Price of being a whore, I guess."

"We don't have time for this, Eric. This whole area, all the derelicts, they're about to go...somewhere else."

"Oh, I know. And if you do what I say, we can all get out of here together."

Amber swallowed her anger, taking one of Lito's long breaths. She didn't trust him, but their only choice was to play along. "What do you want?"

"I want you and my statue, back on the top deck of the cruise ship, ASAP. And my new friend Carlos wants Ponytail to come over and play, too. Who else is with you? I know Cherrywine isn't; she had a little accident of her own. What about Justin, he over there?"

Amber bowed her head at the confirmation of the other girl's death. "No, he...turned into one of those things. He's somewhere on the cruise ship."

"Well, too bad for him then. Get your asses over here, right now. We'll lower a lifeboat for you."

Amber dropped the radio to her side and took the statue out of her pocket. So much trouble for such an ugly little thing.

"Just go," Ray told her. "Drop me off at the cruise ship. I'll do what I can to save Lito. You just take the speedboat and run. Get out while you can."

A sudden rush of determined heat spread across the back of her neck. "I've run away from enough tonight."

14

Another lifeboat waited for them, connected to the deck of the cruise ship high over their heads by its thick cables. The sun was climbing the horizon now, its warm beams reflecting off the water in an amber smear, like an Impressionist painting. The derelicts looked a little less scary in the morning light with their shadows banished.

This time, Amber and Ray tied the speedboat off to one of the massive steel girders showing through the *Atlantic Queen*'s diseased side, then stepped over into the lifeboat.

"No guns," Eric said over the radio. Amber looked up and saw him leaning over the guardrail to watch them. "Let me see you throw them in the water."

The only weapon they had left was Ray's pistol. He tossed it over the side.

"Very good. Now hang on, children."

They were hoisted into the air. The ride was less smooth going up, the rusted cables jerking and bouncing them. The fiberglass hull kept swinging into the side of the cruise liner with bone-jarring thuds. She and Ray held on to the benches until they reached the top. Carlos was there to swivel the boat over the deck. He had to perform this operation with one hand though; the other was wrapped in blood-soaked rags and held to his chest. Not only that, but someone had beaten the holy hell out of the kid. His face was a black and blue landscape of lumps and one eye swollen to a slit.

Somehow, he still managed to sneer at Ray. "Guess I ain't gettin off at the next port after all, homey."

"Go to hell, you weasel. And from the looks of you, somebody already tried to send you there." Ray held his side as Amber helped him back out of the rowboat. His wound was bleeding freely again, and his skin was ice cold and pale. "What did you do with Jericho and Tuan?"

Carlos sidled up closer and patted his cheek. Ray turned his head away. "They both dead, like you 'bout to be. Then I'm findin a way to tow the *Runner* outta here. That bitch is mine, now."

Amber saw a fire come into Ray's eyes. "You really think you're gonna go work for the Dominican? Cause lemme tell ya, him sendin a hit squad after us don't show a lotta confidence."

"He doesn't have to worry about pandering to Caribbean drug lords anymore." A few yards away, next to the empty deck pool, Eric stood with gun in hand, pointed at the sky. "Carlos is thinking bigger now."

Lito lay face down on the wet deck beside him. Amber wanted to go to him, but kept her face a mask. The side of his head was bloody, but he was conscious, blinking up at her and Ray. Eric put a foot on his back and said, "You went into whatever's glowing down there. I saw you come out. What is it?"

"It's an alien spaceship," Amber answered. "The answer to your precious Bermuda Triangle. And in about ten minutes, it's gonna release a burst of radiation that will pull all these ships into another dimension, and give us all a nice, blue suntan."

Eric nodded as if this was just confirming information he already knew. "Then we better hurry this along so we can all go home together."

"You don't have any intention of letting us go."

He grinned. "Give the statue to Carlos."

Amber held the glass figurine up over her head. "Let him go, or I'll toss it into the ocean right now. Swear to Christ I will."

"No." Eric sounded almost bored. "You won't."

"Oh really? And what makes you think that?"

"Because it's not in the cards."

She raised an eyebrow. "The...cards?"

"Yeah, you know, the *cards*. The Big Plan. Fate." He leaned forward, putting weight on the leg resting on Lito's back until he grunted. "You see, Amber, I have a destiny. One you couldn't alter if you wanted to. Cherrywine tried, so I fucking killed her. The universe looks out for people like me. I've become more and more convinced of that in the last 24 hours."

She stared at him, utterly aghast, and let the arm holding the statue fall back to her side. He looked crazed, jittery, nose still crooked and swollen, his eyes swimming out of focus. Amber had a feeling this was the *real* Eric Renquist, the maniac that had been hiding just below the surface of the smarmy veneer his whole life.

He pointed the gun at Lito's head. "But destiny aside, if you don't hand that statue over to Carlos, I'm gonna fucking shoot all of you, starting with your spic boyfriend here."

Feeling numb, Amber passed the statue to Carlos, who walked over to Eric with it held in front of him in his one good hand. "Yo, what is this thing?"

"Your future. After we deliver it for my father, you and I will be working for him. You'll be a *capo* in the Philadelphia mob by the time you're 20. Sounds a lot better than smuggling drugs, right?" He held out his hand.

Carlos frowned and stopped just short of surrendering the statue. "So...it's valuable?"

"Very."

"Then...why don't we just keep it ourselves?"

"Because your new partner always listens to Daddy," Amber said. "Don't you, Eric?"

"Shut the fuck up, slut. Carlos...give it to me."

Carlos hesitated again, looking from the statue to Eric's outstretched hand.

Eric swung the gun up and shot him.

Amber was amazed at how smooth and mechanically the deed was done. Even Carlos seemed surprised as blood spread down the front of his jersey. Eric watched eagerly, taking in every detail as the Hispanic kid went to his knees, then he bent to tear the statue from his grasp, taking his foot off Lito's back as he did. Carlos fell over on his side, wheezing and making feeble clawing motions at the deck. Lito reached over and took his hand. The gesture made Amber's heart ache.

"You're sick," she told Eric.

"Yeah? You a psychology major now too?"

"No. But it doesn't change the fact."

"God, you were always one mouthy bitch. I never did understand what Justin saw in you."

"Cause he's a decent human being, and you're even more of an animal than those things downstairs." Amber shook her head disgustedly. "That's what this whole trip was about, wasn't it? You delivering this statue for your father. I knew you were crazy after what you did to Cherrywine, but now I see you've got more daddy issues than she did."

"If you love her so much, then by all means, let me reunite you two." Eric raised the gun.

Two things happened at once.

Lito let go of Carlos's hand, grabbed Eric's foot, and yanked him off balance.

And a door on the far side of the deck burst open, releasing a flood of irradiated cruise ship passengers.

15

Eric crashed to the deck between Carlos and Lito, his hands too full to catch himself. He chose his precious statue over the Walther; the gun clattered away as he cradled the figurine. Lito heard something in the fucker's side give a satisfying snap. Eric cried out in pain, but the noise was drowned by sudden screeches form the other direction.

The mutants of the *Atlantic Queen* had been lost in its lower decks for a few centuries, trapped by their own deteriorated minds, slumbering as the cruise ship disintegrated around them. Now, they'd finally found their way out.

Or been *led* out.

Justin was at the front of the pack, not as physically repulsive as the rest, but snarling and howling in mindless fury just the same. There must've been just enough of a spark of intelligence left for him to make it all the way up here, and he'd played Pied Piper for the others. The creatures only had to make their way around the corner of the pool before they would reach the group.

Eric performed a strange hobble-crawl toward the gun on his

hands and knees. Lito grabbed his leg to slow him down and received a heel to his already injured head. The world blurred before snapping back into focus. He saw Ray limp forward to help him, but Amber beat him to it, snatching up the pistol and then kicking Eric in his injured side. He screamed again and crumpled to the deck.

She wrenched the statue away from him.

"*PLEASE!*" he pleaded. "*Give it to me, oh god, please, I have to take it back, it's my destiny!*"

"You want this?" Amber demanded, like a master getting ready to play fetch with his dog. "Then *go get it!*"

She threw it into the huge pool. Lito watched it plunk into the murky water at the bottom.

"*You bitch!*" Eric scrambled after it, dumping over the lip and tumbling down the sloped inner wall of the pool. He splashed and flailed below.

"C'mon!" Ray shouted. He offered a hand to Lito, who first paused and checked Carlos before getting to his feet.

The boy was dead, his eyes open and staring at the sky. Lito closed them, giving a silent apology to both the boy and his mother.

The three of them ran as the mob of tourists came around the pool and loped after them.

16

Amber dove back into the lifeboat with Ray. Lito shoved them out to dangle over the water, then swung a leg over the railing and dropped in himself. The bottom of the boat cracked under the stress. Lito had to stretch up to reach the catch on the crank system that would start them lowering toward the water, then pulled back as the creatures surged toward the bulwark above them.

In the sunlight, their glow was dampened, but every detail of their grotesque bodies was revealed, putrid, singed flesh and twisted limbs. They leaned over the *Atlantic Queen*'s guardrail, clawing at the air in a parody of how they had started this voyage, waving goodbye to loved ones they would never see again as the cruise liner sailed away from the dock. A few of them fell over—missing the lifeboat by inches and dropping to smash against the ocean surface far below—but the rest were held against the railing by the press of bodies packed in behind them.

She spotted Justin, his teeth bared like an animal as he howled in frustration.

The thought of him remaining on this cursed ship forever, eventually turning into one of these pathetic freaks, was too much for her to bear.

Wiping at sudden tears, she pointed the gun up at him.

Lito put a hand over hers. "I'll do it."

She gave him the pistol and looked away as the shots rang out.

The lifeboat dropped fast without anyone to control the descent. As they reached the ocean, the sickly glow from the alien ship began to flicker. Arcs of piercing blue electricity surrounded the entire vessel. The air was suddenly so heavy with static, Amber thought she might be able to swim through it.

They reboarded the drug dealers' speedboat. Amber gave the keys to Lito and rushed to cut the mooring.

"You better drive this thing for all it's worth," Ray said, sinking down onto the padded bench with Amber. "I figure we got less than five minutes before we're all goin bye-bye."

Lito brought the engine to life and throttled up. They shot across the band of empty water, back toward the ring of derelict ships. Soon, they were lost in the maze of drifting steel.

An ungodly roar sounded behind them.

Amber looked back as a familiar shape rose from the water in the wake of their boat: a sleek, domed head with jaws big enough to swallow a person whole.

The sea monster. Except now, she knew it was no monster, but some dinosaur-like creature that had never existed in the same time as human beings. A long lost relative—or descendent—of

Loch Ness. Or maybe it came from some other dimension where its species still ruled the oceans, and mankind quaked in fear of it.

Now, it was caught within the Deep's spider web, doomed to forever follow the spacecraft wherever it went, drawn back time and time again by the flashing beacon.

Behind the speedboat, it kept pace with them, opening its crocodile jaws and snapping at their engine. She could see the tip of its tail as it thrashed in the water. Those huge, powerful flippers she'd seen last night during the storm churned the water to either side, propelling its massive body after them. It might've been majestic if its reptilian skin wasn't pitted with radiation burns and stretches of blackened scales.

The beast raised its head and issued another roar at the morning sky, a braying call that sounded like a cross between whale song and an elephant's trumpet.

"*Go faster!*" Amber yelled.

Lito hunched over the wheel, but he was forced to slow down for turns as he navigated through the derelicts. The beast chasing them had no such trouble, submerging briefly to zip under anything that got in its way. In a few seconds, it breached right alongside them, its girth pushing a wall of water in front of it that tipped the speedboat to one side.

Those jaws swung toward them, bashing the side of the boat. Its teeth left gouges in the craft's side. Amber screamed and held on to her bench as they started to tip.

The sky flashed dazzling blue, a color somehow deeper and more exotic—and nauseating—than daylight could ever be. The sea monster slowed, all interest in them lost. It turned around and drifted back toward the bursts of light. The speedboat shot away from it.

Just ahead, the derelicts petered out. Lito steered around the hull of a yacht, then they shot into open water. He opened the boat's throttle to full and then twisted in the pilot's chair to look back.

The sea monster was lost in the field of derelicts now, which stretched out to either side of them as far as they could see. A high pitched whine filled the air, louder even than the boat's droning engine. That sharp tang of burnt ozone hit her nostrils again. Static electricity coursed over them, strong enough to make every hair on her body stand at attention. The flickers of light from somewhere at the center of the ships were getting faster, brighter, so intense they were more white than blue, a hazy color like the interior walls of that ancient craft. Amber caught one last glimpse of the prow of the *Atlantic Queen* stretching high above the other abandoned ships just before the light became too bright to look at. She squeezed her eyes shut and covered her ears, but neither did anything to block out this sensory overload.

And then it stopped. Amber blinked a few times until her vision returned.

The ocean behind them was empty. The derelicts, the cruise liner...all of it gone. In their place was a gigantic hole in the ocean surface, an impossible and perfectly round dimple in the water, like the Sargasso was just one big ice cream carton and someone had removed a scoop. Which was, she realized, exactly what had happened; the Deep had taken a five-mile long chunk of ocean water along to wherever it went next. The hole stayed like that for one precipitous moment, and then, with a pop that Amber felt in her eardrums, the surrounding water and air rushed in to fill the void.

"*Hang on!*" Lito shouted.

Their speed slowed. A sudden current dragged at them. With the boat in motion, there had been a wind blowing over Amber, but now it sucked at her with tornadic force, ripping at her hair and skin as air pressure worked to equalize. A roar like a thousand raging waterfalls assaulted them.

The ocean waters crashed in from all sides in the middle of the depression, creating a foaming waterspout that shot into the air and came down like rain, drenching them. But the sea settled after another minute, and all was calm.

Lito brought the boat to a stop. Turned to face them while wiping saltwater from his eyes.

"That was fun and all, but next year...Disneyland, okay?"

Amber gave a tired chuckle. Ray kicked out at him feebly. Then all three of them grew quiet and went back to studying the sweep of the morning ocean. It seemed so vast and empty again, without the derelicts to break up the horizon.

"Well, I guess that's that then," Lito said. "She was a good ship."

"Still is," Ray told him. He pointed. They followed the direction of his finger.

Far out on the water, several miles off their starboard stern, one lonely ship floated.

17

The *Steel Runner* was as they'd left it. They checked it top to bottom, and found no creatures waiting for them. The engines were still down, but Lito figured the Dominican's luxury speedboat had more than enough torque to tow the ship to land.

He tried to get Ray to lie down, but the man insisted on helping him take the bodies of Mondo and the nameless little girl from the holds and cast them overboard. Amber left them alone for this operation, volunteering to go downstairs and work on mopping up the blood belowdeck.

The sun stood high as they tossed the sheet-wrapped forms over the side. Ray said a short prayer. Though they were only sending off two people, Lito knew the impromptu funeral was also for Jericho, Rabid, and Jorge. And Carlos too; Lito felt the kid deserved at least that much.

"How is it even still here?" Ray asked in Spanish when it was all over, and the last of the bodies had sunk beneath the seaweed. "The *Runner*, I mean. Why didn't it go with the rest of them?"

Lito leaned against the bulwark and gave the railing a loving pat. "Blind, stupid luck, that's what I think. Last night, when we dropped anchor after almost hittin the pontoon boat, we parked right on the damn edge of this *quarantine zone*." Ray and Amber had filled Lito in on their discoveries, some of which he'd already pieced together from his last conversation with Tuan. "We're just lucky it didn't crack up when the ocean collapsed on itself."

Ray was quiet for a moment before saying, "You wanna talk about blind, stupid luck? I've been thinkin about that broadcast the girl and I heard."

"The one from the thousand-year-old alien?" Lito tried not to sound skeptical, but it was hard.

"Yeah, that one." Ray lit a cigarette and dragged deep. "That spaceship...we're all just playin one big game of hot potato. Sooner or later, it's gonna explode, and take out a quarter of whatever planet it's on. We better just hope it's not ours."

"If you'd told me this time yesterday that you and I would be having a serious conversation about alternate dimensions, I'd've busted a gut."

"Then let's talk about how we're gonna find another crew with a death warrant on our heads."

Lito sighed. "Ray...if I never see the Caribbean again, it'll be too soon."

18

After Ray was freshly bandaged and in his bunk, Lito secured the speedboat to the prow of the *Steel Runner* with some heavy steel cord. When he climbed back aboard his ship, Amber was sitting in the wheelhouse, staring out at the water. Her cheeks were wet. He sat down with her, but said nothing for several minutes. The silence wasn't awkward, but he had no idea how to break it.

She saved him the trouble.

"Doing some pirate meditation?" she asked, wiping away the tears caught in her eyelashes.

He smiled. "I'm taking up yoga next."

"Be sure to wear an eye patch with your leotard."

They fell quiet again, and this time he took the lead.

"I'm sorry. About Justin, about...all of it."

She nodded. "I appreciate what you did for him back there. I just...couldn't leave him like that. And, in fourteen years, if there really is a ship called the *Atlantic Queen*, I intend to make sure it doesn't wind up trapped in the Bermuda Triangle forever. Maybe it'll save him. Maybe it'll save *all* of them."

Even though he'd had that thought himself, he briefly considered trying to argue her out of that idea—after all, if that ship never went into the Sargasso, then how had they just escaped from it?—but she seemed resolute. "I better get us moving. If we leave now, we'll be to the Florida coast before nightfall."

He stood, started to walk out, but she grabbed his hand and pulled him to her. Their lips brushed, for just one electric moment, and then she leaned against him.

"You know, *gringa*, you could come with us," he told her. For the first time, Lito admitted to himself how much he wanted to see where things went with this woman.

"Girls can't be pirates, remember?" she said against his shoulder.

"I think Ray and I are givin the whole pirate thing up."

"We'll see. The only good thing about all this is that I have no idea what comes next." He felt her lips move in a way that had to be a smile, but when she spoke again, it was to say, "I know the radiation would've turned him, but...I can't help wondering where Eric ended up."

Lito thought briefly of the rich *pendejo* and his beloved statue. If anybody deserved an eternity in the Triangle, it was him.

"As long as it's somewhere far, far away from here, consider me a happy man."

19

When all was quiet, Eric exited the alien spaceship through the portal on its side.

He'd found the statue in the bottom of the pool, and managed to climb out without attracting the attention of the mutants, who now lined the portside railing as they howled for blood. He launched another lifeboat, then rowed for the UFO. By that point, the craft had been spitting out blue sparks like a chainsaw put to metal. Getting there hadn't been easy with his broken rib, but he'd made it—as he knew he would—just as the glowing cylinder on top of the ship began to emit a whining noise.

His guess that the spaceship would shield him from the blast of radiation was obviously correct. As he left the weird, white interior of the vessel, he felt fine. Better than fine, even considering he still had a broken nose and rib.

After all, he'd been inside an alien spaceship. He knew the secret behind the Bermuda Triangle. All of these would be mere footnotes to his legend, by the time he was finished.

Of course, there was also the question of where (or *when*) the ship had taken him, but he didn't believe it would be a problem. Destiny wouldn't bring him this far just to desert him. Even the ghost of his father inside his head agreed with this assessment.

At first, when Eric stepped outside, he thought it was approaching evening again. But no, that couldn't be it. The sunlight was dim, but not the kind of dimness that comes with twilight. Eric looked up and found the sun was no more than a tiny, red ball floating in a murky brown sky.

And it was *cold*. Much colder than the Caribbean ever got. He could see his breath pluming in front of his face.

He got back in the lifeboat. It took him almost three hours to row his way out of the derelicts, and his arms felt like jelly by the time he was clear.

But he could see land on the horizon to the north, judging by the position of the sun.

He had no idea what it could be other than Bermuda. In which case, he would deliver the statue, call his father, and the man would be so pleased, he'd have a private jet waiting for Eric at the closest airport.

Eric grinned and started rowing.

By the time he reached land—a long stretch of yellow sand bordered by a jungle full of dead, brown vegetation—he was exhausted. It had taken him hours to reach this place, surely long enough for night to fall, but the sun had never really seemed to move from its position.

It didn't matter. He was so thrilled to be on dry land again, he didn't care where he was, as long as there was a bar and five-star resort nearby. He lay on the sand with the statue and closed his eyes, drifting into sleep.

Some time later, he heard the roar.

He opened his eyes. Something big was scrambling through the dead tree line. Like, *dinosaur* big. He could only see quick glances of black, leathery skin and two-foot long spines of jutting bone.

Eric got up from the sand and backed away, but there was no place to run, just the ocean behind him and miles of empty sand to either side.

The trees parted. The thing on the other side shoved its head through, an oblong disc that seemed to be mostly teeth and jaws, and eyes the size of car tires. It caught sight of him...

And smiled.

As the creature charged forward, smacking its gigantic lips, Eric begin to doubt, for the very first time, that this had been his destiny at all.

Like this novel?

YOUR REVIEWS HELP!

In the modern world, customer reviews are essential for any product. The artists who create the work you enjoy need your help growing their audience. Please visit Goodreads or the website of the company that sold you this novel to leave a review, or even just a star rating. Posting about the book on social media is also appreciated.

ABOUT THE AUTHOR

Russell C. Connor has been writing horror since the age of five, and is the author of two short story collections, five eNovellas, and ten novels. His books have won two Independent Publisher Awards and a Readers' Favorite Award. He has been a member of the DFW Writers' Workshop since 2006, and served as president for two years. He lives in Fort Worth, Texas with his rabid dog, demented film collection, mistress of the dark, and demonspawn daughter.

His next novel—*The Halls of Moambati*, Volume IV of *The Dark Filament Ephemeris*—will be available in 2021.